W9-CAM-419

A Change in Altitude

Center Point
Large Print

Also by Cindy Myers and available from Center Point Large Print:

The View from Here
The Mountain Between Us

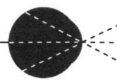

This Large Print Book carries the Seal of Approval of N.A.V.H.

A Change in Altitude

CINDY MYERS

CENTER POINT LARGE PRINT
THORNDIKE, MAINE

This Center Point Large Print edition
is published in the year 2014 by arrangement with
Kensington Publishing Corp.

Copyright © 2014 by Cynthia Myers.

The text of this Large Print edition is unabridged.
In other aspects, this book may vary
from the original edition.
Printed in the United States of America
on permanent paper.
Set in 16-point Times New Roman type.
ISBN: 978-1-62899-224-3

Library of Congress Cataloging-in-Publication Data

Myers, Cindy, author.
A change in altitude / Cindy Myers.
pages cm
Summary: "The town of Eureka, Colorado, has gone through some
        financial hard times, but spring promises to be a time of rebirth
        in more ways than one"—Provided by publisher.
ISBN 978-1-62899-224-3 (library binding : alk. paper)
1. Eureka (Colo.)—Fiction. 2. City and town life—Fiction.
    3. Gold mines and mining—Fiction. 4. Large type books.
    I. Title.
PS3613.Y467C48 2014
813'.6—dc23
                                                            2014019456

For all the wonderful women of
the Bailey Book Club.
Thank you for your friendship and support.

Chapter 1

"Mo-oooom!" The cry rose and fell with the intensity and pitch of a siren's wail, and Sharon Franklin felt the same flood of adrenaline and worry that had once been her response to her infant's wail.

Only now the infant was thirteen years old and glaring at her with the disdain only a teenager can muster.

"What's wrong now?" Sharon asked, her hands tightening on the steering wheel of the Honda Civic. She'd been behind the wheel so long she feared her fingers would remain permanently bent, as if she were always trying to hang on to something that wasn't there.

"You can't be serious about staying here." Alina, bangs she'd been growing out falling forward to half-cover one eye, glowered out the side window of the car at a row of false-fronted buildings on a dirt side street. "If you were so set on living in East Podunk, we could have stayed in Vermont."

We could have stayed in Vermont with Dad and Adan, Sharon completed the thought, and her eyes burned with tears she refused to let fall. "You know we couldn't stay in Vermont," she said softly.

7

Alina glared at her but said nothing. Sharon turned the car down the side street and slowly rolled past a coin laundry, a hardware store, and a place that advertised hunting licenses, firearms, and fishing tackle. A skinny old man in canvas trousers and a brown plaid shirt emerged from the hardware store and openly stared as Sharon eased the car down the street. A shiver rippled up her spine as she felt his eyes on her. Maybe she'd made a mistake coming here. Maybe she and Alina would have been better off in the city. San Francisco, maybe. Or Dallas . . .

"Where are we going?" Alina asked.

"I'm just getting a feel for the layout of the town." She turned left, onto another unpaved street, past a park and a trim white house with lilac bushes flanking the front door and a sign that indicated the library.

"We should go in the library and ask about Uncle Jay," Alina said.

Sharon slowed the car and considered the idea. "My brother was never much of a reader," she said.

"Yeah, but librarians know things. I'll bet the librarian knows everybody in a small town like this. And they might have telephone books and stuff."

"You're right. That's a good idea." She stifled a sigh. Was she ready for this? Not just yet. "Let's eat first. I think better on a full stomach." The coffee and stale muffin she'd had at the motel this morning were a distant memory. And she could use another hour or two to gather her failing courage. When she'd set out on this journey, it had seemed like such a good idea—the strong, right thing to do for her and her daughter.

She wasn't feeling very strong right now. She wanted someone else to tell her what she should do.

"Do you think they'll have anything I can eat?" Alina wrinkled her nose. She'd become a vegetarian last year—a perfectly reasonable choice, Sharon thought, but her father and brother had given her nothing but grief about it. She had struggled all the way across the Midwest, eating mostly salads, French fries, and baked potatoes.

"I'm sure they'll have something," Sharon said.

"Where is there to eat in this town anyway?" Alina looked around. "Uh-oh."

"What?" Sharon followed her daughter's gaze to the black and white sheriff's department cruiser that had pulled in behind her. The officer switched on his rotating overhead lights and she groaned, a surge of adrenaline flooding her with a rush of nausea and dizziness. Was he going to give her a ticket for idling her car in the middle of the otherwise deserted street?

She watched in the side mirror as he approached the car. He was young with short blond hair and dark sunglasses. His brown shirt and pants fit closely to a trim body. She rolled down her window and managed a weak smile. "Hello," she said.

"Hello, ma'am." He touched two fingers to the brim of his Stetson, a salute that was almost courtly. "I saw you stopped here in the street and thought you might need some help. Are you lost or having car trouble?"

"Oh, no. I'm sorry, I was just trying to get my bearings." Her smile was more genuine now. "I just got to town."

"Welcome to Eureka. I'm Sergeant Josh Miller, with the Eureka County Sheriff's Department." He offered his hand and she took it for a brief, firm squeeze.

"I'm Sharon Franklin. And this is my daughter, Alina."

"Hi," Alina said. "We're looking for my uncle, Jay Clarkson. Do you know him?"

Sergeant Miller rubbed his jaw. He had big hands, with short, square fingers. "The name doesn't ring a bell. But then, I've only been in town a month myself, so I don't know a lot of people yet."

That was good news anyway, Sharon thought. There was a time when Jay would have been on a first-name basis with most law enforcement in their town. And not in a good way. "It's nice to meet another newcomer," she said. "We're thinking of relocating here."

"Where are you from?"

"Vermont."

"I've never been there, but I hear it's pretty. Different mountains, though."

Different was exactly what she wanted. "The Green Mountains are less rocky and, well, greener. But this looks pretty."

"It's a good place to live." He had a kind smile, though she couldn't read his eyes behind his sunglasses. She could use a little kindness, so she chose to believe the emotion was genuine. "Is there anything else I can help you with?" he asked.

"Is there any place to eat that would have vegetarian food?" Alina asked.

"The Last Dollar Cafe has pretty much any kind of food you like," he said. "And it's all good." He pointed ahead. "Just go to the corner here and turn left."

"Thank you. It was nice meeting you."

"Same here." He took out a card case. "Here's my card. If you need anything that's not an emergency, you can reach me on that number."

"Thanks."

He hesitated and her heart pounded. For a fleeting moment, she was afraid he might ask for her number. She'd heard about western towns where the men so outnumbered the women that any single female was immediately popular. The last thing she wanted in her life right now was romance. "I guess I'll see you around," he said. He tipped his cap again and walked back to his cruiser.

Relieved, Sharon rolled up the window, put the car in gear, and carefully pulled away. "He was nice," Alina said.

"Yes."

"Cute, too."

"He was nice looking." More importantly, he'd been a friendly—but not too friendly—face in a place that was foreign to her, the first to welcome her to what she hoped would be her new life. She pulled the car into a space in front of the Last Dollar Cafe. Was the name a sign? She wasn't down to her own last dollar yet, but it wouldn't be long. "This looks good, huh?" The cedar-sided building had green shutters, leafy shrubs across the front, and planters full of flowers on either side of the door.

"Let me get my camera." Alina pulled this most treasured possession—a fancy, multiple-lens digital camera—from its case on the floorboard at her feet and slung the strap around her neck. "I might see something good to photograph."

Inside, the café was an attractive, homey place, with tables covered with red-checked cloths and booths with red vinyl benches. A colorful mural filled the back wall, and the other walls were filled with antiques—old skis, skates, and kitchen utensils. A hand-cranked coffee grinder caught

Sharon's eye; she'd had one like it back home.

A pretty dark haired young woman greeted them. "Hello. Y'all can sit anywhere you like."

They chose a booth against the wall. The young woman brought silverware wrapped in paper napkins and two glasses of water. "The menu is on the wall." She indicated a large chalkboard covered in writing in colored chalk.

"Do you have a veggie burger?" Alina asked, her expression guarded.

"We have a great veggie burger," the young woman said. "And killer sweet-potato fries or onion rings. Or I can get you a salad."

Alina made a face. "I've had enough lettuce to last me a lifetime. But the veggie burger sounds good. And sweet-potato fries."

"I'll have the same," Sharon said. "And iced tea."

"I'll have a Coke," Alina said.

"Sounds good." The young woman left and Sharon sagged back against the booth and closed her eyes.

"Are you okay, Mom?"

Sharon's eyes snapped open and she pasted on a confident smile. "I'm fine. Just tired of driving." That was true; they'd been in the car most of four days now. But she was also worn out with worrying—not just about this trip across the country to find a brother she hadn't seen in years, but all the worrying of all the months

13

before that leading up to the decision to leave and come west.

A few moments later a tall blonde brought their drinks. "What brings you two to Eureka?" she asked.

Sharon opened her mouth to say they were just visiting, but Alina answered first. "We're here to visit my uncle. We're thinking about staying, though. If Mom can find a job. Is it nice here?"

"It's pretty nice," the young woman said. "Danielle and I—that's the dark haired woman who waited on you—we weren't sure what to think when we first came here a few years ago. We'd never lived in such a small town. But it feels like home now. I'm Janelle, by the way."

"I'm Alina." Alina offered her hand. Amazing what the promise of a veggie burger could do for a sullen teen. "This is my mom, Sharon."

Sharon took the offered hand and smiled weakly. "Hello."

"Who's your uncle?" Janelle asked.

"Jay Clarkson," Alina said. "Do you know him?"

Janelle looked thoughtful. "The name doesn't ring a bell. Danielle!" She called over her shoulder. "Do we know a Jay Clarkson?"

"I don't think so."

"Anybody else know that name?" Janelle addressed the half dozen other patrons in the restaurant.

14

After some murmuring and brief discussion, it was decided that no one knew of a Jay Clarkson.

Sharon felt hollow. Defeated. Had she driven all the way across the country on a fool's errand?

"We thought about asking at the library," Alina said. "But Mom says Uncle Jay isn't much of a reader."

"Well, I hope you find him. And enjoy your stay in Eureka, however long it ends up being. It's kind of quiet now, but things really pick up come summer."

"Is there a motel in town?" Sharon asked. She'd planned on asking Jay if they could stay with him, but if he wasn't here . . . She was suddenly so exhausted that the thought of getting in the car and driving to the next town was almost enough to make her burst into tears.

"There is. The Eureka Hotel, up by the highway. It's not fancy, but it's clean. We've got a bed-and-breakfast opening this summer, but it's not ready yet."

"The hotel is fine. I'll check it out." She hoped the rooms were cheap. The wad of cash she'd stuffed in her suitcase before she left was getting alarmingly thin. She'd have to find a job soon. She'd counted on Jay to help with that; living here, he'd know who would hire her, where she and Alina could live. . . . But if he wasn't here . . . She fought back the sick, panicked

15

feeling that had threatened to overwhelm her whenever she allowed herself to think of her and her daughter alone. Really alone—something she had never been in her life.

Danielle brought their food, and the aroma of burgers and fries revived Sharon some. She told herself she'd feel better when she'd eaten. She would find Jay, and he would help them. End of story.

"Oh, this is so good," Alina said after a few minutes, pausing to sit back. She took a sip of Coke. "Maybe this place isn't so bad after all. I like Janelle and Danielle."

Sharon nodded. "I was really hoping someone would know where to find Jay."

"When was the last time you heard from him?" Alina asked.

"I talked to him on the phone right before we moved last time."

Alina's eyes widened. "You haven't heard from him in five years?"

"Your father thought it was best to keep to ourselves." Joe had been big on self-sufficiency. That, and his increasing paranoia, had led him to sever relationships with their families and most of their friends.

Alina took a long drink of her soda, then dragged a sweet-potato fry through a pool of ranch dressing on her plate. "He listened to Wilson too much," she said. "Wilson was paranoid that the government was opening all our mail. But Dad isn't that stupid."

Sharon said nothing. Joe wasn't stupid, but he had his own share of paranoia, grown worse since they'd moved next door to his best friend —pretty much his only friend now—Wilson Anderson, a man who trusted no one.

She turned her head to study the mural on the back wall of the café. A miner and his mule stood against a backdrop of majestic peaks, while a stern-faced pioneer woman did laundry in front of a log cabin. On the other end of the painting, a breechcloth-clad Native American crouched beside a stream, watching a rainbow trout.

Janelle stopped by to refill Sharon's iced tea. "Can I take a picture of your mural?" Alina asked.

"Sure. A local artist, Olivia Theriot, painted that for us a few months ago," she said. "She works part time at the bar next door, the Dirty Sally, but she has T-shirts and jewelry and stuff in a shop up on the square."

"Cool," Alina said.

"Maybe you ought to stop in the Dirty Sally and ask about your relative," Janelle said. "If he's not the library type, maybe he's the bar type."

"Definitely the bar type," Sharon said. At least when she'd last seen him, her brother had been a hard-drinking, motorcycle-riding, authority-defying rebel. Maybe he was in jail somewhere.

Janelle moved away. Alina slid out of the booth and went to take pictures of the mural. Sharon stared out the window beside the booth, which looked out onto a neat backyard, complete with a chicken coop and bare raised garden beds.

"Are we going to ask about Jay at the bar?" Alina asked when she returned.

"I don't know." Sharon pushed her almost-empty plate away. "Maybe he isn't here any-more."

"We can't come all this way without at least asking." A whine crept into Alina's voice. "I'm tired of riding. Let's stay here for a day or two, check things out. At least we'll eat good." She nodded to the chalkboard menu. "They have vegetarian lasagna, vegetable soup, stir-fry with the option of tofu instead of chicken, and macaroni and cheese."

Sharon suppressed a smile. Apparently, the way to her daughter's heart was through her stomach. "We'll stay a couple of days," she said. "And we'll keep looking for Jay."

After all, she was running out of options. She needed to find someplace to settle, in case Joe decided to make good on his threats to come after her.

"Have you seen my key chain?" Olivia Theriot asked, as she combed through the box of miscel-laneous junk that had collected beneath the cash register at the Dirty Sally Saloon. "It's a real aspen leaf, encased in resin. D. J. gave it to me."

"Are your keys still attached to it?" Fellow bartender Jameso Clark looked up from the draft beer he was drawing.

"No, I have the keys. But I noticed last night the leaf was missing. I was hoping it had fallen off here and someone had found it."

"I haven't seen it." Jameso finished filling the glass and set the beer in front of Bob Prescott, who sat at the bar eating a bacon cheeseburger.

"Maybe you lost it at the house," Bob said.

"Maybe so, but I looked there." Olivia made a face. "I'm losing everything these days—my favorite pair of earrings, pens, and now my keychain. I think I'm just stressed out with the remodeling and everything."

"How's that coming?" Jameso asked.

"Slow." She and her boyfriend, D. J. Gruber, had bought the old miner's house in a fore-closure sale last month. They'd gotten a sweet deal, but now they spent every spare moment trying to make the place livable. "I can't wait until we can move in together. Maybe then I'll stop misplacing things." D. J.'s rental house was too small for the two of them and her teenage son, Lucas, so she lived with her mother, Eureka mayor Lucille Theriot. Besides, getting their own place and fixing it up together was symbolic of her and D. J. starting over. She was a big believer in symbols. D. J. said that was the artist in her. Lucas just said she was weird.

"Maybe you have a pack rat," Bob said.

"We do not have rats!" She shuddered. Mice were bad enough, but rats were enough to give her nightmares.

"Not a regular rat, a pack rat." Bob set down his burger. In his seventies, he was the picture of the grizzled miner, right down to his canvas pants, checked flannel shirt, and scraggly whiskers. Olivia suspected he cultivated this image carefully. "They're bigger and hairier than your average rat, and they like to collect things and stash them in their nests."

"They're harmless," Jameso said.

She tried to push away the image of a giant, hairy rat wearing her favorite earrings and changed the subject. "How's Maggie?" she asked Jameso. Maggie Stevens, a reporter at the local paper, had moved to town about the same time Olivia had come to Eureka, and had started dating Jameso not too long after.

"Pregnant."

She laughed. "That doesn't answer my question. How's she feeling?"

"She feels fine," Jameso said. "But between the wedding plans and getting Barb's B and B ready to open this summer, she's driving me crazy."

Olivia tried to hide a smile and failed.

"What are you smirking about?" Jameso asked.

"Those two love ordering you around," she said. Barb Stanowski, Maggie's best friend, lived in Houston but spent a lot of time in Eureka. Right now, she was remodeling another of the town's old homes into a fancy bed-and-breakfast inn. "I think they like the idea of domesticating the wild man." Before Maggie had arrived in town, Jameso had a reputation as a hard-partying free spirit, a handsome rogue who refused to settle down. Now that he and Maggie were engaged, with a baby on the way, he'd definitely changed.

"Yeah, well, I'll be glad when the B and B opens and the wedding's over and things settle down." He bent and began detaching the beer keg beneath the bar. "You got the last beer out of this one, Bob."

"I hate to tell you, but with a new baby in the house, your life will be anything but settled," Olivia said. "Have you and Maggie found a place to live yet?"

He scowled. "No, and I don't want to talk about it."

"Maybe you don't have a pack rat." Bob, having finished his burger and drained the beer, pushed his empty plate and glass away. "Maybe you have a ghost. What house did you buy again?"

"It belonged to a woman named Gilroy. She

21

was moving to Florida to live with her daughter."

He nodded. "That's the old McCutcheon place. I wouldn't be at all surprised if it didn't have a ghost. They say old man McCutcheon murdered his wife when she tried to run off with a traveling insurance salesman, and buried her body in the back garden. Of course, they never found the body, but could be she's haunting the place. A woman would like fancy earrings and such."

"Oh, shut up, Bob. Save the tall tales for the tourists." She didn't believe in ghosts. "I'm just losing things because I'm stressed. I'll have to be more careful."

"Don't go scaring her with your ghost stories, Bob." Jameso hefted the empty beer keg to his shoulder. "I have to change this out. Be right back."

As he exited out the back, the front door to the saloon opened and a woman and a girl entered. The woman was of medium height and thin, with dark brown hair falling well past her shoulders. The girl—her daughter, most likely—also had dark hair, worn in two braids on either side of her heart-shaped face. "Can I help you?" Olivia asked.

The woman looked around the almost-empty bar, then finally rested her gaze on Olivia. She had dark circles under her eyes and looked exhausted. "I'm looking for a man named Jay Clarkson," she said. "Have you heard of him?"

22

Olivia shook her head. "I don't know anyone by that name." She turned to Bob. "Sound familiar to you?"

Bob shook his head. "No, and I know everybody. What do you want with this Clarkson fellow?"

She and the girl were already backing toward the door, like wild animals frightened by the questions. "Don't go," Olivia said. "Maybe we can help you."

Jameso emerged from the back room with a fresh keg and Olivia turned to him. "Jameso, do you know—?"

But he was staring at the woman, his face the color of copy paper. "Sharon!" He lowered the keg.

"Jay!" She took a few steps toward him, then stopped. Jameso was frozen in place. "Aren't you happy to see me?" she asked.

"Sure. Of course." He shoved both hands in the front pockets of his jeans. "I'm just surprised. I thought you were in Vermont."

The woman pressed her lips together and took a deep breath, nostrils pinching, then flaring. "I've left Joe." She glanced at the girl, who had hung back, though she kept making furtive glances in Jameso's direction. "It's a long story. Jay, I'm just so glad to see you. I've been asking around town and no one knew you. I—"

"Jay?" Olivia said.

"It's Jameso now," he said, his voice strained. "Jameso Clark."

"You changed your name?" Sharon asked.

He put one hand on the bar, leaning on it. "It's a long story."

The woman crossed her arms over her chest. "I have all the time in the world. Why don't you tell me?"

"Yeah." Olivia copied the woman's pose. "Why don't you tell us?"

Chapter 2

"Everything is going to be fine. You don't have to worry about anything." Barb shifted her Escalade into second gear as she cruised down the steep hill into town.

"Liar." Maggie rested her hands on her bulging belly and felt the baby—Jameso insisted on calling it the Stowaway—kick. So far she'd survived morning sickness, fatigue, cravings, swollen ankles, and indigestion, but whether she'd live through a wedding, a new husband, and a new baby was debatable. "I have plenty to worry about, starting with the fact that Jameso and I don't have a place to live after we're married."

"I don't know why you don't move in with Jameso. Or keep your place and have him move in with you."

"My lease expires June fifteenth and the landlord wants me out so he can collect double the rent from summer tourists. And Jameso's place doesn't have room for a baby."

"A baby doesn't need a lot of room, at least not at first." Barb shifted again and guided the SUV past Living Waters Hot Springs. Steam rose from behind the wooden fence that blocked a view of the clothing-optional hot springs from the road.

"I need for us to find a place to start life together that's just ours," she said. "Call me crazy, but I want a bedroom that Jameso has not already shared with half a dozen other women previously. And a kitchen with a stove that works—Jameso's doesn't."

"That's what you get for falling for the town Casanova." Barb grinned. "Though I like to think Jameso was with all those other women because he was looking for you. Once you came into his life, *bam!* Instant monogamy."

Maggie snorted and plucked at nonexistent lint on the front of her maternity top. "I know he loves me and I love him. I just hate that everything's so unsettled. I don't have a baby bed, or half the things I'll need for the kid, because there's no place to put them. I don't even have a wedding dress, because I don't know what size I'll be a month from now. Plus, I can't get excited about waddling down the aisle, the size of a whale."

"You're the one who wanted to wait until spring to get married," Barb said. "I told you you were cutting it close."

"Now I'm wondering if we shouldn't wait until after the baby is born."

"Jameso will never go for that. It's all I can do to keep him from dragging you off to the justice of the peace now."

Maggie sighed. "I know. He's not a patient person. But he's trying. This is all a big change for him." For a man who'd avoided responsibility for years, Jameso had embraced the prospect of being a husband and father with touching resolve. He made Maggie believe he would have moved mountains for her—so why was she so reluctant to buy a wedding dress and say her vows?

"Maybe I'll buy a dress and surprise you," Barb said. "Consider it a wedding gift."

Maggie glanced at her friend. A former beauty queen, Barb had aged well, thanks to a combination of good genes and the money to afford the best salons, trainers, and plastic surgeons. At forty, she still turned heads wherever they went. Maggie ought to have been jealous, but Barb was unfailingly generous and had excellent taste. "While you're at it, find us a house, too."

"What does the real-estate agent say?"

"That everything in our price range needs too much work or is too far from town."

"There's always your dad's cabin."

Maggie laughed, a short, surprised bark that held no real mirth. The one-room miner's shack perched high on Mount Garnet had no electricity except solar, no heat except for a wood stove, and no access to the house in winter except a snowmobile. She'd lived there when she first came to Eureka after her dad, Jake Murphy, left the place to her in his will. But it was no place for an infant. "Now who's crazy?"

"I'm sure pioneer women raised children in worse conditions," Barb said.

"I am not a pioneer woman."

"Maybe not, but you've certainly blazed a few new trails since you left Houston. The old Maggie would never have chopped her own firewood and snowshoed to the neighbor's house in a blizzard, or half the things you've done here."

She shrugged. "That's just life in a small mountain town." It wasn't a life she'd ever imagined herself living, until she'd come to Eureka to view her inheritance and learn more about her dad. Back then, newly divorced, unemployed, and more than a little lost, the chance to live on her own and rely on her own strength for a while had been exactly what she'd needed. Finding Jameso and a place where she truly felt at home was a bonus.

"You've really blossomed here." Barb patted her hand. "You'll make a beautiful bride and a great mom. No worries, I promise."

Neither woman spoke again as Barb turned onto Eureka's main street. Lucille Theriot waved from the porch in front of her shop, Lacy's. They passed the *Eureka Miner*, the newspaper where Maggie worked, and the library where Cassie

Wynock reigned like a not-so-benevolent despot. So many familiar people and places. To think a year ago Maggie had been a stranger to them all, and now they were like family.

She had new friends, a man who loved her, and the baby she'd always wanted on the way, so why didn't she feel more settled? "I think part of me can't believe I've been so lucky," she said. "I'm waiting for the other shoe to drop."

"Let's hope it's one half of a lovely pair of Manolos." Barb parked between the Last Dollar Cafe and the Dirty Sally Saloon.

"I just want to stop in and say hi to Jameso before we have lunch," Maggie said.

"Of course you do." Barb smiled. "And I need to let that handsome fiancé of yours know the wallpaperers are finished and he can install the shelves in the library at the B and B whenever he's ready."

"Are you sure you don't want to hire a carpenter?" Maggie asked as she slid out of the Escalade. "I know you're anxious to get the remodeling done, and Jameso's schedule is kind of erratic."

"That's all right. I know he'll do exactly what I want."

"You mean, you like ordering him around." The two women met on the sidewalk in front of the saloon.

Barb's smile was enigmatic. "Maybe I just

enjoy watching him work. He does know how to fill out a pair of jeans."

Oh, yes. Jameso did do that. A brisk wind tugged at their clothes and Maggie tried to wrap her coat over her stomach, but it wouldn't close. Was she ready for marriage to a man eight years younger who was better looking than she was?

This time of afternoon on a weekday the bar was far from busy. Bob Prescott nodded from his usual stool, and Olivia Theriot greeted them with a smile. "Hello, ladies. How are things?"

"We just stopped in to say hi." Maggie scanned the bar for some sign of Jameso.

"He's over there." Olivia pointed toward a table by the front window, where Jameso sat with a dark haired woman and a young girl, their three heads close together in intense conversation.

"Oh." Maggie hesitated. The tense expression on Jameso's face—and the fact that he hadn't yet acknowledged her—hinted that she shouldn't interrupt.

But he must have felt her stare on him. He raised his head and met her gaze, and the tips of his ears reddened. "Maggie!" He half-rose from his chair.

She had no choice but to go over to him then. She leaned over and kissed his cheek. "Hello, dear." She looked at the woman and the girl. They both stared at her, openmouthed. "I'm

Maggie. Jameso's fiancée." She offered her hand.

"I'm Sharon." The woman took her hand, her grasp weak. "I'm Jay—his—sister." She looked tired—pale with gray shadows beneath her eyes. But the resemblance to Jameso was evident, in the point of her chin and the thick sable hair. The girl's hair was only a shade lighter, and she had a dusting of freckles across her nose. "This is my daughter, Alina," Sharon said.

"It's good to meet you," Maggie said, shaken but determined not to show it. "I've been curious to know more about Jameso's family." She'd known he had a sister, of course, but he'd told her they weren't close and left it at that. She'd thought it better not to press for details. Jameso tended to clam up under pressure.

"It's so funny to hear everybody calling him Jameso," Alina said, then blushed.

"No one here calls him Jameson," Maggie said. He'd explained that when a clerk at Telluride Ski Resort left the "n" off his name tag, the shortened version had stuck.

Sharon's expression grew more strained. "He didn't tell you he'd changed his name?"

"I really don't think that's important," Jameso said.

"Changed your name?" Maggie studied him, but his expression was more guarded than ever. No answers there. She turned to Sharon again. "What did he change it from?"

31

"He was born Jay Clarkson."

"I changed it when I got out of the army," Jameso said. "I didn't want any connection to that bas—to our father." His eyes met Maggie's, pleading for understanding. "My legal name now really is Jameson Clark."

She nodded, feeling numb. The man she loved hadn't been born with the name she'd always known him by—yet he hadn't thought that was important enough to share with her?

"Hi, I'm Barb Stanowski." Barb slid between Maggie and Sharon, and offered a dazzling smile. "I own a bed-and-breakfast here in town. Maggie and Jameso are helping me with some remodeling. What brings you to Eureka?"

"I wanted to see my brother." Sharon glanced at Jameso, who was staring at the floor between his toes, ignoring all the women around him. "And I'm thinking of relocating here."

"Oh? From where?" Barb asked.

Sharon didn't answer. Alina gave her mother a puzzled look. "We were in Vermont," she said. "My dad and brother are still there."

Maggie guessed there was a story there. She wondered if she'd ever hear it—or did keeping secrets run in Jameso's family?

"Listen, why don't you head on out to the house and get settled and we'll talk later." Jameso fished his keys out of his jeans pocket and worked his house key off the ring. "Head out of town on County Road Four and take the second left. Turn right on Pickax and it's the third house on the right."

"The one painted lavender," Maggie said.

"If they stay at your house, where are you going to stay?" Barb asked.

His ears reddened again. "I thought I'd stay with Maggie."

Everyone looked at her. Even Bob and Olivia had fallen silent, openly eavesdropping. She took a deep breath. For better or worse, right? Even though she and Jameso hadn't said their vows yet, they were going to have a baby together —and she knew a thing or two about complicated family relations, so she ought to cut him some slack.

"Sure," she said. "He's over there all the time anyway." She patted his shoulder and felt some of the stiffness go out of those hard muscles. "I live right next door, in the green house."

"Cute," Alina said. She, at least, didn't seem too put off by the awkwardness between the adults. "When's your baby due?"

"The first week in June." Maggie smiled at the girl. She looked about twelve or thirteen. What did she think of being dragged across the country to a town in the middle of nowhere, to see an uncle she hadn't seen in more than a few years?

"When's the wedding?" Sharon asked. She

addressed the question to Jameso, but he looked to Maggie.

"The first week in June," Maggie said.

"Cutting it a little close, aren't you?" Sharon asked.

"It's going to be a beautiful wedding," Barb said. "At my B and B. Right before my grand opening. I'll be sure you get an invitation, of course." She put one arm around Alina and the other around Sharon. "I was just on my way out to Maggie's place. You can follow me and I'll show you where Jameso lives and you can get settled in. I'm sure you're going to love it here."

"What about Jameso and Maggie?" Alina asked. "Maybe they want to come with us."

"Oh, I don't think so." Barb's gaze met Maggie's, a look that telegraphed *I've got this*. Maggie almost smiled. "I'm sure they have a lot to talk about."

She escorted mother and daughter out of the saloon and suddenly it was quiet enough Maggie imagined she could hear the ice melting in the untouched glasses of water on the table. She moved to a chair and sat, hands folded across her stomach. "So." She looked up at Jameso. "Why don't you tell me what this is all about?"

Lucille Theriot couldn't remember now why she'd wanted to be mayor of Eureka. Something about civic improvement—and maybe a challenge

made to her after too many glasses of wine. Whatever the reason, after almost five years on the
job, she had begun to feel she remained in the
position because she was too stubborn to leave.
She had a dangerous need to fix things and leave
them better. Since small towns always had problems, she could never comfortably leave office.

Which also meant she couldn't do ordinary
things like check a book out of the library without being accosted with more problems to solve.
"Gloria quit," librarian Cassie Wynock said by
way of greeting when Lucille slid the latest best-
seller across the counter to her.

"Gloria Sofelli?" Lucille looked around for
Cassie's wraithlike assistant. The woman hadn't
said three words to Lucille the entire time she'd
known her. Then again, working for Cassie would
cow almost anyone. "I was always amazed she
stayed in the job as long as she did," Lucille
said. "What happened?"

"She eloped with that cameraman who was
filming that cooking show."

"Ah." *What's Cookin'? USA*, a popular cable
show that featured offbeat places to eat around
the country, had picked the local café, the Last
Dollar, for a segment; though in the end the
filming never took place. When the show left,
Gloria had probably seen her chance to get out
of town—and out from under Cassie's thumb.

"She didn't even give notice. She just packed

up and left." Cassie sniffed. "I told her she'd never get a good reference from me and she actually *laughed.* Young people these days."

Cassie and Lucille were near the same age—mid-fifties—but Cassie liked to assume the role of crotchety old woman, dressing like a matron and railing against "young people these days." Maybe she thought she commanded more respect that way. "I guess you'll have to hire someone else for the position," Lucille said. Though who in their right mind would want to work for Cassie? The woman took bossiness to new levels.

"As if I have time to train someone right now," Cassie said. "I'm much too busy."

Busy doing what? It was exactly the question Cassie wanted her to ask, so Lucille kept quiet.

Cassie answered the unspoken query anyway. "I'm working on a new, improved version of the Founders' Day Pageant for this summer. And the state is requiring us to update all our digital records—such a nuisance."

Yes, such a nuisance that her real job was getting in the way of something no one had asked Cassie to do in the first place. "I thought the pageant was fine as it was," Lucille said. "After all, you've only performed it once." And many people had thought once was enough, but Cassie would hear none of that. Unfortunately, since the county commissioners were afraid of her, she got her way a lot. Lucille had learned to live with it. Sometimes watching her take one of her grand ideas and run with it was even entertaining.

Case in point, the pageant, which told the story of Eureka's founding by Cassie's great-grandfather—leaving out the part where he ended up having to sell off most of what he'd owned to pay gambling debts. Cassie had hammed it up with a supporting cast of most of the Eureka Drama Society, only to be upstaged by Bob Prescott's big finale, in which he'd almost burned down the recently restored opera house.

"I'm not letting Bob near the stage this year," Cassie said, as if reading Lucille's mind. "This year, I'm going to focus more on the role women played in settling this area. We don't get nearly enough credit."

"I won't argue with that, but you'll have to tell me about it later." Lucille nudged her book closer. "I'm kind of in a hurry."

Cassie ignored the novel. "I'm never going to find someone to take Gloria's place unless I offer more money," she said. "I don't think any-one else is dumb enough to work that cheap."

"You'll have to take that up with the library board." Cassie was right: She'd have to pay a lot to get anyone to put up with her for forty hours a week.

"The board will just tell me they're broke. They're worse than you for putting on the poor mouth."

"I'm not putting on." Lucille didn't try to hide her exasperation. "The city's pretty much broke."

"Well, we all know whose fault that is."

Lucille's cheeks felt hot, and she gripped the edge of the counter to keep from reaching over and slapping Cassie silly. Yes, everyone knew that Lucille had fallen for a smooth-talking swindler who'd cleaned out the city coffers last fall. Worse, Gerald Pershing was still a fixture in her life, thanks to a swindle they'd cooked up to sell him half of a nonproducing gold mine the city had acquired in payment of back taxes.

"Maybe you should ask Gerald for a donation to the library fund," Lucille said. "Since he seems so sweet on you." Over Christmas, Cassie had had the long-in-the-tooth Lothario running to do her bidding.

"That was only when he thought I was an heiress." She grabbed Lucille's book and ran it across the scanner. She squinted at the computer screen. "Lucas owes a twenty-five-cent fine. He turned in that book about electricity a day late."

Lucille opened her wallet and took out a quarter. Lucas was her grandson, a bookworm. Surprisingly, he got along better with Cassie than most people.

Cassie refused the quarter. "Tell him he can work it off by shelving for an hour for me on Saturday."

Lucille dropped the change back in her wallet.

Lucas, now thirteen, might not want to spend his Saturday morning at the library with a grouchy old woman, but the boy continually surprised her. He might look forward to the arrangement, since he enjoyed browsing the shelves of dusty volumes, some of which hadn't been moved in at least a decade. "I'll give him the message," she said. "And I'll put the word out that you're looking for help."

Cassie made a grunting noise that might have been "thanks." Though Lucille doubted it.

She was on her way out when the door burst open and Bob Prescott sauntered in. As usual, the odor of beer wafted around him like a hoppy aftershave. Dressed in canvas pants and a checked shirt, he looked like a movie extra hired to play a miner. Except Bob was the real thing. He still worked several claims in the mountains above town—when he wasn't propping up the bar at the Dirty Sally. And he'd volunteered as manager of the Lucky Lady, the town's bogus gold mine in which Lucille's former lover Gerald Pershing now held a half interest.

"Good afternoon, Bob," Lucille said.

"Nothing good about it," he said.

"Sorry to hear that." She tried to slip past him, but he took her arm in a surprisingly strong grip. "We've got problems, Madam Mayor. You and I need to talk."

She checked her watch. She needed to get

back to the shop, to meet an antique buyer from Denver who was coming by to look at a folk art piece Lucille had advertised on her Web site. "I can give you ten minutes." She glanced over her shoulder at Cassie, who was leaning over the counter, clearly listening to every word. "Walk with me back to the store."

"Bob, you owe a dollar fine on that book you checked out on how to cheat at blackjack," Cassie called as they headed toward the door.

"It was how to win at blackjack," he said.

Cassie shrugged. "Same difference. My grandmother always said gambling was the work of the devil."

"She would know." He held the door open and motioned Lucille through.

On the sidewalk, a chill wind buffeted them. Lucille drew her coat more closely around her. Though April was almost over, snow still lingered in dirty piles at the edge of the street, and the buds on the trees in the park refused to blossom, closed up like misers' fists. Spring always took so long to come to the mountains and lingered so short a time.

Bob shoved both hands into his pockets and fell into step beside her. "I've been studying up, thinking about taking a trip down to Cripple Creek," he said. "My sister wants me to come see her, and they've got those casinos there—thought I'd give 'em a try."

Bob had a sister? She tried to imagine a female version of the shriveled old man but had to stop. "That's nice, Bob. It's always good to stay in touch with family."

He grunted.

"What's this big problem you wanted to talk about?" she prompted. She prayed it was something small. Something easily—and cheaply—handled. But the problems people brought to her never were small or cheap or easy.

"Oh, yeah. Well, we got the report back this morning from that engineering firm in Denver—the one Gerald hired to do an assessment of the Lucky Lady."

As always when Gerald's name was mentioned, she stiffened. She really needed to get over that. Yes, she'd slept with the guy and let him cheat her and the town, but that was months ago. "I didn't know Gerald had hired anyone to do an assessment."

"I told him he was wasting his money—that I knew more about mining than all those engineers had forgot—but he wouldn't hear anything against it." Bob spat into the brown grass along the edge of the sidewalk.

"And what did they find?" The Lucky Lady Mine was supposed to be a dud—that was the whole reason the city had offered shares for sale—to recoup their lost money by playing on Gerald's greed. What they'd done wasn't exactly

41

legal, but since Gerald had been dancing on the wrong side of the law with his bogus investments, they'd figured they were about even.

Bob looked glum. "The engineers' report says there's gold in there. A good amount of it, too, buried deep and mixed in with a lot of other minerals, but it's there."

She stopped and whirled to face him, heart doing a flamenco stomp in her chest. "How is this bad news?" After all, the city still owned the other half of the mine. "Are you saying we could make money off this after all?"

"It's the 'after all' part that's the kicker," Bob said. "Getting to the gold is going to take a big investment of cash to pay for fancy machinery and processing." He shook his head.

Lucille's mind raced. "Can't we get Gerald to pay for it? He's always talking about how much money he has."

"I tried that already, but he's insisting that each partner in the venture pay an equal share."

"Can we afford it?" She had to ask, though she already knew the answer.

"If we empty the coffers again, maybe."

After paying for plowing during a winter that had seen record amounts of snow, not to mention repairing city streets and paying some other bills they owed, the city budget was already nearly depleted. "What if we refuse?"

"He says he'll sue us for not holding up our

part of the partnership agreement. He could end up with the whole mine." Bob rubbed the back of his neck. "Hell, he could end up with the whole town, for all I know."

"I'll have Reggie look into this." The town's lawyer, Reggie Paxton, might be able to find an angle for them to pursue. "Bob, do you think there's enough gold in the mine to make all this worthwhile? I mean, will the investment eventually pay for itself?"

He scraped a hand over his bristly cheek and worked his jaw back and forth, as if literally chewing on the question. "I don't know. On one hand, why would Pershing waste his money on something that wouldn't pay off? On the other, if he thinks he's been swindled . . ."

She nodded. "He might do it just to get back at the town." To get back at her. Even though Gerald had been the one to run off after their one night together, he'd had the audacity to expect her to pick up where they'd left off when he finally did return to town. She'd told him where he could stick that idea, and he'd acted all hurt and offended. Maybe this was his revenge—to bankrupt the town she loved a second time. She'd always heard that a woman scorned was a terrible thing to behold, but she wasn't so sure that men couldn't be just as bad. Or worse.

Chapter 3

Sharon followed the blonde in the Escalade, Barbara, to a neat street of identical wooden houses a couple of miles from the center of Eureka. She parked in the drive of the lavender house, and she and Alina climbed out and waved to Barbara as she turned her car around and drove off.

"The house is cute," Alina said.

"It is." She didn't normally associate men, especially her brother, with "cute," but the cottage where he lived had lavender-painted wood siding with white gingerbread trim. The sharply pitched roof and tiny front porch made it resemble a doll's house. She glanced at the matching cottage next door—this one painted green and white. Where the fiancée lived. Had being neighbors thrown the two together, or had that come later?

She and Alina carried their suitcases up the front steps, and Sharon used the key Jay—she couldn't get used to thinking of him as Jameso —had given her to open the door. They stepped into a living room dominated by a black wood stove. Light shone through bare windows onto equally unadorned hardwood floors.

"Why doesn't he have any furniture?" Alina asked.

Sharon laughed. The living room was almost empty, save for a leather couch strategically patched with silver duct tape and a television balanced on a stack of crates. Through an open doorway she glimpsed a wooden table and two folding chairs. "Your uncle is just a typical bachelor," she said. "The refrigerator is probably full of beer, and I'll bet there's nothing in the cupboards but cans of soup and chili."

She wondered what other bachelor accoutrements Jay might have stashed about. Note to self: Check under the mattress and in the closet for girlie magazines. She didn't really want her daughter coming across them accidentally.

"But isn't he over thirty?" Alina stood in the middle of the room, clutching her suitcase, as if she was afraid to touch anything.

"It takes longer for some men to grow up than others," Sharon said. Sometimes a lot longer.

"He has a lot of skis," Alina said. They were lined up along one wall of the living room—four pairs of varying widths, from skinny cross-country skis to fat powder boards. A snowboard completed the lineup, along with two pairs of snowshoes, a jumble of poles, two backpacks, and what might have been parts for a snowmobile.

"Men do love their toys," Sharon said.

"At least he doesn't have guns everywhere." Alina set down her suitcase and studied a picture on the wall, a sepia print of a miner with a mule.

Sharon felt a pain in her chest. Right. Her soon-to-be ex-husband had amassed an impressive collection of weaponry in the last few years. She couldn't even go to the bathroom without finding some nasty-looking handgun balanced on the toilet lid. Jameso probably did have a weapon or two somewhere around here, but at least the walls weren't bristling with them.

"Let's check out the bedroom," she said.

The room wasn't as awful as she'd feared. Sheets and blankets trailed from the unmade bed, and a tangle of dirty clothes filled one corner. But she found clean sheets in the closet. And no magazines under the mattress. Alina helped her mother change the bed linens, and Sharon bundled up the old ones and the dirty clothes and stashed them under the bed until she could get to the coin laundry to wash them. She swept the floor and dusted the windowsills, and the room looked habitable.

"Where am I going to sleep?" Alina asked.

"You'll sleep with me." They'd shared a bed in the hotel room on the way down.

Alina made a face. "Mom, I'm thirteen."

And I'm thirty-one, Sharon thought. *Thirty-one and I don't even have my own bed anymore—or a job or house or retirement fund or even a savings account.* How had that happened? "It's just until I find a job and we get a place of our own," she said.

Alina pushed her lip out in a pout and collapsed onto the bed. "When was the last time you had a job?" she asked.

"It's been a few years." She had to force lightness into her voice. She had never actually worked for pay. Joe had never wanted her to work, and Adan had come along exactly ten months after the wedding, so Sharon had been occupied looking after him. Eventually, they'd moved too far from town to make commuting practical and besides, paying for day care was too expensive. She'd stayed home and looked after children and the house. She'd made her own bread and yogurt, planted a garden, sewed her own clothes, and been a regular pioneer woman.

"I did volunteer work," she said. "At your school, remember?"

Alina wrinkled her nose. "I was, like, in third grade."

Five years ago. A lifetime ago. "I'm sure I'll find something," she said with false bravado. She'd have to. Jay—Jameso's—work as a bartender clearly couldn't support them all.

"Why did Uncle Jay change his name?" Alina asked.

"You'll have to ask him that." Though the fact

that he'd grown to hate their father and wanted to distance himself from the past probably had a lot to do with it. She didn't blame him for wanting to start with a completely clean slate. If she didn't have children, she might think of adopting a new name of her own. It would be sort of like going into the witness protection program, with fewer rules and less security.

"I like the name Jameso, though," Alina continued. "It's different. Kind of cool."

That was Jay—always the coolest guy in the room. Untouchable.

"Did you know he was engaged?" Alina asked.

"No, that was a surprise." And the fact that his fiancée was pregnant. Had the child forced Jay's hand, or had the couple been planning to wed all along? Whatever their situation, Sharon's meeting with Maggie just now had been awkward. She'd have to try harder to be friendly. After all, Maggie was going to be family now—maybe the only family, along with Jameso, that she and Alina had left.

She was in the kitchen taking an inventory of the shelves—as she'd expected, there wasn't much to work with—when someone knocked on the front door. "I'll get it!" Alina called.

By the time Sharon made it into the living room, Alina was ushering in Maggie and Barbara. "We stopped by to see if you needed anything," Barbara said. She looked around the room and made a face. "Just as I remembered it —early bachelor pad."

"We planned to buy new furniture for our place together," Maggie said.

"None of us thinks this is a reflection on you," Barb said. "You'll have to visit Maggie's place next door," she told them. "It's very nice."

"I'm sure it is." Sharon studied her future sister-in-law. Maggie looked uncomfortable, as if she didn't want to be here. "I don't guess my brother told you much about me," she said.

"No, Jameso doesn't like to talk about his past. Although I gather his childhood was . . . difficult."

"That's a good word for it. I don't blame him for wanting to start over. Why Jameson?"

"I don't know." Maggie looked tense. "I didn't even know he had changed his name."

"How did you and Uncle Jay—Uncle Jameso, meet?" Alina asked.

"He was a friend of my late father's."

"He came up to check on her father's cabin and Maggie tried to hit him over the head with a stick of firewood," Barb said.

Maggie glared at her.

"Did that really happen?" Sharon asked.

"It was my first night here and I thought he was a burglar or something. He didn't know I was in the cabin and thought I was up to no good. And I only threatened to hit him—I never actually struck a blow."

"But you patched things up and fell in love," Alina said.

"Eventually."

"At Christmas, your uncle skied over a mountain pass in a blizzard to get home for the holiday and bring Maggie an engagement ring he'd had made just for her," Barb said. "The man is a romantic, whether he'll admit it or not."

"Can I see the ring?" Alina asked, eyes alight with eagerness.

Maggie held out her hand and the other three crowded around it. The gold band was studded with old mine-cut diamonds and turquoise. "The turquoise is from the French Mistress," Barb said. "The mine Maggie's father left her."

"It's beautiful," Alina said. "I like that it's not like everyone else's rings."

Maggie tucked her hands back in her coat pocket. "Do you have everything you need here?" she asked.

"I'll go out later and buy some groceries," Sharon said. "I take it my brother doesn't eat many of his meals here."

"No, he generally eats with me, or at the Dirty Sally or the Last Dollar."

Alina giggled. "Everything has such funny names."

"They're named after mines in the area,"

Maggie said. "I guess the miners liked to give their claims colorful names."

"In Vermont, where we're from, most of the places are named after the people who founded them, or after cities in England," Alina said. "Eureka is more interesting."

"And you came all the way from Vermont to here?" Barb said. "Because Jameso is here?"

"I know we haven't been close, but I'm hoping to change that," Sharon said, trying hard not to sound defensive.

"So you're thinking of staying in town?" Maggie asked.

"Yes." She tried to read the tone of the words. Was Maggie welcoming—or warning her off? "I'll need to find a job. Do you know of anyone who's hiring?"

The two women exchanged looks. "There aren't many jobs in a town this small," Maggie said. "What kind of experience do you have?"

"None, really. I've stayed home and raised kids for the last sixteen years."

"Any volunteer work?" Barb asked.

"I was a room mother at the kids' school. And I volunteered at the local library occasionally."

"We'll keep our ears open, let you know if we hear of anything," Barb said. "Something might turn up. It did for Maggie when she came here."

"Where do you work?" Sharon asked.

"The *Eureka Miner*—the local paper." She shrugged. "The pay is lousy, but none of the jobs around here pay much."

"Any job would be good to start. I'm used to scrimping and cutting corners." Sharon waited for one of them to ask why she was here—why show up after years of no contact on her brother's doorstep, with only one of her children and no money or plans?

But they were too polite. And she couldn't find the words to spill her guts in front of Alina. And not to strangers, even if one of them was going to be her sister-in-law. "I'm sure I'll see you again soon," she said.

"Yes, we'd better go," Barb said.

"Let me know if you need anything," Maggie said.

"Thanks." Sharon followed them to the door and shut it behind them. She wanted to lean her head against the cool wood and close her eyes, but she was aware of Alina watching her, so she straightened her shoulders and forced a smile. "Well, they were nice."

"Yeah." The girl flopped onto the sofa, which squeaked in protest. "Are we really going to stay here?"

"I don't know. We'll stay a while, at least."

"Will I have to go to school?"

In Vermont, Sharon had homeschooled the children. "I think you should. If I'm working, I won't have time to teach you. And it would be a good way for you to meet other kids."

"I guess." She picked up the remote control for the television and turned it over and over in her hand. "I miss Dad. And I really miss Adan. I know he's been a jerk lately, but I still miss him."

Sharon sat beside her daughter. "I know, honey. I do too." She missed her son anyway. But at fifteen, he'd declared himself old enough to make his own choices, and he'd chosen to stay with his father. Joe had insisted she leave the boy, too, and in the end she felt she had no choice. Sharon hated to think of the way Joe had turned the boy against her—against everyone really. Joe and Adan and Wilson and the others were sitting up there in that compound with their guns and their dried food, waiting for the apocalypse they were sure was coming.

She took her daughter's hand. "You understand why we had to leave, don't you, honey?"

Alina nodded. "I know. I just . . . I wish things were different."

She smoothed her palm over her daughter's unblemished, baby-soft skin. Alina was growing into a woman, but she was still so young. Bringing her here had been hard, but it had been the right thing to do. "So do I, baby. So do I."

The next morning, Sharon tried to ignore the feeling that everyone was staring at her as she walked down the sidewalk on Eureka's Main Street. Having lived in one small town or another all her life, she was pretty sure everyone who wasn't otherwise occupied was looking out the window at the newcomer, wondering what she was up to. That's what people did in small towns. Some of them probably knew already that she was Jameso Clark's sister, and that would only increase their interest.

She exited the bank—which had no job openings, sorry—and passed under the awning for a florist's, which was closed. At the school where she'd enrolled Alina this morning she'd asked about work, much to her daughter's mortification, but the school secretary had told her they were under a hiring freeze. The grocery store, hardware store, and liquor store didn't need anyone either. She'd really hoped her brother would be more help with this. When Jameso had stopped by last night to pack up some clothes and toiletries he'd told her the saloon where he worked and the café where she'd eaten lunch didn't need help either. "I'll ask around," he said, after she'd pressed him. "If you're sure you want to stay."

She'd gotten the impression that Jameso hoped she'd change her mind about living in the same town. Maybe it made him uncomfortable having someone here who knew his secrets. Well, he'd have to get used to it. She was sticking it out here. It wasn't as if she had anywhere else to go, and he was the only living relative she could have anything to do with. When she'd been younger, he'd always looked after her, so she wasn't being unreasonable to expect him to help her again, was she?

A familiar black and white vehicle pulled to the curb ahead and Sharon slowed her steps. Sergeant Josh Miller emerged from the big SUV, hatless this time, and lifted his hand in a wave. "How are you doing, Sharon?" he asked, when she drew nearer.

"I'm getting settled in," she said. "Thanks for the recommendation of the Last Dollar. The food was delicious."

"I've eaten probably too many meals there myself," he said, patting his flat stomach.

Either his wife didn't cook or there was no wife. He didn't wear a wedding ring, but that didn't mean anything. Joe had never worn a ring either. And she wasn't going to ask. She didn't want him to think she was fishing for information, because she wasn't. His marital status was no concern of hers.

"Did you ever track down your brother?" he asked.

"Yes, he's Jameso Clark—the bartender at the Dirty Sally."

"Well, sure, I know Jameso. We've been climbing together a couple of times."

"Mountain climbing?" That sounded like the daredevil kind of thing Jay had always liked.

"More rock climbing. The canyons around here have some great climbs. I've seen him up at the ski resort at Telluride a few times, too."

"So I guess you're a big outdoorsman," she said.

"That's what brought me to the mountains. Law enforcement pays better in the city, but I prefer the lifestyle here."

"I'm looking for a job," she said. "Do you know if the sheriff's department is hiring?"

He grinned, and fine lines formed around his eyes—nice brown eyes, she noticed, now that he wasn't hiding them behind sunglasses. "You thinking of becoming a deputy?" he asked.

"I'm probably more qualified for clerical work."

"I haven't seen any job postings, but I'll keep my eyes open for you."

"Thanks." She stepped away. "Well, I guess I'd better let you get back to work."

She was aware of his eyes on her as she continued down the sidewalk. Talking to him had lifted her spirits; he was just a pleasant, positive guy. Funny that he was a friend of Jameso's, though maybe not that strange; they were about the same age and obviously shared many of the same interests. She'd have to ask Jameso about him. Maybe it would give them something to talk about. So far all of their relatively brief conversations had been painfully awkward. So much for the sibling closeness she'd hoped for.

She stopped in front of the next store in line. *Lacy's* was written in fancy script on the glass display window. An arrangement of silk sunflowers bloomed in a dented milk can by the door and another sign beckoned—*Come in!*

The jangle of sleigh bells announced her entrance and a tall, angular woman in a white blouse looked up from behind the counter. "Hello," she said, smiling.

"Hello." Sharon took a few steps into the shop, past a child's pedal car and a second milk can. The shop was jammed with the oddest assortment of items, from a seven-foot-tall display case of fine glassware and china, to what looked like a stack of old highway signs, leaning against one wall.

"Some of it's junk and some of it's valuable treasure," the woman behind the counter said. "Which is which sort of depends on the person who's buying. But whatever you're looking for, I've probably got it in here somewhere, or I know someone who does."

"Are you Lacy?" Sharon asked.

"Lucille Theriot." The woman moved out from behind the counter. "I'm also Mayor of Eureka, so welcome to town. Are you visiting or just passing through?"

"I'm staying. Or at least I hope to." She took the hand Lucille offered. "I'm Sharon Franklin. I'm Jameso Clark's sister." She was getting a little more used to referring to her brother by the name he'd chosen. Jameso wasn't so far from Jay.

Lucille's eyebrows shot up and she studied Sharon with the intensity of a crow scrutinizing bread crumbs. "I do see the resemblance now," she said. "You have the same chin, and the same hair." Her smile broadened. "Welcome to Eureka, Sharon. What can I do for you?"

"I'm looking for a job," she said. "You wouldn't by any chance be hiring, would you?"

"I'm sorry to say this is pretty much a one-woman operation. And the city doesn't have any openings either."

"Oh." Sharon didn't even try to hide her disappointment. "Thank you anyway. If you hear of any openings, please keep me in mind." She turned to leave, but Lucille stopped her.

"Wait just a minute. Come sit down over here and let's see what I can come up with." She indicated a tall stool in front of the counter, then returned to her place on the other side. The counter itself turned out to be another glass display case. Sharon looked down and saw a row of sepia print postcards laid out on the shelf. One showed a doe-eyed young woman with a parasol, while another pictured a baby in an old-fashioned pram.

"What kind of work did you do where you're from?" Lucille asked. "And where are you from, if you don't mind my asking?"

"Vermont. And I didn't work outside the home. I was a housewife." It sounded so quaint and old-fashioned. So innocent and simple, when really it had been so complex and difficult at times.

Lucille nodded. "We all know that's hard enough work. I was in the same boat after my divorce. I had a young daughter and a blank résumé."

"I have a daughter, too." Sharon felt a surge of kinship with this woman who was probably old enough to be her mother. Though Sharon's mother had never been this calm and capable. "What did you do?"

"I found work as a cocktail waitress. I was living in Cincinnati at the time. The hours were terrible, and it wasn't good for my daughter. If I had it to do over, I'd have tried for something different. An office job, maybe."

"Are there any offices around here?" Sharon asked.

"Not many, and I don't know of any of them that are hiring. And really, it doesn't matter what you do, you can still be a good parent. My daughter turned out all right. Maybe you've even met her—Olivia Theriot. She works at the Dirty Sally with Jameso."

"The blonde, the artist. One of the women at the café told me she painted the mural there."

Lucille beamed. "That's my girl. She has more talent in her little finger than I have in my whole body. And she was in the same boat you were when she came here—a kid and no job. So we'll find something for you. Instead of employment history, let's think in terms of skills. What can you do?"

Sharon had been over this ground in her head at least a hundred times between Vermont and Colorado. "I'm organized. I can cook and clean and look after children. I volunteered at the children's school, and at the local library."

Lucille drew her expressive brows together in a V. "What did you do at the library?"

"Whatever they needed—I shelved books or entered them into the computer system." She'd enjoyed the work, until they'd moved too far out from town to make the commute practical.

"How are you at handling difficult people?"

Now, that was an odd question. "Difficult?"

"Ill-tempered. Contrary." Lucille leaned closer, eyes locked to Sharon's. "Eccentric."

She bit off a bark of harsh laughter. "You just described my ex-husband." And his friends. The divorce wasn't yet final, but it would be very soon.

"The person I'm talking about is a woman. The town librarian. Her assistant eloped and moved away, so that position is open."

"I'd love to work in a library." Sharon's heart pounded. Talk about a dream job. Libraries kept reasonable hours, so she could be home for Alina at night—and what could be better than working with books?

Lucille shook her head. "Don't get your hopes up until you've met Cassie Wynock. She can be a real dragon and if she takes a dislike to you, forget it."

"I can deal with her." After living with Joe and Wilson for the past two years, she could deal with anyone. "I saw the library when I first got to town. It looks nice."

"Cassie's family used to own the land the library is on, so she behaves as if it's her own private property," Lucille said. "Whatever you do, don't tell her you're related to Jameso until after you have the job."

"Oh? She doesn't like him?"

"She doesn't approve of him. And she has a grudge against a friend of his—who isn't even alive anymore, but that doesn't matter to Cassie. Jameso is tainted by association with Jake."

She'd have to ask her brother about this Jake character. "How can I get her to approve of me?" she asked.

Lucille pressed her lips together. "Are you sure you really want this job?"

"What are my other options?"

Lucille sighed. "Not many, I'm afraid. Not any

this time of year. In summer, the motel hires an extra housekeeper, and some of the businesses that cater to tourists hire seasonal workers, but you need something better than that."

"Does the library job have benefits?"

"Yes, it's a county position, so there's health insurance and retirement."

"Then I really want the job."

"All right." Lucille leaned back against the counter and tapped her chin with one finger. "Cassie appreciates flattery," she said after a moment. "About herself, but also about her family. If I were you, I'd ask if she's related to the Wynocks who founded Eureka. Tell her you're interested in local history."

"I can do that."

"Dress conservatively for your interview and don't wear too much makeup. She's suspicious of beautiful women."

Sharon had never thought of herself as beautiful, but she nodded. It wasn't as if she had a closet full of wild clothes anyway. "Should I go over there now?"

"She'll wonder how you heard about the job. Let me call over there and set something up." She reached for the phone, but the sleigh bells on the door jangled.

Both women turned toward the man who entered—the same grizzled miner Sharon had seen exiting the hardware store the day before.

Come to think of it, he'd been in the saloon yesterday afternoon, too. "Hello, Bob," Lucille said.

"I came by to see if you had a package for me." He scowled at Sharon. Or maybe that was just his normal expression; his face was a mass of crags and wrinkles, worn and roughened by weather.

"UPS did drop off a box yesterday afternoon," Lucille said. "Why did you have it sent here instead of your house?"

"Because I don't necessarily want everybody and his cousin knowing where I live." He leaned on the counter, gaze still fixed on Sharon.

"Sharon, this is Bob Prescott," Lucille said. "Bob, this is Sharon Franklin."

"Jameso's sister." Bob nodded. "I saw her at the Dirty Sally yesterday." He turned to Lucille. "Did you know his name isn't really Jameso Clark? Well, I guess it is now, but he was born Jay Clarkson? Ain't that a kick?"

"My name was Lucille Peyton before I married," Lucille said. "People change their names all the time."

"Women, maybe. Men only do it if they're hiding from something."

Sharon started to tell the old coot that her brother wasn't hiding—but how did she know that? For all she knew, Jameso was wanted on warrants in three states, or had an ex-wife to whom he owed back child support, or he'd stolen drugs or money from the mob, or skipped out on a big debt—there could be any number of reasons a man would come to a small mountain town and take a new name. She and her brother hadn't exactly kept in touch over the years; he really was a stranger to her.

"Says the man who didn't want a package shipped to his house," Lucille said. She reached under the counter and hefted out a large box, about two square feet. "This weighs a ton. What's in it?"

"Survival rations."

Sharon hadn't even realized she'd spoken out loud until Bob and Lucille stared at her. Her cheeks grew hot. "Um, I . . . I recognized the name on the box," she stammered. "My, um, my ex-husband used to order from them."

Lucille looked at Bob. "Survival rations? Are you expecting a disaster?"

"Never hurts to be prepared. Or are you forgetting the blizzard last winter, when no supplies could get to us for four days?"

"Are you planning to have more orders shipped to my shop?" Lucille asked.

"I might." He stuck his jaw out stubbornly. "I figure UPS is in and out of here all the time. What's one more box?"

"Watch it or I'll charge you a handling fee."

"Speaking of handling, we need to talk about how we're going to handle Pershing."

"I'm going to try to set up a meeting with the town council and Reggie and Gerald on Friday morning," Lucille said. "You should be there, too."

Bob hefted the box onto his shoulder. "I'll see you Friday, then." Without a glance at Sharon, he left the shop, the sleigh bells jangling in his wake.

"I don't think he likes me very much," Sharon said.

"Bob doesn't like most people, at least not at first. Don't let him get to you."

"Oh, I won't. So, you'll call the librarian?"

"I'll do it right now." She picked up the phone. "Just don't blame me later if she drives you crazy."

"I won't let her get to me." The last year had given her lots of practice at deflecting harsh words. Nothing anyone said or did to her could hurt her anymore.

Chapter 4

Lucille had thought she'd feel better once the town had turned the tables on Gerald Pershing and swindled some of their money back from him. She'd wanted revenge—vindication, even. Instead, she'd ended up with him more a part of her life than ever. He'd rented an apartment over the hardware store, and she had days when every time she turned around she saw him—at the café, at the library, passing on the street.

She took it as a personal failing that she continued to let him get to her. Though she tried her best not to let it show on the outside, whenever she had to spend time with him, her stomach churned and she wanted to run from the room and go home and take a bath.

Unfortunately, that wasn't an option Friday morning as she sat at a back table in the Last Dollar with the rest of the town council—Junior Dominick, Paul Percival, and Reggie's wife, Katya, as well as Reggie, Bob, and Gerald.

"You're looking lovely as usual, Lucille," Gerald said in the low Texas drawl that had once charmed her but now made her skin crawl. "That color blue is particularly striking on you."

"Save the flattery for someone who cares." She

opened the file folder on the table in front of her, though she'd already read through the paperwork there several times. "About this report the engineers have filed . . . the mine appears to need quite a bit of work to make it viable."

"Bracing of several tunnels, drainage work, ventilation to vent gases." Paul read through his own copy of the engineers' report. "And that's before we even get to the work needed to get to the ore itself."

"The safety requirements are frustrating, but necessary." Gerald nodded sympathetically.

"Skip the bullcrap and let's cut to the chase." Bob leaned forward, hands on his knees. He looked, Lucille thought, as if he was about to spring up and throttle Gerald.

Gerald must have thought so, too, because he leaned back in his chair. "Are you saying a discussion of safety is bullcrap?" he asked. "I doubt the state inspectors would agree."

"All I know is that the safety stuff is only necessary to get to the rest of it," Bob said. "The fancy drills and pneumatic hoists and steam grinders and whatever else these so-called mining engineers have dreamed up to line their pockets."

"This is the twenty-first century, Bob," Gerald said. "The days of taking ore out with a pick and shovel died out with the use of burros and hand trucks."

67

"I always preferred a stick of dynamite myself," Bob said. "But the truth is, we don't have the money to invest in all this fancy machinery. If that's the only way to get to the gold, then it's not worth it to us."

"It's worth it to me, and I own half the mine."

"We know that, Gerald." Reggie, the town's lawyer, who, with his silver ponytail and silver-rimmed granny glasses looked more like a biker than an attorney, spoke up. "The bottom line is, paying for all this will bankrupt the town."

"I really don't see how you can afford not to make the investment," Gerald said. "The payoff stands to be quite profitable."

"Were you listening to a dang thing I said?" Bob practically vibrated in his chair and his voice rose. "If the gold's that hard to get to, it can stay there for all we care."

"But you only have a fifty percent say in how the mine is operated," Gerald said in a tone one might use with a recalcitrant child. "My opinion counts just as much as yours, and I think we should move forward with the project."

"Then you can pay for it," Junior snapped.

Gerald's smile might look pleasant to a casual observer, but Lucille didn't miss the gleam of malice in his blue eyes. "According to the terms of the agreement drawn up when I purchased my shares in the mine, I can sue to force you to pay your half of operating costs," he said. "That includes any investment needed to move forward with acquiring the gold."

Lucille looked to Reggie. "Is he right?"

Reggie looked glum. "It's open to interpretation, but there's a good chance a judge would side with him."

"You can't get blood out of a turnip." Junior tossed the report on the table. "Let him sue. If the money isn't there, it isn't there."

"A judgment against you could force you to sell off all of the town's assets," Gerald said. "I'd hate to see that happen to such a lovely community."

"We wouldn't be in this fix if those Swiss investments of yours had paid off," Paul growled.

"You can't blame me for the performance of the market. I explained the risks and the decision was all yours. And your lovely mayor's."

Lucille wanted to be sick—preferably all over him. "Do you really hate me so much you'd resort to this?" she asked.

His expression was so guileless she knew it had to be an act. "Lucille, darling, why would you ever think this was in any way personal? I told you when I first met you, I'm a businessman. I only want what's best for business."

Still smiling, he stood. "I'll let you all discuss this amongst yourselves, but I'm sure you'll make the right decision."

No one said anything. Lucille listened to

Gerald's boots echoing on the wooden floor as he crossed to the front door of the restaurant and left. When he was gone, Bob was the first to speak. "I know a lot of old mine shafts where no one would ever find his body," he said.

"I didn't hear that," Reggie said.

"What are we going to do?" Lucille looked once more to Reggie.

The lawyer looked grim. "We can try to stall him—give him a little bit of money at a time and hope he grows tired of the game."

"Or we could try to change his mind," Katya said.

"Threats won't work," Lucille said. "I think that would only make him dig in his heels."

"I don't understand it," Paul said. "He's asking us to spend all this money, but that means he has to come up with a big chunk of change, too. Does he really think they're going to be able to pull that much gold out of the mine?" He tapped his copy of the report. "These engineers talk about probabilities and such, but they never come right out and say how much gold is really there."

"The swindler didn't like being swindled, so now he's out for revenge," Bob said. "He'll spend his own money—or more likely, money he stole from some other poor saps—to get back at us."

"I think Bob's right," Lucille said. "He's

determined to take us down. And it's all my fault."

"We've been over that already," Bob said. "He took us all in. What we have to do now is find a way to change his mind, make him think going forward isn't a good idea for him."

"But how do we do that?" Junior asked. "If refusing to cooperate doesn't work and threats don't work—what will?"

"I don't know," Bob said. "But I'm going to think about it. You all do, too. We beat him before; we can do it again."

Lucille stifled a sigh. "In the meantime, Paul, you'd better go over the town budget and see how much we can come up with to stall him for a while." She wondered if other small-town mayors had problems like this. Not the money thing—money was always a problem—but the whole personal romantic mistakes affecting the future of the town you governed.

Probably not. People liked to say Eureka was a unique place, but she'd prefer, in this case, if it wasn't quite so special.

Sharon had never thought of herself as an actress, but she'd faked enthusiasm for Cassie Wynock's ancestors well enough to win the job at the library. The pay wasn't fantastic, but she was used to pinching pennies, so she'd make do.

The role of sycophant wasn't one she relished,

but she'd do what she had to do to put food on the table and pay the rent, though she and Alina were still at Jameso's place for the time being. As long as she thought of it as a role, she could stomach it. Maybe after this she'd even join the local drama society. She knew there was one because her first day on the job, Cassie had recounted— in excruciating detail—the one and only performance of the Founders' Day Pageant of which the librarian had been writer, director, and star of the show.

"Bob Prescott thought it would be a big surprise to set off fireworks at the end of the show," Cassie said, her face growing even more pinched. "It was a surprise all right—he almost burned the place down. You can be sure I won't let him anywhere near this year's production."

"I'll look forward to seeing it," Sharon said. It wasn't a lie; she wanted to learn more about the town she intended to make her home for many years to come.

"The problem is, people just don't respect the sacrifices people like my grandparents made to build this town," Cassie said. "The Founders' Day Pageant is a start, but we could do so much more."

"Mmmm-hmmm." Sharon focused on her computer screen. Keeping Cassie talking about herself was a good way to deflect attention away from Sharon's past, though even this didn't work forever. Today, Sharon's third on the job, the librarian was determined to know her new assistant's life history.

"Of course, I feel this way because I've never lived anywhere else," Cassie said. "We have so many newcomers in town. Like you. What drew you to Eureka? And from Vermont? That's an awfully long way."

"My brother lives here," Sharon said. Now that she had the job, she didn't think Cassie could fire her simply because she was related to Jameso. And the town was so small, the librarian was bound to find out the truth soon anyway.

"He does?" Cassie's gray eyes sharpened. "Who is your brother?"

"Jameso Clark." She kept her eyes on the list of titles she was entering into the computer database, fingers flying over the keys.

"Really." Cassie didn't sound angry, more . . . intrigued. "You don't seem anything like him."

"Jameso is definitely his own person." She had no idea what she meant by that and figured Cassie wouldn't either.

"Still, it's a long way to come."

Sharon felt Cassie's gaze on her, drilling into her, waiting for an answer. She cleared her throat. "There's space on this form for up to six keywords for each book," she said. "Should I add keywords so readers can search for books on similar topics that way?"

"If you like." Cassie leaned over Sharon's shoulder and squinted at the computer screen. "I don't know why the state decided we needed this new system, when the old one worked fine. How long have you been divorced?"

Sharon choked back a protest. Her marital status was none of Cassie's business, but saying so wouldn't make working with her any easier. Telling the truth—that the divorce wasn't yet final—would only open the door to more questions. "Not long," she said. That was true enough.

"You must have really wanted to get away from him, if you came all this way."

She had, and maybe that was obvious, but she didn't want to talk about her marriage, especially not with her boss. "I wanted to make a fresh start," she said. And she'd wanted to reconnect with her brother—the only family she had left really. Maybe that idea had been foolish; Jameso wasn't exactly bending over backward to spend time with her. She'd seen him exactly twice in the five days she'd been in town. She hoped closeness would come later, when he'd grown more used to the idea of her being in his life.

"What do you think of that woman Jameso is marrying? Maggie Stevens."

"She seems very nice." What else could she say? She'd spent even less time with Maggie, who had been polite but distant. Then again, Maggie was pregnant, planning a wedding, and obviously hadn't known much at all about her fiancé's past. The name thing had clearly been a shock. The two women would have plenty of time to get to know each other later.

"She's older than him, you know. A divorcée."

Sharon almost laughed. As if divorce was a scandal in this day and age. "I think an older woman will be good for him," she said.

"I think it's disgraceful, her putting off the marriage so long, with a baby on the way."

"Hmmm." Time to change the subject. "I've been meaning to ask you, you live in that beautiful old house on Fourth Street, don't you?" Lucille had pointed the place out to her after they'd had lunch together the other day.

Cassie brightened. "Why yes. That house has been in my family for three generations. My great-grandmother . . ." And she was off. Sharon smiled to herself. She'd do just fine in this job. It was all a matter of knowing how to handle people.

Cassie was describing the antique furniture in her dining room when Alina breezed in. Pigtails flying, cheeks flushed from her walk from school, Sharon's daughter looked happier than she had in a while. Sharon's heart felt too big for her chest as she rose to greet her daughter. "Hello, darling," she said, and kissed her cheek.

"Hey, Mom."

Cassie made a disapproving noise in her throat. Sharon turned to her. "This is my daughter, Alina. Alina, this is Miss Wynock, the head librarian."

Alina held out her hand. "It's nice to meet you, Miss Wynock. I love libraries."

"As you should." Cassie briefly touched the girl's hand. "But you mustn't come around distracting your mother while she's working."

"I won't, I promise." Alina slung her backpack to the floor. "I need to do research for a paper for school."

Cassie clearly couldn't object to this. "Be quiet and get to work, then. If you need any help, ask."

"Sure thing." Alina winked at her mother, then carried her backpack to one of the wooden tables in the center of the room. Sharon returned her attention to the database, though she could have floated out of the chair. Seeing her daughter so happy was like having weights removed from around her ankles. She'd made the right decision coming here, she was sure.

The door to the library burst open and a whirlwind—in the form of one teenage boy— swept in. He slammed the door, launched his backpack onto the table where Alina sat, and rushed up to the counter. "Hey, Miss W," he called. "I'm here to shelve books to work off my fine."

"Lucas, lower your voice please." Cassie's words were scolding, but she was clearly pleased to see the boy. He was thin and angular, like someone who isn't tall yet, but will be. A mop of honey-colored hair drooped into his eyes, which peered out from behind round, wire-rimmed glasses. He wasn't boy-band handsome by any means, but he looked intelligent and interesting.

"Sorry. I'll use my indoor voice," he said, softening his tone slightly. He turned and spotted Alina and strode over to her. "Hey, you're the new girl, aren't you? I'm Lucas."

"Hi, Lucas, I'm Alina. My mom and I just moved here from Vermont."

He slid into the chair next to her. "Are you working on that paper for English class?"

"Yeah, I'm still trying to decide what to write, though."

Sharon forced her attention back to her work, still smiling to herself. Alina was going to be all right.

A few moments later, she heard giggling at the table and looked over to see Alina with the camera. "It was a going-away present from my dad," Alina said as she handed it over to Lucas.

"It's really great," Lucas said. "When the wildflowers start blooming in a few weeks, you should be able to get some great pictures. I can show you where to find some really pretty ones if you like."

"I'd like that."

Joe had given Alina the camera? That didn't sound like him; he wasn't the generous type, especially not with his daughter. But Alina had made a big deal out of wanting a camera at Christmas, so maybe he'd felt guilty about how things had worked out and he'd bought it for her. Funny that Alina hadn't said anything to Sharon, though. She'd just shown up with the camera the day they left. When Sharon had asked about it, Alina had said, "It's just a camera; don't make a big deal about it."

"Hey, Miss W?" Lucas called.

Cassie looked up from her desk. "Yes, Lucas?"

"Does the town park have a name?"

"A name?" Cassie frowned. "I believe everyone just refers to it as the town park."

"That's what I thought. I was telling Alina about all the flowers that bloom there every year."

"My grandmother started the tradition of planting flowers in the park every spring," Cassie said. "In fact, the land on which the park sits once belonged to my family."

"Most of the town used to belong to Miss Wynock's family," Lucas said.

"You are correct, Lucas." She stood, a broad smile on her face. "And it's really time Eureka acknowledged the contribution the Wynocks have made. You've given me a brilliant idea."

She slipped her purse over her arm. "Sharon, watch the front desk. I have an errand to run."

"Sure." Sharon set aside the computer print-out and watched as Cassie hurried out the door. "Where's she off to in such a hurry?" she wondered out loud.

"I don't know." Lucas frowned. "But it's not always such a good thing when Miss Wynock gets an idea."

Maggie set the plate in front of Jameso, then slid into the chair opposite. The house was so small that what passed for her dining room was merely a space between the kitchen wall and the back of the sofa that was just wide enough to accommodate a small table and two chairs. One more thing on her wish list: a house big enough to have a real dining room.

Jameso eyed the plate warily. "I told you you didn't have to cook for me," he said. "I could get take-out."

"I like to cook. Besides, it's expensive to eat out all the time."

"You're right. I just don't want to make more work for you."

"You're going to be my husband. I don't mind cooking for you."

"That's great. I just don't want you to think you *have* to cook for me." He picked up his fork. "What is it?"

"Thai noodles. I got the recipe from Barb."

"Barb cooks?" He eyed the plate warily.

"All right, she got it from her caterer, but it's good. Try it."

He shoveled in a forkful of the noodles in a spicy peanut sauce and nodded. "It is good." He chewed, swallowed, and seemed to relax a little. "What did you do today? Anything interesting going on at the paper?"

"Cassie Wynock is on a tear about the town park."

"What? Are people not picking up after their dogs again? Does she not like the flowers the garden club planted?"

"Better than that—she wants the town to change the name from Town Park to Ernestine Wynock Park."

"Who is Ernestine Wynock?"

"Her grandmother."

"The one in the play?"

"No, that was Emmaline, her great-grandmother. Ernestine was Emmaline's daughter-in-law, I think."

"What's so special about her that she should have a park named after her?"

"Ernestine Wynock was on the board of the women's club that established the park and planted the first flowers there. And apparently a lot of other flowers around town, including the lilacs in front of the library. Cassie came by the office today, demanding that Rick write an article promoting the idea of renaming the park." She grinned, remembering the newspaper editor's reaction to Cassie's badgering.

"I'll bet that went over really well," Jameso said.

"Oh, yes. Rick went on a rant about the free press and no one telling him what to print in his paper."

"What did Cassie do?"

"I thought at first she was going to hit him with her purse. But then she pulled herself together. She sat down at an empty desk and wrote out a letter to the editor on the subject." As much as Cassie annoyed Maggie, she admired how the librarian never let obstacles defeat her. Maybe she got that from her pioneer ancestors.

"Is Rick going to print it?"

"Oh, yes. It's sure to start people talking, and there's nothing Rick likes better."

"Should be interesting to see how it plays out," Jameso said.

"Yes." She toyed with the noodles on her plate. "What did you do today?"

"I finished the wallpaper at the B and B this afternoon."

"And you're still sane. That's something." Really, the man deserved a medal for putting up with Barb's constant "supervising" and interfering. Maggie adored her best friend, but the Houston socialite was used to ordering around the men in her life, and she treated Jameso the same way she treated her husband and son. Funny thing was, none of the guys ever seemed to really resent it.

"Barb was giving me the silent treatment."

"Oh?" She fixed her gaze on him, watching a flush rise from his neck, up past his beard to his cheeks.

He put down his fork and cleared his throat. "I'm sorry I didn't tell you about the name change," he said. "I just . . ."

"I know. You don't like to talk about the past." She'd been okay with that, mostly. What mattered most was right now, and the future she and Jameso would have together. But maybe he needed to talk about this. "I know you didn't have a happy childhood. Taking a new name is a good way to make a fresh start."

"My father was a bastard and my mom refused to admit that anything he did was wrong. I got away as soon as I could, went into the army." He took another forkful of noodles and chewed, his expression intense.

"You're a survivor," Maggie said. "I admire that. I think it's why my father liked you, too." Her father, Jacob Murphy, had battled his own demons after the Vietnam War. In a way, he'd been the father Jameso had never had, and Jameso had been his surrogate son. They'd helped heal each other, she was sure.

"I always felt guilty about Sharon," Jameso's voice was rough, his face suffused with sadness. "When I left home she was fourteen. She was stuck there."

"She seems to have turned out all right. I mean, she has her daughter and she seems, I don't know—strong. Together." A lot more together than Maggie had been when she'd come to Eureka after her own divorce.

"She has a son, too. Adan. Apparently, he stayed with her ex, Joe."

"Did you know him—Joe, I mean?"

"I saw him a couple of times. Big guy with a loud voice and a lot of loud opinions. I wanted to punch him about five minutes after I met him. I never understood what she saw in him."

"I can't answer for her, but sometimes, when a person has been bullied, they're drawn to someone strong, someone they think will protect them."

"Another bully."

"You really think so?" Her stomach knotted and she rested her hand on the mound of her abdomen. "Do you think he abused her?"

"I don't know. But I don't think she'd have left her son unless she had to."

"Have you asked her?"

"No." He filled his mouth with food again, a convenient way to avoid answering her question. Oh, she knew all his methods by now.

"You need to talk to her," she said. "She came all this way to see you."

He looked down at his plate and said nothing.

She nudged his leg under the table. "Jameso, she's you're only relative. And I think she loves you, or she wouldn't be here now."

"I don't know what to say to her. You know I'm not good with all that emotional stuff."

"You don't have to say a lot. Just listen. Let her know you're here for her." She leaned across the table and patted his hand. "The way you let me know you're here for me."

He turned his hand palm up to clasp hers. "We're going to make this work, right? The baby and the marriage and the whole nine yards?"

Relationships were unpredictable. She knew that better than anyone. But no one would ever get married if they focused on everything that could go wrong. She loved Jameso and he loved her. She'd seen how hard he tried, how much he'd changed for her and for their baby. She squeezed his hand. And she'd changed, too. She wouldn't make the same mistakes with Jameso she'd made with her first husband.

"Yeah, we are," she said. "We're going to make it."

"Okay. Just hold that right there a little bit longer."

Kneeling on the kitchen counter, shoulder

shoved underneath the cabinet D. J. was endeavoring to mount to the wall, Olivia strained to hold steady. "Hurry," she pleaded. "This thing is heavy."

"I'm hurrying."

She gritted her teeth at the sound of the drill driver, which always made her think of the dentist. "Okay, you can let go now," he said.

Relieved, she wiggled out of her awkward position and admired the new cabinet. "It looks great," she said. It was the last in the row of upper cabinets they'd spent all afternoon installing. They'd had to completely gut the kitchen of the old house they'd bought, but it was finally coming together.

"Pass over those handles and I'll put them on," he said.

"Where are they?" She looked around the clutter—boxes, tools, and bits of junk were everywhere.

"I put them on the windowsill when we unpacked the boxes yesterday."

She found the tiny plastic bags of door hardware scattered across the windowsill and the floor below. "There are only seven here," she said. "One's missing."

"It was there yesterday. I counted."

"It's not here, D. J."

Muttering under his breath, he stomped over.

"I'm not stupid," she said, as she watched

him paw through the construction debris scattered around. "It's not here."

He reached out and caressed her shoulder with one big, calloused hand. "I never said you were stupid. I must have put it someplace else."

She leaned in and slid her arms around his waist. "Maybe the ghost took it."

He laughed. "So we have a ghost now?"

"That's what Bob thinks is behind all the things that keep disappearing here."

"Oh, well, I'm sure Bob Prescott is an expert."

"I don't believe in ghosts, but he did tell me some interesting history about this place. He said the man who lived here before Mrs. Gilroy supposedly murdered his wife and buried her in the backyard."

"Grisly. And probably untrue." D. J. patted her back and released her. "Even way back when, if your wife disappeared, people asked questions. They'd notice a fresh grave in the backyard. I think Bob's pulling your leg."

"Probably." She looked back at the row of cabinets. "What are you going to do about the missing door hardware?"

"If I don't find it, we can order another one."

She leaned back against the counter and watched him install the handles on the other seven doors. "Everything is looking really good."

"Yeah, especially considering what a dump this place was." He pressed the trigger on the drill driver and drove a screw into place. "I'm looking forward to spending my nights and weekends doing something besides construction work."

"There's always yard work and home repairs," she said. "When you have a house, the upkeep never stops."

He looked over his shoulder at her. "You're not sorry we got the house, are you?"

"No." She moved over and put her arms around him again. "We're going to be happy here."

"I'd be happy anywhere with you." He set aside the drill and kissed the top of her head.

"I know. But it's just so crazy sometimes, how things turn out."

"What do you mean?"

She closed her eyes and breathed deeply of the dust, cotton, and soap scent of him. Why did that combination smell so good to her? "I always thought of myself as a city girl. Yet here I am in a small town in the mountains, and I'm happier than I've ever been," she said. "I'm starting to earn some money from my art. Lucas is doing well in school. . . ."

"Don't forget the wonderful man who loves you."

"Oh yeah, him, too." She stood on tiptoes to kiss him, a long, satisfying kiss that might have turned into more if she hadn't pulled away.

"Seriously," she said. "If you'd told me two

years ago that I'd end up living near my mother, I'd have spit in your face. She and I never got along."

"Sometimes you have to grow up to appreciate your parents."

"Yeah." She reluctantly straightened and began gathering up the cardboard and plastic the cabinets had been packed in. D. J. returned to attaching the cabinet hardware.

"Hey, speaking of unexpected family relationships, have you met Jameso's sister?" she asked.

"The new librarian, right? I saw her when I stopped by to pick up Lucas the other day. She looks like Jameso."

"Divorced, one kid, new in town—she reminds me of me." Olivia hoped for her sake that Sharon hadn't been as messed up. Olivia had been running away from the only man who'd really loved her, planning to hide out in the mountains for a while to lick her wounds. She'd thought she was tough and smart, and that she knew what was best for herself and her son. She'd turned out to be wrong on so many levels.

"She getting settled in okay?" D. J. asked.

"I guess. She and her daughter are living in Jameso's place and he moved in with Maggie."

"That's going to be a tight fit when the baby's born."

"They're looking for a place to live, but I guess they're not having any luck."

88

"We were lucky to get this place."

She looked around the kitchen again. They'd replaced all the cabinets, the sink, and the appliances, and refinished the original wood floor, which had been covered with ugly gray linoleum. D. J. had poured concrete for the countertops, which sounded so industrial but ended up looking great. In other rooms, they'd plastered, rewired, and replumbed. "Yeah, the old dump is shaping up," she said. "I can't wait until we move in—the three of us, together. Lucas is so excited he can hardly stand it. He worships you, you know."

"I'm crazy about him, too. And about you." He finished attaching the last piece of hardware and shut the cabinet door.

"It looks great," she said, as he pulled her to his side once more.

He kissed her again. "When are you going to let me make an honest woman of you?"

She forced herself not to fidget. "You know I want to get married," she said. "It's just a matter of timing. I don't want anything fancy, but I feel like I need to do something special—for my mom, and for Lucas, too. And we've been so busy with the house and everything. . . ."

"I know, but the house is almost done. And whatever we do, it will be special."

She nodded. "I promise, I'll decide on a date soon. I won't keep you waiting forever."

His expression grew more tense. "There's something else I've been wanting to talk to you about."

"Oh?" Her heart beat a little faster. "What is that?"

"First, are you going to change your name when we get married? You don't have to," he rushed to add before she could even answer. "Whatever you want is cool with me."

"I don't know. I'd kind of like to be Mrs. Gruber, old-fashioned as that might be. And if we have a baby . . ."

"I hope we will have babies. As many as you want."

She did squirm then, shifting from foot to foot. She couldn't help it; she wanted nothing more than to have D. J.'s baby. "Then *when* we have a baby, Theriot-Gruber is too much of a mouthful. But Lucas's name is Theriot, and I don't want him to feel left out."

"That's what I want to talk to you about." He smoothed his hand down her back. "I'd really like to adopt him . . . if that's okay with you."

"Oh, D. J." She couldn't speak for the knot of tears that rose in her throat. "That's wonderful. Have you said anything to Lucas?"

"I wanted to talk to you first."

"I think it's a wonderful idea. And I think he'll be thrilled. But you should ask him, to make sure."

"I will, now that I know it's okay with you."
He straightened, the strain gone from his face.
"Okay, now that that's settled, back to work.
Have you seen the tape measure? I need to
measure the bathrooms again and make sure that
new vanity is going to fit."

"The last time I saw it, it was on the end of
the counter." They both looked in the direction
she indicated, but there was no sign of the tape
measure. He began to laugh.

"What's so funny?" she asked.

"I'm just trying to imagine what a ghost would
want with a tape measure."

Chapter 5

Maggie studied her reflection critically in the full-length mirror attached to the closet door. The white lace dress, which Barb had promised would float over her baby bump, making her look goddess-like and alluring and not fat, clung in all the wrong places. "I look like I swallowed a beach ball," she said to no one in particular. She'd deliberately waited until she was alone for this little fashion show.

With difficulty, she reached back and slid down the zipper on the dress and picked up the next candidate. This one was pink—a color Barb had declared would emphasize Maggie's "glow" and featured ruffles around the neck "to draw attention to your face." Unfortunately, that face was forty years old and beginning to sag, not the dewy twenty-something the maternity designers had probably had in mind. Maggie shook her head and began to wrestle her way out of reject number two.

Maybe she'd get married in maternity jeans and the extra-large "Eureka! Colorado's Great Discovery" T-shirt she'd won at the Chamber of Commerce mixer last month. Jameso could wear his Dirty Sally T-shirt, and all the guests could sport the slogan or logo of their choice. No fuss, and they'd all be so busy reading each other's chests they wouldn't notice the pregnant woman at the front of the room.

She studied the next candidate—a cream colored summer-weight wool suit that probably cost a month's salary. The color made her think of vanilla ice cream, which set her mouth to watering. Did they have any Blue Bell left in the freezer?

A timid tapping on the front door made her jump. She reached for her robe, and waited for the sound to repeat itself. Was that someone knocking or just a flicker attacking a knothole in the cabin's siding?

The knock came again—definitely the door. With a sigh, she sashed the robe over her belly and waddled into the front room.

"Oh, hello, Maggie." Sharon looked like a startled rabbit—all big dark eyes and twitching nose. "I'm looking for Jameso."

"He's at work. But come on in." She held the door open wider.

Sharon squeezed between Maggie and a stack of half-packed boxes. A backpack and camping equipment fought for space with a half-assembled baby bed and a lamp with its shade knocked askew. "Excuse the mess," Maggie said. "Things have been sort of crazy around here."

"No thanks to me, I'm sure. I feel terrible,

intruding on you this way." Sharon shoved her hands in her pockets and looked everywhere but at Maggie.

"You're not intruding. I've been meaning to get by to see you. How are you doing?"

"Okay."

"How's the job?"

"Good."

"That's good." She waited, but Sharon didn't elaborate. This wasn't exactly the heart-to-heart between soon-to-be sisters-in-law that Maggie had hoped for.

"So, Jameso's at the Dirty Sally?" Sharon asked.

"No, he's at his other job, with Mountain View Tours?" At Sharon's blank look, she added, "He's a driver and guide for a Jeep tour company in the summer. It's too early for tourists yet, but they had some kind of meeting. Is there something I can help you with?"

Sharon chewed her lower lip. "You're going to think I'm really stupid," she said after a long silence.

Nervous, standoffish, maybe shy. But not stupid. "I won't, I promise."

"I need to find a place to live. A house or apartment to rent, I mean. I feel terrible, kicking Jameso out of his house. Now that I have a job, I can afford a place of my own."

"As long as you're not looking for anything very big—pickings are a little slim right now.

Jameso and I have been looking for a place to move into together for months now."

"Two bedrooms would be nice, but it doesn't have to be big or fancy. And I don't have to be right in town. Alina and I are used to living out in the country."

"I can introduce you to my real-estate agent," Maggie said. "I'm sure she'd be happy to help. And there's nothing stupid about wanting your own place."

"It's not that, it's just—" Her voice faded.

"Just what?"

"I've never rented my own place before." Her face reddened. "I don't know what I need to do, what I should watch out for. I don't even know how to get the electricity turned on or the phone connected." She gave a shaky laugh. "I'm thirty-one years old and I've never even had my own checking account. Isn't that pathetic?"

"Maybe a little unusual, but you can learn about those things. Why don't we sit down?" She moved a pile of magazines from one end of the sofa and Jameso's shirt from the other, and motioned for Sharon to join her. "Jameso said you married young. I take it your husband took care of the money."

"Yes." She perched on the edge of the sofa, as if prepared to spring up again at the slightest alarm. "What did Jameso tell you about Joe?"

"He said he didn't know him well."

"He didn't like him. It's all right. None of the family did. I think that's why I liked him, at first. My father hated him, but Joe was bigger and tougher than my dad. He was the first man I'd met who would actually stand up to our father, and that impressed me."

"And he promised to take care of you," Maggie said.

"Yes!" Sharon's eyes widened. "How did you know?"

Maggie shrugged. "It makes sense—if you were afraid of your father and someone promised to protect you, of course you'd want to be with him."

"Joe did protect me. And I didn't mind that he took care of all the money and business stuff. I wasn't interested in all that." She waved her hand, as if brushing aside a pesky fly. "And I don't want you to think I'm useless; I can do a lot of things. I can shoot a gun as well as any man, dress a deer, make bread and candles, and tell poisonous mushrooms from ones that are good to eat."

"There are plenty of people around here who would be impressed with those accomplishments," Maggie said. "I can't do any of those things. When I first came to Eureka, I had to learn how to build a fire in a wood stove, how to start a snowmobile, how to walk in snowshoes, and a lot of other things."

Sharon wrinkled her nose. "All the things I can do are fine if you want to pretend you're still living in the nineteenth century, but they're not much use in the twenty-first."

"You know how to use a computer." It had been one of the requirements for the library job, apparently.

"Oh, yes. Even living off the grid, we had Internet. That was the one modern invention Joe approved of. Well, that and automatic weapons."

Maggie must have looked as confused as she felt. "I guess you'd call Joe a survivalist," Sharon said. "A prepper. He and his friends thought civilization as we know it was going to end any day now—and good riddance to it. They were going to hole up in their compound and start over with their own rules."

Maggie had heard of these survivalist groups —some were even rumored to live in the mountains around Eureka. But she'd always pictured them as single men. Never women and children—families.

"Is that why you left?" she asked. "Because you didn't want to live that way?"

"I didn't mind at first. I like living in the country and I enjoy doing things for myself, like baking bread. The last few years I home-schooled the children and I enjoyed that, too, spending so much time with them. For a long time the prepper thing was just something Joe did on weekends. We still lived close to town and he worked in a factory that made skis. The kids belonged to 4-H and went to the local school. I volunteered at the local library. We were a pretty average family."

"And that changed?" Maggie asked.

She nodded. "About five years ago, Joe started hanging out with a different group—more hard-core and radical. He quit his job and we moved farther out. The kids couldn't go to school anymore. We were supposed to be completely self-sufficient. I didn't like it and we argued more." She pressed her lips together.

"That would be hard," Maggie said.

"Yes, too hard." She sighed. "One day I took Alina and went to a hotel in a nearby town. I tried to convince my son, Adan, to come with me, but he refused. I was afraid to wait any longer, so Alina and I left. I had some money I had saved and I paid a lawyer to file for divorce."

"Where did you get the money?" Maggie asked. "I mean, if you didn't work outside the home and your husband controlled the finances?"

She smiled. "I made money writing for different Web sites on the Internet. I put everything I made into an online savings account Joe didn't know about. That's how I found the lawyer, too—online. She was very good. She threatened to report Joe to the police—he had some illegal weapons and hunted without a license. He didn't believe in paying taxes or having a driver's license or anything like that. If she'd pressed charges, she could have sent him to jail for a long time. Instead, she persuaded him to agree to a divorce."

Her face clouded. "But I couldn't force him to give up Adan, not unless Adan wanted to come with me. He didn't."

"That must have been heartbreaking for you." Maggie's own heart hurt, thinking of this mother having to give up her child.

Sharon nodded.

"You don't sound stupid to me at all," Maggie said. "You sound like a very smart, resourceful woman."

"Thank you. I am, I guess—but it's hard. Doing everything by myself." She shrugged. "I guess I thought by coming here I'd have Jameso to help me. I can see now that wasn't very realistic. He has you and the baby to think about." She stood. "And I've taken enough of your time. I'd better go."

"No, stay." She didn't want them to part on this sad note. "As long as you're here, I could use your opinion."

"What do you need my opinion about?" Sharon looked wary.

"I'm trying to choose a wedding dress. Come look."

Maggie led the way into the bedroom, where several dresses were strewn across the bed. "They're from my friend Barb—you met her the first day you were in town—she owns the new bed-and-breakfast that's due to open this summer?"

"I remember Barb."

Maggie laughed. "Barb's a hard woman to forget. She and I have known each other for twenty years, at least. She's married to an oil executive in Houston and wastes more money than I've ever made, so when she said she wanted to buy my wedding dress, I agreed."

Sharon reached out and touched the soft, cool fabric of a pink dress, the color of apple blossoms. "They're all beautiful," she said.

"I'm at the point where I think I look awful in everything," Maggie said. "So I could really use an honest opinion."

"I remember that feeling." Sharon transferred her attention from the dresses to Maggie. "You look really great. Not all bloated and blotchy like I was."

"I feel bloated and blotchy." Maggie sat on the end of the bed. "I was nineteen when I married my first husband. I wore a white lace dress from the wedding department at J. C. Penney and a veil I'd made out of tulle, white satin roses, a hair band, and hot glue. I weighed one hundred and eight pounds soaking wet."

"I didn't realize you were married before. Do you have any children?"

"No, my ex didn't want any and I let him convince me that that's what I wanted, too." She rubbed her hand back and forth over her swollen belly. "When I found out I was pregnant, I couldn't believe it."

"How did Jameso take the news?"

"He fainted."

Sharon couldn't keep back the laughter. "He fainted?"

Maggie laughed, too. "He swears hearing about the baby had nothing to do with it, but of course it did. He was living the ideal life: single, working just enough to pay for beer and gas for his motorcycle—no ties, no commitments."

Sharon sobered. "But he's sticking by you and the baby."

"Oh, he loves me," Maggie said. "I'm sure of that. And this is probably what he needed to settle down. But we didn't exactly plan anything. I never thought I'd be forty and pregnant and planning a wedding."

Sharon did the math in her head—Maggie was eight years older than Jameso. She was watching Sharon, waiting for a reaction to this revelation. "Joe was twelve years older than me," Sharon said. "I was barely fifteen when we got married." A lifetime ago.

Maggie's eyes widened. "You were a baby!"

"I was. And the thought of Alina marrying at that age makes me break out in hives." She sat on the bed next to Maggie, careful not to crush the dresses. "I was so desperate to change my life. Even without planning, you and Jameso are in much better shape than I was."

"Jameso doesn't like to talk about the past, but he did say the two of you had it hard growing up." Maggie's voice was soft and she spoke slowly, as if searching for the right words. "You did what you had to do, and you turned out all right."

Sharon nodded. "I guess so." She turned and studied the dresses. "Which one of these do you like the best?" She didn't want to talk about Joe anymore. The subject made her so tired.

"I can't decide," Maggie said. "What do you think? I can try them on, if you like."

Sharon considered the options and tried to picture them on Maggie's small frame. "What time of day is the wedding?" she asked.

"Morning. With brunch afterward. I know that's unusual, but I know I'll be too nervous to wait all day, and there's less chance of rain in the mountains in the morning."

"A morning wedding will be nice. I think the suit, then." She smoothed a hand down the cream-colored wool. "The others are too frilly and girlish. Not that you wouldn't look pretty in them, but you seem classier. The suit will look dressy and beautiful."

"You're right." Maggie let out a long sigh. "I thought that one looked the best of the three, but I wasn't sure. Thank you. You've been a big help. I'll tell Barb to send the other two back."

"What is Jameso going to wear?" Sharon asked.

"I'm hoping I can persuade him to put aside his motorcycle jacket and T-shirts, and wear a suit for the ceremony. I might need your help with that, too."

Sharon doubted she had any influence over her brother; he hadn't looked all that thrilled to see her, and he hadn't gone out of his way to get together with her now that she was here. She'd told herself he was very busy, with work and the upcoming wedding and baby. But in the tender places she kept locked away inside, his rejection hurt. She'd spent all morning gathering the courage to confront him. But maybe it was better that she'd found Maggie home alone. Maybe the way to reach her brother was through the woman he loved. "I have a feeling he'd do anything for you," she said. "How did the two of you meet?"

"He was my father's best friend. After my father, Jake, died, he left me everything he had, including his property here in Eureka." She looked around the cabin's cramped bedroom. "Not this place—a cabin in the mountains and an old gold mine. I'd just gotten divorced and was unemployed, so I decided to come up here and check it out. The first night I spent at my dad's cabin, Jameso came by to check on the place. He thought I was a squatter or something and I thought he was a serial killer, come to prey on a woman alone."

"So you really did try to hit him with a stick of firewood?" Sharon asked, remembering Barb's pronouncement.

"I just waved it around a little. He had the grace not to laugh in my face."

Sharon smiled, picturing the scene. Jameso had probably looked pretty scary, but Maggie hadn't backed down. "And you fell in love."

"Not right away." Maggie shook her head. "I really didn't want anything to do with him, but he was persistent."

Yes, that sounded like Jay. "He was always stubborn, even as a little kid," she said. "It's one reason he had such a hard time with my father—he would never back down, even when it cost him."

Maggie's face clouded. "He told me his father was abusive. He was afraid he'd be that way with our baby—that it was something he could inherit. I told him he was crazy, that I knew he'd never hurt me."

"I don't think he would either. He hated our father—that alone would make him work hard not to be like him."

104

And here they were again, back to depressing subjects she didn't want to talk about. Maggie must have felt it, too. "It's almost lunchtime," she said. "Are you hungry?"

Not really. She hadn't had much of an appetite for months, but she went through the motions. "I could eat."

"Then come to lunch with me." Maggie shoved to her feet. "I'm eating everything in sight these days and it looks better if someone else is sitting at the table when Janelle and Danielle bring out all that food."

The Last Dollar was busier than it had been Sharon's first day in town. Almost every table and booth was filled, and people waved and greeted Maggie by name as the two women passed. "You must know everyone in town," Sharon said when they were seated in a booth near the back.

"You will soon, too," Maggie said. "At least all the ones who frequent the library."

"I guess so." She spread her napkin in her lap. It would be nice to have friends. The only other woman in the camp with Joe and Wilson— a Russian emigrant named Oksana who was married to a man named Earl—didn't speak much English and in any case hadn't been friendly to Sharon. She seemed to have developed the idea that Sharon was after Earl—as if the paunchy old man who was missing half his teeth was such a great catch.

"Hello, Maggie, Sharon." Danielle glided up to the table, order pad in hand. "What can I get you two and the baby today?"

"I'll have the cheeseburger, no onions, curly fries, and a glass of milk," Maggie said.

Sharon studied the chalkboard menu. "The vegetable soup sounds good. And a small spinach salad."

"Coming right up."

"Their soup is wonderful," Maggie said. "But then, everything here is."

"Alina fell in love with the place as soon as she saw they had veggie burgers." Sharon smiled her thanks as Janelle set two glasses of water in front of them. "She decided to become a vegetarian last year and you'd have thought she'd declared she was a communist the way Joe reacted, or overreacted."

"I don't think it's that unusual for young teenagers to do things like that," Maggie said.

"Joe was big on living off the land—killing our own food and stuff. But he took it too far with the kids. When Alina was twelve, he made her go out in the woods by herself and kill and butcher a deer. The poor girl was traumatized. She swore she'd never eat anything with a face again." She rotated the water glass, watching the beads of condensation form on the sides. "I think I knew then that I'd have to get her away from there sooner or later."

"It does sound a little grim. Are you a vegetarian, too?" Maggie asked.

"Sort of. I'm not as committed as Alina, but a steady diet of wild game did give me an appreciation for fresh vegetables." And she really didn't want to talk about this. She searched the room for another topic of conversation and spotted Lucille.

"There's the mayor," she said, and waved.

Lucille headed toward them. "Hello, Maggie, Sharon. May I join you?"

"Please do." Sharon slid over so that Lucille could sit beside her.

"How are things at the library?" Lucille asked. "Are you plotting revenge against me yet?"

"Things are fine. No need for you to worry."

"Really? You're getting along with Cassie?"

"She's all right. She likes to boss people around, but I'm used to that." After Joe and Wilson, Cassie was easy to manage. Sharon had perfected the art of seeming compliant while ignoring two thirds of what she said.

"Have you heard her latest scheme?" Lucille asked.

"You mean her drive to rename the park?" Maggie nodded. "I heard she was circulating a petition."

"Yes, and she's asked me to put the item on the

agenda for the next town council meeting. I tried to put her off, told her we had too many other pressing concerns, but you know her. She won't give up. And as a citizen, she's entitled to be heard."

"Is there any reason not to rename the park for her grandmother?" Sharon asked. "I mean, if the woman really did all the things Cassie says . . ."

"Her and half a dozen other women who are just as worthy of being remembered," Lucille said. "For instance, Irene Kildaire, who is a hundred years old and living in a nursing home in Montrose, founded the first day school in the area. And she was on the board of the same women's club as Cassie's grandmother, the board that founded the park. Cassie makes it sound like Ernestine did everything all by herself."

"So you think by naming the park after Cassie's grandmother, you'll be slighting other families," Sharon said.

"Exactly. Not to mention I'm afraid this will set a dangerous precedent. First, she wants the park named after her grandmother. Next, she'll be lobbying to have the school christened for her grandfather, and the ball fields dedicated to the memory of her uncle. If she could, she'd change the name of the town from Eureka to Wynock."

Janelle stopped by the table. "What can I get you, Madam Mayor?"

"Iced tea, a winning lottery ticket, and a chicken Caesar salad," Lucille said.

"I'll have the tea and salad right out," Janelle said. "You're on your own for the lottery ticket."

"It's always something," Lucille said.

"How is the budget battle?" Maggie asked after Janelle had left.

"Money has always been tight, but the new expenses with the mine are putting a whole new strain on things."

"The town owns half interest in a gold mine," Maggie explained to Sharon.

"And the other half is owned by a man I was once involved with," Lucille said. "Much to my regret."

"We received a press release last week about an engineering report that showed the presence of high-grade gold ore in the mine," Maggie said. "I've been waiting for someone on the council to say something. In fact, I was planning to call you tomorrow."

"The report shows a high probability of ore that's only accessible with a lot of expensive equipment we can't afford. Investing in all that would be another big gamble, with no guarantee of a payoff."

"So what's going to happen with the mine?" Maggie asked.

"I don't know. Gerald is insisting we put up half the money for the improvements, per the partnership agreement." She leaned closer and lowered her voice. "This is strictly off the record, but he says if we don't comply, he'll sue."

"Can he do that?" Sharon asked.

"Reggie, our lawyer, says he can. He could bankrupt us."

"But what good would that do him?" Maggie asked.

"Allow him to buy us out cheap? Though I have a feeling his real motivation is revenge." She paused while Danielle delivered a glass of tea, then glanced at Sharon. "The man dumped me—after he swindled the town out of a lot of money. And now he has the nerve to act the part of the wounded lover." She squeezed lemon into her tea, a seed flying across the table and striking the window.

"What are you going to do?" Maggie asked.

"I don't know. I need to find a way to bring more money into the town. Know any successful businesses we can invite to town—preferably ones that will generate big tax revenues? Factories? Giant tourist attractions?"

"I'd hate to see anything like that spoil the town," Sharon said. "Eureka looks like something off a movie set. It's so perfect."

Lucille froze. "That's it." She dropped her teaspoon and retrieved her tote bag from beside her chair.

"What is it?" Maggie asked. "What's wrong?"

"Nothing's wrong." She pawed through the papers in her tote bag and pulled out a glossy flyer. She shoved aside the salt and pepper shakers and spread the flyer out in front of them. "This is from the Colorado Film Commission, inviting towns to submit an invitation to film-makers to make a movie in their town."

Sharon tilted her head to read the brochure. "Tell us ten reasons your town would make the perfect movie set," she read.

"Eureka would be the great setting for a western or a period piece," Maggie said.

"Or one of those post-apocalyptic stories, where civilization is destroyed and people have to revert to doing things the pioneer way," Sharon said. Joe had loved those stories; he had a whole wall of books like that.

"I'm going to send in our application today," Lucille said. "A movie might be just what we need to keep the wolf from the door. Or Gerald Pershing off our backs."

Chapter 6

"You don't really believe in ghosts, do you?" Alina huddled with Lucas Theriot in a back corner of the school library. They were supposed to be working on a social studies project on space exploration, but Lucas had brought up the subject of haunted houses.

"I'm not saying I believe in ghosts," he said. "But it's not beyond the realm of possibility that humans might leave behind some sort of energy field if they succumb to sudden death. Whether that's the same as an otherworldly spirit would be interesting to investigate."

She couldn't decide if Lucas was the smartest kid she'd ever met or just the geekiest. He was certainly the most interesting, and that had to count for something. He had also been the first one to make friends with her when she enrolled in Eureka Middle School, and that counted for something, too. "But do you think this house your parents are fixing up is haunted?" she asked.

"Not my parents—my mother and her boy-friend. But they're engaged, so he'll be my step-father, which is a kind of parent, I guess."

She nodded. Lucas always explained things—

even things that didn't need explaining. "But have you seen the ghost?" she asked.

"No, but things keep disappearing from the house. We'll leave tools or stuff behind and the next day they're gone. Once I left a half a peanut butter and pickle sandwich, and the next day it was gone."

"Peanut butter and pickle? Seriously?"

"It's really good. The sweetness of the pickles complements the saltiness of the peanuts."

She made a face. "So your ghost has weird taste in food, too. Maybe it's just a thief."

"But a thief would take big stuff that was worth money—power tools and stuff. Everything that's gone missing so far is little stuff."

"Maybe some animal is taking them."

He nodded. "I thought of that. Which is why I want to set up a camera to catch it."

"So why do you need my help?"

"I don't have a camera," he said. "You do."

She leaned back, as if that would put enough distance between them. "You can't have my camera."

"I just want to borrow it. For one night. I'll give it back, I promise."

"What if your ghost steals it? My father gave me that camera." She loved the way the words sounded. As if her father was this loving, generous person who lavished her with expensive gifts. He wasn't, but maybe he would have been, if his

113

circumstances had been different. The camera proved that.

"Then you could come with me. We could wait together for the ghost—or whatever it is—to show up; then you could snap the picture."

"You mean, spend the night at the house with you?" A haunted house?

"We probably wouldn't have to wait the whole night," he said.

"Like my mom is going to let me do that."

"You'd have to sneak out." He moved his chair closer, his voice scarcely above a whisper. "You could do it. Wait until she's asleep and climb out the window. I can meet you on my bike. Haven't you ever snuck out before?"

"No." What would have been the point? Where they'd lived, there was nowhere to go.

"At least say you'll come to the house with me this afternoon, after school."

"Do you think we'll see the ghost in daylight?"

"Probably not, but at least you can see the house. I'll show you my room, and the ride over there is pretty cool."

"I don't have a bike."

"You can ride on my handlebars. It'll be fun."

She chewed her lower lip. Her mom was working late and she'd be home alone with nothing really to do. Homework never took long, and they didn't even have a TV. "Okay. But I have to be back before seven."

"Great. I'll meet you at your house at four."

"Okay." She looked down at her notebook. "But for now we'd better work on the social studies project."

"I was thinking we could make a rocket," he said. "One that really flew."

If she could make a rocket, she'd fly back to Vermont and bring her brother back to Eureka with them. He'd said he wanted to stay with their father, to run around in the woods shooting animals and pretend enemies. He repeated things their dad said, about the government and the end of the world, as if they were his own opinions. But if she could just get Adan away from there, back to things he used to enjoy, like books and music and talking about traveling other places, she knew she could make him change his mind. She could make him love her again, and they could be a family once more.

The lavender house Jameso had loaned Sharon and Alina was small and old, but she was grateful to have the privacy of her own place. She had an appointment to meet with Maggie's real-estate agent tomorrow. If she found something she liked, she'd try to get Jameso to go with her for a second look. She wanted his opinion about what was a good value in this area, and she hated to make this big of a decision on her own. She needed at least two bedrooms, so that Alina could have her own room, but maybe three would be better, if she could afford it—the third bedroom for Adan when he came to visit, or maybe if he decided to stay.

Her heart felt too big for her chest as she anticipated this. She was working her first job. About to rent her first house. So many firsts; so much excitement to go with the fear.

She pulled into the driveway and cut the engine, then took a deep breath. She and Alina would be much better for all of this. She could do this, for both of them.

She was surprised to find the house dark. "Alina, why are all the lights out?" she called as she pushed open the front door and fumbled for the light switch. "What are you doing sitting around in the dark, silly?" But even as she flipped the switch to flood the small front room with light, she knew the house was empty. An unoccupied house has a feeling unlike one filled with life.

"Alina!" She dropped her purse and hurried farther into the house—to the single bedroom she and her daughter shared, then back to the kitchen. She even checked the bathroom. Fighting panic, she stood in the middle of the room. "Think," she said out loud. "What do you see?"

Alina's backpack rested on the floor at the end of the sofa. The jacket she usually wore was missing from the nail on the wall by the door.

Sharon returned to the bedroom. Alina's clothes were still here, but she didn't see her daughter's treasured camera. She searched for a note, saying where Alina had gone, but found nothing.

With shaking hands, she punched Jameso's number into her cell phone.

"Hey!" he answered. "What up?"

In the background, she heard laughter and the clink of glasses. He must be at the Dirty Sally. "Have you seen or heard from Alina?" she asked. "I just got home and she's not here."

"I haven't seen her, but I haven't been out there all day. Maybe she went to a friend's house."

"Maybe, but I think she would have told me." She fought to keep her voice from shaking.

"I'll ask if anyone here has seen her. Do you think she'd have run away?"

Oh, God—run away? The words hit like a blow to the stomach. She sank onto the sofa, suddenly too weak to stand. "I don't think so. I mean, I think she was happy here. She likes school, and she's making friends. . . ." *She misses her old home and her brother.*

"But you're not sure."

"She's a kid—a teenager. Who knows what they're really thinking?"

"Right. What about Joe?"

"What about him?"

"Would he have taken her?"

She moaned. "Oh, God, no!"

"Look, you know the man better than I do. Was he upset about you leaving town with his daughter? Would he try to get her back?"

"I don't think so." Yes, he had made some threats when he was angry, when she'd first declared her intention to leave, but by the time she and Alina had packed up, Joe had seemed almost happy to see them go.

"One of his survivalist buddies, then?" Jameso asked.

Wilson—would he stoop to this? "I can't believe it," she said. She didn't want to believe it.

"Let me know if you want to call the police. I'll send them right out there."

"Your friend, Sergeant Miller, gave me his card. Maybe I should call him."

"You know Josh?"

"We met my first day in town. He saw me stopped in the street and asked if I needed help."

"Maybe you should call him. He can organize people to look for Alina."

A search party? The thought made her even queasier. "No, not yet. She's probably just at a friend's house." She had to be.

"All right. But, Sharon?"

"Yes?"

"Let me know when she gets in, okay? In the meantime, I'll ask around."

"I will. Thanks." She hung up the phone and sagged onto the sofa. What to do now? She didn't know who Alina's friends were. She'd mentioned a few boys and girls she'd met in school, but Sharon had been too preoccupied to pay much attention to their names.

The camera worried and reassured her. If Alina had taken the time to collect her precious camera and take it with her, she probably hadn't been abducted suddenly. And if she'd run away, she would have at least packed some clothes, right?

Maybe she should call the police. They'd send people out looking. Better to be embarrassed by a false alarm than learn she'd waited too late to save her little girl.

Heart pounding, she took out her phone. She'd punched in a nine and a one when she heard a noise at the back of the house. She froze, every nerve alert, and heard it again—muffled voices and a scrabbling sound.

Phone in hand, she tiptoed to the dark bedroom, the room closest to where the noises were coming from. Definitely voices—one low and one high-pitched and urgent. Like her daughter's voice. She sat on the end of the bed and waited.

She didn't have to wait long. The sash of the window flew up and Alina's voice very clearly said, "You're going to have to boost me higher than that."

Sharon leaned over and switched on the bed-side lamp. "Oh, crap," Alina said.

If Sharon hadn't been so angry, she might have

laughed at the idea that this was the most serious curse word her daughter could think of. Alina had indeed led a sheltered life.

But not sheltered enough, apparently. She hung, half-in and half-out of the bedroom window, her face white as a ghost. Sharon stood and helped her daughter into the room. Then she stuck her head out the window and looked down at the boy who stood on the ground below, the light from the open window illuminating his face. "Lucas Theriot, what do you think you're doing?" she asked.

"I brought Alina home, Mrs. Franklin. I was showing her the house my mom and her fiancé are remodeling and we sort of lost track of time. We didn't mean to be so late. It's all my fault."

"You'd better go now, Lucas," she said.

"Yes, ma'am. Good night, Alina."

"Good night," she called. She removed the camera strap from around her neck and slumped onto the end of the bed.

Sharon closed the window and sat beside her daughter. "If Lucas's bike hadn't had a flat tire, we'd have been home before you," Alina said.

"But you weren't. So you thought sneaking in the bedroom window was the answer."

"I was hoping you hadn't looked in the bedroom yet. I could tell you I'd been taking a nap."

"Alina Michelle Franklin!"

The girl winced. "Mom! I didn't do anything

wrong. Lucas and I just went to see his new house. His mom and her fiancé are remodeling it. It was cool."

"You didn't have permission to go anywhere. You didn't tell me. You came home late and tried to sneak in. You intended to lie about what you'd been doing—how is that nothing wrong?" Sharon tried to keep her voice even, but relief over finding her daughter safe was swiftly being overtaken by anger.

"I'm sorry, okay? You don't have to make such a big deal about it."

"It is a big deal, Alina. Lying and sneaking around are big deals. And you're not really sorry—you're only sorry you got caught."

"I'll ask next time before I go, okay? I didn't mean to worry you."

"Worry me? I was frantic. I didn't know if someone had kidnapped you, or if you'd run away. . . ." Sharon sat on her hands. It was the only way she could be sure she wouldn't reach out and shake Alina.

"I wouldn't run away, Mom. Where would I go?"

Back to Vermont. Back to your father. But Sharon couldn't say those words. What if she gave the girl ideas? "I didn't think you were the type to climb in windows when you were late either," she said.

"Mo-om!"

"You're grounded for the next month."

121

"A month! Mom! That's not fair."

"After school, you'll come to the library and you'll sit there doing your homework or reading until it's time for me to get off work."

"Mom! I never have that much homework. You're just being mean."

"Obviously, I can't trust you home alone. And whatever you may think, it's my job to keep you safe."

"Why do you hate me so much?" Alina wailed. "Why did you even bring me here if you were just going to make me a prisoner?"

"You're not a prisoner. But you have to earn responsibility. You don't do that by going off without telling anyone."

Tears streamed down Alina's reddened face. "Why did you even bring me here, where I can't do anything and I can't have friends? Why did you take me away from Dad and Adan?"

All the fury and energy deserted Sharon. She reached for her daughter, but Alina scooted away, her body bent into a C of despair. "You know why we had to leave," Sharon said softly.

Alina said nothing, merely jutted out her chin and sniffed.

"I had to protect you," Sharon said.

"Nothing would have happened," Alina said. "Dad wouldn't have let it."

Sharon knew Alina wanted to believe that. She needed to believe that her father would have protected her, no matter what. But Joe had different ideas about what that protection meant.

"I couldn't take that chance," Sharon said. "I had to leave and take you with me. You don't appreciate now how hard that was, but you will one day. I know you will."

She stood and left the room, and shut the door behind her. Alina lay sobbing against the pillows. Maybe crying would do her good, help her sort out her crazy emotions.

Sharon went into the kitchen and made a cup of tea, then carried it to a chair by the window. She left the lights off and stared out at the darkness, and the swatch of star-spangled sky visible between the trees. She scarcely saw their beauty, her mind too full of that night in Vermont, when she'd found Wilson with Alina.

Sharon had needed another egg for the frittata she was making for dinner, so she'd gone out to the henhouse to see if one of the chickens had laid an extra egg after she'd collected them that morning. Alina had gone out earlier to feed and water the lamb she was raising for 4-H, and Sharon realized she hadn't come back up to the house yet.

She was probably sitting on a bale of hay, singing or talking to the lamb, or lost in a daydream, making up stories or songs in her head. Sharon would remind her she had laundry to fold before supper.

The barn door opened without a sound. Joe kept up on things like that, everything in repair and shipshape. Straw muffled Sharon's footsteps as she made her way past the neat rows of stalls, toward the storage room at the rear, where the light from a kerosene lantern cast a pool of gold onto the floor.

She heard him before she saw him, his words making her skin rise up with gooseflesh. "You're turning into a pretty young woman, did you know that?" Wilson's voice was low, but with a gravelly timbre that was unmistakable.

Alina's answer was a mumble, uncertain. Timid.

"How old are you now—fourteen?" he asked.

"Thirteen," Alina said.

"Fourteen before you know it. Did you know your mama married your daddy when she was only a little older than you are now?"

Again, some unintelligible noise from Alina.

"I always thought it was a good thing for a girl to marry young. That way she'd grow into the marriage. That's why your mama and daddy get on so well."

No sound from Alina.

"Come over here a little closer. I won't bite. You know me. I'm your daddy's best friend and I know he wants the two of us to be friends, too." Sounds of movement. Sharon told herself she should move forward. She should stop this. But she remained frozen. Stunned.

"There now, that's not so bad, is it?" Wilson said. "Do you like the way that feels? I know I do."

Sharon picked up a milk pail that was sitting by the door and dropped it, sending it clattering down the aisle between the stalls. "Alina!" she shouted, her voice high-pitched and strained. "Quit your daydreaming and come help me with supper."

"Yes, Mama!" Alina's voice was equally strained. She ran from the storeroom, leaving the lantern behind. She ran to Sharon and threw her arms around her and buried her face against her mother's shoulder. Sharon held her close, feeling her child's heart racing, but also feeling Wilson's eyes on them. He didn't step out of the storeroom, but she knew he was there, and the knowledge made her skin crawl. "Let's go back up to the house," she said softly. "It's going to be all right."

That night, as they lay in bed, she'd tried to talk to Joe about what she'd overheard in the barn. "There's nothing wrong with Wilson taking an interest in the girl," Joe said.

"He's old enough to be her father." Wilson was at least as old as Joe, who was forty-two. "And she's just a child."

"She's growing up fast. I'd like to see her stay here, in the family, so to speak, instead of going away. She could do worse than a man like Wilson."

"Joe, she's thirteen."

"And in a couple years she'll be fifteen—the same age you were when we got married."

And I was an idiot, she thought. But, of course, she didn't say so. "I want Alina to get an education," she said. "To go to college, even."

"So the godless liberals can fill her head full of nonsense? She'll be better off here."

Of course he would think something like that. He didn't trust the outside world. "Talk to Wilson," she pleaded. "Tell him to keep his hands off your daughter. She's too young."

"I'll talk to him." He rolled over and punched his pillow. "Now go to sleep."

But she couldn't sleep. She lay awake most of the night, replaying the scene in the barn over and over. She doubted Joe would warn Wilson off. The two men would chuckle about nervous women and Joe would all but give his blessing to his best friend's pursuit of his barely-a-teen daughter.

Sharon knew then she had to leave. It had meant giving up her son and her home and every bit of security she'd ever had. But she had to do it. She had to protect her daughter. What kind of mother would she be if she didn't?

Chapter 7

"I know how we're going to get rid of Gerald Pershing once and for all."

Lucille and Olivia looked up from the stack of T-shirts they were examining, at Bob's scrawny figure silhouetted in the open doorway of Lacy's.

"Hello, Bob." Lucille went back to unfolding T-shirts. "I don't have any packages for you today."

"Didn't you hear what I said?" He joined them at the store's front counter. "I know how to get Pershing out of our hair for good."

"I heard you, Bob." The old man was infamous for his wild schemes—the majority of which didn't end well.

"I think we should set Gerald up with a rich heiress online," Olivia said. "If we could find one who could be interested in him, he'd leave town to pursue her. And hopefully, never come back."

"What is some rich woman going to see in that old goat?" Bob propped one elbow on the glass display case that served as Lacy's checkout counter. "My plan is better."

"Bob, weren't you the one who came up with

the idea to sell him half interest in the mine?" Lucille asked.

He scowled more than ever. "It would have worked, too, if the mine had been a real dud. And it got most of the town's money back, didn't it?"

"Yes, the problem is, Gerald is trying to force us to spend most of that money on the mine."

"I know about that. The thing we have to do is get him to abandon the project altogether."

Lucille folded her hands on the stack of shirts and sighed. "Okay, I'll bite. How are we going to do that?"

"We scare him away."

Of course. Why hadn't Lucille thought of that? She shook her head.

"He doesn't strike me as the type to scare easily," Olivia said. She slipped a T-shirt over the head of a female mannequin and turned it toward Bob. The T-shirt was pale blue, painted with a stylized hummingbird hovering over a columbine blossom. "What do you think?"

"I always preferred a live woman myself," Bob said. "Though I've known a fellow or two who liked those sex dolls."

"I mean the T-shirt, Bob. It's my own design. I had a bunch of them screen-printed to sell here and around town."

"The shirt looks nice." His expression might have been a smile; it was hard to tell with all the facial hair. "I just don't like to encourage you. If you get too successful at your art, you won't have to work at the Dirty Sally anymore, and Jameso don't put near as nice a head on a mug of beer as you do."

"Thank you. I think."

"Olivia's jewelry already sells like crazy, and Barb Stanowski hired her to paint a mural in the dining room of her new B and B." Lucille fell easily into the role of proud mom. "You and the rest of the regulars at the Dirty Sally may have to learn to do without her sooner rather than later."

"Then you should teach Jameso how to pull a decent beer before you leave," he said. "Now, about my plan for Pershing."

She should have known he wouldn't drop the subject. "How do you think we could scare Gerald enough to convince him to leave town and not come back?" she asked.

"We convince him that the mine is haunted."

Olivia snorted. "You and your ghosts." She turned to her mother. "He told me the house D. J. and I bought is haunted."

"You're the one who said things keep disappearing for no reason. That sounds like a ghost to me, especially given the history of the place."

"My house is not haunted," Olivia said. "What makes you think the mine is?"

"It's not, at least as far as I know," he said. "But

it doesn't matter if it is or it isn't, as long as Pershing thinks it is."

"You have to believe in ghosts in order to be afraid of them," Lucille said. "I doubt Gerald is a believer." He made a point of playing the savvy sophisticate for the mountain bumpkins; to think that act had once impressed her.

"The skeptics are the easiest to fool," Bob said. "Make a few noises, let them feel a clammy hand on the back of their neck in the dark, and they piss their pants and run away, gibbering."

"You talk as if you've had experience with fake hauntings," Olivia said.

"Well, I'll tell you." Bob leaned in closer, settling in for a long story.

Lucille stifled a groan. She really didn't have time for this. She still had to complete the town's application for the Film Commission and unpack a shipment of pottery from the estate of a collector in Hotchkiss. "Bob, maybe you should wait and tell this to the town council. I'm sure they'll want to hear, and I can put you on the agenda at the next meeting."

"I can tell them, sure. But first, I'm going to tell you."

Lucille looked to her daughter for help. Olivia shrugged. "Give us the story, Bob," she said.

"It was back about 1974. I had a claim up above Creede. I was working it just fine, starting to see a little color, when this other fellow comes along and says the mine belonged to him first. He waved a lot of papers around and talked about lawyers, but I just ignored him and kept working. Of course, that just made him madder, and he started screaming about an injunction."

"Bob, was the mine his?" Olivia asked. "I mean, legally."

"It may have belonged to him at one time, but he'd abandoned it," Bob said. "The only reason he showed up when he did was because I was finding pay dirt in the thing. He wanted the spoils without having to do any of the work. I told him to get his injunction, but meantime, I was going to keep working and taking out gold.

"That didn't set well with him at all. He called me a lot of names that aren't fit to repeat in mixed company and said he'd be back in a few hours with the sheriff. He left and I went back to work."

"You weren't worried?" Olivia asked. This was why the customers at the Dirty Sally loved her, Lucille thought. She was such a patient listener.

"Nah, I knew the sheriff had gone over to Grand Junction that morning and wouldn't be back until late. I figured this guy—Tothe was his name, Bart Tothe—would get a bunch of his friends to come up and try to run me off. So I planned a little surprise for them when they did show up."

"What did you do?" Lucille asked. She might as well play along.

Bob's grin was clearly visible behind the

drooping moustache now. "I rigged up an old blanket to look like a spirit, hovering just in the entrance to the mine. I could stand over to one side and tug at a string to make it flap around. Then I set up a piece of pipe so the wind would blow over it and make a moaning sound."

"You scared him off with an old blanket and sound effects?" Olivia's doubt showed clearly on her face.

"Those were just the props. The key is to have the ghost say something only a spirit would supposedly know. I'd done my homework, and I knew this Tothe fellow had a secret. You see, mine tunnels don't just give you access to the ore—they're good places to hide stuff. Some people prefer a mine shaft to a bank vault or a safe deposit box for hiding things they don't want anyone to know about."

"And you'd found something Tothe was hiding?" Olivia asked.

"Hold your horses, I'll get to that." He shifted, leaning back with his elbows on the counter. "Sure enough, just after dark Tothe comes striding up the path with half a dozen of his friends behind him. They're all waving shotguns and flashlights, and from the sounds of 'em, they'd probably shared a little liquid courage on their way up. He stops in front of the mine and hollers, 'Prescott, you old so-and-so, you come out of there with your hands up.'

"I didn't answer, just stayed back in the shadows. He shone his light into the mine and when the beam hit that blanket hanging up, he jumped back. I pulled the string and the blanket danced; then I blew across the bottle and it made a high-pitched moan. But I'll give old Tothe credit; he didn't back down. 'I don't have time for games, Prescott,' he said. 'You come out of there.'

"I jerked the blanket harder, hard enough to let loosen the papers I'd tucked up inside. They drifted to the ground like dry leaves, and I could hear the men behind Tothe murmuring. 'What's that?' somebody asked.

" 'It's just Prescott, playing games,' Tothe said. 'Come out of there and fight like a man!'

"One of the men with him walked up and picked some of the papers off the ground. 'Who's Hiram Jacoby?' he asked.

"Tothe looked like he was going to be sick. 'I never heard of him,' he said. 'Prescott, come out, or I'm coming in after you.'

"I slipped up behind the blanket, and in a low, spooky voice, said, 'Hiram Jacoby, do you hear how your children weep for you? Do you hear the wails of your wife, abandoned by the man who had pledged to take care of her? Do you hear the curses of the employer you stole from? Do you feel the heat of the devil's breath on your shoulder?'

"There was a lot of murmuring from the other men; they didn't know what to make of this. But Tothe knew. And he was afraid."

"Who was Hiram Jacoby?" Olivia asked.

"He was Bart Tothe," Bob said. "I found a trunk full of his stuff in the mine—pictures and paperwork. From what I could tell, he'd been married with four children, working for a shipping company. One day he walked out with all the money in the company safe, came to Colorado, and started using another name. There was probably a warrant out for his arrest somewhere, not to mention a wife anxious to find him and see him strung up."

"So he ran away?" Lucille said.

"He did, indeed. I started moaning about Hiram and the money and the kiddies, and he turned heel and fled. The others ran right after him. I heard he left town the next day, and I went on mining in peace."

"It's a good story, Bob, but you didn't scare him off with ghosts," Olivia said. "You scared him off because you had something on him he didn't want everyone to know. We don't have anything like that on Gerald."

"I know he's a coward," Bob said. "I knew it the first day I laid eyes on him, and we can use that to our advantage." He turned to Lucille. "I figure you get him up to the mine some evening. I'll be waiting there and I'll commence to haunting. You run away and leave him to get the full benefit of my treatment. Next thing we know, he's packing to leave town."

"I don't know, Bob. I don't think he'll leave that easily."

"And I think you're wrong."

"I think you'd better both be quiet," Olivia said. "Gerald's ears must have been burning."

Just then, the man himself walked through the front door to Lacy's. He wore a gray Stetson, western-cut suit coat over pressed jeans, and gray eel-skin boots. "Just the folks I was looking for," he said cheerfully.

"Pershing." Bob nodded curtly.

"What do you want, Gerald?" Lucille asked.

"I've spent a very productive morning on the phone with the safety engineers," he said. "As soon as we give them the go-ahead, they're ready to install the new ventilation system and bracing in the Lucky Lady Mine. All I need is for you to write me a check for your half of the first payment and they can get started day after tomorrow."

"I can't just write you a check, Gerald," she said. "You'll need to submit a requisition to the town council. We'll consider it and if it's approved, the town treasurer will submit payment directly to the contractor."

His face folded in an expression of hurt. "Lucille, you talk as if you don't trust me."

Bob snorted. "She doesn't trust you as far as she could throw you, and neither do I."

Gerald ignored him and turned to Olivia. "You're looking lovely today," he said. "So much like your beautiful mother."

Lucille resisted the urge to make a gagging gesture. Olivia only smiled. "Thank you, Gerald. You know, I was thinking, before you get any contractors up to the mine, you ought to have some sort of religious ceremony—an exorcism or a native American blessing or something."

Gerald looked amused. "Why is that?"

Olivia's eyes widened. "You didn't know? Everyone at the Dirty Sally says the Lucky Lady Mine is haunted. It's the reason no one has worked the claim for years."

Gerald laughed. "Haunted! Oh, that's a good one." He leaned toward her, his voice low, confiding. "The reason the mine hasn't been worked for years, my dear, is that all the easy gold has already been taken out. The ore that remains is more difficult to reach, and requires technology and equipment that has only recently been developed."

"I don't know, Gerald," Olivia said. "People around here usually know about these things. I've heard that if you don't honor the ghosts, they'll get in there and wreck your expensive machinery, and then where will you be?"

Gerald drew back, eyes narrowed. "Don't think

I don't know what you're trying to do." He shifted his gaze to Lucille, then Bob. "All of you. But you won't scare me away so easily. I'll present the payment request to the town board," he said. "And if it is not paid promptly, you'll be hearing from my lawyers."

He left, and none of them said anything until he was well out of earshot. "That didn't go so well," Olivia said.

"No, you did good." Bob patted her hand. "You planted the idea in his head. That's the first step."

"This isn't going to work," Lucille said. "You can't frighten a man like Gerald with ghost stories."

"I still think it's worth a try," Bob said. "What have we got to lose?"

"Only the last shred of my dignity, Bob. At least let me keep that."

"Make twenty more copies of the petition, and use the heavy cotton copy paper, not that cheap recycled stuff. I don't want these falling apart before they're full of signatures." Cassie dropped the petition form on Sharon's desk. **HELP NAME TOWN PARK AFTER PIONEER WOMAN ERNESTINE WYNOCK** stood out in bold capitals across the top of the paper. Cassie had plastered the town with the flyers, and yesterday she'd spent all afternoon going door to door, persuading people to sign her petition. Sharon imagined Cassie could be very persuasive.

"How's the petition drive coming?" Sharon asked, as she carried the sheet to the copy machine.

"People around here are too afraid of change." Cassie moved aside the Date Due stamp, which she still insisted on using on every book, despite the computerized checkout system. "Half of them I talk to want to argue about the need to change the name of the park at all—as if 'Town Park' was ever an appropriate name in the first place. The other half are just plain ignorant. 'I didn't even know the park had a name,' they say." She rolled her eyes.

"Still, it looks like you've collected a lot of signatures." Sharon nodded to the folder on the corner of Cassie's desk, which bulged with a stack of signed petitions.

"Not all of them are legitimate." Cassie plucked a sheet from the folder and scowled at it. "I don't think Elmer Fudd is going to impress the town council. And the tourist signatures won't count either."

"How did your presentation to the town council go?" Sharon asked. The older woman had been in a state yesterday. She'd finally persuaded Lucille to put her on the meeting agenda, but she had only three minutes to make her pitch to rename the park. She'd made Sharon listen to her presentation so many times Sharon practically had the few lines memorized.

"I was doing fine until Junior Dominick interrupted me to say he didn't think the park needed to be named after anyone at all. I told him we might as well change the name of Eureka to 'Generic Mountain Town' and call the Last Dollar 'the café,' the Dirty Sally 'the bar,' and everything else by a similar label."

"How did he react to that?" Sharon asked.

The scowl deepened; it looked as if Cassie's face was folding in on itself. "Lucille told me my time was up and I needed more legitimate signatures to prove I wasn't the only one who thought changing the park name was a good idea."

"I'm sorry things didn't go better." Sharon straightened the stack of blank petitions and handed them to Cassie. For one thing, she'd have to hear about the park all day long for more days or weeks to come. She was becoming expert at feigning interest while tuning out, but the effort was tiring.

"They're more concerned with getting someone here to make movies than honoring the people who really matter," Cassie said.

"Someone is making a movie in Eureka?" Now this sounded interesting.

"Not yet. But they're hoping to lure someone here. As if Hollywood is dying to relocate to small mountain towns." Cassie sniffed.

"Yeah, why would anyone want to move *here?*"

Sharon cringed at the words, and half a second later her daughter slouched around the corner, the picture of the tortured teen. Alina hefted her backpack onto the wooden table at the center of the room with a resounding *thunk!* and dropped into a chair. Day four of the I'm-so-put-upon hit parade. How was Sharon going to survive a whole month?

"Treat library property with more care or you will not be allowed to use it." Cassie peered down her nose at Alina, the picture of the dour schoolmarm. Truly, the woman belonged in another century.

"Yes, ma'am." Alina moved her backpack to the floor and sat up a little straighter. Though Cassie showed little warmth to any young person other than Lucas, and treated most of her patrons with disdain, Alina didn't seem to mind her. "If she bans me from the library, you'll have to let me come home after school," she'd pointed out after her first day serving her punishment.

"If she bans you, she'll probably fire me," Sharon said. "Then you won't have a home to come to, after school or any time."

The threat was extreme; they were still living in Jameso's little rental, Sharon's meeting with the real-estate agent not having yielded anything suitable or affordable in the Eureka housing market. "Something will come along," the agent had warbled breezily. "It always does."

In any case, the specter of homelessness had induced Alina to sullen quiet in the library, which satisfied Cassie, if not Sharon. Meanwhile, Sharon was doing her best to ignore Alina's pouting.

"Hello, Alina," Sharon said evenly. "How was school?"

"School is dumb. If we still lived in Vermont, I wouldn't have to go to school."

"So you'd rather go back to being home-schooled and stay at the house all the time, with me as your teacher?"

Alina moaned and laid her head on the table. "Are you studying drama now?" Sharon asked.

"No, I don't get to do anything fun."

"I just wondered, because you're seriously overacting." She nudged the back of Alina's chair. "Sit up and do your homework. Then you can help me shelve books."

"Oh, joy."

"Oh, come on. You like shelving." Alina, like her friend Lucas, enjoyed perusing the titles and discovering unusual gems among the dusty volumes. Cassie apparently didn't believe in culling the shelves, and thus the Eureka County Library had books dating back to the turn of the twentieth century scattered among the modern novels and technical manuals.

Alina glared, the message in her eyes simple: *I don't like you.*

The sound of sneakers squeaking on the polished wood floors signaled the approach of another patron. Sharon turned in time to see Lucas Theriot lean his lanky frame against the checkout counter. "Good afternoon, Miss Wynock, Mrs. Franklin." His smile broadened. "Hey, Alina. You beat me here."

"I'm not allowed to stop anywhere between here and school," Alina said.

This wasn't exactly true; Sharon had agreed that Alina could go home to change and grab a snack, as long as she was at the library one hour after school let out. But she supposed the girl thought it sounded more dramatic to picture herself as not even allowed a bathroom break before she had to hit the books under the eye of her slave-driving mother.

"I think you just ride faster than me." He sat across from her at the big table. "I keep telling my mom and D. J. that I need a new bike—the one I have used to belong to my grandmother! But they're too caught up in all this house stuff to pay attention." He smiled up at Sharon. "That's a great bike you got, Alina."

"It belongs to my uncle," Alina said. "So it's not even really mine; he just lets me use it."

"Maybe when you're older, he'll let you borrow his motorcycle," Lucas said. "That's such a cool bike."

Jameso had explained, on one of his brief visits to the house, that the 1948 Indian Chief was a rare and valuable motorcycle. Maggie had added that she sometimes thought Jameso loved the bike more than he did her. He'd denied this, but the pained look on his face told Sharon that his devotion to the bike was a close second to his love for his fiancée.

"Jameso Clark is a menace on that motorcycle," Cassie said. "I've complained more than once about him speeding through town on that thing at all hours."

"Motorcycles always sound like they're going faster than they are," Lucas said. "You should ask Jameso to give you a ride sometime, Miss Wynock. I bet you'd like it."

Sharon had to look away, afraid her face would give away how hard she was fighting not to laugh at the ludicrous picture of Cassie, in her modest skirt and blouse and sensible shoes, perched on the back of a motorcycle behind a black-leather-clad Jameso.

Alina had no such reserve. She laughed out loud. "I'd like to see that."

"Enough of this nonsense." Cassie turned to Lucas. "What are you doing here?"

"Alina and I have to work on our social studies project."

The fond look the two young people exchanged made Sharon's stomach hurt. Not that she didn't like Lucas—he was smart and had good manners and even Cassie, who had a low opinion of most people, thought highly of Lucas. But she didn't like the idea that her daughter would fall under the sway of a boy at such a young age. She knew from personal experience how a man could lead a young girl astray.

What was she thinking—Lucas wasn't a man, and other than making Alina go off without telling Sharon, he hadn't done anything bad. When she'd met Joe, he had been twenty-seven to her fifteen, positively ancient in some ways, but he had a man's confidence and a man's strength, and he'd stood up to her father, threatening to slit his throat if he laid a hand on Sharon again. That had been enough to make her love him—to make her believe he was the one who could save her, now that her brother, Jay, had joined the army and left her alone.

She shoved the painful memories back into the corner of her mind where she kept them locked away. Alina didn't need anyone to protect her; she simply needed a friend her age, and Lucas fit that role. Sharon shouldn't worry. "What's your project about?" she asked.

"Rockets," Lucas answered. "Mr. Ames is letting us use the science lab at school to make one that really flies. But we also have to write a paper and do a presentation."

"We're going to get an A," Alina said. "Nobody else is going to the trouble to actually build a rocket." She glared at her mother again. "If I wasn't grounded, we could work on the rocket after school, instead of just during our study period."

"I'm sure we can arrange a special dispensation to work on a school project," Sharon said.

"I told you it would be all right." Lucas nudged Alina, but she continued to frown.

"Lucas, I believe you wanted to see more about the history of Eureka from our historical collection?" Cassie, either bored with talk of rockets or eager to once more be the focus of Lucas's attention—Sharon suspected a little of both—held out a hefty scrapbook. A stack of sheets of black paper five inches thick was sandwiched between embossed cardboard covers, yellowed bits of lace and faded flower petals sticking out on all sides.

"Wow, look at this, Alina." Lucas took the book and carefully opened it on the table between them.

"That scrapbook was compiled in 1961 by my grandmother and the other members of the Eureka Women's Society," Cassie said. "I have others, but this one is most closely focused on local history."

"There's your house." Lucas pointed to a fuzzy black-and-white photograph of a white house with upper and lower porches across the front and pillars like the posts that support wedding cake tiers. It was set back on a large lot, landscaped with abundant flowering shrubs.

"The yard was much larger then," Cassie said. "My grandmother had two gardeners to tend the plants. Of course, that sort of thing isn't practical now."

Or affordable, Sharon thought. Though she had not been invited to visit Cassie in her home, Lucille had pointed the house out to her: a faded version of the mansion in this photo, on a small plot of land, flanked by other houses and the street. Cassie's grandparents or parents must have sold off their excess acreage long ago, judging by the age of the neighboring houses. But in this photograph, at least, the house reigned as a fine estate, befitting the founder of a town.

"I think it's wonderful that you know so much about your family's history," Sharon said. "Few people these days have roots that run so deep." The flattering words came easily, maybe because part of her meant them; she did envy Cassie her deep roots in the town. Sharon had never lived in any one place long enough to truly feel at home.

"Yes, I'm very fortunate." Cassie smoothed her hand over the page with the picture of her family home; then she gave Sharon a sharp look. "What about your family? Where are you from? Are your parents and grandparents still alive? Jameso never talks about them; I always suspected it was because he had something to be ashamed of."

"Not ashamed," Sharon said, aware of Alina listening intently. "Ours was never a close family. I guess you could say Jameso and I are the only family we have left."

Cassie sniffed. "It's a disgrace how many people don't know anything about their heritage. Knowing where you come from gives you pride not merely in what you yourself have accomplished, but in your history, and all your family has done and represents."

"But other people don't care so much what your family did or who they are," Alina said. "They look at you and what you do and what you stand for."

"I stand for the same values and achievements my ancestors stood for," Cassie said. "They have established an example I strive to live up to. It's another reason it's important for us to remember what those who came before us did, and to remember them with acknowledgments, such as naming the park for my grandmother."

Lucas nodded, but he appeared to have lost interest in the subject. He turned the pages of the scrapbook. "Do you know if there's a picture of the house my mom and D. J. bought?" he asked.

"Let's see." Cassie leaned over him and flipped through a few more pages. "What was the name of the woman you bought it from?"

"Mrs. Gilroy. She was really old."

"Mavis Gilroy is eighty-five," Cassie said. "She taught home economics when I was in school. She was famous for her meringue pies. She and her husband bought that house after he left mining and opened a hardware store, about 1969. Before that, the house belonged to Cecil McCutcheon." She turned more pages, then stopped and put a stubby finger on a photograph. "There it is."

Everyone—including Sharon—leaned forward to study the picture of a two-story wood-sided house with some kind of blooming bushes flanking the narrow front stoop. Unadorned with shutters or porches, the house had an air of simple dignity, but no luxuries.

"Is it true that Mr. McCutcheon murdered his wife?" Alina asked.

Cassie's head shot up. "Where did you hear that?" she demanded.

"Mr. Prescott told my mom," Lucas said. "Is it true?"

"I've never heard such nonsense," Cassie said. "The McCutcheons were perfectly respectable people."

"So you knew them?" Lucas asked.

"Not well. But I believe Adelaide McCutcheon

was in the Women's Society with my grand-mother." Cassie flipped to the front of the scrapbook, to a group photo showing a dozen women in long white dresses arranged on the steps of what appeared to be a church. Cassie adjusted her glasses and peered at the photo, then at the accompanying roster. "I think that's her, third from the left in the second row."

Mrs. McCutcheon was a thin, pale woman with a narrow face and an impressive bouffant of blond hair. She stared solemnly into the camera, a high lace collar almost covering her chin. Sharon thought she looked as if she was holding her breath. "But did her husband kill her and bury the body in the back garden?" Lucas asked.

Cassie closed the scrapbook. "Bob Prescott should be ashamed of himself for making up such wild stories," she said. "First of all, Eureka was always a law-abiding, peaceful town. I don't believe we've had a single murder in the history of the town. And second, if Cecil had killed his wife, someone would have found out about it."

"But why would Mr. Prescott say it if it wasn't true?" Lucas asked.

"Because Bob Prescott enjoys putting people on," Cassie said.

"Do you have any other scrapbooks from the Women's Society?" Alina asked.

"We have several in the collection here at the

library," Cassie said. "Are you interested in local history, young lady?"

Alina at least had the grace to look sheepish. "I was just thinking that if we had a scrapbook that was from later on, after this one, we could look and see if Mrs. McCutcheon's picture was in there, too. If she wasn't, maybe it was because she was dead."

"Or, it could mean she decided to leave the club," Sharon said.

"Members did not leave the Women's Society," Cassie said. "Membership was a great honor, and by invitation only. A member might die, or move away, but she did not quit."

"Then we should look at the other scrapbooks," Lucas said.

Cassie hesitated, then nodded. "All right, I'll get them. But I'm sure she's there." She cradled the scrapbook to her chest and left.

Alina looked up at Sharon. "Mom, don't you have work to do?"

She'd been thinking of waiting around for Cassie's return, but she saw Alina's point. "I do have work to do," she said. "And you and Lucas have homework."

Alina let out another tortured moan.

"We could work on the outline for our paper while we wait for Miss Wynock," Lucas said. "Then we won't have to worry about it later."

When Sharon left to return to her desk, the

two young scholars had their heads together, pouring over a chapter in a textbook on jet propulsion or some similar topic. Sharon returned to the task of updating the library inventory for the state's computer system. The idea was to catalog all the books in the collection so that they'd be available for other libraries to request for their patrons. But Cassie had decided to exclude anything she considered "rare" or "of historical value." "I learned the hard way never to let those books leave this premises," she said when Sharon had questioned the exclusions. "I'm certainly not going to send them through the mail to people I don't even know."

But it made Sharon's task more tedious, since she had to cross-reference the inventory master list against Cassie's exclusion list.

"I found four more scrapbooks." Though Cassie was a pro at shushing anyone who dared raise their voice within the sacred confines of the library, her own voice carried clearly in the silence. Sharon looked up in time to see her deposit a stack of scrapbooks on the table between the two kids. She resisted the urge to join them—she really did need to finish entering these books—but she kept one ear tuned to the conversation, and she couldn't resist glancing their way every few minutes.

"There she is," Lucas said. He pointed to

something in one of the scrapbooks. "Get a load of that hat."

Alina laughed. "They all have funny hats. That one's almost like a turban. And look at the white gloves."

"A lady wasn't considered properly dressed unless she wore a hat and gloves," Cassie said. "Such a shame the custom has passed. I still have several of my grandmother's hats. Little works of art, I tell you."

"You should wear them," Lucas said. "You might start a new fashion trend."

"That's nice of you to say so, Lucas, but I don't think so." Cassie flipped through one of the scrapbooks. "Though maybe for special occasions . . ."

"Do it, Miss W," Lucas said. "I want to see your hats."

"Is that her?" Alina pointed to a page in the book Cassie was reviewing.

"Why, yes, I think it is," Cassie said.

"What year is that book?" Lucas asked.

"1963."

"This one says 1966." He pulled another volume from the stack. "Let's look in here."

Sharon focused on her computer once more. If nothing else, the kids were learning a little local history, though in the guise of investigating a fifty-year-old ghost story. Of course, pulling off a murder in a small town like Eureka would be almost impossible. It wasn't as if no one would notice if a prominent woman in the community suddenly turned up missing.

"She's not here," Alina announced.

"You must have overlooked her," Cassie said.

"She's not. Look. This is the official photograph of all the members, next to a program with everyone's name, from something called a Spring Tea."

Sharon gave up and joined the others at the table. Over Cassie's shoulder she studied the photos of the rows of women arranged on the church steps. More color in the dresses and different hats, but clearly the same bunch. Except that the thin-faced woman from the previous photograph was nowhere in sight.

"Maybe they moved away," Sharon said.

"What year did Mrs. Gilroy and her husband buy the house?" Lucas asked.

"The county keeps real-estate records that could tell you that," Cassie said. "We don't have that information here."

Lucas glanced at the big clock that hung behind the checkout desk. "It's after four. If we hurry, we can get to the courthouse before they close at five."

"Can I go, Mom, please?" Alina stood and began shoving books into her backpack before Sharon even answered.

"You have a social studies project to work on," Sharon said. "And you're still grounded."

"Mo-om!"

"Young lady, you will lower your voice in the library." Cassie's frosty tone would have quieted Attila the Hun.

Alina looked as if she was about to cry, and Sharon braced for a fight.

But Lucas ended the battle before it began—and earned points from Sharon—when he said, "She's right. We can check the real-estate records anytime. I mean, she probably did just move away. Real life is never as exciting as fiction."

Alina gave her mother one more reproachful look, but settled back into her chair. "It's still more interesting than sitting here doing homework," she grumbled.

"I don't know," Lucas said. "This rocket propulsion stuff is pretty interesting."

"You're such a geek," she said, but a smile tugged at the corners of her mouth.

Sharon returned to her workstation. Maybe she'd modify Alina's punishment so that she could work on the rocket—and visit the courthouse—after school with Lucas. Parenting, like pretty much everything else in life, was all about compromise, the perfect ideal warring with flawed reality. If the worst thing Alina wanted to do was build rockets and hunt ghosts, Sharon had no right to complain.

Chapter 8

"Barb, it's just beautiful. I can't believe how you've transformed this old place." Maggie squeezed her friend's hand as they admired the new wallpaper and refinished wood floors in the entryway of the house Barb was converting to a bed-and-breakfast inn. A chandelier hung from the high ceiling, crystal prisms sparkling, and through an arched doorway Maggie could see the elegant yet comfortable sitting room, with its cherry-wood wainscoting and antique furniture, including a red velvet Victorian fainting couch. Upstairs, each bedroom featured big antique beds and luxurious linens, gas fireplaces, and views of the mountains.

"I'm almost sorry to see the remodeling end." Barb ran a hand along the polished mahogany table in the entryway. "I haven't had this much fun since I decorated our first home—and we won't talk about how long ago that was."

"You'll do great at running a B and B," Maggie said. "You're a terrific hostess—nobody puts on parties like you do. And you get along with all kinds of people; it's the reason all those charities and other organizations in Houston want you to be in charge of fund-raising and outreach, and anything else they can talk you into."

"I did those things because I wanted to help," Barb said. "But also because I was bored. It's nice to have a business to focus on for a change, now that Michael is grown and sort of on his own."

"How is that going, Michael working with his dad?" The previous fall, Barb's husband had left his job with the oil company and started a business with his son.

"Surprisingly well. Jimmy says Michael actually has some really good ideas for the business, and he's great with the golf course owners and store managers. But who would have guessed they could make a living washing and selling used golf balls?"

"I'm glad they're making a go of it, but it doesn't sound like the kind of thing that would do well in the mountains. So how is that going to work, with his business in Houston and you up here?"

"We're still trying to figure that out. As much as I love Eureka and being closer to you, I'm a Texas gal at heart and I don't want to leave. And the thought of spending winter here makes me want to crawl under the covers and stay there. I had enough snow when we got stuck here at Christmas, thank you very much."

"I'd just as soon not see a repeat of that either," Maggie agreed. A blizzard had closed the roads for several days, isolating the town, trapping Jameso on the other side of the pass, and forcing Barb and her husband, Jimmy, to spend the holiday as refugees at a fishing camp.

"I figure I'll find a manager to take care of day-to-day operations here and I'll visit every few weeks to do the fun stuff," Barb said. "That way I won't get bored, and I can spend more time with Jimmy."

"That's a good idea. It shouldn't be tough to find someone in this economy."

"Sure you don't want to quit your job at the paper and work for me?"

Maggie shook her head. "It's nice of you to offer, but I like writing for the paper, and I'll have my hands full with the new baby."

"How are you feeling?" Barb squeezed her arm. "You look tired."

"I am tired. My back hurts. I have to pee every ten minutes. I'm hungry all the time, but everything I eat gives me indigestion." She smiled. "But other than that I'm wonderful. I'll just be glad when the wedding is done, we have a house, and the baby is born. Right now it feels like I'm just waiting for so much to happen."

"Where do you want this?" Jameso came through the door, carrying a stack of boxes so high they obscured his face. But Maggie would have recognized those muscular arms—and the deep voice—anywhere. How had she—who had always dated the ordinary, quiet, "safe" guys—ended up with such a stud?

"Just sit them down over there." Barb gestured to a space at the bottom of the stairs. "I'll open them later."

"Whatever they are, they're heavy." He set the boxes on the floor and straightened.

"Oh, you know you love showing off those muscles," Barb said. "And you're just the man I've been looking for."

"Sorry, Barb, but I'm already taken." He winked at Maggie and warmth skittered through her. Would she ever get over the thrill and wonder of being in love with this man? She hoped not.

"Be serious now," Barb said. "We need to plan the wedding."

"I thought that's what you two have been doing for weeks now," he said.

"I have a dress," Maggie said. "That's something." But they hadn't done much nitty-gritty planning. She told herself it was because Barb was busy with the remodeling, and she had work and the baby to think about. She wanted to marry Jameso—she truly did. But a wedding was so big and so much work. Thank God for Barb, or their baby might be in high school before they got around to making things official.

"We need your input," Barb said.

He shoved his hands in the pockets of his jeans. "Whatever Maggie wants is fine with me."

"I thought we could have the ceremony here in the front sitting room," Barb said.

"Fine with me," he said.

"Though I'm worried the room might be a little too small for all the guests," Barb continued. "Do you think the weather would be nice enough to have the ceremony outside, in the garden?"

"That sounds good."

"But will there be many flowers blooming that early in the summer?"

Jameso shrugged. "Could be iffy in June."

Maggie wanted to shake him. "Jameso, we asked you here because we wanted your opinion," she said. "It's your wedding, too."

He blew out a breath. "If it were up to me, we'd elope."

"Elope!" To her horror, she burst into tears.

"What did I say?" Jameso reached for her, then drew away, as if thinking better of the gesture. "Why are you crying?"

She shook her head. She didn't know really. Stress. Hormones. Or maybe just that he was being so unhelpful. Such a *man.* "You want me to do everything while you just keep going like you always have," she said. "If we have a wedding, I have to make all the decisions. If we want a house, I have to find it. Is this how it's going to be when we're married and have a baby to look after?" Was life with Jameso going to be the same as life with her first husband—

159

where she ended up doing all the work in the relationship? Was that simply the way marriage worked?

"I'm letting you take care of the wedding and the house because those things matter more to you," he said. "I don't care what kind of ceremony we have or where we live. What comes after—the marriage and spending the rest of my life with you—is important to me."

"But the wedding is important, too." She dug in her purse for a tissue. Barb handed her one, and she scrubbed at her nose and tried to regain her composure. Jameso was looking at her as if she were a bomb about to explode. "A wedding is a public commitment and a symbol of our love," she said. "And . . . and it ought to mean something."

"It will mean something, I promise." He patted her shoulder tentatively. "When I say those vows, I'll mean them; but it doesn't matter to me if I say them in front of a preacher and a room full of people or a judge and no one but you. Because I'm saying the vows to you. Not anyone else."

He knew the right words to say, but did he mean them? Part of marriage was accepting each other as you were. But it was also important to work together—to be partners. "You're right," she said. "The wedding and the house are more important to me than they are to you. But you

160

need to care about them because I care about them. And I can't keep doing everything to make this work. You've got to pick up some of the slack and help."

Jameso looked at Barb. She held up her hands. "I can't help you. You two are going to have to work this out amongst yourselves."

He turned back to Maggie. "Fine. Tell me what you want me to do."

"That's the point!" Her voice rose and a fresh wave of tears threatened. "I shouldn't have to tell you."

"Now I'm supposed to be a mind reader?" Jameso threw up his hands. "Women!" He turned on his heel and stormed out, slamming the door behind him.

Maggie gave in to the tears. Barb came and put her arm around her, and Maggie leaned into the embrace of her friend. "Now I've done it," she said. "He'll probably head for the hills—literally."

"He probably would have a few months ago," she said. "But not now. I think he's going to stick it out."

Maggie mopped at her eyes and blew her nose. "Do you think he understood what I was trying to say?"

"It'll probably sink in after a while. It's good that you said it anyway. You probably never told Carter anything like that, did you?"

"No." She couldn't remember ever standing up

161

to her first husband, Carter Stevens. "Whenever I was angry with him, I told myself it wasn't worth rocking the boat, that my anger was my problem and I had to learn to adjust my expectations, that I was responsible for my own feelings."

"Sounds like something from one of those books about how to be the perfect wife—the subservient kind who focused on pleasing her man."

"It probably was."

"Can you believe we were ever so dumb?" Barb patted her shoulder. "So see, blowing up at Jameso was a good thing. You can say what you need to to him and trust that he won't run away or pout like a little boy."

"Do you really think so?"

"Well, he might pout for a little while, but he'll get over it. Now, come on. I know just what will cheer you up."

"What's that?"

"Homemade pie from the Last Dollar. I hear Danielle's making strawberry rhubarb today."

The baby inside her gave a mighty kick. Maggie laughed and rubbed her belly. "I think the baby likes that idea."

"Then we'd better go, or she'll keep you up all night. And don't worry about Jameso. He'll come around."

"You always have more confidence in him

than I do." Barb had been Jameso's champion from the first day they met; it had taken Maggie a lot longer to see his good qualities.

"I have confidence in both of you." One hand on the doorknob, Barb looked back over her shoulder at her friend. "Remember—I was a cheerleader in high school."

"Obviously, you were a natural." She followed Barb out the door, toward pie and whatever other sweetness life could offer. She and Jameso would make up later; they'd figure out how to negotiate marriage—how to be together and yet separate, which she supposed was really the big puzzle of marriage, after all.

Olivia marveled at how much a year could change a person. When she'd first arrived in Eureka the year before and started work at the Dirty Sally, she liked the night shifts best. The bar was always busy and she served up drinks, cleared tables, flirted with the customers, and scarcely had a moment to think about anything. Avoiding her thoughts was better than wrestling with them, she'd believed. The work had bought her the time she needed to face her fears and straighten out her life.

Now she preferred afternoons, before the evening rush, when sometimes she and whoever else was on duty were the only people in the place. The customers who did come in were quiet, undemanding, and low-key. She had time to let her mind wander, or to talk to her coworkers.

Or, as was the case this afternoon, to listen to them talk. She and Jameso were inventorying the liquor supply behind the bar, checking the level of each bottle, wiping it down and returning it to the shelf, grouping like spirits together, and making note of anything they needed to reorder. While this occupied their hands, Jameso was telling about his fight with Maggie over the wedding preparations.

"I told her we could do whatever she wanted —that I only wanted her to be happy, and she accused me of not caring." He shoved a bottle of bourbon back onto the shelf. "How is that not caring?"

Olivia wiped down the next bottle and handed it to him. "Do you really want to know?" she asked.

He glared at her, his darkly handsome face forbidding, though she'd long ago learned there was little venom behind the black looks. "Of course I want to know," he said. "Why would she think I don't care?"

"You were taking the easy way out—you want her to do all the work, and all you have to do is show up and put the ring on her finger. It sets a bad precedent."

"What precedent? We're only going to do this once."

She grabbed the next bottle in line and began wiping it. "It sets a bad precedent for the marriage," she said. "First, Maggie plans and executes the wedding. Then, she decides what's for dinner every night. The next thing you know, she's buying all the clothes and dealing with the kid's teachers and planning all the vacations."

At his blank look, she shook her head. "You still don't get it, do you?"

"Get what? Isn't that stuff what women do? What they want to do?"

"In a lot of marriages, yes. But Maggie has been there and done that, and now she wants a different kind of marriage. One where the two of you are equal partners, and you share responsibility. And she wants to start with the wedding." She handed him the bottle. "It makes perfect sense to me."

"It makes sense to you because you're a woman."

"What do you want—a partner and a lover, or a live-in housekeeper and surrogate mother?"

"Maggie is not my mother. That's sick."

"Then stop acting like a kid. Grow up and speak up. Have an opinion about the wedding—and saying you want to elope does not qualify as a valid opinion."

He clammed up, shoving bottles into place with so much force she feared one might break. But his agitation soon subsided. He turned to face her. "The problem is," he said, "I never had a model for what a marriage is supposed to be. My parents certainly didn't know."

"Don't look at me, my parents split when I was a kid. But that doesn't mean I don't think I can't figure things out on my own."

"You and D. J. don't seem to be in any hurry to rush to the altar."

"We're just waiting for the right time. After the house is done and we can live together." She and D. J. knew they were staying together. Rushing to get a piece of paper that said so wasn't as important to her.

"So are you going to have a big ceremony with the white dress and the bridesmaids and the whole nine yards?" he asked.

"No, we're thinking of something quieter."

He shook his head. "So why didn't I marry you?"

"You don't want me."

"No, I want Maggie." His shoulders slumped. "I just want her without so many complications."

"Relationships are all about complications."

"Not all of them. Guys can be friends without all the drama."

"Ha! So your friendship with Maggie's dad, Jake, never had any drama? From the stories people tell around here, he was all about the drama." Though Jacob Murphy had died before Olivia had even come to town, he'd made a big impression on people. All the bar regulars had Jake stories—wild things he'd done or said. But

Jameso had known the man better than most. They'd been best friends for years.

Jameso's frown was more thoughtful. "Okay. Jake had his problems. It made things . . . tense between us sometimes."

"Is Maggie like him?"

"They're both just as stubborn, but then so am I." He shook his head. "But they aren't alike —no. Jake didn't trust people. Hell, he didn't trust himself. He had a mean temper and a drinking problem, and things in the past he could never quite overcome. I used to think the two of us were friends because *we* were so much alike."

"You're not like that," she said. "You're not mean or a drunk. As for the past . . . you can't undo it, so you have to get over it. History doesn't have to repeat itself." A lesson she was trying hard to learn herself.

"I want Maggie and me and the baby to be a real family," Jameso said. "I'm afraid of screwing it up. I've been on my own so long, I'm not used to having other people depending on me."

"Don't be so hard on yourself." She handed him another bottle. "You're a good guy and you'll figure this out. Speaking of family, how's your sister?"

He turned back to the shelves. "She's doing okay, I guess."

"You don't know?"

"I haven't even talked to her in years. Just because she suddenly showed up in town doesn't mean we're going to be close."

"She came to town to see you. To be near you."

"She came to town to get away from that jerk of a husband of hers."

"She told you that?"

"She didn't have to. The guy's one of these survivalist/militia/right-wing nuts. He dragged her and the kids to the middle of nowhere to live off the land. She finally woke up and had enough, and decided to get out of Dodge. I guess she figured Eureka, Colorado, is far enough from Vermont he wouldn't come after her."

Olivia felt a shiver of alarm. "Do you think he will? Come after her, I mean?"

"I don't know. I told you, I hadn't spoken to her in five years when she showed up here."

So it was back to being grouchy. The man was definitely touchy. "Her daughter and Lucas are friends," she said.

"Oh yeah?" He glanced over his shoulder at her. "Like girlfriend-boyfriend?"

"I don't think it's to that stage yet. Though I did ask D. J. if he thought we should talk to Lucas about sex."

Jameso laughed. "You're joking, right? Olivia, he's almost what—fourteen? Don't you think it's a little late for that?"

"You sound like D. J. He said the same thing.

But then he told me not to worry, that he sounded Lucas out on the subject on one of their overnights last winter. The boy knows more than I ever did at his age, that's for sure."

"Tell him if he ends up getting my niece in trouble, he'll have to answer to me."

"That ought to be real effective, considering Maggie's going to be walking down the aisle nine months' pregnant."

At the stricken look on his face, she laughed. "I'm just kidding. Lucas already thinks you're the town badass. It won't hurt him to be reminded that you're Alina's uncle—though I don't think he thinks of her in that way."

"He probably does. You just don't want to admit that your baby thinks about having sex."

She covered her ears with her hands. "La, la, la . . . I can't hear you."

"Hey? Anybody home?" Someone called from the back.

Olivia leaned around the corner and saw Alina herself, peeking in the half-open back door. "Can I come in?" the girl asked.

"Come on up." Olivia waved her forward.

Alina hurried to join them. Dressed in jeans with ripped knees, pink Keds, and a pink polo shirt, her long hair in pigtails, she definitely looked more like a tomboy than a glamour girl. "Hey, Ms. Theriot." She waved. "Hey, Uncle Jay—I mean Uncle Jameso."

Olivia bit back a laugh. She still couldn't get over the idea that Jameso had changed his name. "What brings you here?" she asked. "Lucas told me you were grounded."

"Mom decided one week was enough misery for both of us. I think after she got over being scared and mad she realized she may have overreacted a little. I was only a few minutes late, and I promised to call her before I went anywhere again."

"I'm sorry my son got you into trouble."

"It's okay." She smiled shyly, looking up through her bangs. "My mom really likes him, so that helps, actually."

"That's good to know. What can we do for you?"

"I came to see Uncle Jameso." She glanced his way.

Olivia nudged Jameso, who was intently rearranging liquor bottles, as if unaware of Alina's arrival. "Your niece is here to see you," she said.

"Oh. Hey, Alina." He leaned against the bar, an uber-casual pose, but Olivia felt the tension radiating from him. Mr. Cool was nervous around this *girl*. "How are you liking Eureka?" he asked.

"It's okay. The people are nice."

"What can I do for you?"

Olivia moved down the bar, though she stayed close enough to eavesdrop.

"I just wanted to say hi," Alina said. "We haven't seen too much of you since we got to town."

"Well, your mom and I are both busy."

"I was hoping we could maybe, you know, hang out."

The look on Jameso's face was priceless—a mixture of surprise and fear and confusion. "You want to hang out with me? Why?"

"You're the only uncle I have, and I don't have any aunts or cousins." She shoved her hands in her pockets, shoulders hunched. "I just thought it would be good if we got to know each other better."

"Uh, sure." Jameso looked around the bar, as if someone might arrive to rescue him from this awkwardness. Everyone, including Olivia, avoided his gaze. "What do you want to do?" he asked the girl after a moment.

"Maybe you could show me more of the town. Take me to your favorite places or something. Sometime when you're not busy."

"He's not busy now," Olivia said.

"I'm working," he protested.

"Tuesdays are always slow." She indicated the half dozen customers. "If I need help, Bob can pitch in."

"Sure, I can do that," Bob said from his end of the bar.

"Or I'll call Reggie upstairs at his law office,"

Olivia said. "He likes to play bartender when he can." She reached out and pulled off Jameso's apron. "Go."

"Cool!" Alina said as she followed Jameso toward the door. "Can I ride on your motorcycle?"

"Wear a helmet," Olivia called after them.

"I will, I promise," Alina said.

At least one member of the family had her head on straight.

"Jameso doesn't know the first thing about looking after a kid," Bob said when they were gone.

"Considering he's about to have one of his own, it's time he found out," Olivia said. He'd said he wanted family. Maybe his niece was a good place to start.

Chapter 9

Jameso handed Alina his spare helmet, the one Maggie usually wore. "Put this on."

"Cool." She slipped the helmet on, then fumbled with the latch.

He reached out and fastened it for her. "I'll get on first," he said. "Then you climb on behind me." She did so and he showed her where to put her feet. "And hang on to me."

He could barely feel her small hands and slight body, yet every nerve was aware of her. "Your mother will probably kill me when she finds out I had you on my bike," he said.

"She'll get over it."

He choked back a laugh. That was exactly the sort of thing *he* would have said if Sharon had complained to him. "So where do you want to go?" he asked.

"Take me to your favorite place in Eureka."

Did he have a favorite place? She'd already seen the Dirty Sally and the Last Dollar. There was only one other place he really liked to spend time. "My favorite place isn't in town," he said. "It's in the mountains."

"So take me there."

He couldn't think of a reason not to. "Hang

on," he said. The bike started with a familiar, comforting rumble, and he turned it into the street and headed toward the highway out of town.

After the long winter, the road was rough, pocked with holes, worn into ruts. He had to slow the bike and steer carefully. Alina leaned forward to talk to him, her voice raised above the motorcycle's engine. "This is so much fun," she said. "I love flying along so close to everything."

They weren't exactly flying, but he knew what she meant. "Maybe later on, when we get to a better stretch of road, I'll show you what it's like to really fly," he said.

"Awesome!"

He turned the bike onto the even more narrow and rutted road up to Jake's cabin. Even though it belonged to Maggie now, he'd always think of the renovated miner's cabin as Jake's place. If there were such a thing as ghosts, Jake would haunt this place he'd loved so much.

Fifteen minutes later, he pulled in front of the cabin and cut the engine. "Who lives here?" Alina asked.

"No one right now. It belongs to Maggie. Her father owned it."

Alina climbed off the bike and stood staring at the cabin. The place had been old when Jake had bought it, and most of the improvements he'd made didn't show. Weather and time had burnished the wood siding to silver, some pieces cracked and curled. Stone crumbled from the pillars that supported the porch across the front, and the stovepipe had rusted dark red. "He lived way up here?" Alina asked.

"He did. He liked the solitude, and the view. Come on, I'll show you." He found the key on his ring and unlocked the front door. "Jake never locked it when he lived here," he said. He pushed open the door and motioned for Alina to enter ahead of him.

"Wow!" she gasped, and froze in the middle of the cabin's main room.

Jameso laughed. "It leaves most people at a loss for words, the first time they see it," he said. Oversized picture windows filled the back wall, which jutted out over the canyon. More windows on the sides flooded the space with light and views of blue sky, white clouds, and soaring mountains. Alina turned slowly all the way around, her mouth open. "It's like floating in space," she said finally. "Or maybe being in a really, really tall tree house."

"The first time Maggie saw this place, she fainted." At Alina's horrified look, he added, "She was new to Colorado and wasn't used to the altitude."

"I think it would be an awesome place to live." She put her hand on the railing at the bottom of the steps. "What's upstairs?"

"A bedroom. You can go on up."

Maggie had left most of the furniture, so the big bed, stripped of sheets and comforter, still sat in the middle of the room, flanked by large windows. Maggie had covered the windows with drapes she'd made from old red velvet theater curtains, but right now they were pulled back. Alina sat on the side of the bed and gaped at the view. "Why did she move into town?" she asked after a moment.

"The only way to get here in winter is on a snowmobile," Jameso said. "Jake did it for years, but he didn't have a job he had to be at every day."

"I guess that would be kind of tough. Hey, look at that." She pointed out the window.

He followed her gaze toward a bighorn sheep that was ambling its way down the slope behind the house. "That's Winston," he said.

"He has a name?"

"Jake—Maggie's dad—named him. Come downstairs and you can meet him."

He led the way downstairs and outside, with a brief stop by the kitchen to retrieve a package of Lorna Doones from the cabinet. "Want a cookie?" He offered one to Alina.

"Um, sure." She took the cookie and crunched it. "A little stale."

"Winston won't mind." He hooked two fingers over his lower lip and let out a loud whistle. Seconds later, the mountain sheep trotted around the corner of the house and headed straight toward them.

"What's he doing?" Alina stepped behind Jameso.

"It's okay. Here, offer him a cookie." He showed her how to place the cookie on her open palm and hold it out toward the sheep. The animal eagerly swiped up first Jameso's offering, then Alina's.

"Oh my gosh. His tongue feels so weird." She giggled and smiled up at him, eyes shining.

He felt about ten feet tall, as if he'd done something heroic, instead of merely letting her feed cookies to a mountain sheep. "You look just like your mom when she was your age," he said.

"Really?" She brushed her hands on her jeans and shook her head at the sheep. "No more cookies. Sorry."

They watched the ram wander back the way he'd come. Alina fixed Jameso once more with a look of intense interest. "What was my mom like when she was a kid?"

Sharon had been a sweet, sensitive girl who hid in the closet when their parents fought. He'd find her there, shaking and crying without making a sound, tears slipping down her cheeks, making a wet spot on her T-shirt. He'd hold her and rock her and tell her everything was going to be okay.

He'd been a good liar, even then. Really, he'd

been just as scared and upset as she was, but the compulsion to protect her had been stronger than his fear, so he'd pretended, for her sake. Somehow, that made them both feel better. "She was smart, like you. Quiet, but with a wicked sense of humor." Sometimes the lie wasn't in what you said, but in all you left out.

"She never talks about her childhood." She hugged her arms across her chest. "She told me once her father was mean and that was why she married my dad when she was so young. I figure it must have been pretty bad."

"It was. But your mom turned out okay in spite of that. She's a good woman."

"She is. The best."

He wanted to ask why Sharon had left Joe and come all this way—and without Adan. But maybe that wasn't his business. Or maybe he shouldn't ask a kid to explain a parent's action.

"She didn't like that my dad kept us so isolated from everyone," she said, as if she'd read his mind. "She said it wasn't right—that we couldn't go to school or have friends. He was always so paranoid. He thought everyone was bad, while Mom thought most people were good."

That was Sharon—while he was much more like Joe. He used to think she was just naïve, while he was being realistic. Now he wished he shared more of her optimism about life. He wanted to set aside some of his cynicism, to focus on all the good things that had come his way. "What did you think?" he asked.

"I missed going to school and having kids my own age to hang out with," she said. "I didn't like it when my dad would get mad and go on about the government and stuff like that. It didn't make sense to me."

"Sometimes people get angry about things they can't control." Jake had been like that—a man with rages he couldn't talk about. Jameso had learned to stay away until the storms passed, but a wife and kids didn't have that option.

"Now that we're here, I miss him sometimes," she said. "And I really miss Adan."

Here was the opening he'd been waiting for. "Why didn't Adan come with you?"

"He wanted to stay with Dad. He's almost fifteen and bigger than Mom. She couldn't make him come." She hunched her shoulders, as if warding off a blow. The air practically hummed with tension.

"Is there something else?" he asked gently. "Something you aren't telling me?"

She shrugged, shoulders still hunched, eyes downcast. "I think as long as Adan stayed behind, Dad didn't care what Mom and I did."

He pulled her close in a rough hug. "Some guys are just jerks."

She buried her face in his chest. "You're not a jerk."

"I try not to be, but sometimes even I am." He thought of his argument with Maggie, and how Olivia had accused him of wanting to take the easy way out. Maybe she was right.

He patted Alina's shoulder. "Come on, let's go see if your mom wants to go have dinner with us."

"Really? With you and Maggie?"

"Maggie has to cover a town council meeting for the paper, so you're stuck with me. Is that all right?"

"That would be great. Mom will be so happy."

One more way he'd been a jerk—avoiding his sister when she asked so little of him. "It's time we spent more time together," he said. "After all, we're family." For too long, he'd treated the idea of family like a dirty word. Time to rethink that and try again.

"Tell me again why we're meeting at the library?" Junior Dominick asked as he settled his bulky frame into a chair at the table in the center of the book-lined space.

"Because our charter requires we meet in a public place and the Last Dollar was booked by a car club out of Denver who are passing through on their way to Telluride," Lucille said. She picked up the gavel. "I now call this meeting of the Eureka Town Council to order."

"You should have just moved the meeting to the Dirty Sally," Bob said.

"You'd have certainly been at home there," Cassie Wynock said from one of the side chairs she'd arranged for spectators. So far, these consisted of Cassie, Josh Miller, and Maggie Stevens, who was here to report on the proceedings for the *Eureka Miner.* "The library is a much more suitable space in which to conduct official business."

Lucille banged the gavel again. "Why don't we get down to that business. Katya, do you have the minutes?"

Katya Paxton, wife of the town lawyer, Reggie Paxton, handed out the single sheet of typed minutes. Bob fitted a pair of wire-rimmed glasses over his ears and scowled at the page. "You ought to just make a generic form you fill in each month," he said. "The town is broke, some piece of machinery needs repairing, Cassie complained about something, then we adjourned for pie and coffee."

"You left out Bob Prescott was drunk—as usual," Cassie said.

Lucille banged the gavel again, though her temptation was to start banging heads. First Bob. Then maybe Cassie. "May I have a motion to approve the minutes?"

Paul Percival made the motion and Junior seconded. "Now, to tonight's agenda." Lucille consulted the paper in front of her. "The first item."

"I'm the first item and I have my petitions right here." Cassie jumped up and deposited a sheaf of paper in the center of the table. The council members stared at the pile, none of them daring to meet Cassie's eyes.

"How many signatures do you have there, Cassie?" Reggie asked.

"Three hundred and seventy-eight," she announced.

She must have gotten everyone who came into the library—and all their relatives, maybe even their pets, to sign. "Do we even have that many people in the town?" Katya asked.

"I included people from the county also. After all, they use the park, too."

"Someone will have to count and verify the signatures," Lucille said. Most likely meaning she'd have to do it—everyone else would find an excuse why they couldn't possibly do so. "Then we'll get back to you."

"Oh, please. Do you think I was born yesterday?" Cassie asked.

Bob hooted with laughter, but a quelling look from Cassie silenced him. "You all think you can keep putting me off and I'll forget about this," she said. "But I won't forget. The town park needs a name, and my grandmother's is the perfect name for it."

"Other people might think their grandmother— or their grandfather or uncle or mom or dad—

need the park named after them," Lucille said.

"My grandmother was president of the Women's Society the year they dedicated the park to the town," Cassie said.

"She makes a good point," Junior said. "I always thought calling the place Town Park made us look uncreative."

"Cassie's grandmother obviously thought the name was fine," Katya said. "Since that's what the Women's Society called it."

Cassie flushed but wouldn't be cowed. "Grandmother Ernestine was far too modest to name the park for herself, but she would be pleased. It's only fitting."

"I promise, Cassie, we'll get back to you once we've reviewed the petitions," Lucille said. She banged the gavel. "If that's all the old business, we'll move on to new business. . . ."

"We still have one more item of old business," Katya said. "The improvements to the Lucky Lady Mine."

"So we weren't able to talk Pershing out of that scheme?" Paul asked.

"We authorized the basic safety upgrades," Lucille said. "We couldn't very well get away without those."

"Pershing thinks we ought to spring for an upgrade on the ventilation system," Bob said. "I told him I'd worked forty years in mines and if we had a ventilation system at all, it was a length of stovepipe and a blower, and that was good enough for me."

"That explains a lot," Cassie said. "Not enough oxygen to your brain."

Lucille raised her voice to be heard over the chuckles at Bob's expense. "I think the best approach is to keep stalling and pay as little as possible until we see some income from the mine," Lucille said.

"I agree," Paul said. "If Pershing wants a lot of fancy upgrades, he can pay for them himself."

Lucille looked at Reg. "Do we need a formal vote on that?"

He shook his head. "No, since you didn't take any specific action."

"Fine." She took a deep breath. Here was the moment she'd been waiting for all night. "Now, on to new business."

"It just says movie." Junior tapped his copy of the agenda. "What movie?"

"I've had a reply from the state movie commission." Lucille had to hold back a grin as she made the announcement.

"Already?" Reggie said. "That was quick."

"Apparently, they had a director contact them the same week they received our application. He thinks we'd be perfect for the movie he has planned."

"Who's the director?"

"What movie?"

"Who are the stars?"

"What's it about?"

The questions came all at once, overlapping into gibberish. Lucille pounded the gavel, but no one paid attention.

"Silence!"

The voice of the librarian in the hall where she reigned supreme was enough to cut them off in midsentence. Cassie fixed them with an icy stare. "Remember where you are," she said.

"We're in a town council meeting, not a ladies' club tea," Bob groused. "Lucille, what's this about a movie?"

"The director's name is Chris Amesbury, and I don't know anything about the movie. But he wants to come to Eureka in two weeks to see the town and talk to us about his movie."

"What's in it for us?" Bob asked.

"If the movie is a hit, it could mean more tourist traffic." Paul, who owned the local gas station, looked pleased.

"The last thing we need is more tourists," Bob said. Bob complaining about tourists was nothing new, so no one paid any attention to him.

"A movie takes several weeks to months to film," Lucille said. "During that time, we'd have a whole movie crew staying in town, eating and drinking and shopping here. It could be a big boost for our economy."

"And they would probably hire locals to work as extras in the film," Cassie said. She wore a dreamy expression, her eyes bright and feverish.

"Thinking of trying out, are you?" Bob asked.

"Everyone did say I gave a remarkable performance in the Founders' Day Pageant," she said.

"I never said it," Bob grumbled.

"I think we should plan a real Eureka welcome for Mr. Amesbury," Lucille said. "A dinner at the Last Dollar with the town council. A Jeep tour in the mountains. I'll ask Jameso Clark about that. And I'm going to ask Barb Stanowski to put him up at her new B and B."

"But she isn't open for business yet," Maggie said. "The house won't be ready for guests for another three weeks, at least."

"It's almost complete," Lucille said. "And all we need is one really nice room. Her place is by far the most upscale in town."

"Put him up at the motel, send him to the Dirty Sally for a burger, and let him see what we're really like," Bob said.

"Maybe we should buy Bob a ticket out of town for the duration of Mr. Amesbury's visit," Paul said.

"I second the motion," Junior said.

"We can't do that," Lucille said, though she secretly agreed it was a good idea. "Now, who will help me plan a warm reception for Mr. Amesbury?"

Most of the hands in the room went up. "Great.

I'll be in touch to make plans. Is there any more new business?" This was always a tense time in any meeting, as everyone held his or her breath, hoping someone didn't pop up with a problem or complaint that needed to be addressed right away.

Tonight, they were lucky. "I make a motion we adjourn," Katya said.

"I second," said Paul.

"Motion carries." As soon as Lucille lowered the gavel, chairs scraped back and people stood.

Maggie headed straight for Lucille. "Do you know anything else about Chris Amesbury?" she asked.

"His Wikipedia entry shows a few documentaries for the Discovery Channel and a low-budget horror picture," Lucille said. She lowered her voice and leaned closer to Maggie. "But for God's sake, don't put that in your article. Someone will start a rumor he's coming here to make a zombie picture."

"How do you know that he's not?"

"We don't. And frankly, I don't really care what he wants to do—as long as it's not porn, of course. But anything would help our economy."

"Maybe Gerald will find gold in the Lucky Lady and you won't have to worry," Maggie said.

"That would be lovely, but in the meantime I'm going to do my best to impress this director.

Will you help me persuade Barb to give him a room?"

"I'm sure she'll help if she can." Maggie stashed her tape recorder and notebook in her bag. "I'll call you tomorrow."

"Thanks."

"Lucille, I just had a wonderful idea."

Lucille closed her eyes. "What is that, Cassie?"

"We can ask the director to dedicate the park with its new name."

"We haven't determined that the park is going to have a new name," Lucille said.

"Then you'd better get busy if we're going to have everything ready by the time Mr. Amesbury arrives."

"He's coming here as a guest, not to work," Lucille said.

"These famous people always like to be recognized," she said. "He'll be flattered."

Flattered to be asked to cut the ribbon or raise a toast or whatever on the renaming of a small village park—named for a woman he never heard of. "I think we'll allow Mr. Amesbury to relax and get a feel for the town," Lucille said. "Maybe some other time we'll give him the opportunity to participate more."

"Honestly, I don't know how you've managed to remain mayor for so long," Cassie huffed. "You're so obstructionist."

"Trust me, I've been called worse," Lucille

188

said to Cassie's back as the librarian stalked away.

"If you make Eureka famous, you'll be called a hero," Maggie said.

"That would be a nice change." She gathered up her papers. "Come on. Let's get out of here before Cassie thinks of another great idea."

Chapter 10

Sharon pressed the phone tightly to her ear and listened to the ringing on the other end of the line. It sounded so far away—the way she felt. After the sixth ring, the call disconnected. No explanation. No message. Nothing.

She clutched the phone to her chest and pictured her son, Adan—all long limbs, knobby knees, and elbows, like a colt that hasn't yet grown accustomed to his size. He had inherited his father's height and his mother's slimness. He wore his hair long, falling into his eyes, which were the dark brown of polished chestnut. Girls watched him, and giggled behind their hands; he pretended not to notice, though the tips of his ears burned red.

Why wasn't he answering the phone? She'd bought it for him before she left, so that they could keep in touch. Joe didn't believe in cell phones; he was convinced the government used them to track people and to record their conversations. But Adan was enough of a teen that he was excited to have his own phone. She'd spoken with him a couple of times since they'd come to Eureka, but for the past two days he hadn't answered.

She stood and went into the living room, where Alina was reading, one leg draped over the arm of the sofa. Petite like Sharon, she had Joe's thick, dark hair and high cheekbones. Whatever else she thought of her marriage, Sharon had to admit she and Joe had made beautiful children. "Have you heard from your brother?" she asked.

"No." She laid aside her book and looked up at her mother. "How would I have heard from him? I don't have a phone." The fact that Sharon had bought a phone for Adan and not for Alina was a sore spot.

"He might have called the house when I wasn't here."

"I haven't heard from him. Why?"

"I've been trying to reach him and can't."

"Maybe Dad took his phone away."

Sharon's stomach clenched. It would be like Joe to do something like that, though he'd promised that, as Adan's mother, she'd still be allowed to stay in touch with her son, and that Adan could visit whenever he liked. He'd never mentioned wanting to see Alina again, or have her visit, things Sharon had kept from her daughter.

The sound of tires on gravel distracted her from these thoughts. Alina jumped up. "Mail's here," she said, and raced out the door. Almost everything that arrived was for Jameso—and most of that was junk that went straight into the

191

recycling bin—but Alina still delighted in racing to the mail box, as she had when she was a little girl. Maybe today would bring a free sample or an interesting magazine or an offer that would change her life.

Sharon stared at her phone. Should she try again? Maybe Adan had forgotten to charge his phone or had misplaced it in his room. He was bound to discover the mistake sooner or later. But why couldn't she even leave a message?

The door banged open and Alina bounced inside. "There's a couple of things for you," she announced, and held out two envelopes—one large and brown, the other small and white. A small thrill of anticipation raced through Sharon as she studied the white envelope. Neither of these looked like bills, so maybe that meant something good.

"Who's it from?" Alina looked over Sharon's shoulder.

"Barbara Stanowski."

"That's Maggie's friend, right? The one with the bed-and-breakfast."

Sharon nodded and slit open the envelope. A pink card shaped like a rattle slipped out. "It's an invitation to a baby shower for Maggie," she said.

"How cute. What are you going to get her?"

"I don't know." She didn't have the money to buy anything very impressive, and even though

Maggie had been very nice to her, Sharon didn't know her well. Buying a gift for her felt awkward. "Maybe we'll find a cute baby outfit." A new mom could never have too many bibs and diaper shirts.

"What's in that other big envelope?" Alina asked.

Sharon's previous elation vanished, incinerated by the return address stamp with the name of the law firm she'd hired to handle her divorce. Heart pounding, she slit open the flap and eased out a sheaf of papers. She flipped through to the bottom of the last page:

The bonds of matrimony now existing between the Plaintiff and the Defendant are dissolved on the grounds of irreconcilable differences, and the Plaintiff is awarded an absolute decree of divorce from the Defendant.

Alina had been reading, too. "So you and Dad aren't married anymore," she said. Sharon tried to gauge her daughter's mood. Was Alina happy? Sad? She sounded more stunned. Exactly the way Sharon herself felt.

"When your father and I married, we meant our vows," she said carefully. "I'm sorry we weren't able to keep them. It's not easy to split up a family, but I think, in this case, it's for the best."

"I know." Alina plopped onto the sofa and

hugged a pillow to her stomach. "Lots of kids don't live with both parents," she said. "Lucas's parents are divorced. He hasn't even seen his father since he was really little."

Sharon sat beside her daughter. She wanted to gather Alina to her and hold her close, but resisted the impulse. Either Alina would pull away or they'd both burst into tears, and neither outcome she wanted right now. "I'm glad you've made friends," she said instead. "I know moving to a new place can be hard."

"I like Eureka," Alina said. "I like going to school again, and the kids are mostly okay. Some of them are really nice. And Uncle Jameso is nice."

"Yes, he is." She hadn't known what to expect from her brother. They'd been apart so long, separated by physical distance and their own problems, and a past neither wanted to remember. At first, she was sure she'd made a mistake coming here; that Jameso didn't want them in his life. She hadn't pushed him, and her patience had been rewarded.

Or maybe she should say Alina's impatience had been rewarded. She'd sought him out and he'd responded. "Last night was fun," Sharon said. At dinner, Jameso had been warm and funny, gently teasing Alina and making them all laugh. She'd felt such a surge of warmth and love, confirmation that she'd made the right decision, coming here.

"Uncle Jameso had a friend who sounds a lot like Dad." Alina pushed the pillow aside. "He was Maggie's dad, but he died. He lived by himself in a cabin in the mountains with no electricity or running water. Uncle Jameso took me up there. It's a really neat place, perched on the side of a mountain. And there's a tame bighorn sheep that likes to eat cookies."

"So Maggie's dad was a kind of hermit?"

"I guess." She shrugged, and cast a sideways, questioning look at her mother. "Is Dad crazy?"

The question startled Sharon, and she fumbled for the right answer. "I don't think your father is mentally ill, no," she said slowly. "He just has different ideas."

"But they're not normal ideas. Normal people don't refuse to talk on the phone or let their kids go to school or think the government controls the weather and is putting stuff in our food to make us sick on purpose."

Sharon realized how naïve she'd been, believing she'd done a good job of shielding her children from the worst of Joe's paranoia and conspiracy theories. Maybe Joe *was* crazy. "You're right," she said. "I don't know why your father does the things he does."

And without her there to serve as a buffer, Adan was getting a steady diet of Joe's slanted worldview. Would he turn out to be as bad as his father? In trying to protect her daughter, had she failed her son? The guilt almost made her double over in pain. She clutched her phone. "Maybe I should try to call your brother again."

"You could call Mrs. Phillips and ask her if she's seen him," Alina said. "Maybe she knows what happened to his phone."

Eden Phillips was their closest neighbor; she'd sometimes bought eggs from Sharon, and she'd delivered soup when she'd learned the kids both had the flu. Joe thought she was a nosy busybody, but Sharon had appreciated the woman's efforts at friendship. "That's a great idea," she said.

She had to call directory assistance for the Phillips' number, then she punched it in with shaking hands. She thought her heart would leap out of her chest when Eden finally answered the phone. "Hello!" she said, too loudly. Then, more calmly, "This is Sharon Franklin. Is this Eden?"

"Sharon?" Eden sounded startled. "Are you all right? How are the children?"

Was she alarmed? Relieved? "I'm fine," Sharon said. "I guess you know Joe and I split up."

"I knew you weren't around anymore. I thought maybe you'd decided to leave—at least I hoped it was voluntary."

Maybe Joe had been telling people the divorce was his idea, that he'd kicked Sharon out. That would be just like him, to save face. "It was for the best," she said. "Alina is here with me and Adan stayed with Joe. He wanted to stay and since he's fifteen . . ." She let the sentence trail away. She'd tried to persuade Adan to come with her, she really had. But his refusal, coupled with Joe's insistence on keeping the boy with him, had tied her hands. If she wanted to get Alina away, she had to leave Adan.

"Oh, that's too bad."

Sharon wasn't sure whether the sympathy was over Sharon having to leave her son behind, the end of her marriage, or the situation as a whole. "Adan's the reason I'm calling really," she said. "I've been trying to reach him on the phone, but he's not answering. Have you seen him recently?"

"Not in a couple of weeks, since they all moved out."

Sharon wasn't sure she'd heard Eden right. "Moved out of where?"

"Their place. They're not living there any-more. Didn't you know?"

"I talked to Adan last week and he didn't say anything about moving."

"Probably his father told him not to say. You know how Joe is about people knowing his business."

Yes, she knew. "Where did they go?" she asked.

"I don't know. If you don't either, then I doubt anyone knows."

"They're all gone?" Her brain refused to accept this. "Everyone?"

"I went down there two days ago to make sure they hadn't left any animals behind, but they took it all—chickens and dogs and goats and the pigs that Russian couple was raising. All they left was a lot of trash, and the buildings are a mess. Whoever buys it will probably have to tear down the house and start over."

"Oh, God." Sharon clutched her stomach and sank into a chair, her legs too weak to support her. "I didn't know. And he has Adan."

"I'm sorry," Eden said. She sounded as if she meant it. "If I find out anything, I'll call you. Is this a good number?"

"Yes. Yes, call me if you find out anything."

"I will. And I'll pray for you, dear. And for all Joe's odd ideas, he does think a lot of the boy."

"I know. Thank you, Eden. For everything."

Alina had been watching Sharon and as soon as she hung up the phone, she launched herself at her mother. "What's wrong?" she asked. "What's happened to Dad and Adan?"

"Eden said they moved away. They moved and didn't tell us."

"Where did they go?"

Sharon shook her head. "She doesn't know."

"That must be why you can't reach Adan—his phone doesn't work wherever they are."

"Joe should have told me. I have a right to know." Anger was edging out panic and fear, making her feel stronger.

"Maybe he wrote you a letter and you haven't gotten it yet."

She didn't believe that, but for Alina's sake, she nodded. "Yes, maybe that's it. Would you bring me my purse, hon? It's on the dresser in the bedroom."

While Alina fetched her purse, Sharon tried to think. Surely Joe was breaking some law, not notifying a mother of her son's address. Even if Sharon didn't have custody of Adan, she still had rights, didn't she? Had he done this to spite her—as revenge for the divorce? Is that why he'd waited until the papers were signed and everything was final, so she'd know that she'd brought this on herself?

Or had something else driven them away—a new paranoia or real trouble with the law?

Alina returned and handed Sharon the bag. "What are you going to do?" she asked.

"I'm going to call Deputy Miller." She found the business card in her wallet and punched in the number.

"The sheriff?" Alina wrinkled her nose. "Dad isn't in trouble with the police, is he?"

"I don't think so, but maybe Deputy Miller knows someone I should contact."

He answered on the second ring, his voice pleasant and calm. "Deputy Miller."

"This is Sharon Franklin. I . . . I have a problem and I'm hoping you can help me."

"Of course, Sharon. What can I do?"

"My son . . . he's fifteen and he lives with his father. In Vermont. I've been trying to reach him for a few days and he doesn't answer his phone. I just spoke to a neighbor and she tells me Joe— my ex—moved a couple of weeks ago. He didn't tell me and I don't have an address or . . . or a way to contact my son." Her voice broke and she struggled to maintain control. "I'm worried."

"I'll be right over. Just hang on."

"Oh, thank you." She hung up and leaned back against the sofa. Only Alina's tense presence beside her kept her from bursting into tears. "He's coming over," she said.

"Does he think he can help us?"

"I'm sure he will." She patted her daughter's leg. "Of course he will." She couldn't afford to think otherwise. Her son couldn't be lost to her.

Lucille had always liked living alone. After a day of dealing with customers at her store and the demands of running a small town, her little house on Fourth Street offered a quiet retreat. The Victorian cottage had three small bedrooms, a cranky furnace, and scarred wood floors, but she'd fixed it up to suit her, and it was neat and peaceful.

Or it had been, before the arrival of her daughter, Olivia, and teenage grandson, Lucas. These days a bicycle, soccer ball, and the remains of a firewood fort littered the front yard, and the house was strewn with discarded shoes and clothes, half-eaten sandwiches, magazines, school books, and the other detritus of the messy, busy occupants. Soon, she'd have her house back, she thought as she collected dirty socks and two T-shirts on her way through the living room. In a few weeks, when Olivia and Lucas moved in with her fiancé, D. J., things would be neat and peaceful again.

And Lucille was going to hate it. She dropped the dirty clothes in the hamper in the laundry room behind the kitchen, then returned to boil water for tea. After so many years by herself, she'd cherished the time with her family. She didn't know if she knew how to be alone anymore. The thought of evenings of silence and solitude depressed her. How had she gotten to be fifty-five with no one in her life? Not that she believed a woman needed a man to be happy, but did life have to be so lonely?

Right. Next thing she knew she'd be spending her evenings watching old movies and crying into her popcorn. *Get a grip,* she told herself. *Your life could be a lot worse.*

She was measuring honey into her tea when a knock sounded on the front door. The heavy, hollow sound echoed through the old house and, tea cup in hand, she hurried to answer the summons. But when she saw who was on the other side of the door, she debated retreating to the kitchen and pretending she wasn't home.

"I know you're in there," Gerald Pershing called. "I can see your shadow on the other side of that curtain."

Sighing, she opened the door. "What do you want, Gerald?"

"I need to talk to you about an urgent matter at the Lucky Lady."

"Come to my office tomorrow." She tried to close the door, but he wedged his foot in the gap.

"I really must speak to you now," he said.

She looked down at the ostrich cowboy boot blocking the door and at the cup of hot tea in her hand. Would throwing the tea in his face qualify as assault if he was trying to force his way into her house? A local jury certainly wouldn't convict her.

"I just want to talk," he said in the smooth drawl that still sent tingles up her spine. "You can't begrudge me that."

She could, and should, begrudge him anything she liked, considering what he'd done to her. But she was the mayor, and had a responsibility to take care of any problems at what was, at the moment anyway, Eureka's largest investment and potential source of income. "We can talk out here," she said, and stepped onto the porch, shutting the door firmly behind her.

If he was disappointed, he didn't show it. He

followed her to the old-fashioned wooden porch swing at one end of the columned veranda. "You're looking lovely this evening, Lucille." His standard opening line.

"I don't have time for idle chitchat," she said. "What's this problem that can't wait until tomorrow?"

"No need to rush on a beautiful evening like this." He settled onto the swing next to her, hands on his knees, and looked around, as if he'd never seen her house before. Purple clematis climbed the trellis at the end of the porch, dark green leaves just beginning to unfold. Later in the summer the star-shaped blooms would fill the air with their perfume. "After the tensions of a busy day, it's good to relax and recenter yourself," Gerald said.

She restrained a snort. "This isn't a yoga class. What's going on at the mine?"

He turned to her, his lined but still-handsome face grave. "I have some concerns about Bob."

"What has he done this time?" Bob was mean, stubborn, unpredictable, and contrary, but he shared her disdain for the man beside her, which made him her ally.

"I caught him moving a number of large boxes into one of the abandoned mine tunnels," Gerald said. "When I confronted him about this, he threatened me."

"What did he threaten to do?"

"He offered to skin me alive and make a blanket out of my hide if I didn't mind my own business."

Lucille bit back a laugh. "Bob's bark is much worse than his bite. He might throw a punch if he's really riled, but he wouldn't skin you."

"I reminded him that the mine is my business. It's your business, too, so you should take this seriously."

She sobered. Yes, the mine was her business. "Do you know what was in the boxes?"

"He said it was supplies."

"He's been ordering dried food from some survivalist outfit," she said. "It was probably that. If the world ends tomorrow, he probably plans to retreat to the mine."

"We are an operating mine, not a storage facility."

"I'll talk to him about it tomorrow." She stood. "Good night."

She started to move past him, but he grabbed her hand and held it. "That's not the only reason I stopped by tonight, Lucille," he said.

She stiffened. "What else?"

"You and I have unfinished business between us."

"You're wrong. We're definitely finished."

"Please. Sit down. Hear me out. You at least owe me that."

She didn't owe him anything, but she sat. She

wanted to cross her arms over her chest, but it was such a defensive posture. She was immune to his blandishments and she wanted him to know it, so she kept her hands at her sides and waited, unspeaking.

"I've already apologized for leaving you so abruptly after our wonderful night together," he said. "But I'll say it again—I'm sorry I ran out that way. I know how it must have looked, but when I received the call from Texas, I seized the opportunity to flee."

She didn't believe there had been a call; the cad had seduced her, then left before she woke, after scamming the town out of most of its money. Greed was the only thing that had brought him back to Eureka, not any affection for her.

"I left because I was afraid." His eyes filled with such sadness, mouth drooping. Really, he deserved an Oscar for such a performance. If she didn't know better, she'd almost believe he was sincere. "What I felt for you—what I still feel for you—is so intense it frightens me."

"It's a nice line, but you should sell it to someone else. I'm not buying."

He scooted closer to her. "You can't deny that we had something special," he said. "When we made love I felt more whole than I've felt in years . . . as if I finally found something precious I'd been searching for for years."

That night had been pretty incredible. But then, considering it was the first time she'd had sex in more than a decade, a night with almost any living, breathing man would have been memorable. And the fact that she was still attracted—physically—to this despicable snake of a man didn't mean anything. "You're going to have to keep looking," she said. "I'm not interested."

"Lucille, don't you understand? I'm admitting I made a mistake. I want to try again. I'll do anything to make things right with you."

She stood, almost dumping him out the swing with the force of her movement. "You can't make it right for me," she said. "How much clearer do I have to be? I don't want you."

Liar, whispered a voice in the back of her head, but she told the voice to shut up. She was too smart to give in to a con like Gerald.

She moved past him, and this time he let her go. He sat in the swing, hands hanging loose between his splayed knees, looking old and tired—the way she felt. She walked quickly into the house and shut the door behind her. For good measure, she turned the deadbolt, then rested her forehead against the cool, smooth wood. Oh, she was smart all right. Smart and alone. Which was really the better choice?

Chapter 11

Josh was at Sharon's door in less than ten minutes. Seeing him dressed in jeans and a polo shirt, instead of the uniform she'd expected, caught her off guard. "I didn't realize you weren't on duty or I wouldn't have called," she said.

"You were right to call me," he said. "I came as a friend."

That this man she scarcely knew considered her a friend further unsettled her, but she stepped back to let him in. "I didn't even think to give you the address," she said. "But you got here so quickly."

"I saw Jameso in the Dirty Sally the other evening and he told me you were staying here. And I live in the apartments over the hardware store, so it's close by."

"There are apartments over the hardware store?"

"Yes, they're new. Very nice, with a good view of the mountains."

She filed this information away in the tiny corner of her brain that wasn't filled with worry for her son. "Can you help me find Adan?" she asked.

"I can try." He turned to Alina, who had retreated

to the couch, knees drawn up to her chest, arms wrapped around them. "Hello, Alina. How are you?"

"I'm mad at Adan for going away without telling us," she said.

Sharon wondered why Alina wasn't angry with her father. After all, Joe was the one who'd made the decision to move; this was all his fault. But maybe admitting that her father was to blame hurt too much for the girl. A sibling felt less like a part of yourself than a parent whose approval you'd spent all your life seeking.

"Let's go into the kitchen," Sharon said. "I'll make coffee."

He followed her into the small room and waited while she measured grounds into the coffee maker and filled the reservoir with water. When she'd started the machine and turned to face him, he asked the question she'd been dreading. "Do you have any reason to believe your ex-husband would hurt your son?"

She gripped the edge of the counter, the ridge of tile digging into her palms. "I don't think so. Or maybe I don't want to believe so."

"How old is your son?"

"He's fifteen." The age she'd been when she had him—the idea seemed shocking, even to her.

"When was the last time you talked to him—Adan, is that his name?"

"Yes. It means 'little fire.' He was such a lively baby." She squeezed her eyes shut against the tears that threatened as she remembered her firstborn as an infant, always alert and curious, eager to explore the world.

"I know this is hard. Take your time." Josh's voice was so soft and soothing. When she opened her eyes, he regarded her with a calm compassion that washed over her like a healing balm. She released her hold on the counter. Now was no time to fall apart. She had a job to do; she had to find her son.

"The last time I talked to him was last week, so . . . five days ago?" She nodded. "Yes, I'm sure it was Wednesday."

"Did you call him, or did he call you?"

"I called him. It was about nine in the morning here, before I went to work, so eleven there."

"How did he sound?"

She wished she could lie and tell this kind man that she'd had a wonderful conversation with her son, that he'd been glad to hear from her and told her he missed her and he loved her. It was the kind of conversation she'd imagined having when she'd given Adan the phone, but the reality was much harder to acknowledge. "He was annoyed. He was angry with me for leaving, and he didn't want to talk. But he said he was fine, and he never mentioned that they'd moved, though my neighbor tells me they'd been gone at least a week by that time."

"Did your husband ever mention wanting to live someplace else? Did he have friends or relatives he might have gone to?"

"Joe wasn't in contact with his family. They were somewhere in the Midwest—Iowa or Nebraska or someplace—but he hadn't spoken to any of them in years." That was something they'd had in common, a desire to cut all ties with the people who had raised them. She felt physically ill when she thought that Adan might want the same thing when it came to her.

"And friends?" Josh prompted.

"All his friends were with him."

Josh's puzzled expression required an answer. She tried to sort out the right words to explain the strange life she'd lived too long. "Joe believed in doing things for himself, in being independent. When we first married, that meant planting a big garden and making our own furniture and stuff. But over the years, he gravitated toward more extreme groups. He began stockpiling food and ammunition. He spent a lot of time online, reading about various conspiracy theories. He became more and more paranoid, believing horrible, ridiculous things about the government. He met others who believed the same things, and about five years ago, they decided to all live together in a kind of compound on some land they bought in upstate Vermont."

She sighed. Now that she had put some time and physical distance between herself and all that had happened, she saw how naïve and complacent she'd been. She'd told herself it was her duty to follow her husband and look after her children and yes, she'd been drawn in by the picture Joe had painted of their little family making a way for themselves, living life on their own terms, free of the interference of anyone else. "He made it sound like paradise. Our own little Eden. We moved out there and built a house and barn. We planted a garden and hunted for meat, and I homeschooled the children. I thought everything would be all right."

"And these friends moved there, too."

"Yes, a man named Wilson Anderson. He was a little older than Joe and had been in the military. The navy, I think. He had a lot of tattoos he said he'd gotten in the service. And there was a couple from Russia—Earl and Oksana Petricoff. They were older, too, and not very friendly. There were two other couples originally, but they moved on after a few years. I think they didn't like Wilson and Joe telling them what to do."

"So, your husband and this Wilson were the leaders of the group?"

"Yes, he liked that—being in charge." Joe was not a physical bully—he'd never raised his hand to her or the children. But he'd raised his voice, and he knew how to use words as weapons, belittling the opinions of others, dismissing their concerns or beliefs. With his words he'd reduced them all to lesser beings than himself. Away from his sphere of influence, Sharon could see how much power he'd wielded over them all— how much power she'd given away to him. The realization made her feel sick. How could she have left her son behind to endure that? How had she allowed Joe to convince her that she was doing the right thing in abandoning her oldest child?

Josh made no comment, and tension built as the silence lengthened. Josh said nothing, and his face betrayed no emotion beyond quiet concern. Finally, he spoke. "Is there anything else you can think of that might help us locate your son?"

She took a deep, shuddering breath, pushing aside the grief and guilt that threatened to overwhelm her. She had to be strong. She had to focus on Adan, on helping him. "Wherever they went, it was probably more remote even than where we'd been. Joe wanted to be off the grid and off the map, he used to say. He wouldn't use cell phones because he believed the government could use them to track people. He wouldn't register to vote or buy a hunting license or renew his driver's license." They hadn't paid taxes in years, but then, they'd had so little income she hadn't thought it mattered.

"You said he spent time on the Internet. Do you know a name he might have used on the conspiracy group Web sites?"

"He called himself Badger." Badgers, he'd explained to her, were wild and fierce loners, who fought off even much larger attackers to protect what was theirs. No mention of the badger's mate and children; they were on their own.

"That's a place to start, then. We can go on some of the sites and see if he's posted, maybe track him that way. He probably hasn't left the country. Even if he has legal custody of your son, he'd need permission from you to take him overseas or into Canada. He might be able to slip into Mexico, but it's a long way from Vermont."

"He wouldn't have gone to Mexico. He was horribly prejudiced, and despite his hatred for the United States government, he thought of himself as a true patriot."

"We should contact the National Center for Missing and Exploited Children and alert them. They can start circulating Adan's picture. And I'll talk to the police in Vermont. They may know something."

In her heart, she knew all of these actions were unlikely to be of much help, but having a plan made her feel so much more steady on her feet. "Aren't you going to ask me why I left him there?" she asked. "How could a mother abandon her child to that kind of life?"

"It's not my place to judge you, Sharon."

"Why not? I judge myself every day." She pressed the heels of her hands to her eyes and choked back a sob.

"Hey, this is not your fault." He gently pulled her hands away from her face, his arm tight around her shoulder, supporting her.

"How is it not my fault? I left him. No wonder he hated me."

"Split custody isn't that unusual in divorce," he said. "And plenty of teenage boys would choose a life of freedom running around in the woods over days spent in the classroom. I probably would have at Adan's age."

"Yes." She tore a paper towel from a roll on the counter and blew her nose. "He said he wanted to stay with Joe, and Joe wouldn't agree to the divorce unless I let Adan stay. I didn't want to do it, but I didn't feel I had a choice."

"It doesn't sound like you did."

"My lawyer told me Adan was old enough to choose—that a court would grant Joe custody anyway, even if I tried to fight it. I didn't have the money to do that, in any case."

"You don't have to justify your actions to me."

Maybe not. But she was still trying to justify them to herself. "I couldn't stay with Joe anymore. I hadn't loved him for years." She glanced toward the living room; Alina still sat on the sofa, huddled against the cushions, staring into space. She lowered her voice. "Wilson was after Alina. He hadn't done anything yet, but I'd caught him with her in the barn. . . . Joe didn't see anything wrong with it. That's when I knew I had to go."

"Your ex better hope I never meet him in a dark alley."

The anger behind the words touched her even more than his previous compassion. No one else had cared what happened to her for so long— maybe never, really. She had to turn away to keep the emotion from showing on her face. "What do I need to do now?" she asked.

"Nothing yet. Other law enforcement may contact you for more information. And if you have a picture of Adan, I'll need that."

"Of course. I have a photo album in my bedroom."

He waited while she retrieved the photo. "It's a couple years old," she said when she handed him the snapshot a friend had taken at a picnic. "Adan is taller now, and his hair is longer, past his shoulders."

"This will be fine." He tucked the picture in his pocket. "I'd better go now. Do you want me to call someone to stay with you? Jameso?"

If her brother came, what could he do? She'd headed to Eureka with the idea that Jameso would look after her, the way he had when they were kids. Because all the other men who'd been important in her life—her father and her husband—had told her she wasn't capable of looking after herself, she'd believed them. She shook her head. "I'll be all right now. Thank you. You've already helped so much, just coming here tonight."

"Hang in there. I'll let you know what I find out." He squeezed her shoulder, a brief, reassuring gesture. She walked with him to the door, then stood at the front window and watched until the taillights of his car were no longer visible.

She felt like someone coming out of anesthesia after surgery. Away from the belittling words men had showered her with all her life, she was finally waking up. She felt new pain, but she was alive and building up her strength. She had to take care of herself and her daughter; no one else would care as much about them as she did.

"It feels so great not to have to sit at the library all afternoon," Alina said as she peddled hard after Lucas up the slight hill leading to the Eureka County offices. She squinted into the bright sun, and a breeze blew back her hair, bringing the scents of cedar and vanilla, which Lucas had explained was the smell of ponderosa pine trees. Just ahead of her, Lucas stood on the pedals of his bike to blast up the steepest part of the hill, long legs pumping, shoulders straining against a black T-shirt with the logo for the Drive-By Truckers, which he said he'd borrowed from his mom's boyfriend.

"I'm glad your mom finally lifted your punishment," Lucas said, when she joined him at the top of the hill. "I was waiting for you to do this."

"Thanks." She slid off the seat of the mountain bike Uncle Jameso had said she could use as long as she liked. "And thanks for your help with the science project. I never would have gotten an A without your help. I don't know anything about rockets."

"You'd have done all right. You're smart." They walked their bikes into the gravel lot in front of the brick building that served as courthouse and clerk's office for tiny Eureka County.

She liked it when he said things like that. Her mother told her all the time that she was smart and pretty and good, but mothers always thought those things. No one else had ever given her compliments, not and really meant them. "Do you know where we go to find out about your house?"

"Miss Wynock said I had to ask for the tax records in the clerk's office." He held the door open and they stepped into a wood-floored room flanked on one side by a long counter.

"May I help you?" A sandy-haired woman with a long face and deep grooves on either side of her mouth asked.

"We'd like to see the property tax records for 116 Pinion Lane . . . as far back as you have them, please." Lucas looked the woman in the eye and spoke firmly and politely, his voice, which was still changing and had a tendency to break and rise alarmingly at times, modulated to its lowest bass.

"And why do you want that information?" the woman asked.

"My parents just bought the property and as a housewarming surprise, I'm researching its history. The librarian told me this was the place to start."

"Oh, she did, did she?" The lines around the woman's mouth deepened. She turned to Alina. "Who are you?"

"I'm his friend. I'm here to help." She had to force herself not to fidget. She hated adults who looked at kids as if they were all about to steal or break something.

"The older records are not computerized," the woman said. "They're filed in ledgers, which are quite old and fragile."

"We'll be very careful." To Alina's surprise, Lucas pulled a pair of thin white gloves from his pocket. "I'm used to looking through rare books in the library's collections, so I know how to handle them," he said. He handed a second pair of gloves to Alina. "You don't want the oil from your hands getting on the paper."

The woman clearly didn't know what to say to this, but she soon recovered. "I'm not allowed to show that information to minors."

"The property tax records are public records," Lucas said. "They're not X-rated or in any way unsuitable for children, though most children wouldn't be interested. I am and if you won't show them to me, I'll ask Mr. Paxton to file a request with the court. You could be charged with obstruction, or at the least your boss probably wouldn't appreciate the judge's attention on this office."

The woman looked ready to spit nails. Alina had to bite the inside of her cheek to keep from laughing. Lucas, with his round glasses and serious expression, plus his formal manner of speaking, looked like a kid lawyer. He also sounded like he knew what he was talking about. Mr. Paxton was the lawyer who had offices over the Last Dollar Cafe. He looked more like a biker than an attorney, but Alina guessed he really was one, because as soon as Lucas said his name, the woman behind the counter turned white, then red.

She opened a half door at one end of the counter and motioned them through. "I'll show you where the records are kept, but you'll have to find what you need yourself," she said. "I have other work to do."

"Thank you."

They followed her into a windowless, musty room that was scarcely bigger than a closet. The clerk switched on the light and pointed to shelves of thick, leather-bound books. "The records are arranged by year, beginning in 1887, when the county was established. Properties are listed according to their legal description, not by address. Be sure to put everything back the way you found it."

With a stiff nod, she left them, leaving the door open behind her. Alina moved closer to Lucas. "Do you know the legal description of your folks' place?" she whispered.

"No, we'll just have to read through everything until we find it." He leaned forward and squinted at the top row of books. "Let's start with 1966. That's the first year Adelaide shows up missing in the Women's Society scrapbooks."

Alina slipped on the gloves and helped him lift down the massive book. It was probably two feet high and almost as wide. When they opened it, she let out a groan. "How are we going to read this?" she asked, staring at line after line of spidery handwriting.

"It's not too hard after you get used to it." He pointed to the top of the page. "This must be the legal description—section and lot numbers from when the town was platted. If we can figure out how it's organized, we can turn to the part of town where the house is located and find it that way."

"Or we could look for the name, McCutcheon." She pointed to a column on the left side of the page. "This looks like it might be listings of the property owners."

He nodded. "I think you're right. Come on. Help me look."

Lucas was right; after a while the handwriting wasn't so difficult to make out. Whoever had written this was neat, and wrote with a lot of extra curlicues, but it was like cracking a code. She skimmed over numbers and looked for names, nodding when Lucas should turn the page. Ten pages in, she spotted it. "There!" She pointed to a line halfway down the page. "Cecil McCutcheon. That's him."

"And there's the lot description." Lucas wrote down the section and lot number while Alina hurried to pull down the book for 1967. He helped her wrestle it down, and they opened it to the page for the McCutcheon home. Lucas took notes, and they moved on to the next book. Within half an hour, they'd examined the records all the way up to 1969, when the Gilroys became the owners of the house.

They replaced the last book on the shelf and returned to sit side by side at the little table. "The house didn't sell until three years after Mrs. McCutcheon disappears from the Women's Society yearbooks," Lucas said.

"So did Mr. McCutcheon kill her and bury her

body in the garden and live there three more years?" Alina said. "In a small town, people would have noticed."

"Maybe he told them she'd gone to stay with a sick relative."

"Not for three years."

"Maybe they divorced."

"Maybe . . . but that would have been a scandal, too, I bet. People didn't divorce as much back then."

"Maybe that's why she wasn't in the Women's Society," Lucas said. "She was a scandalous divorcée and all the proper ladies didn't want to associate with her."

"There must be some other way we can find out this stuff," Alina said.

"We should look at old newspapers on microfiche to see if there's any mention of Adelaide McCutcheon's death or disappearance or a divorce," Lucas said. "They have copies at the library."

She covered her face with her hands and moaned. "Not the library, please. I've had enough of that place." She lowered her hands and pushed back from the table. "And enough of being indoors. Let's ride out to your house and see how the remodeling is coming."

"That's a great idea. We finished painting in my room over the weekend. It looks awesome."

The sour-faced clerk was just as glum when

they told her they were leaving as she had been when they arrived. She insisted on inspecting the records room and seemed surprised to find everything in order. "Well, everything looks as it should," she said. "Did you find the information you needed?"

"We did," Lucas said. "Thank you."

Alina mumbled thank you, then followed him sedately out the door. But as soon as they hit the parking lot, they raced to their bikes and flew down the hill, toward the other end of town, and the former Gilroy house, soon to be home to the Gruber-Theriots.

They crossed Main, past a crew who was painting the old-fashioned light posts with a fresh coat of dark green enamel. Word at school was that the town was sprucing up for the arrival of some big-shot movie director who was thinking of making a movie in Eureka.

"Do you think they'll really make a movie here?" Alina asked, when they stopped to let a delivery truck rumble past.

"Why not?" Lucas said. "It would make a cool setting, don't you think?"

"I don't know. I don't know much about movies."

"What's your favorite movie? Mine's *Lord of the Rings*." Not waiting for her answer, he set off pedaling again, but slower, so that she could keep up and they could talk.

"I don't really have one," she said. "I haven't

seen many." As in, hardly any. "My dad didn't believe in TV or movies."

"So you didn't have a television—even for educational stuff like the History channel or public television?"

He didn't look at her like she was a freak, the way some people did. He was just being Lucas —interested in everything. "Nope," she said. "And we lived too far from a movie theater to ever go."

"Then I guess you've got a lot of catching up to do," he said. "That could be fun. You can skip the dumb stuff that's a waste of time and concentrate on the classics worth seeing."

"I guess so. Though right now, with school and everything, I don't have a lot of time for watching stuff. And I'm reading *The Hunger Games* trilogy. I think I'd rather read than watch TV."

"Those are awesome books," Lucas said.

"My dad definitely would have approved of them. He would have loved it if I'd decided to hunt with a bow. He thought I was a freak for wanting to be a vegetarian."

"You're not a freak," Lucas said. "I think being a vegetarian is cool—I just like hamburgers too much."

He made a face and she laughed. They pulled up in front of his house. Though the yard was still overgrown and neglected, the house itself had received a fresh coat of olive green paint, with cream-colored trim. "D. J. put in new, energy-efficient windows and more insulation," Lucas said. "Mom refinished the floors and painted stencils and stuff in some of the rooms. She said that was something the Victorians did—that was the time period when the house was first built. She said she's going to paint a mural in the dining room when she has the time." He led the way up the front walk.

"I saw the mural she did in the Last Dollar," Alina said. "It's gorgeous."

"That was the first artwork she ever got paid for," he said. "Now she does a lot of stuff like that. She did a ton of painting over at Mrs. Stanowski's new B and B."

He opened the front door, which was unlocked, and led the way into the open front room. When he and Alina had been here the other night, it had been dark, and they hadn't been able to see much. "It's beautiful," she said, admiring the golden oak floors and high ceilings. It was four times the size of her uncle's cottage where she was staying with her mom, and way bigger than the house where they'd lived in Vermont.

"My room is upstairs."

Lucas's bedroom was at the back corner of the house, with big windows overlooking a side alley and an empty pasture, with mountains beyond. "There's a bathroom next door, and three other bedrooms. My mom and D. J. will have the biggest room, at the other end of the house, with their own bathroom."

"What about the other two bedrooms?" she asked.

He leaned against the windowsill, hands shoved in the pockets of his jeans. "They haven't said, but I'm pretty sure they plan to fix up the one closest to their room as a nursery, then when the kid gets bigger, he or she can move down to the room next to mine."

"So your mom is going to have another kid?"

"I know she's always wanted more kids, and I think D. J. would like to have some. And she's still young."

"How do you feel about that?" she asked.

"I always wanted brothers or sisters," he said. "Being the only kid can be good, but it sucks sometimes, too. The only thing is, I'll be a lot older than these kids. I mean, even if my mom gets pregnant now, I'll be fifteen by the time the baby's born. Still, it'll be cool being the big brother."

A pain lanced through Alina as she thought of her own big brother. When they'd first left Vermont, she'd tried hard to put him out of her mind. He was where he wanted to be, with their dad, and he was fine. She didn't have to waste a lot of her time missing him.

But now she didn't know where he was, or if he was all right, and she couldn't stop thinking about him. "I have an older brother," she said. "His name is Adan. He stayed in Vermont, to live with my dad."

"You must miss him," Lucas said.

She nodded. "The thing is, we don't know where he is right now. Or my dad either. My mom tried to call the other day and Adan wouldn't answer his phone. She finally talked to a neighbor, who said my dad moved and didn't tell anyone where he was going. The police are trying to find them, to make sure Adan is all right."

"Oh, Alina."

She nodded. "I know. It sucks."

"What's your brother like?"

"He's different from me. Quieter, not as friendly. Kind of like my dad. Sometimes he's really sweet to me, teaching me things or talking to me. But he can be really mean, too. He'll say stupid stuff." Stuff their dad would say—that girls were useless and it would have been better if she was a boy, for instance. "I think sometimes he's just trying really hard to impress my dad. That's important to him."

"I never knew my dad, so I didn't have anyone to impress," Lucas said. "But I guess, when you look up to someone, the way I look up to D. J., you want them to be proud of you."

"They should be proud just because you're their kid," she said. "You shouldn't have to earn a parent's love."

He moved away from the window and put his arm around her shoulders. "No, you shouldn't have to earn love. It should just be there. The way my mom loves me. The way your mom loves you."

She nodded and swallowed back tears. It was nice standing here, with his arms around her. It made her feel less like she was going to fall apart. Safe.

"If I tell you a secret, will you promise not to tell anyone?"

"I promise." She studied his face, looking for clues as to what this big secret might be.

"After Mom and D. J. are married, he's going to adopt me. They have to file some legal paperwork and stuff, but when it's done, I won't be Lucas Theriot anymore. I'll be Lucas Gruber."

She thought Theriot was a prettier name than Gruber, but clearly Lucas didn't see it that way. He loved D. J., and having him for a father was probably a dream come true. She squeezed his arm. "That's so great," she said. "I'm really happy for you. But why is it a secret?"

He made a face. "I just don't want to jinx it. I'd rather wait until it happens, then let everybody know."

She nodded. "You can go around correcting everyone—'my name's not Theriot, it's Gruber.'" She slipped out of his arms and punched his shoulder lightly. "Though you know somebody

228

is going to end up calling you 'Goober' instead."

He laughed. "Then I guess I'll be a goober. I've been called worse." He moved over to the window and looked out across the alley. "D. J. says we can move in in a couple more weeks. I can't wait."

"Has your ghost been up to anything lately?" she asked.

"D. J.'s missing a pocketknife and my mom's favorite paintbrush is gone. I told them maybe the ghost is going to open a hardware store on the other side."

She smiled, because she knew he was trying hard to cheer her up.

"I still wish we could spend the night here and take photos," he said. "That would be so cool."

"It would. But I'd better not risk it now."

"Yeah, I know." He glanced out the window. "It's getting late. We'd better get home before you're sentenced to another month at the library."

"No!" She waved her hands in mock horror. "Not that!"

They'd just crossed Main when a sheriff's SUV pulled alongside them. Sergeant Miller rolled down the window. "Hello, Alina, Lucas," he said. "How's it going?"

"Have you heard anything about my brother?" Alina asked.

"I wish I had good news for you, but I haven't

heard anything. I did contact the police in Vermont, and they're looking. And we haven't heard anything to make us think anything bad has happened. Your dad just moved and neglected to tell anyone. We'll find him."

"Thanks." She wanted to believe him—that Adan was safe and happy, hiding out with their paranoid dad, playing survivalists who didn't need anyone or anything. It was all so stupid and pointless. Friends, and especially family, were important. Why couldn't they see that?

They skidded to a stop in front of the lilac house. "I'll see you in school tomorrow," Lucas said.

"Can you wait here for half a second?" she asked. "I just have to run inside and get something."

"Okay." He looked puzzled, but he didn't pump her with questions. That was another thing she liked about Lucas—he accepted you wherever you were. And he was patient.

She found the camera case in her room and ran out to him with it. "Here." She thrust it at him. "You can borrow this and try to take pictures of your ghost."

"Alina, I don't like to take your camera. I know it means a lot to you."

She shook her head. "It doesn't mean anything. My dad didn't really give it to me. I stole it."

His eyes widened. "You stole it?"

"I took it from a guy named Wilson—my dad's friend who lived with us. I was mad because he was the reason we had to leave—because my mom caught him trying to kiss me . . . and stuff." She shuddered, remembering Wilson running his hand over the top of her breast and pinching her bottom whenever she walked by. "And I was mad at my dad because he stood up for Wilson instead of for me. He wouldn't have given me a camera. He didn't think girls were worth anything."

"I think you're worth a lot. And I'll take good care of this camera, I promise." He stowed the case in his backpack and zipped it up, then reached out to pat her shoulder. "You're really special, Alina. Don't let anyone ever tell you different."

She nodded, afraid if she said anything, she'd burst into tears. Sometimes having people be nice to you was even harder than when they were mean. You could build up walls against the meanness.

"I'll let you know what I find." He mounted his bike again. "And I'll say a prayer that your brother is okay."

"Thanks," she whispered. She hugged her arms to herself and watched him ride away, blond hair blowing in the wind, long legs pumping.

Chapter 12

When she was younger, Sharon had believed that the gift of getting older would be letting go of the angst and self-doubt that had plagued her teenaged self. She'd envisioned a day when she'd be so calm and put together that she could look in the mirror in the morning and not fret about her hair or the shape of her nose or an impending zit on her chin. She'd imagined nights not spent lying awake worrying about what people thought of her, or what she should have said to the man who cut her off in traffic, or replaying in an endless loop the stupid mistakes she'd made that day.

She might as well have continued to believe in Santa Claus and the tooth fairy. Adult Sharon was just as angsty and self-doubting as teen Sharon. Only with adulthood came more things to stress over—parenting mistakes, relationship flaws, job crises, and general bad decisions. Now she believed she was doomed to spend her retirement reviewing a lifetime of missed opportunities and poor choices—worrying about her weight or her hair or things she should have said, long past the point they really mattered.

Neuroticism might play well in television comedies, but in real life it was just, well, exhausting. Proof: the fact that she spent ten minutes the morning before Maggie's baby shower trying unsuccessfully to cover the circles under her eyes with a tube labeled "concealer" that did nothing to hide the dark smudges but only seemed to highlight them.

She'd tossed and turned all night, imagining half a dozen terrible scenarios at the shower. She had told Jameso about Adan, and he had, of course, shared the news with Maggie, who had probably told Barb and everyone else, so now all these women knew she was a mother who'd abandoned her son to a man who she could see now was probably unstable. She was a terrible mother, and they all knew it and they would hate her for it.

In the light of day those fears seemed a little extreme, but she still couldn't think about Adan without wanting to throw up. Her baby—her firstborn. Maybe he looked and talked and acted too much like a man now, but he was still her boy. He'd insisted on staying with his father, but she was his mother—she knew better how to take care of him. And now he was gone. Vanished. She gripped the edge of the sink and watched the tears fall into the basin, smearing her freshly applied makeup. Oh God, how was she going to get through this?

She grabbed her phone and punched in the number for Sergeant Miller, which she'd already memorized. It rang three times before going to voice mail. "Um, hi. This is Sharon Franklin. I'm just wondering if you've found out anything about my son." She hung up, feeling foolish. If he'd heard anything, he would have called her.

Her gaze shifted to the mirror and she groaned. Now she looked like something out of a horror movie. She'd have to start over, and be quick about it or she'd be late to the shower.

Thirty minutes later, she parked on the street down from Barb's bed-and-breakfast. As far as she knew, the business as yet had no other name, and no doubt even after it was christened, locals would continue to refer to it this way. On her third day in town she'd asked someone how to find the office to register her car and they'd told her to turn "where the yellow barn used to be," as if, of course, she knew where that was. Every town was filled with these ghosts of places and names that, though changed or vanished, remained fixed in the memories of long-time locals.

The bed-and-breakfast definitely stood out from its neighbors, with its fresh white siding and new Victorian gingerbread highlighted with green and purple paint. A stone path led to the front door, which was inset with stained glass in a wisteria pattern. The effect was both opulent and homey.

As she'd feared, Sharon was the last guest to

arrive. "We were getting worried about you," Barb said as she ushered her inside. "If you didn't show up soon, I was going to send Jameso to fetch you."

"Jameso's here?" She looked around the circle of women gathered in the front room on sofas and folding chairs.

Barb laughed. "He wouldn't come near this much estrogen, but I have the man on speed dial."

"Hello, Sharon." Maggie heaved herself out of a chair to embrace her future sister-in-law. She patted Sharon's shoulder. "How are you doing?"

"Okay." Sharon bit her lip. "Okay," she repeated, forcing a smile. "How are you doing? You look ready to deliver any day now."

"Oh, no. I'm definitely not ready." Maggie returned to her chair. "I doubt I'll be ready even when the baby gets here."

"You'll be ready," Barb said. "You've been waiting most of your life for this little one."

"That's true enough," Maggie agreed. She addressed Sharon. "My first husband didn't want children, so he made me think I didn't want any either."

"Amazing how men can brainwash us sometimes," another woman, her hair a cloud of baby-fine blond around her pale features, said. "When we first married, my husband convinced me that if we didn't have sex every day, he'd get some horrible disease and die."

"How long did it take you to figure out he was wrong?" Barb asked.

"We'd been married about three months when I came down with the flu. I told him he'd just have to die, since I obviously was—but there was no way I was letting him anywhere near me. He lived and so did I, and he never tried that line on me again."

"That's one of the benefits of getting married at my age," Maggie said. "I hope I'm not quite as naïve as I was in my twenties."

"Do you know if you're having a boy or a girl?" Danielle took a cookie from the tray on the coffee table and broke off a bite.

"It's a girl." Maggie smoothed the front of her maternity top. "We've picked a name, but we're not telling anyone yet."

"Is Jameso excited?" A middle-aged woman with a German accent asked.

"It's hard to tell with him, but I think so, yes," Maggie said. "I was worried he'd be disappointed in a girl, but he seems thrilled. He said he wouldn't know how to handle a boy like him."

"Boys have their challenges, but so do girls," Sharon said.

"I heard about your son," Janelle said. "We're all praying they'll find him safe."

"Thank you." She had a hard time getting the words out around the sudden lump in her throat.

"Now that everyone's here, let's get this party started," Barb said.

"You promised no silly games." Maggie gave her friend a stern look.

"Since when do I listen to you?" Barb shook her head. "I promise nothing too silly."

"I was once at a baby shower where we had to bob for nipples," Olivia said.

Everyone stared. "Seriously," she said. "There was this big punch bowl full of baby bottle nipples and we had to try to snag them with our teeth."

"Baby bottle nipples." Lucille put a hand to her chest. "I don't even want to tell you the images that went through my mind."

"I thought we could just eat all the wonderful food Janelle and Danielle brought and talk," Maggie said.

"And open gifts—you can't forget that," Olivia said. "We want to see all the great stuff you got for the baby."

"But don't you want to guess what's in the diaper bag or play baby charades?" Barb asked.

A groan went up from the assembled crowd. Barb stuck out her lips in an exaggerated pout, but Maggie patted her arm. "You know you'd rather eat, drink, and talk, too. And you can keep track of the gifts for me."

"Well, all right." Barb led the way into the dining room, where the table was laden with food, and soda and liquor bottles filled a sideboard. "Help yourselves, ladies. Then we'll look at all of Maggie's loot."

"I want to see the rest of the B and B," Janelle said. "Downstairs is gorgeous."

"Only one of the bedrooms is finished," Barb said. "I'm still waiting on some of the bedding for the others."

"I'm trying to talk her into opening up that one bedroom for Chris Amesbury," Lucille said.

"Who's Chris Amesbury?" Sharon asked.

"He's a director who thinks Eureka would make a great location for his next movie." Olivia selected a raspberry tartlet and added it to her plate.

"You should definitely put him up here," the fair blonde, whom Sharon remembered was named Tamara, said. "It's the classiest place in town. He might even end up using it in his movie."

"I say all we need to do is feed him Danielle's baked goods and he'll never want to leave." Maggie popped a bite of lemon bar into her mouth, closed her eyes, and moaned.

"We'll do all of that and more if it will convince him to bring a film crew here to pour some money into the town coffers," Lucille said. "We're not proud."

"Eureka in the movies." Olivia shook her head. "I can't imagine."

"I'll do my best to impress this director," Barb said. "Though I was really hoping Maggie and Jameso would be my first guests, on their wedding night."

"We'll still have the wedding here," Maggie said. "Having this other guy stay here first won't spoil that." She winced and put a hand to her belly.

"What is it?" Barb asked. "You're not going to go into labor right now are you?"

"Before the presents are opened?" Maggie shook her head and rubbed her stomach. "No, the baby just kicked me in the kidneys."

"She's reminding us who the real guest of honor is." Barb took Maggie's arm and led her back toward the living room. "All right, everybody. Let's open the gifts. You can bring your food and drinks with you."

For the next half hour they all "oohed" and "aahed" over the diapers, stroller, baby seat, and other items Maggie received. The clothes were Sharon's favorite—delicate little shirts, pajamas printed with images of kittens, dresses trimmed in lace and ribbon. She fingered the soft fabric and longed for a return to her own time as a new mother, when she'd been too absorbed by the wonder of her new baby to notice or care about anything else.

If she had the chance to start over with Adan, she would have done things differently. She would have found a way to keep him with her. To keep him safe.

"Thank you, everyone," Maggie said when the last box was open, the last ribbon carefully tucked away. "Now all I need is a house to put everything in."

"You still haven't found a place to live?" the woman with the German accent, who Sharon had learned was a massage therapist named Katya, said.

"Not yet." Maggie sighed. "And neither of us really has time to look. If worse comes to worse, we'll make do with my dad's cabin, I guess. Babies are little and don't take up much room." She looked at the items stacked around her and laughed. "Though apparently their stuff does."

The party began to break up. Sharon stayed to help clean up. As she stacked plates to carry to the kitchen, Maggie touched her arm. "Thank you for coming this afternoon," she said. "I know you have a lot on your mind."

"It was good to have a distraction. Though seeing all the baby things reminded me of when mine were little."

"You were still a baby yourself when your children were born, from what Jameso tells me," she said.

Sharon smiled. "I was and I wasn't. I was always mature for my age. And I liked being a mother. For me, that was the best part about marriage."

"Have you heard anything from the police?" Barb joined them beside the now-cleared table.

Sharon shook her head. "Joe knows how to cover his tracks. He's not going to be easy to find." It was the first time she'd said the words out loud, admitted that she might not see her son again anytime soon. She wouldn't say never. Surely he'd want to find his mother again. She had to cling to that one hope at least.

"But he wouldn't hurt his son—would he?" Barb asked.

"Not physically." She had to believe this. Joe was a lot of things, but he'd never been violent with her or the children. "But he's paranoid about the government, and about other people, too. I'm afraid he'll pass along those crazy ideas to Adan, who really worships his father." Her voice caught and she looked away.

Maggie rubbed her shoulders. "You did what you had to do," she said. "What I'm sure any of us would have done."

Barb pressed her lips together. Sharon recalled that she had a son; maybe she didn't agree with Maggie's assessment of the situation. Sharon didn't blame her; if they had changed places, she might have judged harshly, too.

Maggie continued to rub Sharon's back. "You have to believe everything will work out all right," she said.

Sharon nodded. To do otherwise meant giving

in to despair, and she had Alina to think about, too. Her daughter needed her.

A musical chime sounded and she looked up, grateful for the distraction. The kindness of these women, whom she barely knew, overwhelmed her. They eased her pain, but also made it impossible to escape from her feelings for even a moment.

"The party's over!" Barb called, as she headed for the door.

Lucille and Olivia came in from the kitchen. "Is that everything?" Olivia asked.

"I think so," Maggie said. She put a hand to her back and grimaced. "Time to go home and take a nap. I'll let Jameso come by later and get all the gifts."

"Don't leave yet, ladies," Barb called. "We have a visitor." She ushered Officer Miller into the room.

He removed his Stetson, and nodded. "Hello, ladies."

Sharon's heart thudded hard and she took a step toward him. "I got your message," he said. "I still haven't heard anything. I'm sorry." He turned to Lucille. "I really came here to see you, Madam Mayor."

The lines around Lucille's eyes and mouth deepened. "What's wrong now, Josh?"

"I drove by the park just now and saw some activity there. I wanted to double-check that you'd authorized it."

"Activity? What kind of activity?"

"It looked like Miss Wynock was there, with a couple of young people. They were up on ladders by the sign at the entrance to the park."

Cassie had really done it this time, Lucille thought as she and Olivia, followed by Maggie, Barb, Josh Miller, and no telling who else, headed toward the town park in a caravan that wound through the streets of Eureka. A small crowd, including Bob and Reggie, had already gathered at the entrance, drawn by the spectacle of Cassie Wynock on a ladder, shouting directions to Lucas Theriot and Alina Franklin, who were also on ladders, a large vinyl banner stretched between them.

Lucille stopped her car a scant two feet from the base of Cassie's perch and jumped out. "Cassie," she called up. "What do you think you're doing?"

"I'm doing what the town should have done years ago." She turned back to the two teens, who were eyeing the gathering crowd apprehensively. "Pull the banner tight and tie on the ends. The sign company said it should fit perfectly."

A gasp rose from the crowd as the banner straightened to reveal the words *Ernestine Wynock Park*.

"You do know it's a crime to deface public property," Lucille said.

"I'm not defacing anything. Think of it as righting an old wrong."

Lucille searched and found Reggie in the crowd of onlookers and beckoned him. "Where do we stand legally on this?" she asked.

"Well, she's not actually defacing anything, so you couldn't get her for vandalism. It's public property, so she's not trespassing. Maybe littering, but that's only a fifty-dollar fine, and the judge usually lets folks work that off by cleaning up alongside the highway one Saturday."

The image of Cassie, dressed in orange jail coveralls and brandishing a trash-picking stick, flashed through Lucille's mind and she shuddered. "What's our liability if we don't do anything?" she asked.

"If she falls off that ladder, she could sue us, and depending on how good a lawyer she hired and how sympathetic the jury, she might actually win."

Lucille never thought of Cassie as sympathetic, but the woman was determined, and even a decent actress, so who knew what she could get a jury to believe.

A flash went off to Lucille's right. She looked over to see Maggie, her camera aimed up at the sign and the trio holding it. "Rick is going to be sorry he chose today to go fishing over in Norwood," Maggie said, as she repositioned the camera for another shot.

No question what would be on the front page of the next issue of the *Eureka Miner*, probably with a headline along the lines of REBELS TAKE OVER TOWN PARK. Rick tended to like military references. When it was his turn to write up the report of the town council meeting, council members never discussed issues, they always battled or fought.

"Do you want me to order them to stop?" Josh Miller had worked his way over to Lucille's side and spoke softly.

She probably should have Cassie arrested. The librarian was ignoring the town board's decision —or lack of one—and making a ridiculous show of getting her own way. On the other hand, "Town Park" was a dud of a name, and Ernestine Wynock had been a driving force for good in the town at one time. "Where did you get that banner?" she called up to Cassie.

"I had it printed in Montrose. It's guaranteed for a year, though they said it could last longer."

"And you paid for it?"

"Of course." She gave a very unladylike snort. "If I waited for the city to pay for it, I'd be in my grave before you ever got around to fitting it into the budget."

"Alina, what do you think you're doing?" Sharon Franklin, a little out of breath, ran up to join them. She stared, white-faced, at her daughter, who was balanced on the tall step ladder, struggling to lift the heavy vinyl banner.

"Miss Wynock said she needed our help, Mom," Alina called. "You always said we should help people, especially old people."

"Do not speak of me as if I am in my dotage, young lady," Cassie admonished. "And make sure you tie that banner tightly."

"Don't be too hard on your daughter," Olivia said. "I blame Lucas." She looked amused. "For some reason, he actually likes Cassie. I sometimes think he even encourages her schemes."

"Oh, let her hang her silly banner," Bob said. "Everybody will still call it the town park, no matter whose name is on it. And it'll save you having to repaint the old sign before the movie fellow shows up."

Discussion spread among the crowd; from what Lucille could tell, opinions were about fifty-fifty for and against the name change. "You can keep the banner up for now," she called to Cassie. "But we won't be changing the permanent sign anytime soon—not until the town council has voted on the matter."

"You heard what she said, Lucas," Cassie said. "How are you coming with your end?"

"Almost done." He strained against the ropes that held the banner in place, red-faced.

"I can't get my end tight," Alina said.

"Maybe I'd better help." Josh handed Sharon

his hat and climbed the ladder to help Alina fasten her end of the sign.

Maggie took another photograph. "You aren't going to print that one, are you?" Sharon asked. "I mean, he might get into trouble, since he's on duty."

"I won't print it." Maggie checked the shot on her camera's screen. "But I'll give you a copy if you like."

"Oh." Sharon flushed pink. "No, why would I want that?"

"I just thought, since she's your daughter . . ."

"Oh, yes. Of course. Sure, you can send me a copy."

Maggie grinned. "Oh, I will."

Together, Alina and Officer Miller succeeded in fastening their end of the sign. They climbed down and met Cassie and Lucas on the ground.

"It looks really good," Lucas pronounced.

"But we need some kind of plaque in the park, to let people know who Ernestine was and what she did," Alina said.

Cassie beamed at the girl. "That's an excellent idea. The historical society has some money in their funds. I'll persuade them a plaque would be a worthy expenditure."

Lucille could have protested that there was no sense erecting a plaque when the sign was neither official nor permanent. But she could have suggested the sun stop shining or the wind stop blowing with about the same effect.

"Take another picture, now that we're done," Cassie ordered Maggie. "And tell Rick I'll be sending over a press release, with all the information he needs to include in his story."

"Rick always looks forward to your press releases," Maggie said with a straight face as she raised the camera for another shot of the sign in place.

Someone in the crowd started clapping and others joined in. Cassie's cheeks pinked and she looked almost happy.

"It is kind of nice to see something named for a woman for a change," Olivia said, as she and Lucille headed back to Lucille's car.

"There are lots of things around Eureka named after women," Bob protested. "There's the French Mistress, the Irene McGraw, Washerwoman Hill, and don't forget the Dirty Sally."

"Old mines and a saloon named after a mine," Lucille said. "Forgive us if we're not flattered."

"There wouldn't be a town here if it weren't for those mines," Bob said.

"Speaking of mines, how are things at the Lucky Lady?" Lucille asked. "Have the engineers finished installing the safety gear to Gerald's satisfaction?"

Bob spat a stream of tobacco juice into the flower bed alongside the parking lot. "In case you haven't figured it out, there's almost nothing

Pershing likes better than putting on airs and ordering people around. He keeps finding new work for the contractors—and I keep reminding him that until we get in there and start actually mining, none of us is going to be making any money."

"What does he say to that?" Olivia asked.

"He tells me a good investment requires patience, or some such balderdash. He needs to watch it or I'll teach him a thing or two about patience."

"Bob, promise me you won't do anything illegal," Lucille said.

"Who's the proven shyster in this partnership?" Bob asked. "I'm not the one you need to worry about."

"I'm pretty sure it's in the job description of the mayor to worry about everything." She didn't point out that he hadn't promised not to break the law; Bob might pretend to be a loony old codger when it suited him, but the man's mind was still razor sharp, and he never did anything that wasn't deliberate. He'd probably broken more than a few laws when it suited him, and he had certainly bent plenty. "Be careful," she said. "Eureka doesn't need any more problems."

"I can handle Pershing," Bob said. "Lesser men than him have tried to get the better of me and lived to regret it."

She had plenty of regrets where Gerald Pershing was concerned, but it was too late to do anything about any of them. She could only move forward and hope things turned out for the best. She opened her car door. "Where's Lucas?" she asked Olivia.

"He asked if he could hang out with Alina and make sure she doesn't get into too much trouble with her mom," Olivia said.

"How gallant," Lucille said. "Is Alina Lucas's girlfriend?"

Olivia made a face. "He says she's just a friend. I don't know if he's really ready for romance. I know I'm not."

"As if any of us are ever ready for that." Lucille climbed into her car and stared out the windshield at the banner that now hung over the entrance. Ernestine Wynock Park.

"What are you thinking?" Olivia asked as she fastened her seat belt.

"That we could do worse than follow Cassie's example."

Olivia frowned. "What example is that?"

"I'm not sure—maybe 'Don't take no for an answer,' or 'When someone puts an obstacle in your way, climb over it.' "

"Or maybe the lesson is, 'Don't be the person everyone expects you to be,' " Olivia said.

"What do you mean by that?"

"I mean, did you ever expect Cassie to pay for

her own banner and then climb up a ladder to hang it? I didn't. I thought she was all about manipulating other people to do what she wanted."

"Well, she did recruit Alina and Lucas to do most of the work."

"Still, she paid for the banner. She stopped whining and just did something for a change."

"That probably ought to go on a bumper sticker." Lucille started the car, then glanced at the banner one more time. "It looks nice," she said. "I think I'll vote for it to stay."

"Tell Cassie she owes you one," Olivia said. "Who knows? It might pay off one day."

Chapter 13

Sharon smoothed the hair back out of Alina's eyes. "What were you thinking—up on that ladder with that heavy sign?" she asked. "You could have fallen and broken your neck." She'd brought the young people back to her house, proud of herself for remaining calm.

"It wasn't that heavy." Alina squirmed away from her mother and pretended to focus on the sandwich her mother had fixed as a makeshift supper. "And I couldn't let old Miss Wynock climb up on the ladder, could I?"

"She's really not that old, you know." Sharon sat at the end of the table and contemplated her own sandwich. Cassie was technically old enough to be Sharon's mother, and thus Alina's grandmother, but she wasn't ancient and decrepit.

"What's dotage?" Alina asked.

"It means somebody who's really old and maybe not altogether with it. You know, like when they say somebody is dotty?" Lucas looked up from his tuna sandwich, then flushed. "Sorry, Mrs. Franklin. I shouldn't have interrupted."

"I don't mind the interrupting as much as I mind you involving Alina in these schemes of yours," Sharon said. But there was no malice behind her words, and without being asked, she added more tea to Lucas's glass.

"I tried to talk Miss Wynock out of it," Lucas said. "Nobody believes me, but I did. But she was really determined."

"I thought it was a good idea," Alina said. "The town should do more to honor the women who were so important in settling the area. All anyone remembers is the men."

"When the police came to tell the mayor you were up there on that ladder I couldn't believe it," Sharon said, not ready yet to let her daughter off the hook.

"We weren't breaking any law." Alina's voice rose. "Officer Miller even helped me with the sign."

"Maggie took our picture for the paper," Lucas said. "I'll bet we make the front page."

"Cool!"

"Just how I want everyone in town to get to know my daughter," Sharon said.

"Oh, Mom—people in Eureka are nice. They won't think you're a bad mom or anything."

"How was the baby shower?" Lucas asked, clearly trying to change the subject.

Sharon should have been annoyed, but maybe it was time to leave this topic for now. "The shower was nice. Maggie got a lot of things she needed for the baby. Some pretty clothes."

"I can't wait to see them. All those little shirts and tiny socks—so cute."

Lucas rolled his eyes and pushed back from the table. "Thanks for the sandwich, Mrs. Franklin," he said. "I'd better get home or I'll be late for dinner."

She could have pointed out that the sandwich was dinner, but for a teenage boy that was probably irrelevant. "You're welcome, Lucas."

"See you tomorrow," he said to Alina.

When Lucas was gone, Alina started clearing the table without being asked. "Don't be mad, Mom," she said. "I was just trying to help Miss Wynock."

"I know Cassie can be . . . persuasive." She'd been about to say "bossy," but maybe that wasn't the best way to describe her supervisor in front of her daughter. "But next time, check with me before you do something like this. Let me deal with Cassie. With school out next week, maybe we need to set some rules for you."

Alina slumped. "I'm thirteen, Mom. I can look after myself while you're at work."

"What are you going to do with yourself all day?"

"I can hang out with Lucas."

"I don't know if I like you spending so much time alone with a boy."

More eye rolling. "Lucas and I are just friends."

"I know, dear, but sometimes friends can

develop . . . feelings for one another, and that can lead to experimenting and . . ." Oh, this wasn't going well. Sharon's face was hot and Alina looked torn between laughter and tears.

"Mom! Lucas and I aren't going to have sex. We're just going to, you know, ride our bikes and talk and stuff. He has to paint and stuff at his mom's new house and I could help with that."

"All right. I don't want you to think I don't trust you."

"But you don't trust me." Alina patted Sharon's arm. "It's okay. But honestly, Lucas and I are just friends."

"And I'm glad you've made friends here in Eureka. I really am."

"I have girlfriends, too, but none of them are as fun as Lucas."

"Whatever came of that research project you were working on with him, searching the tax records to find more about the history of his house?"

"We found the records, but it was crazy. Mrs. McCutcheon just disappears after 1966. Maybe her husband really did murder her and bury her in the backyard."

Sharon rubbed her shoulders against a sudden chill. "I hope that's not really the case."

"Well, it did happen years and years ago. But it would be cool to know . . . like solving a mystery."

Sharon had never been a fan of mysteries. But she'd welcome any detective, amateur or professional, who could find her son for her.

A knock on the door distracted her from her brooding. "I'll get it!" Alina shouted, and popped up from the table.

By the time Sharon made it into the living room, Officer Josh Miller had stepped inside. "Hello, Sharon," he said.

She wondered what had happened to "Mrs. Franklin," but she liked the way he said her name, and she'd never been a very formal person anyway.

"Hello, Josh." She hesitated only a little over the name, and his smile told her she'd made the right decision.

Alina collected her backpack from where she'd dropped it by the door when she'd come in from school on Friday. "I have homework," she said. "Thanks for helping me with the sign, Officer Miller. That banner was a lot heavier than it looks."

"You're welcome, Alina."

And then he and Sharon were alone, with two feet of space and a much larger silence between them. "She's a good girl," he said.

"Yes, she is." Sharon tried not to fidget. "Can I get you anything? I have iced tea."

"Tea would be nice."

"It's in the kitchen." She turned and he

followed. She hastily cleared the remains of dinner and put fresh ice in glasses.

He pulled out a chair and sat as if he'd spent hours in her kitchen, perfectly at home. "I'm beginning to get a complex," he said. "You look so hopeful every time you see me; then you always end up disappointed."

She clutched an empty ice tray to her chest. "It's not you. I—"

"I know. And that was my poor attempt at a joke."

"I'm not good company right now, I'm afraid."

"It's all right." He shifted in the chair, enough to remove his wallet from his hip pocket, and withdrew a folded scrap of paper. "Tell me what you think of this."

The paper was a classified ad.

Wanted: Self-sufficient, skilled patriots to form a society for a new Republic.

While others struggle to survive in the new reality, we will thrive and lead the way to the new millennium. Reply to Box 70.

A shiver raced up her spine. She looked up at Josh. "Where did you get this?"

"It's from the classified section of a magazine for preppers. Does that sound like something your ex-husband would have responded to?"

"It sounds like something he would have written." She sank into a chair. "Where did you get a prepper magazine?"

"Bob Prescott subscribes. I saw him with it at the post office the other day and asked if I could take a look. I was really just curious, but for some reason the ad caught my eye."

She read the ad again. "It doesn't say where this supposed community is."

"I can check with the magazine. They may not know either, but it's worth a shot."

"It sounds innocent enough," she said. "All patriotic and peaceful."

"Was your husband ever violent?"

"Yes and no."

He leaned toward her. "Care to elaborate on that?"

"He had a lot of guns. He taught us all how to shoot, so we'd know how to defend ourselves."

"Against what—or whom?"

"No specific threat—foreign invaders, people who tried to destroy our home—no one in particular."

"But you don't think he'd hurt your son?"

It was the second time today someone had asked that question, but her answer was the same. "No, Joe loved Adan. As much as Joe could love anyone. His son was an extension of himself, a chance to live out his hopes and dreams."

"That's a lot of pressure to put on a kid."

"Yes." She sighed. "Adan adores his father, but I worry about the long-term effect of Joe's influence."

"He has your influence to counteract that."

"Had." She met his gaze, hoping, perhaps, for some reassurance or comfort from those warm brown eyes. "What if he thinks I let him go too easily? What if he believes—and Joe lets him believe—that I didn't love him enough to fight for him? That I willingly abandoned him." Saying the words out loud made her stomach clench.

"You had to make an awful choice," Josh said. "You did your best—it's all any of us can do. If it helps, my father raised me after my mother died, and I like to think I turned out okay." He held out his hand. "Let me have that back and I'll see what I can find out."

"Of course." She returned the little square of paper, then looked around, trying to remember what she was supposed to be doing. Her gaze landed on the glasses of ice still sitting on the counter. "Your tea."

"That's all right." He stood. "I have to go, but I'll let you know as soon as I hear anything."

"Thanks for stopping by." She stood also. "And thanks for listening."

"Anytime." He touched her arm—a brief contact that carried with it a great deal of reassurance. "I'll talk to you soon."

She walked him to the front door and watched him climb into his cruiser and drive away. She couldn't afford to get her hopes up that the ad would lead to anything; Josh probably didn't think so either, but she was touched that he'd gone to the trouble to cut it out. Knowing he'd done so made her feel less alone, and that was a gift in and of itself; but at the same time, the feeling made her nervous.

She was fighting hard to stand on her own two feet, to avoid years of conditioning that told her to look to a man to make decisions for her. Jameso refusing to do that was probably the best thing that could have happened to her, but she was still trying to find her way. It would be so easy to surrender the small bit of independence she'd gained to rely on a man like Josh for help and comfort. Like an addict who needed to avoid drink or drugs, she needed to spend some time alone, making friends with herself and discovering her own strengths.

Chris Amesbury turned out to be a lanky surfer dude whose long blond hair wasn't combed quite artfully enough to hide his bald spot, and whose blond goatee was heavily sprinkled with gray. His uniform of board shorts, Mexican guayabera shirt, and rubber sandals stood out even among the tourists on Eureka's streets, but his enthusiasm for the town won over the welcoming committee that greeted his car and driver on the steps of the Idlewilde B and B Inn, otherwise known as Barb's place.

"Welcome to Eureka, Mr. Amesbury." Lucille, who'd unearthed an actual blazer from dry cleaner's bags at the back of her closet, greeted the VIP with a firm handshake.

"The town is perfect," he said in a voice an octave higher than she'd expected. "So charming. And the scenery!"

"Thank you," Lucille said, then had to hold back a snort of nervous laughter. As if she herself were personally responsible for the scenery. "Most people who come here end up falling in love with the place. I'd like you to meet Barbara and James Stanowski. They own this bed-and-breakfast."

"So pleased to meet you." Barb, dressed in a chic pantsuit, looked every inch the former beauty queen and current socialite. Beside her, Jimmy fidgeted in the suit she'd made him wear, despite his protests that he'd come to Eureka to relax and see his wife, not fawn over Hollywood directors. "I hope you'll be comfortable during your stay."

"As long as you have room service and plenty of drinks, I'll be great," Amesbury said.

Barb's smile never faltered. "We don't have room service, but I can give you directions to all the restaurants and a wonderful bar. It will be the perfect way for you to get to know some of the townspeople."

"Oh. That's, uh, very thoughtful of you."

"We try to think of everything." She put a well-manicured hand on his arm, the red lacquer standing out against skin that was surprisingly pale for someone from California. "Let me show you to your room."

The welcoming party, which consisted of Lucille, Maggie, Reggie, Katya, Junior Dominick, and Paul Percival, flowed up the stairs after the director and his hosts. Though most of the bedrooms remained unfurnished, the rest of the house looked amazing, like something straight out of a luxury home brochure. Plush carpet in a deep shade of rose muffled their footsteps, and paintings that looked real and valuable filled the walls.

"Putting him here might have been a wrong move," Reggie whispered in Lucille's ear. "The rest of the town is going to look like Dogpatch after this luxury."

"Hush." Lucille sent him a quelling look. "The rest of the town is authentic. He said he wanted authentic."

"This is your room." Barb opened the door to a large bedroom that overlooked the front of the house. It was furnished in a cherry four-poster, a red-velvet fainting couch, and had its own fireplace. She ushered the director inside, then turned to the others. "Perhaps you'd like to wait downstairs while Mr. Amesbury freshens up for lunch."

Right. What kind of rubes followed a guy into his bedroom? Lucille thought as she did an about face and headed toward the stairs. Dogpatch indeed.

Downstairs, they filed outside to wait in what Barb referred to as "the front garden," though it was actually a narrow strip of grass flanked by two small rose bushes and a handful of zinnias. Bees buzzed around the flowers and Lucille slipped on sunglasses to fight the glare off the home's white siding.

"What did you think?" Junior asked.

"He said he liked the town. That was good."

Junior shoved both hands in his pants pockets and frowned up at the house. "Has he said yet what kind of movie he wants to make?"

"He's only been here ten minutes," Lucille said. "Give him time."

Which may have been a poor choice of words, she thought thirty minutes later when they were still waiting for Amesbury to join them. The front door opened and they all perked up like school-children at the final bell, but it was only Barb.

"What's taking him so long?" Paul demanded. "He's not taking a nap, is he?"

Barb's smile had vanished, and her poise was frayed at the edges. "He asked for ice, then he wanted a different pillow, then he didn't like the toilet paper." She gave a delicate shudder. "I now know far too much about the man's hemorrhoids, but I was finally able to satisfy him."

"Thank you, Barb. The town appreciates everything you're doing," Reggie said.

"They'd better." She glanced over her shoulder. "Jimmy's with him now, talking golf and trying to ease him toward the door. He said he's eager to soak up the 'atmosphere.' "

"He'll have plenty of opportunity to do that," Lucille said. "After lunch at the Last Dollar he gets the VIP tour of the town."

"And he's agreed to an interview for the paper," Maggie said. "I'm hoping I can get him to talk more about his movie."

"What's the big secret about the movie anyway?" Junior asked.

"He said it was such a fabulous idea he's afraid someone will steal it from him if he talks about it too much," Lucille said. "But he's promised to tell us all about it before he leaves town."

"I hope it's a western," Reggie said. "I love a good western; they don't make enough of those."

"I hope whatever it is, it takes a long time to film and requires a big crew and a lot of actors who'll need to stay in town and spend money," Lucille said.

The front door opened and Jimmy emerged, followed by the director, who'd added a battered cowboy hat and a leather satchel to his outfit. "I'm at your disposal, Madam Mayor," he said.

"We thought lunch first, then a short tour of the town," she said, leading the way to the SUV she'd borrowed from Olivia and D. J. for the day.

"Lunch sounds marvelous. And I'm really hoping to get to meet more of the locals while I'm in town. I want to get a real flavor for Eureka's personality."

"I'm sure that won't be a problem," she said. "People here are very curious about you."

"I don't imagine celebrities make it this far back in the hinterlands, do they?"

Lucille didn't know if a director she'd never heard of counted as a celebrity, but she wisely kept her mouth shut while Amesbury and Reg made small talk about the flight from Hollywood to Denver to Montrose. She pulled into the reserved parking spot in front of the Last Dollar ahead of a crowd of townspeople hoping to catch a glimpse of the man himself. He emerged from the SUV smiling and waving like the grand marshal at a parade and people responded with applause, which seemed to please him.

Inside the Last Dollar, Danielle and Janelle, wearing matching Betty Boop T-shirts, ushered the welcoming party and their guest to a long table in the center of the room. "How perfectly quaint," Amesbury said, looking around the room. "You've gone all out with the rustic theme."

Danielle's smile grew strained. "It's not really a theme," she said. "It's just things people have given us to display."

Amesbury's grin widened as he surveyed a trio of singing trout mounted on the wall behind his head. "I know designers in Hollywood who would kill for this kind of kitsch." He handed back the menu Danielle gave him. "Just serve me whatever you have that's local, organic, fresh, and a specialty of the house."

"Vegetarian or carnivore?" Danielle asked.

"I'm not afraid of meat. What have you got?"

"The elk steak is fresh, and you can't get much more local and organic. Junior took it off his lease up near Garnet Mountain. It comes with home fries and the soup of the day or vegetable. We've got broccoli from our garden."

"It sounds divine." He looked her up and down wolfishly. "I can see I'm going to be eating here a lot while I'm in town."

"We have the best food in the county." Janelle set a glass of water in front of him. "Save room for dessert. Danielle's a wizard in the kitchen."

"I'll just bet she is." He looked around Janelle to watch Danielle as she walked back toward the kitchen.

"Uh-oh," Maggie whispered to Lucille. "He's going to be disappointed if he goes after Danielle."

"Let's hope Janelle doesn't dump a pot of hot

coffee in his lap first." Lucille leaned toward the director. "We're all very curious to know more about the movie you're planning," she said.

"It's not a movie," he said.

"Oh?" Across the table, Reggie raised his eyebrows.

"It's a TV series."

"So you have to film a pilot and sell the network on the idea?" Barb asked.

"That's how some people do it, but in my case the network's crazy about the idea, and they're familiar with my work, so they've already given me the green light. I just have to find the right location to film—and the right cast, of course."

"Who do you have in mind for the cast?" Katya asked.

"I prefer to use unknowns in a project like this." He smiled up at Danielle as she set a bowl of vegetable soup in front of him. "Did you make this yourself, darling?" he asked.

"Janelle makes the soup."

"I get it. And you're in charge of the hot buns."

Maggie, who sat on Lucille's right, made a choking sound and reached for her iced tea.

Danielle ignored him and moved down the table to serve the others. "So I gather your proposed television series is set in a small town in the mountains?" Barb asked the director.

"It doesn't have to be in the mountains, but I'm looking for a small village with a slower pace of life, removed from life's modern conveniences."

"If you mean things like movie theaters and fast-food chains, Eureka doesn't have those," Lucille said.

"I noticed my 4G smartphone connection doesn't work at the bed-and-breakfast," he said. "I can't tell you how happy that made me. And I didn't see a single Starbucks downtown."

"Some people consider that to be one of Eureka's advantages," Junior said.

"Oh, it's ideal for my purposes."

Janelle arrived with his steak and he took a moment to contemplate the large slab of meat. "That's certainly impressive," he said. "I'm sure a vegetarian would choke."

"We serve vegetarian food also," Janelle said. "And vegan, if you like."

"Well, we won't tell anyone about that. Why ruin the tension?" With this strange statement, he cut into the meat.

Lucille picked at her chopped salad. She ought to be thrilled at the idea of a television show setting up home in Eureka. If the show was a hit, they could look forward to years of filming, not to mention an influx of tourists who'd want to see the real town behind the series.

But Amesbury's glee at Eureka's "quaintness" annoyed her. He acted as if they were backward, or a bunch of hicks.

He was finishing up the last of his steak when

a strident voice from the front of the room destroyed any appetite Lucille might have had left. "I don't need you to show me to a table, Danielle," Cassie said. "I see exactly the person I need to talk to right over there."

The librarian made a beeline for Amesbury at the head of the table. Lucille noted Cassie had pulled out all the stops today: She wore her grandmother's pearls and matching drop earrings with a wide-collared white blouse, gray pencil skirt, and sensible pumps, and she'd added pink lipstick and two spots of pink blush to her normally pale face. Call it librarian chic, as only Cassie knew how to do it. "Welcome to Eureka, Mr. Amesbury," she said.

Still chewing, Amesbury regarded Cassie. He swallowed. "Thank you, ma'am. And you are?"

"Cassie Wynock. Town librarian and president of the Eureka County Historical Society."

Amesbury wiped his hand on his napkin and offered it. "The pleasure is all mine, Ms. Wynock."

Cassie shook his hand, then just stood there, staring at him. The others looked on, too stunned —or perhaps too afraid—to say anything.

"Is there something else I can do for you?" Amesbury asked.

"Yes, I want to audition for a part in your movie."

"It's not a movie. It's a television show."

"Even better. A continuing drama allows much

more opportunity to truly develop a character."

"Uh, yes." His mouth twitched. "Have you acted before Ms., uh, what was your name again?"

"Wynock. *Miss* Cassie Wynock. And yes. I was the lead in our town's Founders' Day Pageant, which I not only starred in, but wrote and directed. You can ask anyone and they'll tell you the program was a popular triumph."

"Well, I'll definitely take that into consideration when I sit down to cast the production. Thank you for stopping by."

"Here's your dessert, Mr. Amesbury." Danielle inserted herself between Cassie and the director. "Linzer torte."

"It looks almost as delicious as you." He beamed at her.

Cassie frowned at the slab of sugar-dusted pastry. "She stole the recipe from my grandmother," she said. "I don't know how she did it, but I swear it's the same."

"Well, I'm sure it will be delicious."

Reggie stood. "Cassie, perhaps Mr. Amesbury can stop by the library later to continue this conversation."

"That would be lovely." She gave him a thin smile, pink lips pressed tightly together. "I'll be looking forward to it."

She had been gone a full minute before Amesbury looked up from the crumbs of his torte and noticed the rest of the table was staring at him. "Is something wrong?" he asked.

"I apologize for Cassie interrupting like that," Lucille said. "She can be a little eccentric at times."

"Is she really the town librarian?"

"Oh yes."

"She looks like she could be a real tartar."

"Yes, she can be," Lucille agreed.

"Then she'll be perfect. I'll have to find a way to work her into the show."

"You think Cassie would be right for your show?" Lucille felt a little light-headed. "But you don't even know if she can act."

"It doesn't matter. She thinks she can, and people like that are some of the best participants. I want real characters who will rub up against the other cast members. The more unique, the better."

"Yes, Cassie is unique," Reggie said.

"So you think you might choose Eureka as the location for filming?" Maggie asked.

"Nothing's certain yet. I'll need to see more of the town, and there are a lot of logistics to work out. We'll need somewhere for the cast to stay."

"I'm sure I could accommodate some of them at the B and B," Barb said.

"Oh, no, we'll need something much more rustic. An old barn, maybe. Heated by a wood stove, with an outdoor privy. Is there anything like that around here?"

"Well, I don't know . . ." Lucille stopped trying to hide her confusion.

"I knew it—this is a historical show." Reggie slapped his knee. "You want period authenticity."

"Oh, no, it's a contemporary piece. I just want to be sure I convey the primitive nature of the surroundings to the audience."

"Mr. Amesbury, Eureka has indoor plumbing and has for over a century." Lucille couldn't quite keep the snippiness out of her tone.

"Well, yes, but our viewers don't have to know that."

"What kind of show—exactly—is this going to be?" she asked.

He smacked his lips over the last of the torte, then dabbed at the corners of his mouth with the napkin. "The idea is to take a group of twenty-somethings from the city—attractive, hip up-and-comers—and dump them off in the middle of nowheresville America, and show them struggling to cope without their iPads and skinny mocha lattes and hipster hangouts. It'll make for some fantastic drama and comedy. The network's crazy about the idea."

"You want to shoot a reality TV show in Eureka?" She had trouble getting the words out.

"Killer, isn't it? We'll make the kids chop

wood and eat elk steak and interact with people like Miss Wynock—audiences will eat it up."

"And we'll come off looking like a bunch of dumb hicks." Junior threw down his napkin and stood up. "I won't be a part of it."

"On the contrary," Amesbury said. "You could all come off looking like heroes—the salt of the earth simple people who make this country great."

The only answer was the sound of Maggie's pen as she furiously scribbled in her reporter's notebook. "What do we do now, Lucille?" Reggie asked.

She swallowed. Once again, she was responsible for putting the town in a predicament. "If everyone is finished eating, we'll show Mr. Amesbury some more of the town," she said. "After all, that's what he came to see." Even if he viewed everything through a filter that alarmed her, he might find something positive to showcase. Or maybe he'd choose some other town to play host to his spoiled hipsters.

Chapter 14

"He wants to film a reality TV show about a bunch of hipsters who have to survive in a small town without coffee shops and sushi bars." Maggie wedged another pillow behind her back and tried to decide if that helped or not. At this point in her pregnancy, no position was truly comfortable.

"Who would want to watch something like that?" Jameso climbed into bed beside her.

"Apparently a lot of people. He said 'the network' was excited about the project."

"Then let him do it. His money spends as well as the next guy's." He arranged his own stack of pillows and picked up a suspense novel from the bedside table.

"He wants to stick these people from the city in a barn with a wood stove for heat and an outhouse, and let viewers think that's how we all live in the mountains."

"It's almost how you lived when you first came here, up in Jake's cabin."

"I had indoor plumbing!" She punched the pillow and wedged it more firmly against the small of her back. "And that's not the point.

He wants to make Eureka the butt of a joke. He even wants to cast Cassie in the show."

"Cassie Wynock?"

"Yes, she interrupted lunch to introduce herself and tell him she wanted a part in the show. You know how Cassie is—she can't help but come off as abrasive and, well, weird."

"That's because she is. Abrasive and weird."

"Yes, but Chris Amesbury wants to exploit her weirdness and play it up. He'll make her think she's going to be a star or something, but she'll end up looking foolish."

"Cassie doesn't need his help to do that." He opened his book.

She hated it when he was so calm and reasonable when she was annoyed. He was supposed to get incensed right along with her. "It's not right to use people that way," she said.

"If people get pulled into a scheme like this by their own vanity and greed, why not let them go?" he asked. "I might even tune in to see Cassie confront a bunch of hipsters who want to use the library computers without first jumping through all her hoops. It would be hilarious."

"Lucille is so upset. She wanted to do this to help the town."

"If this guy brings in money, and tourists who want to come here and spend their money, it will help."

"Not if it turns Eureka into a joke."

He set aside the book and turned on his side toward her. "Since when do you care so much about what people think of Eureka?" he asked.

She smoothed the blankets over the mound of her belly. "This is my home now. Of course I care about it. Or I care about the people in it. No one likes to be made to look backward or ignorant or foolish—and that's what this director wants to do to all of us."

"I'm supposed to take him on a Jeep tour tomorrow. Should I dump him off a cliff?"

The offer surprised a laugh from her. "That might be a little bit extreme."

"If Jake were alive, he'd regale the guy with stories about people who had gotten on the wrong side of folks around here and disappeared down a mine shaft. He'd have him packing to leave before nightfall."

"Amesbury would have made Jake the star of his show. He's just the kind of 'character' he's looking for."

"And Jake would have loved it," Jameso said. "He'd have gone out of his way to make the director and the hipsters look foolish. And it's what we'll do if he tries to come in here and manipulate us." He squeezed her knee. "This could still work out good—we'll get Amesbury's money and a little notoriety, but he won't get the best of us."

He sounded so certain. So reassuring. Maybe he

was worth keeping around after all. "I suppose you're right. I worry too much. Rick's happy anyway. He's putting the story about this possible reality show on the front page."

"It will be hard to top the picture of Cassie up on a ladder on the front page of this week's issue." He laughed. "I cut it out and pinned it on the wall behind the bar at the Dirty Sally."

"Your niece was in that picture, too. I don't think Sharon was too happy about that."

"Sharon worries too much, too. Alina's a good kid."

"You've been spending more time with her lately, haven't you?"

"I have. I thought at first I wouldn't know what to say to a kid, but she's smart and fun to be around." He rolled onto his back again, eyes focused on the ceiling. "She reminds me of hanging out with Sharon when we were younger."

Did she imagine the wistfulness in his voice? A longing for old connections that had been severed? He'd probably say she was being too sentimental. "It's good that you can be there for Alina now," she said. "She needs another adult besides her mom whom she can talk to."

"Did you have someone like that when you were her age?"

"No, it was just my mom and me." She'd had plenty of conversations with her imaginary father—a man as different from the reclusive, troubled Jake Murphy as he could be.

"Jake shouldn't have walked out the way he did."

"No, he shouldn't have. But that's old news." In this last year, as she'd learned more about Jake, she'd been able to forgive him for leaving her and her mother. She didn't fully understand his reasoning, and she'd never condone his behavior; she wasn't even sure she'd have liked the man much if she'd had the chance to know him. But he was her father, and she believed he'd tried to do right by her. Not hard enough, and he'd ended up missing the mark by a wide margin, but he had tried. "I don't know what kind of man Alina's father is, but I'm sure she misses him," she said.

"She does. She misses her brother, too."

The mention of Sharon's missing boy set up an ache in Maggie's chest. Was it because she was so soon to be a mother herself? "I hope they find Adan soon," she said. "For his sake, but for Sharon's, too. This must be so hard on her."

"Alina talks to me more than her mother does. Sharon just says she's fine when I ask her if there's anything I can do to help."

"That's because there's nothing you can do. Some things even tough mountain men can't fix."

"I'd fix Joe, if I could find him."

"What do you think happened to him? Do the police have any idea?"

"I think Joe wanted to retreat even farther from society and he took Adan with him," Jameso said. "They're hiding out in the Great North Woods somewhere, living off the land and stockpiling ammunition for the end times."

"That's no way for a teenager to live. Can you imagine?"

"Adan probably thinks it's great—he doesn't have to go to school or clean his room or any of that stuff. But one day he'll get tired of being under Joe's thumb, and there'll be trouble."

"Is that what happened to you, with your father?" She held her breath, waiting for his answer. Jameso so seldom talked about his family, only that his father had been an abuser and that Jameso had left home as soon as he could.

His expression darkened, closed off. "I finally got big enough that he couldn't hurt me anymore," he said. "That's when I left. Sharon left later that year, too. Maybe without me around she felt like she had to marry Joe in order to be safe."

Guilt was such a powerful, terrible thing. She heard the shame and regret behind Jameso's words, though he'd probably never admit to those feelings out loud. "She stayed with Joe a long time," she said. "I think there must have been something there besides fear."

279

"I hope so." He crossed his arms over his chest, gaze fixed on the ceiling still. She could feel him closing her off and wanted to shake him.

She stroked his arm. "You're going to be a great dad, you know."

He didn't answer for a long moment. When he did finally speak, his voice was soft. "I hope so. I want to be. It feels like I have a lot working against me—history, a lot of bad examples."

"You're your own person. That's what made me fall in love with you."

She felt some of the tension drain out of him. "I thought it was the motorcycle leathers." He sat up and pulled her close.

She settled against him. "Mmm. That, too."

"I love you, Maggie. You know that, right?"

"I do know it." There had been a time when she'd doubted the truth behind those words, but no more. "It'll be all right, Jameso. We'll be all right, and so will Sharon and Alina." And Adan too, she hoped.

Sharon eyed the man on the other side of the circulation desk. Chris Amesbury wore an Indiana Jones–style fedora and a denim work shirt with the sleeves rolled up, over skinny jeans and hiking books that were so new they squeaked. "I'm sorry, I'm not sure I understand what you're looking for," she said.

"I'm compiling a list of the most interesting people in Eureka," he said. "People with unusual hobbies or habits that might interest television viewers. Obviously, this is a difficult task for someone who doesn't live here. But as a librarian, you know all your patrons and their reading tastes, so I thought you might point me in the direction of some Eurekians who might be good candidates for my list."

She suspected *interesting people* was code for eccentrics and nuts. Didn't he think it might be just a bit insulting for him to pick out the oddest people in town as representatives of "typical Eurekians"? He had a lot of nerve, asking her to help him in his quest. "Information about the books people check out is confidential," she said.

"Of course." He leaned across the counter and looked into her eyes, in a way he probably thought was charming. "I'm not asking you to divulge state secrets, just give me a little help. For instance, who, in your professional opinion, is the most eccentric person in town?"

In her short time in Eureka, she'd become acquainted with more than a few people who might qualify as "most eccentric." The mountains attracted people who marched to a different drummer. "I don't have a professional opinion on that subject," she said.

The buzzer on the back door sounded and Cassie entered, returning from her lunch break.

"The lilacs are going to be truly spectacular this year," she called. "Another week and the bushes here at the library will be in their full glory." She emerged from the back hallway and froze when she spotted their visitor. "Mr. Amesbury! Such a pleasure to see you." She sent Sharon a look that clearly said, *You can leave now, I'll take care of him.* Sharon gladly took a few steps back toward her desk. Speaking of eccentrics, Cassie could be number one on Amesbury's list.

"Miss Wynock! Or may I call you Cassie? I was hoping I'd find you here."

Twin spots of pink bloomed on Cassie's cheeks. "So nice of you to stop by. I hope you're enjoying your visit to Eureka so far."

"I am. This morning I was taken on a guided tour of the surrounding mountains by one of the locals, who regaled me with tales of an area legend named Jake Murphy. Quite the character. I wish I could have met him."

The wattage on Cassie's smile dimmed at the mention of Jake Murphy. Sharon had heard her share of stories about Maggie's father—about how he built Janelle and Danielle a fireproof chicken house after bigots destroyed their first one; how he climbed Mount Garnet every Fourth of July to hang the flag at the pioneer cabin there; how he'd won the trophy at the Hard Rock Days competition three years running, and about how he'd abandoned Maggie and her mother three days after Maggie was born, then left her everything he owned in his will. None of the stories Sharon had heard involved Cassie, but clearly the librarian had little love for Jake or his memory.

"I'm sure you're not really interested in someone who isn't even around anymore," Cassie said. "Can I help you with something else? Do you need to use one of our computers, or would you like to do some research about the town?"

"Research, yes! That's exactly why I'm here." He explained his mission to ferret out information about the town's most eccentric "characters." Sharon sat frozen, fingers poised over her keyboard, waiting for Cassie to launch into a speech about privacy rights and rules and the impropriety of divulging information about the library's patrons.

"I'd love to help you," she said, and Sharon almost fell out of her chair. Who had replaced the real, acerbic, rule-enforcing Cassie with this compliant, even pleasant version?

"I knew I could count on you." Amesbury opened a small notebook and clicked his pen, poised for any information she could provide.

"Bob Prescott ought to be on your list," Cassie said. "He isn't rowing with all his oars in the water."

"In what way, exactly, is Mr. Prescott distinctive?"

"He reads all those survivalist books. He's got a stash of food and ammo big enough to wait out the end times—or so he says."

Thanks to Joe, Sharon knew plenty of people like Bob. Some of them were odder than others, but none of them was outright nuts—just a little more cautious, or a little more suspicious, than everyone in the mainstream.

"All right, I've got Prescott." Amesbury looked up from his notebook. "Who else?"

"Let me see." Cassie touched the tip of one finger to the corner of her mouth in a coquettish pose. "There are so many to choose from."

The front door to the library opened and a breeze swept through the building, ruffling the papers on Sharon's desk. "Hello, Miss W, Mrs. Franklin." Lucas Theriot shambled in, followed by Alina, both bent under the burden of backpacks.

"Hi, Mom. Hello, Miss Wynock," Alina waved and deposited her pack on the center table between the shelves.

Lucas joined her and took a camera from his pack and handed it across to Alina. "Thanks for letting me borrow it," he said. "I didn't have any luck."

"Any luck with what?" Sharon asked. Alina gave her a pained look, but she ignored it. A mother had a right to be nosy.

Lucas didn't seem to mind the question, though. "I was trying to get a picture of whoever—or whatever—is stealing stuff at the house my mom and D. J. are remodeling," he said, turning in his chair to face her. "I set up this motion detector thingie so the camera would take a picture if anyone came into the room. But all I got were pictures of my mom and D. J. and workmen and stuff."

"Are things still going missing?" Sharon asked. As mysteries went, this wasn't a big one, but it was curious.

Lucas nodded. "I've been keeping track. This week a fork, another earring, and a tin of snuff have disappeared."

"Maybe your folks are just careless." Alina stuffed the camera in her pack. "Those are all items that are easy to misplace."

"I think the ghost is taking them," he said.

"There are no such things as ghosts." Cassie had apparently decided not to be left out of the conversation.

"Wait. I want to hear more about this ghost." Amesbury moved over to join the two teenagers at the table. "I'm Chris Amesbury, director. I'm thinking of filming a television show in Eureka."

"Hi." Lucas shook the director's hand. "Uh, I'm Lucas Theriot. And this is Alina Franklin."

Amesbury scarcely glanced at Alina. "Tell me about your ghost, Lucas."

"My mom and her fiancé are fixing up this old

house that used to belong to an old woman who had to go into a nursing home. But before she lived there, the house belonged to a man named McCutcheon. He was married to a woman named Adelaide, but she disappeared about 1966, and some people think her husband murdered her and buried her in the backyard and now she haunts the house."

"Now, that is interesting." Amesbury scribbled furiously in his notebook. "Have you seen the ghost?"

"No," Lucas admitted. "But stuff keeps turning up missing. Little stuff like jewelry and door-knobs and bolts and stuff. Whatever it is, it managed to steal more stuff without tripping the camera we set up."

"I still don't see what Adelaide would want with forks and single earrings," Alina said. "You wouldn't think a ghost would need anything really."

"This is her way of communicating," Lucas said. "Of letting us know she's here."

"I thought you were too sensible to believe in nonsense like this," Cassie said.

"We-ell, yeah." He grinned. "But wouldn't it be fun if it was true?"

"I'd still like to know what happened to Mrs. McCutcheon," Alina said. "We looked at the courthouse, but we didn't really learn anything. She was here in 1965, and she wasn't here in

1966, but Mr. McCutcheon lived in the house another three years before he sold it to the Gilroys."

"We checked the death records, too," Lucas said. "She's not in there."

"A murder mystery!" Amesbury said, and wrote more in his notebook.

Sharon glared at him. She wanted to tell him to mind his own business, but with Cassie encouraging him, she had to keep her mouth shut.

"What's this show you want to film in Eureka?" Lucas asked.

"I'm envisioning a documentary format that examines what happens when you bring young people from the city and put them in a small mountain town to interact with the local citizens and absorb the culture."

Lucas frowned. "You mean, like a reality TV series."

Amesbury clicked his pen three times. "Some people react badly to the words 'reality TV.' I picture this production as being a cut above the ordinary. And I'll be looking for local talent to participate." He grinned at Sharon. "Perhaps you'd like to audition for a role. You definitely have the looks to be a star."

"No, thank you." Sharon refrained from making a face. "Though I'm sure Cassie would be perfect for a role in the show." Might as well score points with the boss while she was at it.

"Chris has already promised me a part." Cassie didn't exactly preen, but she couldn't have looked any smugger.

"Oh, definitely," Amesbury said. "I'll want to feature as many Eurekians as possible."

Alina giggled. "Eurekians? That sounds so funny."

Amesbury flushed. "What else would you call the people who live here?"

"I don't know." She shrugged. "People who live in Eureka, I guess."

"I don't think—"

But they never learned what he didn't think, because a loud siren's wail split the air. "What is that?" Sharon called over the din.

"Emergency siren." Cassie headed for the door. "It's used to summon the volunteer firemen and EMTs."

They all followed her to the door and out onto the sidewalk in front of the library. Cassie put up her hand as if she was hailing a taxi, and to Sharon's amusement, a car screeched to a halt at the curb. "Paul, what's going on?" Cassie addressed the driver.

"There's been an accident up at Lucky Lady Mine," he said. "Word is people are trapped inside."

Chapter 15

"Remind me why I ever wanted to be mayor?" Lucille asked Reggie as she gunned her Jeep up the steep grade leading to Lucky Lady Mine. The lawyer had shown up at Lacy's seconds after the emergency siren sounded, with the news that Bob Prescott and Gerald Pershing were trapped in one of the tunnels after an explosion.

Reg clenched his jaw and braced one hand against the dash as the Jeep jounced over deep ruts. "I thought they fixed this road when they reopened the mine."

"They hauled three truckloads of road base up here and the first hard rain washed it all back down." She steered the Jeep around a particularly deep gully. "There are a lot of reasons no one's ever developed the land up here, and access is one of them. And you didn't answer my question."

"I didn't think you were serious. When you ran for mayor, I think you said something about wanting to give back to the town."

"Well, I think I've given enough. Can I turn in my resignation now?"

"Not in the middle of a crisis. It wouldn't look good."

"When are we ever not in a crisis these days?" She steered around a big boulder, then braked hard and brought the Jeep to a halt next to a sheriff's department cruiser. The crowd of men gathered at the mine entrance turned to stare as she stalked up to them, Reg hurrying after her. "What's the situation?" she asked.

"An explosion at the north end of the main shaft caused the midsection of the tunnel to collapse, blocking the entrance," Charlie Frazier, head of the local Search and Rescue volunteers, said.

"But there's a back way out, right? An escape route?"

The men looked at her blankly.

She turned to Reg. "It was part of the new safety features Gerald was so insistent about installing. The features we paid for."

"There's no escape route," Charlie said.

A sick feeling swept over—one she'd experienced before. "But I saw it. It was on the engineers' drawings Gerald submitted to the town council."

"Well, yeah, it was on the drawings," Charlie said. "It just isn't in the mine."

"Why not?"

The men exchanged glances. "We don't know why not. Maybe they hadn't gotten around to installing it yet."

"Or maybe Gerald Pershing took the money we paid and put it in his own pocket. Where is he?" She looked around. "I want to personally strangle him."

"He's trapped in the mine. At least, that's his car over there." Charlie pointed to the silver Cadillac Gerald drove.

"There is some justice in the world," Lucille said. "Who's in there with him?"

"Bob Prescott, we think." Charlie nodded toward the battered pickup that was a familiar sight around town.

"What caused the explosion?" Reggie asked.

"We're not sure," Charlie said. "Though we suspect dynamite."

"They weren't using dynamite in the mine," Lucille said.

"They weren't supposed to be," Charlie agreed. "But you know, Bob's kind of old-fashioned. He's used dynamite before to blast away rock. Maybe he decided to use it again."

She clenched her hands into fists. "If he's still alive, I'll strangle him, too. What are we doing to get them out?"

"Search and Rescue is trying to establish where they are in the mine, and a crew is on its way from Lake City to try to either clear the blockage in the tunnel or drill a new exit," Charlie said. "That could take a couple of days or more."

"Wait, could you repeat that for me?" a familiar voice called from the parking area.

Lucille turned and gaped at Maggie, who was

struggling up the path to the mine entrance. "You shouldn't be up here in your condition," she scolded. "Where's Rick?" One more man she'd have to give a piece of her mind. What did the publisher of the *Eureka Miner* mean, letting his pregnant reporter trek up the mountains like this?

"He's at the dentist . . . in Montrose. He had . . . an abscess." She stopped next to Lucille, panting, one hand cradling her belly.

"You're not going to go into labor right here, are you?" Reg asked.

"At least if I do there are plenty of people here who are qualified to help." She nodded toward the crew of EMTs. She switched on her tape recorder and extended it toward Lucille. "Madam Mayor, what's the situation?" she asked.

"Right now we don't know much," Lucille said. "There may or may not have been an explosion, and Bob and Gerald may or may not be trapped in the mine. If they are trapped, we don't know if they're injured or not, and we don't know how long it will take to rescue them."

The roar of an engine accelerating up the grade announced a new arrival. A black Escalade hove into view in a cloud of dust and parked haphazardly. Chris Amesbury, in an Indiana Jones hat and aviator sunglasses, stepped out of the driver's side, while Cassie Wynock, looking more than a little flushed and disheveled, slid out of the passenger seat.

"What are you two doing here?" Lucille asked.

"A mine tragedy is great drama," the director said. "I couldn't stay away."

"And what about you?" Lucille asked Cassie, who was straightening her skirt and smoothing her hair. "Don't you have a library to run?"

"Sharon is there. I came to show Chris the way." She adjusted her sunglasses and looked around. "It doesn't look like much is going on up here."

"All of you need to stay back." Charlie ushered them some distance from the mine. "We don't know if there's more explosives in there or not."

"Explosives?" Amesbury took out his notebook. "What kind of explosives?"

Everyone ignored him. "What were Bob and Gerald doing with explosives?" Maggie asked.

"We don't know," Charlie said. "Maybe cutting a new tunnel the old-fashioned way."

"More likely he had a stash of the stuff just in case," Cassie said.

"Just in case of what?" Lucille asked.

"Just in case of the end of the world or the crash of civilization or invasion by foreigners or natural disaster—you name it, Bob was prepared for it." Cassie shrugged. "He had a stash of supplies he said was hidden in a secret storage area in the mountains."

"He was hiding things in the Lucky Lady?" Lucille asked. She'd thought Gerald had merely used his report of Bob storing things in the mine as an excuse to talk to her. She'd meant to ask Bob about the accusation, but it had slipped her mind. If the old man survived this disaster, she was going to kill him!

"It would be a good place—out of the weather, underground, hidden," Charlie said. "He wouldn't have put the supplies in a tunnel where they were working, but in a more remote shaft. You know these old mines, they have tunnels running every which way underground."

"A mine would make a good place to wait out dangerous times," Reggie said. "A man with enough supplies could hold out a long time underground."

"Then let's hope Bob and Gerald can reach some of those supplies, if it's going to take a few days to get them out," Charlie said.

"This is perfect," Amesbury said. "I must get a film crew out to capture this."

"Mr. Amesbury, two men are buried alive in a mine," Lucille said. "In no way is that perfect."

"Not perfect for the men certainly. But it is perfect television. There's nothing like life-or-death real-life drama to pull in the ratings." He pulled out his phone and frowned at the screen. "There's no signal? What kind of place doesn't have a signal?"

The kind of place where people—even people like Gerald Pershing—matter more than ratings, Lucille thought. But she didn't bother saying so to Amesbury.

He turned away. "Cassie! We need to drive back to town. Pronto."

Some other time it might have been amusing to see Cassie, who was so adept at ordering others to do her bidding, jump to wait on the imperious director. Maybe there is justice in this world, Lucille thought, as she turned back to confer with the rescue crew. If so, maybe it would help them get Bob and Gerald out of the mine alive. And then she'd give them both a lecture that would make them wish they were dead.

Bob woke coughing, his head pounding, muscles aching. He hadn't tied one on like this in a long time—not since Jacob Murphy's wake. But as his vision cleared and he was able to draw a clear breath, he remembered that the pain had nothing to do with alcohol. He was in the Lucky Lady Mine. He'd been arguing with Pershing (he and the man never seemed to have a civil conversation) when the roof had caved in.

With effort, he heaved to his knees and shoved aside a pile of loose rubble. The backpack he wore had protected him from the worst of the impact and his headlamp still worked, so that was something. In the dim glow he could make out a jumble of boulders and splintered timbers. The tunnel was blocked, though the passage he was in was mostly intact, littered with debris.

A groan from said debris near the wall indicated that Pershing was coming to. Bob crawled toward the sound until he encountered a shoe. He tugged at it and was rewarded with a louder groan. He worked his way up the body, shoving aside rocks and dirt, until he unearthed the Texan's face, gray as a statue with dust. "What happened?" Pershing croaked.

"The damn mine caved in, that's what happened."

Pershing shoved himself into a sitting position, his back against the tunnel wall, and looked around them. "I remember now. It sounded like an explosion."

"It was an explosion and it's your fault." He pulled a bottle of water from his battered pack, drank half of it, then handed it to Pershing.

Pershing drained the water and sat holding the empty bottle. "My fault. How is it my fault?"

"You went and made the Tommyknockers mad."

"The who?"

"You decide to go into mining and you don't bother finding out the first thing about it." Bob coughed and spat. He was definitely getting too old for this. "The Tommyknockers are the spirits who live in the mine. They've been known to help a miner who gets into trouble; but rile them and there'll be hell to pay."

"You're talking nonsense." Gerald brushed dust from his clothing. "Do you have any more water?"

"If I did, why should I give it to you? You didn't even say thank you."

"Forgive me for forgetting my drawing-room manners. Now, what do you really think happened, and what are we going to do about it?"

"I told you what happened—The 'knockers got fed up with your lying and cheating and decided to do something about it, and I was unlucky enough to get caught in the crossfire." He took inventory of the pack: two sandwiches, another bottle of water, a pack of chewing tobacco, his phone, and a map of the mine. The phone was useless under all this rock. He'd save the sandwiches and water for later. He took a pinch of tobacco.

"There's no such thing as mine spirits," Pershing said.

"How do you know?"

"I know because superstitions like that are nonsense." He shoved himself to his feet, though he had to duck his head to avoid cracking it on the ceiling. Timbers groaned and a fresh shower of rubble rained down. Bob couldn't have timed it better himself. Beneath the dust, Pershing's face paled.

"If you'd spent as much time underground as I

have," Bob said, "you'd have more respect for the Tommyknockers. This world is full of things you can't explain with science."

"There's a scientific explanation for everything, even if you're too ignorant to know it." He sat back down. "We probably hit a pocket of methane. And a spark off the rocks ignited it."

More likely a rat had chewed into the casing around the detonating cord Bob had stashed in his storage tunnel. He'd heard of something similar when he was working over near Leadville, back in the seventies. He should have wrapped it better. "You believe what you want to believe," he said. "But I know what I know."

"What are we going to do to get out of here?" Pershing asked.

"We wait."

"For what?"

"When that crew of engineers you hired to put in the escape tunnel on those plans the council approved shows up, they'll dig us out."

He wished he had a camera to record the sick look on Pershing's face. "Well, now, about that crew . . ." He swallowed, his Adam's apple bobbing, and a fine sheen of sweat shone on his forehead.

"There isn't one, is there?" Bob glared, though inside he was holding back a grin. He'd suspected for a while now that Pershing was concocting another swindle; nice to be proved right, though the circumstances were less than ideal.

"Um . . . no," Pershing admitted.

"What were you going to tell me—that they'd canceled?"

"I was going to say they needed more drawings and a geological survey."

Bob nodded. "I imagine that would cost a lot of money."

"At least another ten thousand dollars."

The man had solid-brass balls, Bob would give him that. "How much of that would end up in your pocket?" he asked.

"You don't understand. I have obligations to meet, debts. My ex-wife was talking about court action if I didn't pay her the money I owed, and a former business partner made certain threats I couldn't ignore. I had investors expecting payments, and a certain lifestyle to maintain. I was going to pay it all back once the mine started producing."

Bob glanced up at the ceiling. What he really wanted to do was grab a good-sized rock and attempt to knock some sense into this old fool. But that probably wasn't possible, though he might be able to scare him onto the straight and narrow—at least temporarily. "Good thing you had that extra ventilation put in," he said. "At least we won't suffocate."

Gerald put his head in his hands and moaned.

"One of those falling rocks hit you?" Bob asked.

"I only had half as many ventilation outlets installed as were on the plans I submitted to the town council," he said.

Half was probably plenty, Bob thought, but let Pershing sweat. "You know how to work every swindle, don't you?" he said. "Guess you'll pay for it now."

"What do you mean?"

"Maybe a rescue crew will get here before we run out of air. I guess we'll find out." He folded his arms across his chest and closed his eyes.

"Are you just going to sit there doing nothing?" Pershing asked.

"What do you think I should do instead?"

"Dig. Try to summon help."

"You think we're going to bust through a wall of rock with our bare hands? And who's going to hear us way down here?"

Pershing rose to his knees and began pulling aside the rubble around him. "We might be able to break through if we both work. We can't just sit here and wait to die."

"I'm not waiting to die. I'm waiting for the rescuers. Someone will notice me missing eventually."

Pershing stilled, and for once he was silent. But he didn't have to say anything for Bob to read his thoughts—no one would miss the old swindler. "You don't think we should at least try to dig out?" he asked after a long moment.

"All that work uses up oxygen faster, and it's a waste of time and energy. They'll need heavy machinery to get us out."

Pershing slumped back against the wall. "Isn't there anything we can do?"

"You might try apologizing to the Tommyknockers."

"There is no such thing as Tommyknockers!" Pershing's shout echoed in the small space, and another chunk of rock broke loose from overhead and glanced off his shoulder.

Bob laughed. "They do have a sense of humor." He switched off his headlamp and tried to get comfortable on the hard floor.

"What are you doing?" Pershing demanded.

"I'm saving the battery."

Pershing said nothing and Bob dozed. He wasn't thrilled about being stuck down here, especially with Pershing, but there was no sense panicking. Somebody was going to notice when he didn't show up at the Dirty Sally, and he was supposed to give the town council a report tomorrow night. With luck, he and Pershing wouldn't strangle each other before then.

"Have you been trapped in a mine before?"

Gerald's words cut the profound silence and jerked Bob out of a hazy half sleep. He opened his eyes but could see nothing in the blackness.

If not for the sharp rock at his back, he could imagine he was floating in nothingness. Disconcerting, but not unpleasant.

"I said—have you been trapped in a mine accident before?"

"I heard you. Yes, I've been caught once. In 1967. I hadn't been in the business long." And he hadn't thought about that time for years. He had been so young and sure of himself in those days; only now, looking back, he saw how foolish he'd been.

"What happened?" Pershing asked.

"Another fellow and I were working for a bigger outfit, taking ore out of a shaft on the back side of a mountain. I got lazy. Greedy. I thought I'd cut corners on safety to get at the ore quicker, and I almost killed us both." He closed his eyes. He could still see the other man, his face gray and silent, when they dug him out from the rubble, both legs crushed. He'd never work a mine again. Bob wondered if the man was still alive. He'd worked hard to forget the guy, and his own part in the accident, but of course he never had. Guilt was like that. You could push it down below the surface, but it always rose up again, like a body filled with gas.

"Then that had nothing to do with your mythical Tommyknockers," Pershing said.

"It had everything to do with Tommyknockers," Bob said. "They don't like cheaters and they don't care for greed. Wanting gold is one thing, but cheating other people to get it doesn't set well with them. They punished me for it."

"Your carelessness caused the accident, not spirits."

"If you don't believe in spirits, do you believe in the concept of karma?"

"The idea that everyone gets what he deserves? Just look around at all the good people who suffer and you'll see that's a joke."

"You don't believe you'll reap what you sow? Maybe all those suffering good people get a higher reward in the next life."

"I don't believe in that either."

"What do you believe in?"

"The power of the individual to make his own destiny," he said without hesitation.

"Even if that means stepping on other people and taking advantage of them?"

"If they're naïve enough to be taken in by a scam, they'll learn a lesson and be smarter next time."

"And you'll be long gone, spending your ill-gotten gains. Or maybe you'll end up rotting at the bottom of a mine shaft, the victim of the shortcuts you took."

Silence. Nothing like contemplating his own death to shut up a man. Bob closed his eyes again. He believed someone would come for them, but what if the collapse was worse than he thought and rescuers couldn't reach them in time? Was karma deciding that he should die in the company of a man he detested? Had the sins he'd committed in his life—and he could admit there had been plenty, if mostly petty—doomed him to such a miserable end?

So be it. He'd passed by his "three score and ten" a couple years back, and though he'd imagined living to be a hundred or more, he supposed he couldn't complain. His only regret was the role he'd played in his own demise. He'd taken a risk, hiding all that ammo in a mine with the gunpowder and detonator rope. He hoped people didn't think he was some nutcase terrorist, planning to blow up the government or anything. He was just a miner, and he'd wanted enough supplies to keep practicing his trade even if the world went to hell in a handbasket.

"What do you care about the money I took anyway?"

Pershing again. The man could not go five minutes without the sound of his own voice. "You took that money from people I like and respect," Bob said.

"From Lucille, you mean. It isn't even her money. It belongs to the city. And I like and respect Lucille. She might even be the woman I've come closest to really loving. I never intended for her to take this so personally."

"You may know a lot about money, but you don't know jack about women," Bob said. "And I wasn't talking about Lucille in particular. I was talking about the town. You stole from Eureka. From the people who work for the town, and those who rely on it for services. You took a community's sense of trust and security. If it was up to me, they'd hang you up by your toes and let people take turns taking shots at you for that."

"Then I guess it's good that you don't make the laws."

"No, but I know the people who do." And now that Pershing had confessed to taking the city's money and pocketing it, he'd make sure the old fraud got what was coming to him.

"Are you threatening me?" Pershing asked.

"I wouldn't waste my breath."

Fraud or not, Pershing wasn't a dummy. It took about two seconds for him to realize what Bob had in mind. Bob switched on his headlamp in time to see the Texan leaning over him with a large rock. The light blinded them both, but Pershing didn't have to see to feel the blade of Bob's knife against his throat. "I didn't have to dig you out of that rubble and I can put you back in there," Bob said.

Pershing dropped the rock and backed away. When he reached the wall, he slid down to a sitting position again. Bob kept the light on and studied the other man. "Do you really think they'll find us?" Pershing asked.

"Unless the Tommyknockers don't want us found."

Pershing winced, but made no protest. Bob took his first really good look around the chamber where they were trapped. The space was maybe eight feet on each side, the ceiling too low for a man to stand upright. Where the rock had sheared off in the explosion, the walls were a sandy beige color, mica sparkling in the light from his lamp. Jagged timbers showed like broken teeth in the ceiling, and a tumble of rock, dirt, and broken wood clogged the only exit.

Bob tilted his head back to aim the light up. A dark, heavy beam spanned the chamber—the only thing that had saved them from being crushed. Alongside the beam, chunks of rock had broken loose and fallen, revealing a six-inch-wide band of quartz. Bob's heart beat a little faster as he stood and walked over for a closer look at this find.

"What is it?" Pershing stood also and joined him in looking up at the beam. "Is it a way out? Can we dig to the surface?"

"Can you dig through twenty or more feet of solid rock?" Bob reached up and scratched at the quartz, then shone the light again. A bright glint on the surface of the white quartz made him grin.

"What is it?" Pershing demanded.

"Gold." With the tip of his knife, Bob chipped at the quartz and succeeded in dislodging a chunk about the size of his knuckle. He held it between his thumb and forefinger, admiring the shine. "Way more than I ever thought this old mine would yield. It could be our luck hasn't run out yet after all."

Chapter 16

"I'm just saying that, with Bob and Gerald trapped in the mine and everyone focused on that, maybe we should postpone the wedding." Maggie shifted on the hard bar stool at the Dirty Sally. Her back hurt, her feet were swollen, she had indigestion, and she was sure she looked like hell. She had intended to have this discussion with Jameso at home, but as with everything else in her life these days, things hadn't gone as planned and she'd ended up blurting out the idea in the saloon, where Jameso was stuck working a double shift to serve the influx of rescue workers, reporters, and curious hangers-on who'd flooded into town to cover the tragedy.

"We're getting married Saturday morning." Jameso lined up three pint glasses on the bar and began filling them from the tap. "Your due date is Monday. I want to be able to tell my daughter that her parents were married *before* she was born."

"A due date isn't exact. It doesn't mean I'm going to have the baby then." Maggie put a hand to her back and winced. Frankly, she was over being pregnant and wouldn't mind if her little girl decided to make an entrance early. "And it doesn't matter anyway. You're the father, and that's what the birth certificate will say."

He released the tap handle and looked her in the eye. "It's important to me. Isn't that enough?"

"Of course, I just thought it would be easier this way."

"I don't care about easier. Easier would be going to the courthouse in Montrose and letting a judge make us legal. But we can get married with everyone who cares about us on Saturday. Here in Eureka. I don't want to wait."

Clearly, there was no sense arguing the point with him. "Fine," she said. "When you get a chance, could you bring me a ginger ale?"

"What do you look so glum about?" Barb, the few strands of blond hair escaping from her updo the only sign that she was frazzled, joined Maggie and Jameso at the bar. "You don't have anything to be glum about. You're going to have a beautiful baby and you're getting married in three days."

"Maggie thinks we should put off the wedding because of everything that's going on at the mine." Jameso set the three beers on a tray.

"You have to have the wedding Saturday," Barb said. "It's the only way I'll get Chris Amesbury out of my bed-and-breakfast. He promised to be gone by then because I told him he's in the honeymoon suite. If you don't have the wedding Saturday, he'll never leave."

"We're not putting off the wedding." She gratefully accepted a glass of ginger ale from Jameso. "It was just an idea. It just feels so strange, with all these strangers in town—including Amesbury."

"The man looks at everyone here like we're exhibits in a zoo." Barb slid onto a stool next to Maggie. "I've stopped changing his sheets and I'm limiting his fresh towels, hoping he'll get the message and pack up."

"What does the mayor think of you hassling the town's guest of honor?" Maggie asked.

"My mother wishes she'd never heard the name Chris Amesbury." Olivia deposited a tray of empty beer bottles and glasses in a bus tub behind the bar. "Now that he's decided to put his reality show idea on hold in favor of a documentary about the mine explosion, he's even more annoying."

"The Eureka Mine Disaster." Maggie snagged a pretzel from the bowl at the end of the bar. "Just what Lucille wants the public to associate with the town."

"Amesbury asked me this morning if I could find him half a dozen donkeys to use in his film," Barb said.

"Donkeys?" Maggie ate another pretzel.

"You know, those burros miners used to use to haul equipment and ore and stuff," Barb said. "He thought it would be 'quaint' to re-create a scene of an early miner for his movie. I told him that, present company excepted, I did not normally associate with jackasses."

"Oh, Barb." Olivia laughed. "You're too much."

"Speaking of mines and miners, what's the latest word from the Lucky Lady?" Barb asked.

"They think they know where the men are trapped, but there's no way to communicate with them to know if they're okay," Maggie said. "They've got crews working around the clock to move rock and try to get to them."

"I never thought I'd say this, but I miss Bob," Olivia said. "This place isn't the same without him holding up the bar every afternoon."

"If anyone can make it through something like this, it will be Bob." Jameso opened the cash register and stuffed in a handful of bills. "He's too stubborn to die."

"Yes, but can you imagine being trapped for two days with Gerald Pershing?" Olivia made a face. "If they survived the explosion and cave-in, they might have killed each other by now."

"Do they know what caused the explosion?" Barb asked.

"Rick heard they found in one of the side tunnels enough ammunition and powder to start a small war," Maggie said.

"That was Bob's survival supplies," Olivia said. "He also had a bunch of canned food and

311

bottles of water. He used to say civilization was going to hell in a handbasket, but he wasn't going to go with it."

"Mainly, I think he liked the idea of being prepared for anything," Jameso said.

"One of the investigators told Rick they think an animal got into the explosives and accidentally set them off," Maggie said.

"Maybe when he gets out, he'll decide to take up a less dangerous hobby," Barb said.

"I just hope when they get out, Gerald Pershing decides to leave town for good," Maggie said.

"You can't say Gerald hasn't done something good for the town, in a roundabout way." Barb crunched on her own pretzel. "Business is booming with all these people around. I could rent out every room of the B and B if I had beds to put them in."

"When are those mattresses arriving?" Olivia asked.

Barb shrugged. "I'm not sure. But really, I'm just as happy not to have to deal with guests until after the wedding."

"You do realize that running a bed-and-breakfast is all about dealing with guests, don't you?" Maggie nudged her friend. "It's not just decorating and menu planning."

"But those are the fun parts. Changing sheets and fetching ice are the drudge work. I'm not a drudge work kind of person."

"That would be me." Olivia hefted a full tray of drinks. "One drudge coming through."

The door to the saloon opened and Lucille slipped in. She removed her sunglasses and searched the room, then headed toward Maggie and Barb. "So this is where everyone interesting is hiding," she said. "Have you seen Reggie? He's not in his office."

"I thought I saw him earlier," Barb said. "Headed out of town on that Harley of his."

"Probably avoiding me." Lucille nudged Barb. "You're little. Share your bar stool with me."

"Notice she didn't ask me," Maggie said.

Barb moved over and Lucille leaned against the stool. "Why would Reggie be avoiding you?" Barb asked.

"Every half hour I have a new question for him about the town's liability, in case Gerald or Bob decides to sue."

"Bob wouldn't sue, would he?" Maggie asked.

"It's not Bob I'm so worried about. But if Gerald smells money, he'll go after it."

"Maybe you won't have to worry about that." Maggie drained the last of her ginger ale and pushed the glass aside. "In fact, you might be the one suing Gerald when this is all over with."

"Oh?" Lucille leaned toward her. "What have you heard?"

"Nothing official, but Rick and I have been talking to the investigators and rescue crews, and some things don't add up. I haven't had a chance to compare the plans Gerald drew up for the town council with the map of the mine the rescuers are using, but just from memory, some things are missing."

"Like the emergency exit the engineers were supposed to install," Lucille said. "It could be they hadn't gotten around to that yet."

"The town had to put up money for a bunch of safety improvements to the mine, right?" Maggie asked. She'd written the story for the paper, so she knew coming up with the money had been a hardship.

"Yes," Lucille said. "An emergency exit and more ventilation, things like that. There have been engineers and crews up there for weeks, working on everything."

"They were doing some work, but I don't think they were doing everything you paid for," Maggie said. "Charlie told me he didn't see any sign of ongoing work—to him it looked like everything had been done that was going to be done. Which sounds like they never had any intention of installing that emergency exit."

"But they must have known we'd do a final inspection before we paid," Lucille said. "And their liability would be extreme. No one from the company has bothered to contact me, despite the fact that the mine collapse has been all over the news."

"Maybe they've been paid everything that was owed them," Maggie said. "And maybe they weren't hired to oversee the safety of the mine, but just to do a few specific jobs—enough for Gerald to string the town council along and keep asking for more money."

"And Gerald kept the rest." Lucille made two fists. "I will kill him. I don't care who hears me say that."

"You can't hurt him physically," Maggie said. "Better to go after him where it really hurts—in his pocketbook."

"I'm missing something here," Barb said. "What happened?"

"The town paid Gerald our half of the cost of all the improvements to the mine," Lucille said. "Instead of using the money to pay for the work, he pocketed it, or at least most of it."

"Talk about your own greed coming back to bite you in the butt," Barb said.

"Trust me, when they haul him out of that mine, we will be pressing charges," Lucille said. She leaned against the bar, head in her hands. "Honestly, I can't decide if this makes me feel better or worse."

"Wasn't Bob supposed to be overseeing Gerald?" Maggie asked. "I mean, you just didn't hand the money over to him, right?"

"Yes, Bob was supposed to be overseeing him," Lucille said. "And despite his eccentricities, Bob does know a lot about mining. He tried to hold Gerald's feet to the fire, but Gerald is very good at talking a lot and saying nothing. Whenever Bob pressed him for results, Gerald always had an excuse—the contractors were slow, the engineers needed more information, etcetera, etcetera."

"He was stringing you along," Barb said.

"Yes, and we had the sense to refuse to pay him any more until we got results, but still, he pocketed a good amount."

"So you sue him," Barb said. "If Reggie doesn't want to handle it, I know a few good lawyers."

"I'll keep that in mind. Meanwhile, let's talk about a more pleasant topic of conversation. Are you ready for the wedding?"

"I don't know," Maggie said. "I was thinking maybe we should put it off until things are calmer."

"We're not putting it off," Jameso said as he walked by on his way to deliver a tray of drinks to a table full of reporters.

Barb leaned closer and spoke in a low voice. "What's wrong?" she asked. "Are you getting cold feet?"

No, she had swollen feet. She loved Jameso and she definitely wanted to marry him. She just didn't necessarily want to do it right now. "It's a little overwhelming. The baby and marriage all at once," she said.

Barb patted her hand. "You'll do all right. You and Jameso are already living together and that's worked out okay, hasn't it?"

"Yes, I hadn't planned on that either; but when his sister showed up, we couldn't put her on the street. But the house is really too small, and my dad's cabin is even smaller. How are we ever going to manage with the baby?"

"You still haven't found a place to move to?" Lucille asked.

"Eve Fairview with Eureka County Realty thinks she's found something for us, but it's quite a ways out of town. Still, at this point we can't be too picky." She tipped up the pretzel bowl and peered at it hopefully. Empty.

"Don't sign a lease for something that isn't right," Barb said. "I might have a lead on something."

"What?" Maggie asked. "Where?"

Barb waved away the questions. "Never mind. I'll tell you when I know something definite. Just don't be in such a rush."

"Barb, I'm getting married on Saturday and I have a baby due Monday. I don't think I'm rushing."

"Fine. Don't think of it as rushing," Barb said. "Think of it as right on time. You'll find your house when the time is right, too." She snagged Jameso as he passed with a bus tub full of empties. "Be a dear and bring me a Bombay sapphire and tonic when you get a chance."

"Nice to see at least one of you ladies came to the bar to drink," he said.

"I came here because you're here," Maggie said.

He leaned over and kissed her cheek. "You're exactly where you belong." The soft brush of his beard against her skin sent a pleasant shiver up her spine. The baby kicked and she put her hand to her belly to soothe it and smiled. The agitation she'd felt when she'd come in here in search of him had dissipated like an afternoon thunderstorm, giving way to a feeling of deep contentment. For so many years she'd been searching for the place where she belonged, where she fit. To think she'd found it here in this quirky, remote town.

Still smiling, she looked out onto the crowd of familiar and unfamiliar faces, and spotted Sharon working her way toward them. She wore an expression Maggie recognized—that of a woman determined to hold herself together. She was lost and uncertain, but determined not to show it. Exactly how Maggie had felt when she'd arrived in Eureka last year. She thought at the time she'd done a good job of hiding her uncertainty, of appearing competent and content to those around her. But now she judged herself a fraud. She'd been balancing on the edge; one slip and it was breakdown city.

She rose to greet Sharon and took her by the

arm. "What is it?" she asked softly. "What's wrong?"

Sharon's eyes met hers, and for a brief moment Maggie glimpsed such sadness and despair. Then she blinked and Sharon had rallied. She gently pushed Maggie's hand away. "I need to talk to Jameso," she said.

Maggie turned to call him, but he was already there. "What is it?" he demanded, in that direct way men had that could be, in spite of its brusqueness, comforting in its strength.

"The police in Vermont found Joe." Sharon's voice had the flat affect of someone who has worked hard to strip all emotion from her words. "But they didn't find Adan."

People surrounded Sharon and led her to a chair at a table near the bar. Someone put a drink in her hand—something dark and potent that she swallowed without question. She yielded, disconnected from herself, from the grief and fear that threatened to overwhelm her. Jameso put a hand on her shoulder and bent to look her in the eye. "Tell me what happened," he commanded.

"Someone from the Orleans County Sheriff's Department called and asked to speak to me. He said they'd located Joseph Franklin, but that there were no minors living with him. According to Joe, Adan left over a week ago, and Joe has no idea where he's gone." The words sounded so foreign, as if she were discussing some other

319

Joseph Franklin, a stranger or a character in a television show.

"Adan left?" Jameso scowled. "Do you mean he ran away?"

"The police seem to think so. They wanted to know if I'd heard from him." She hugged her arms across her chest, wishing she could squeeze out the fear that threatened to overwhelm her. "I can't believe Joe didn't tell me. I'm Adan's mother. I have a right to know."

"Why did he leave?" Maggie asked. "Do they know where he was headed?"

"Joe wouldn't tell them anything. I know how he can be. He clams up around authorities, or he starts spouting off about his rights."

"So the police are just guessing?" Jameso's voice rose in anger. "Are they charging Joe with anything in connection with the boy's disappearance?"

"I guess they questioned the others—Wilson and the Russians and a couple of other hangers-on they picked up. They all said Adan left last Saturday morning. He and Joe had argued over something, though no one would say what the argument was about."

"Sharon!" She looked up and Josh Miller was there, his Stetson slightly crooked on his head, the fine lines around his eyes deepened by concern. "I just heard the news about Adan," he said. "I'm sorry."

"Thank you," she said, and had to look away from the kindness in his eyes. Everyone was being so kind, going out of their way to avoid blaming her for what had happened. But she couldn't push away the guilt so easily.

"Can you tell us more about what happened?" Jameso asked Josh.

"It took me a few calls to find out what little I know," Josh said. "That's why I wasn't here sooner. I was hoping to have some good information for you."

"What did you find out?" she asked.

"Not much. Joe and his followers had hooked up with another bunch of hard-core preppers and were squatting on National Forest land up near the Canadian border. The deputy I talked to said it was pretty rough conditions: tents and an old camper, though they were cutting timber—illegally, of course—to build some cabins. Joe had already rubbed some of the others the wrong way, and he and Adan had some clashes. The next thing everybody knew, Adan had packed a backpack and headed out."

"Didn't Joe try to stop him?" Sharon asked.

"The others said he didn't." Josh moved closer to her. "Do you have any idea where he might go? Do you have any relatives in the area? Friends?"

She shook her head. "Neither Joe nor I are close to our parents. The children weren't in school, and we lived away from children their own age." She grabbed her purse and pulled out her cell phone. "I gave Adan a phone before I left. I've been calling and calling, but it always goes straight to voice mail and I never get an answer."

"He might have lost the phone, or left it behind," Josh said. "They're looking for Adan." Josh squeezed her shoulder. "They'll find him."

She wanted to believe him but couldn't. Anything could happen to a fifteen-year-old boy, on his own among strangers. Adan knew a lot about hunting and fishing and living off the land, but he'd been sheltered from things other kids his age knew about, such as how to drive a car or navigate in a city.

"If you want me to go up there and look myself, I will," Jameso said.

This declaration brought a lump to her throat. She took his hand and squeezed it, unable to speak. Part of her did want him to do just that, but she still had it together enough to realize the foolishness of this. Jameso had never lived in Vermont. He didn't know the area or the people. And he had obligations here.

"No," she said after a moment. "You're getting married in a few days. And your baby will be born soon. You need to stay here. With your family."

"You're my family, too." His voice was rough

with emotion. "I know I haven't always acted like it, but I love you. And I hate anyone who would hurt you."

Something gave way within her at those words —a restraint that had been binding for too long fell away. This is why she'd come to Eureka, what she'd driven all the way across the country to hear. She hugged his neck and pulled him close. "You're a good brother," she said. "And I love you for wanting to help me, even if you can't. No one can. All I can do is wait."

"Then we'll wait with you." Maggie patted her arm.

She looked at Maggie, her face flushed and her body rounded with the promise of new life; at Jameso, torn between anger and dismay; then at Josh, all concern and tenderness and the same powerlessness she felt.

In leaving Vermont, Sharon had lost her son, though she prayed not for forever. But she'd gained a new family and a second chance, here in Eureka. That had to count for something, and when she did find Adan again, he'd be a part of that family. She wouldn't give up hope for him, or for herself.

Chapter 17

"I'm really sorry about your brother," Lucas said after he rode over to Alina's house the next morning. In ripped jeans and a baggy T-shirt, his hair drooping into his eyes, he reminded her so much of Adan she wanted to cry.

But she'd done enough crying. Her eyes felt like they had sand in them from crying so much last night. But this morning she just felt—numb. She drooped against the door frame. "Yeah, it sucks," she said. Missing Adan had been the worst thing about coming to Eureka, but she'd always been able to think of him safe at home with their dad—only a phone call or a plane ride away. Not knowing where he was, or if he was even safe, left a whole different void in her heart, a jagged pain that couldn't be soothed.

"If you don't want to paint today, that's okay," he said.

"Painting sounds good." She straightened. "I need to do something and I don't want to be alone."

He waited while she retrieved her bike; then they pedaled slowly toward Main. "If you want to talk about it, that's okay," Lucas said. "But if you'd rather not, that's cool, too."

She didn't know what she wanted. "It just . . . it doesn't seem real. I mean, I haven't seen him or even talked to him in weeks, so I'd kind of gotten used to not having him around. But still, I always knew he was there. I could have picked up the phone and called him if I wanted."

But she hadn't called him. She'd been too afraid he hadn't wanted her. After all, her father hadn't said a word against her going away, and Adan wanted so much to be like their dad. He talked like their father and chose to stay in the woods with him instead of coming to Colorado with Alina and her mother. As if he didn't care. She bit the inside of her cheek hard, tasting blood. But it was better than letting loose a flood of useless tears again.

"Do they know what happened?" Lucas asked.

She shook her head. "Mom said the police think he and Dad argued, and Adan either left on his own or Dad sent him away." Her voice broke and she swallowed hard. Where would Adan have gone? How could her brother have just disappeared?

Lucas looked miserable, as if he might cry himself. "I wish there was something I could do," he said.

"Just hanging out with me is good." She took a deep breath and felt a little steadier. "It helps, having something else to think about. So, what are we going to paint today?"

"Mom said we should do that old shed out back. I don't think she trusts me with anything inside the house; but it'll be more fun being outside anyway. But I've got a surprise for you first."

"Oh?" Lucas's surprises were good.

"Yeah, I took your advice and put out a bunch of flour around the windows and table and counters." His expression cleared and he was once again the eager Lucas she was used to. "I had to wait until Mom wasn't around. I thought I could get out there and clean it up with D. J.'s shop vac before she found out."

"Where did you get the flour?"

"From my grandma's pantry. That's another thing—I need to stop on the way home and buy another bag to replace it."

"Did you get any footprints?"

"I haven't checked yet. I thought we could do that together."

"Cool." She pedaled harder, surging ahead, but he raced to catch up. They turned onto Main, past the Last Dollar, where Danielle waved from the front porch; past the Dirty Sally, closed at this hour. Flowers bloomed in yards along Oak Street, and an apple tree was studded with dozens of little green fruit, like tennis balls tied to the branches.

They slowed and pumped hard to climb the hill up Fourth, breathing hard, muscles straining. The exertion felt good, all that blood flowing letting some of the sadness burn off. At the top, they each took their feet from the pedals at the same time and coasted down the long incline, the cool air blowing through her hair.

They turned onto Pinion and skidded the turn into the drive of Lucas's house. Next door, Reverend Kinkaid looked up from tending his vegetable garden, then walked over to greet them. "Good morning," he said. He wore khakis and a faded T-shirt advertising a barbecue place, Hog Heaven. The shirt made her want to giggle, but she managed to keep a straight face.

"Good morning," she said.

"I was very sorry to hear about your brother, Alina," he said.

"Uh, thank you."

"If there is anything I can do to help you or your family, let me know."

"Thanks. Right now we're just waiting to see what happens next."

"I'll be praying for you."

"Thanks." She wasn't sure if she believed in prayer, but it was kind of nice, thinking of other people petitioning God for her. It couldn't hurt, right?

She and Lucas left their bikes by the front steps and went into the house, which was unlocked. "How does everybody already know about my brother?" she asked. "How did you know?"

"I heard it from my mom, who heard it from Jameso at the Dirty Sally." He shoved a ladder to the side so they could get to the kitchen. "Reverend Kinkaid probably heard it from someone who was there, too."

"How are things going up at the mine?" She felt bad for not asking before. "Have they found the guys that are trapped yet?"

"Not yet. D. J. is helping, running a back hoe to dig."

She hugged her arms across her chest and shivered. "I can't imagine being trapped underground like that. Like being buried alive."

"We hope they're alive anyway." He picked up a glass doorknob, the old-fashioned, faceted kind. "Mom found these at Grandma's store. She wants to put them on all the interior doors."

"They're like big jewels." She picked up another knob and held it as she looked around the room. Lucas's mom had painted a geometric border near the top of the high ceilings. Oak wainscoting and refinished hardwood floors added to the look of something old that had been made new. "This is a beautiful room," she said.

"It'll be our living room. And these steps go up to the bedrooms. Four of them."

"And you'll have the tower to yourself," she said. "Like your own apartment."

"They're letting me fix it up like I want. One

room's going to be my bedroom and the other a kind of study and workshop, with tables and my PlayStation and stuff. We can go up there after we check the flour."

The flour. She'd almost forgotten. She set the doorknob aside. "Do you think we'll find anything?"

"Let's find out." He pushed open the door into the kitchen.

The kitchen looked the way her bathroom had when she'd dropped a whole box of dusting powder once. White covered the floor and most of the table and countertops, as well as the tools, scraps of lumber, paint cans, and assorted construction debris that littered the room. "It's going to take you forever to clean this up," Alina said as she followed him into the room, their tennis shoes leaving tracks in the flour.

"Look!" He pointed to a pair of much smaller footprints in the flour. About four inches long, with distinct toes.

"Oh my gosh!" Alina stared at the trail of prints across the table. "What do you think made them?" Definitely not a ghost, but an animal of some kind.

"I have a book. Let me get it." He turned and raced from the room.

Of course he had a book. She smiled. He was such a geek. The kind of guy you'd want to be stranded on a desert island with. He'd know how to build a raft, which plants you could eat, and stuff like that.

"I think it's a raccoon." He returned, the book open. "Look."

She studied the page he pointed to, which showed tracks very like the ones in the flour. "It says they're attracted to small objects," he read.

"Look, he went out the window." She pointed to the trail of white footprints leading across to the window.

"Maybe we can follow it." Lucas closed the book and laid it on top of a paint can.

They raced outside and around the house. At first, Alina thought they'd lost the trail; then she spotted a smudge of white. "The flour stuck to the grass in places," she said.

Bent at the waist, eyes focused on the ground, they followed the trail of flour to the leaning shed in the back corner of the yard. Covered in board and batten siding like the house, the shed was gray with age and slanted a little to one side. The door stood open and Alina could see a jumble of boxes, tools, and what looked like trash filling the small space.

"It doesn't look like anyone's used this for decades," she said.

"The raccoon's been using it." Lucas walked around the side and pointed to a broken window. Flour dotted the sill below the broken pain. "I think he went in here."

She leaned toward the window, careful to keep her distance, in case the raccoon decided to jump out suddenly. "It's too dark to see anything in there," she said.

"I'll get a flashlight."

He ran toward the house, long legs stretched out, tennis shoes making muffled thumps in the weeds. Alina waited in the shade. She was curious to know what they'd find in the shed, but not as excited as Lucas. That was okay. Watching him get excited was almost as much fun as being excited herself.

He returned a few moments later with the flashlight and shone it through the window. The first thing Alina saw was a big spider web. She drew back. "I really don't like spiders," she said.

"They won't hurt you. At least, most of them won't." He shone the light on the web. "It doesn't look like anyone's home. Come on. Let's go inside."

She followed him to the door of the shed but hung back, letting him dive in first. He shoved aside an old lawnmower, a bookcase, and a stack of boxes, until he reached the section of the shed beneath the broken window. When he shoved the last box aside, he shone the light down onto a kind of nest. Alina braced herself to flee an angry raccoon, but the animal was nowhere in sight.

"Maybe he just uses this for storage," Lucas

said. He bent and retrieved a piece of shiny metal from the pile of detritus piled on a faded quilt. "This is my mom's key fob that went missing a couple months ago."

While she watched, Lucas sorted through a pile of screws, a teaspoon, a door handle that matched the ones on the kitchen cabinets, thirty-three cents in change, and a bunch of other small, metallic objects the raccoon had apparently collected.

"There's a hole in the wall," she said.

Lucas shifted his attention to the hole. "Funny, it doesn't look like an animal gnawed it," he said. "It looks like someone cut it out on purpose."

He bent and shone the flashlight into the space. "There's something here."

"More raccoon treasure?" she asked.

He reached in and pulled out a blackened object, about the size of a paperback book. "It's a purse," he said. "One of those fancy ones."

"An evening purse," Alina said. She reached out and Lucas handed her the object. The black was tarnish—the purse had once been silver. It was heavy, covered all over with little silver scales. What might have been jewels trimmed the frame and the clasp. "I'll bet this was really fancy a long time ago," she said.

"Do you think someone put it in the wall to hide it from thieves or something?"

She fumbled with the clasp but was able to force it open. The purse was lined in blue satin, surprisingly bright and clean. "There's papers in here. Letters."

She tugged out one small, square envelope, covered in spidery writing.

"That stamp looks old." Lucas looked over her shoulder. His eyes behind his glasses grew wide. "What does it say?"

Alina carefully took out a single sheet of stationery and unfolded it. The page was brittle, and the spidery writing was faded. "I can't read it," she said. "We need a magnifying glass or something. And better light."

"I have a magnifying glass up in my room," he said. "We can go there."

She tucked the letter back into the envelope. "First, we'd better clean up that mess in the kitchen. And then we have to paint the shed."

He looked as if he was about to argue, but finally nodded. "My mom will have kittens if she comes in and sees flour everywhere. And even D. J. will be upset if I don't paint the shed, after I begged him to let me."

Alina patted the purse. "This will give us something to look forward to." The letters would probably turn out to be nothing important, but they would be one more distraction from her real-life problems, better than TV or home-work.

• • •

When Lucille walked into the Last Dollar and saw Chris Amesbury occupying the front booth, she was tempted to turn and leave. The director had managed to annoy and/or offend almost everyone in town, and at least half of them had complained to the mayor about his presence.

But she wasn't a coward, and she'd learned long ago that ignoring a problem didn't make it go away. So she hitched her purse more firmly onto her shoulder and strode to his table. "May I join you, Mr. Amesbury?" she asked.

He looked up from the remains of his lunch special (BLT and homemade potato salad) and blinked, like someone coming out of a doze. "Oh, hello, Mayor Theriot."

"May I join you?" she asked again.

"Uh, sure." He hastened to move aside a pile of notebooks.

"What can I get for you, Lucille?" Danielle stopped beside their table. She wore a peasant blouse and a flowered jumper. With her hair in twin ponytails, she looked like a milk maid, or possibly the buxom model on the label of a German beer.

"The special is fine. And iced tea."

"Save room for blackberry cobbler," she said. "I made it this morning." She turned to Amesbury. "Would you like some dessert?"

"Could I persuade you to feed it to me?" He

gave her what he probably thought was a win-some smile.

"One pie in the face, coming right up." She winked at Lucille and moved away.

"I can't believe someone so lovely is hidden away here in the mountains," he said.

"You do know Danielle is already involved with someone else," Lucille said.

"You mean Janelle?" He waved his hand as if brushing aside this bit of information. "I'm a very open-minded kind of guy. I don't mind sharing."

Just when she thought he couldn't get any more loathsome. She cleared her throat. "I didn't mean to interrupt your lunch," she said. "You look absorbed in your work."

He nibbled a crust and rested an open palm on the stack of notebooks. "I'm just trying to work out on paper how best to present this story."

"Which story is that?" Was he still stuck on his reality TV idea, or was he focused on the rescue drama?

"I'm thinking of tweaking the reality show idea to make it more of a modern-day gold-mining story," he said. "I mean, we still have the hipsters, and we still put them together in rustic accommodations, only this time, they're hunting gold. There's enough old mines around here I figure we could probably even stage somebody being trapped in one. That would really pull in the viewers."

"But if you stage something, then it's not really reality TV, is it?" Not to mention the liability involved in a stunt like that.

"Oh, they'd be really trapped. What I can't figure out is how to make the rescue really dramatic."

"I'm not following."

"I've been spending a lot of time up at the Lucky Lady, thinking it would be good to capture the rescue proceedings on film. But there's so little going on—a little digging, a lot of standing around."

"What did you think would happen?" she asked.

"I don't know . . . dynamite. Grieving wives and wailing children. Fighting mistresses. You know—drama."

She tried to hold back laughter, but in the end it was impossible.

"What's so funny?" he asked.

"I'm sorry," she said between gasps of laughter. "It's just that I know the two men who are in the mine and neither of them is the type to induce that kind of reaction from the people in their lives."

"So I gather. And hey, that must be hell, being trapped under there. I hope everything turns out all right. But some young dude with three chicks fighting over him would make for much better TV."

She thought about reassuring him they'd try to do better next time, but suspected the sarcasm would be lost on him. And she had a more pressing matter to broach with him. "Otherwise, are you enjoying your stay in Eureka?" she asked, as Danielle delivered her lunch.

"Pretty much. The food is great and the bartenders at the Dirty Sally pour a mean drink. But my hostess at the B and B has let me know I've worn out my welcome. She needs my room for a pair of honeymooners or something." He snorted. "As if anybody comes here for a honeymoon."

"I believe the couple live here in town and plan to spend their wedding night at the inn," Lucille said.

"Well, I told her not to get her panties in a knot. I plan on checking out in a couple of days. I thought I'd stick around and see if anything interesting happened when they pull those two old guys out of the mine."

"So, will you head back to Hollywood?" Perhaps permanently?

"I'm going to have to meet with my producers. No offense, but I'm not sure Eureka is really what I'm looking for with this show. It's a little too, well, comfortable."

A mouthful of BLT saved her from having to

reply to that, though she was silently thanking God for this change of heart. Sad as she was to see the town lose the money a television show might have brought in, she couldn't help thinking they'd be better off without a Hollywood invasion.

Janelle came to take Amesbury's empty dishes and leave his check. "Any news from the mine?" she asked Lucille.

"The last I heard they'd pinpointed the location where they think Bob and Gerald are trapped," she said. "But the rock is still too thick to communicate."

"We're praying they're all right," Janelle said.

"Me too."

"I'm headed up there this afternoon." Amesbury slid out of the booth and gathered his notebooks. "Who knows? Maybe we'll all get lucky."

"He was hoping for a little more drama," Lucille explained when he was gone.

"He might get plenty," Janelle said. "After being trapped together for three days, I figure Bob and Gerald are either going to be best buddies, or they're going to come out brawling."

"If they haven't already done each other in." A customer entered and Janelle went to greet him while Lucille finished her meal. As long as she was praying for Bob and, yes, Gerald's safety, was it too much to ask for a break from any more town crises? She'd really love a truly relaxing summer for a change.

Olivia spent the morning painting a new series of T-shirts, since the shops in town were almost sold out of the others. Only yesterday, she'd finished a mural in the upstairs parlor of Barb's B and B, and the historical society wanted to talk to her about doing some restoration work at a building they were converting to a museum. If this kept up, she'd have to quit her job at the Dirty Sally. And D. J.'s job was going well. He'd transitioned from driving a snowplow this winter to running heavy equipment for the county this summer, hauling gravel and road base and, for the past few days anyway, helping with the rescue operation at the Lucky Lady. It was a good time to cut back a little.

She checked the clock and was surprised to find it was almost noon. Lucas and Alina were supposed to be out at the house, painting the shed. Not that she didn't trust her son, but it wouldn't hurt to check on those two.

Two bikes leaned against the railing of the front porch, and a check of the backyard revealed one freshly painted shed and two teenagers squirting each other with the water hose as they cleaned up their painting supplies. "The shed looks great," she called, and Lucas shut off the water.

"Hi, Mom," he said.

"Hi, Mrs. Theriot."

"Hi, Alina." The girl looked a little pale, but not bad, considering she'd just found out her brother was missing. Olivia had no idea if Alina and her brother were close, but still, that had to hurt.

"We know what's been taking your earrings and spoons and stuff," Lucas said.

"Please don't tell me it's a ghost." She followed the two kids up the back steps and into the kitchen.

"No, not a ghost. A raccoon."

"A raccoon?" She stared at her son and realized she had to look up. He was growing up too fast. "Are you sure?"

"We put flour all over the floor and it left tracks. Then we followed the tracks to the shed, where it's been hiding everything. We have it all, see?" He took an empty paint can from the counter and showed her the collection of missing items.

She plucked out the aspen leaf key fob and stared at it. No harm done. "But how is a raccoon getting into the house?" she asked.

"The sash on the kitchen window is really loose." He ran to the window and demonstrated how easy it was to raise it. "I think the raccoon just pushes it up and climbs in."

"I'll ask D. J. to nail it shut." Nothing against

340

raccoons, but they didn't belong in her kitchen. She pocketed the key fob. "I think you two detectives deserve lunch out. My treat."

"That's not the only mystery we solved today," Lucas said.

"Well, *maybe* solved," Alina said. "We don't know for sure." She glanced at Olivia. "We found a bunch of letters stuffed into an evening purse in the shed. I sneaked a peak at the address and the writing's awfully hard to read, but I think they might be written to Adelaide McCutcheon."

"You peeked?" Lucas said. "That's cheating."

"I'm not certain the letters are hers," Alina said. "I just looked for a second while you were in the bathroom earlier."

"If they're her letters, maybe they'll help us figure out what happened to her," Lucas said.

"Can I see?" Olivia asked.

"We'll show you at lunch, Mom." Lucas slung one arm around her shoulder. "I'm starved."

Chapter 18

As usual these days, the Last Dollar was crammed with tourists, media sent to cover the mine rescue and hungry locals. Olivia froze in the doorway, stomach heaving.

"Are you okay?" Danielle asked when she came to greet them. "You look a little pale."

"I'm sorry." Olivia covered her nose with her hand. The last thing she wanted was to insult Danielle or Janelle, but she couldn't help her reaction. "What is that smell?"

Danielle made a face. "Liver and onions. We sell out every time we make it, even though I know it smells strong." She touched Olivia's hand. "I can seat you by the front window—there's a nice breeze coming in and you'll hardly smell it there."

She nodded. "Okay. And bring me a Sprite."

"Are you coming down with something?" Lucas looked worried. "Maybe you've been working too hard."

"I'm fine." She forced a smile and took the chair closest to the open window. More than fine, really. "Let's take a look at these letters you found."

Alina opened the tarnished evening purse and

drew out a half-inch-thick bundle of letters. "Look, they have five-cent stamps." Lucas pointed to the canceled postage.

"You would notice the stamps." Alina slid a letter from one of the envelopes. "The writing is so loopy and small, I don't know if we can read it."

Danielle arrived with Olivia's soft drink. "What do you have there?" she asked.

"Some old letters we found," Alina said. "But we need a magnifying glass to read them."

"I think we have one of those up by the register. I'll check. What can I get y'all to drink?"

They ordered sodas and burgers—veggie for Alina—then leaned forward to study the spidery handwriting. "I think it's a love letter," Alina said. "See." She pointed to the words above the signature at the bottom of the missive. "I'm pretty sure that says 'all my love.' "

"Maybe she was writing her mother. Or her sister," Olivia said.

"But why save letters to your mother?" Alina asked. "I mean, I guess you could. But people usually save love letters, don't they?"

"I suppose some people do." Olivia had once burned all the letters D. J. had sent her from Iraq. The memory pained her, but she couldn't undo the past. Maybe the two of them were stronger because of that time apart; she hoped so. She sipped the soda, the bubbles settling her stomach, and watched out the window as a news van rolled slowly down the street.

"Have you heard anything from D. J.?" Lucas asked. "How's the rescue work coming?"

"Nothing new to report," she said. "I guess it's pretty slow going." She still couldn't believe Bob was trapped in the mine. The stubborn old coot had better not die on her. Who would she find to argue with at the Dirty Sally?

"I hope Bob's okay," Lucas said. "He was grouchy sometimes, but I kind of like him."

"You have a thing for grouchy old people, don't you?" she teased. He was one of the few people who got along with Cassie Wynock, though she'd never understand what he saw in the old bat.

"They usually have interesting stories." He pushed his glasses up on his nose.

"I'll bet these letters have an interesting story," Alina said. She frowned at the small pile of papers. "I just wish they weren't so hard to read. Why would anybody write that small?"

"Maybe she was trying to save paper," Lucas said.

"Maybe she was keeping a secret and didn't want anyone to know what she was writing," Alina said.

"Here are your drinks." Danielle delivered the sodas. "And a magnifying glass." She slipped the glass from her pocket and handed it to Lucas. "Your food will be out soon."

Lucas studied the magnifying glass while Alina spread the letter open on the table between them. The two put their heads together. *"My darling Andrew,"* Lucas read.

"Definitely a love letter," Alina said. "What did I tell you?"

"The hours apart from you stretch like years," Lucas continued. *"I don't know how I can bear it much longer."* He wrinkled his nose. "This is going to get mushy, isn't it?"

"Is Andrew her husband?" Olivia asked.

"No, his name was Cecil," Lucas said.

"Uh-huh." Alina leaned closer to the letter. "So who is Andrew?"

"Mr. McCutcheon's business takes him to Denver next week," Lucas read. *"I plan to take the train to Grand Junction to do some shopping."*

"She's letting Andrew know he can meet her there," Alina said.

"How do you know that?" Lucas asked. "She said she was going shopping."

"She couldn't come right out and say they should meet up—in case someone else found the letter and read it," Alina said. "But I'm sure that's what she means."

Lucas looked at his mother. "What do you think?"

"I think Alina could be right. What elsc does the letter say?"

He scanned the rest of the page. "Nothing

interesting. She asks him when he thinks he will be transferred to Montrose, and if he's found a house there yet."

Both young people looked to Olivia. "What do you think it means?" Alina asked the question this time.

"I don't know. Maybe they were planning to run away together."

"We can't find any mention of her in Eureka after 1966, so maybe they did run away," Alina said.

"Or maybe her husband found out and murdered her," Lucas said.

"Maybe you'll never know," Olivia said.

"I'll bet Miss Wynock can help us," Lucas said. "She knows how to research census records and stuff, for genealogy research. We could look for Adelaide and see if she and this Andrew guy ended up together."

"But we don't know Andrew's last name," Alina pointed out. "There's no return address on these letters."

"But we know her name and we can start with that," Lucas said. "I don't know why I didn't think of it before. Don't you think it's worth a shot?"

"I guess so." She shrugged. "It's better than sitting around all summer anyway."

Olivia wanted to reach over and brush the girl's hair out of her eyes, to pat her on the shoulder and offer sympathy. The poor kid had lost so much—her home and her brother and father. Olivia wanted to reassure her that life would get better—it almost always did. But when you were only thirteen it was hard to look very far down the road. When Olivia had been Alina's age she'd pretty much hated everyone—including herself. When she looked back at how awful she'd felt and behaved then, she was amazed she'd come so far.

She settled for tapping the back of Alina's hand. "If you start feeling too bad, remember you've got friends and people who love you," she said. "That helps."

Alina's eyes sparkled, but she held back the tears and nodded. "Yeah. Yeah, it does." She looked at the packet of letters. "Maybe that's all Adelaide wanted—to go somewhere she was loved."

"I think that's pretty much what we all want," Olivia said. What she'd been lucky enough to find. She hoped Alina had, too, even if she didn't quite believe it yet.

Worry over Adan ate at Sharon's gut and robbed her of sleep, but work was a welcome distraction. Cassie did not hover or try to make things better; her self-centeredness became a virtue as she trained Sharon to make reports and shelve volumes and in any other job Cassie herself found boring.

Alina found solace in her friends, especially Lucas. She'd shown her mother the packet of letters from the mysterious Andrew to Adelaide McCutcheon, and this morning the two friends had shown up at the library to pester Cassie into helping them learn more about the ghost woman. This left Sharon to man the front desk, though in the afternoon stillness she could clearly hear the conversation in Cassie's office.

"We need you to show us how to look up information in the census records," Lucas said. "So we can find out if Adelaide was living in another city in 1966, since we know she wasn't in Eureka."

"We should have thought of that before." Cassie sat at the computer and rubbed her hands together, as if she were preparing to drive nails or saw wood or some other manual labor. "Let me take you to the database; then it's a simple matter to search for people with that last name."

"What if there is more than one person with that name?" Alina asked.

"We know how old she is. We can cross-reference that." The keyboard clicked as she typed, the only sound in the building, where only a handful of patrons browsed the shelves, read, or worked on laptops. Sharon loved that people respected the silence of this place; that the library could still be a sanctuary from chaos.

"I'm not finding anything," Cassie said. "What about the man? What was his name?"

"All we have is Andrew," Lucas said. "No last name."

"Do the letters give us any clue what he did for a living or how they met?" Cassie asked. "That might help us."

Alina, who had taken the letters home and read them over and over, like an engrossing novel, said, "He was a pharmacist. They might have met in Eureka, but I'm not sure."

"Let's try the 1960 census for Eureka. We know Adelaide McCutcheon was here then. That was the year the Women's Society planted lilac bushes all over town, including those in front of this very library." She typed for several seconds.

"Wow," Alina said after a moment. "I never realized so many people lived in Eureka."

"More people lived here then than do now," Cassie said. "At one time Eureka was one of the key communities in the Rockies—rich with gold and bustling with people."

"Look! There he is," Lucas said. "Andrew Reason. Occupation: pharmacist."

"Look for his name in Grand Junction," Alina said. "She mentions that town."

A few minutes of more furious typing passed. "Here he is," Cassie said. "Andrew Reason. Pharmacist. His marital status is listed as single."

"Try 1970," Alina said.

More typing. "He isn't here then."

"What about Montrose?" Lucas asked. "She mentions him moving there in one of the letters."

"Of course," Alina said. "I forgot."

"Here he is," Cassie said. "Andrew Reason. And his wife, Adelaide."

"Wow," Alina said. "I can't believe we found them."

"So she did leave her husband and run away with Andrew?" Lucas asked.

"It looks that way," Cassie said.

"Then why the rumors that he killed her?" Alina asked.

"Divorce was a huge scandal," Cassie said. "He probably preferred for people to think she'd died."

No one had reacted negatively at all when Sharon had divorced Joe. Was it a good or bad thing to accept that two people who'd started out loving each other weren't compatible anymore? She was grateful she hadn't had to stay trapped in her marriage, but the idea that maybe " 'til death do us part" didn't exist anymore saddened her.

Boot heels on the polished hardwood floor signaled a new arrival. Sharon stood up straighter, ready to assist this new patron. But this wasn't a customer needing her help, but Josh. And a second uniformed man followed him. "Hello, Sharon." Josh removed his Stetson and nodded to

350

his companion. "This is Parker Roberts, from the Vermont State Police."

Sharon's heart pounded, and she gripped the edge of the counter for support.

"What do you two want?" Cassie spoke from over her shoulder, in the stern, schoolteacher's voice she used with disruptive teens and trouble-making tourists.

"We need to speak to Sharon for a few minutes," Josh said. "Maybe we could use one of the meeting rooms."

"She's working. You should come back later," Cassie said.

"I'm only here for a short time," Officer Roberts said. "It would be a great help if I could talk to her now. I won't take too much of her time."

Whether it was his courtly manner or his badge that won Cassie over, Sharon couldn't tell, but she pointed him toward one of the meeting rooms at the back. "You can talk in there."

"Mom?" Alina was half out of her chair, both the tone of her voice and her expression tele-graphing her worry.

"It's okay, hon. You stay out here with Lucas." Determined to remain composed, she followed Officer Roberts and Josh to the meeting room.

Josh switched on the light and motioned for Sharon to sit at the conference table. "Have you found my son?" Sharon asked, before Roberts could say anything.

"No, we have not," Roberts said. "But we don't have any indication that he's come to any harm. We're hoping he's hiding or staying with friends and that we'll locate him soon."

Not the answer she'd wanted to hear, but the news could have been so much worse. "What can I do for you?" she asked.

Roberts took a small notebook from his pocket. "What was your relationship with Wilson Anderson?" he asked.

"He and my ex-husband, Joe, were friends. He lived on the same property, right next door to us, for the past twelve years."

"Then you didn't know that he had a criminal record?"

"No." The news didn't surprise her either. "My husband wanted to get away from the mainstream world and live on his own because he was paranoid and worried about the future. But I wasn't naïve enough to believe everyone wanted to live without connections to society for the same reasons. Wilson never talked about his past, and I wouldn't have asked. But he probably wasn't the first person we'd associated with who had a record. What did he do?"

"I don't think that's really pertinent," Roberts said.

"He was a teacher. A girls' soccer coach. He was convicted of molesting several of his players." Josh returned Roberts' scowl. "She has a young daughter. She has a right to know."

Sharon lowered herself into a chair, her knees suddenly too weak to support her. "He was a child molester?" And he'd been going after her daughter. Her fears about what could have happened—what *would* have happened if she'd stayed—hadn't been overprotective fantasies, as Joe had claimed.

"You were right to get Alina away from him," Josh said.

She focused on Officer Roberts once more. "Do you think Wilson had something to do with Adan—my son's—disappearance?"

"We don't believe so. From what we've been able to piece together, your ex-husband and your son argued and the boy ran away. Is it possible he's hiding somewhere? With a friend?"

She shook her head. "He doesn't have any friends his age—not that I know of. Not someone he could go to. Why doesn't he call and tell me where he is? I bought him a phone."

"We found a Nokia cell phone at the campground where the group was staying." He consulted his notebook. "The cell-phone number assigned to it was 555-8972."

"That's Adan's phone." She'd heard of people saying their hearts sank at bad news, but she felt hollowed out. Empty.

Roberts tucked the notebook back into his pocket. "We'll keep looking for your son, Mrs. Franklin. Someone will be in touch."

He left the room, but Josh lingered. "Are you all right?" he asked.

No. But there was nothing he could do to change that. "Why would they send someone all the way from Vermont to ask me a few questions?" she asked.

Josh's frown deepened. "They're treating this as more than a runaway. I don't know this for sure, but some things Roberts has said lead me to believe they think Wilson—and Joe, too—may be connected with some domestic terrorist groups."

"Terrorists?" She choked on the word.

"Groups advocating the overthrow of the United States Government."

"Joe didn't want anything to do with the government. He just wanted to be left alone."

"Maybe not. But they'll probably have more questions for you. And you might have to go to Vermont to testify."

"Only if I have to."

A tapping sounded on the door and it opened a few inches. "Mom? Can I come in?"

"Of course, honey."

Alina came to her side. Josh replaced his hat on his head. "If you need anything, call me."

"Let me know if you find out anything else— about any of this."

"I will."

Alina leaned into her mother. "Is everything okay?" she asked.

Sharon slipped her arm around her daughter's waist. "The police think Adan and your father argued, and Adan ran away."

"What were they arguing about? Was it . . . was it about me?" Her face crumpled, as if she was about to cry.

"About you? Honey, no!" She pulled her daughter close and smoothed back her hair. "Why would you think that?"

"You left after you and Daddy argued about me."

"That was only one reason we split up," she said. "Listen to me." She waited until Alina lifted her head and met her gaze. "The police have arrested Wilson. He had a criminal record. He was wanted for molesting some young girls who were on a soccer team he coached. I'm not telling you this to frighten you, but I want you to understand I did the right thing in taking you away."

Alina nodded and swallowed hard. "Dad didn't believe what Wilson did—what he tried to do with me—was wrong."

"I think he didn't want to believe his friend would ever hurt you," Sharon said. "But the divorce was not your fault. Even without Wilson, I think I would have left, though maybe not as soon as I did."

"Why?"

The question had probably haunted the girl since Sharon had broken the news about the

355

family split. "I didn't want the same things your dad wanted," Sharon said. "He wanted to be farther and farther away from people. I wanted to belong—to be part of a community. To be in a family where I wasn't just the cook and the maid."

"I think we can have that here in Eureka."

"I hope so." She wanted Alina to be happy— and she wanted to be happy herself. But her family would never be complete until her son was home.

"Do they know what happened to Adan?" Alina asked.

"Only that he probably ran away. But why doesn't he call me? Even without his phone, he could borrow someone else's."

"Maybe he can't remember the phone number."

She looked at her daughter. Alina shrugged. "He's a teenage boy. They're not that good at paying attention."

She almost smiled. Adan paid attention to the things that interested him, but he'd tuned her out whenever she'd talked about going away. Maybe that was his way of coping. Maybe some of his rejection hadn't been because he didn't love her, but because he did. He was pulling away to try to lessen the hurt.

The idea was something to hold on to. She nursed it like a precious spark, a hope of warmth in the wet and cold.

She hoped wherever Adan was tonight, he was

warm and dry. She hoped he knew how much she loved him, and how much she wanted to be with him right now. If he'd run away from his father and the lifestyle he'd chosen, she prayed he knew he could run to her. She sent out the thought, counting on some connection across the miles between a mother and the child she'd carried inside of her all those years ago. *Adan, come home. Whatever was lost between us, we can find it again.*

Chapter 19

Lucille knew something was up as soon as Maggie burst into Lacy's on Friday afternoon. "Are you all right?" She rushed around the counter to meet her friend. "You're not going into labor, are you?"

"Why does everyone automatically assume that any time I look the least big flustered, it's because I'm going into labor?" Maggie shoved her bangs back off her forehead and leaned against the front counter, catching her breath.

"Probably because you're nine months' pregnant." Lucille regarded Maggie's protruding belly. That baby looked as if it was ready to pop out at any moment. "But if it's not the baby, what's got you looking so excited?"

"I just heard on the police scanner that the rescue crew has made contact with Bob and Gerald. They're alive and apparently okay. The crew might have them out as early as this afternoon."

"That's wonderful news." Lucille felt lighter than she had in days. "Oh, thank God."

"I was headed up there to see what I could find out for the paper. Do you want to come with me?"

"Absolutely." She turned the Closed sign to face

outward and went to fetch her purse. She was getting ready to lock up when Reggie jogged down the sidewalk toward them.

"Did you hear the news about Bob and Gerald?" he called.

"We did and we're on our way up there right now," Lucille said.

"Me too." He grinned. "We should have known those two were too ornery to let a little thing like being buried under a ton of rock keep them down."

"I'm just amazed they didn't kill each other," Maggie said as she wiggled under the steering wheel of the Jeep she'd inherited from Jake. The battered red vehicle still carried the faint scent of the cigars Jake liked to smoke. Lucille smiled at the memory. If he'd been alive, Jake would have been in the thick of the rescue efforts, even though he and Bob had fought like badgers on more than one occasion.

"Can you imagine, being buried like that for almost a week?" Maggie asked as she raced the Jeep up the road out of town.

"Better not stand downwind of them," Lucille said. "Bob doesn't always smell that great when he's aboveground."

They clearly weren't the only ones to have heard the news about the trapped men. A caravan of vehicles wound up the road toward the mine. Maggie parked next to a dozen other cars along the roadside and Reg swung in behind her.

The first person she spotted when they reached the crowd gathered around the entrance to the Lucky Lady was Chris Amesbury. He was gesturing and giving directions to another man, who balanced a video camera on his shoulder. "He's capturing the big moment for posterity, I see," Maggie said.

"I'm guessing it won't be as dramatic as he hopes," Lucille said. "No anxious women here to throw themselves at either man."

"I'm half-tempted to play the part myself." Maggie rubbed her belly. "I'm sure the director would love it."

Lucille stood on tiptoe. "I can't tell what's happening."

"I'll find out." She edged toward the front of the crowd. "Pregnant woman coming through."

Lucille and Reggie fell in behind her, and thus managed to make their way to the edge of the hole rescuers were digging in the rubble of the explosion. D. J. spotted them and waved. "I understand you've talked to Bob and Gerald," Maggie said. "How do they sound?"

"They sounded a lot better than I would after a week underground," D. J. said. He hefted a pick onto his shoulder. "You might want to stand back a little. Sometimes rock shards fly about."

They retreated a few feet and watched as he and another man took turns striking the dense rock. Suddenly, their target gave way and collapsed into the hole. D. J. stumbled, then caught himself. On his knees, he peered into the opening. "Bob!" he shouted. "Can you hear me?"

A muffled sound came from below, followed by scrabbling. A gasp rose from the crowd as a figure, covered in white rock dust, emerged from the hole.

Half a dozen hands reached out to help the man, who turned out to be Bob, his hair and beard matted, his clothes filthy. But he looked none the worse for wear. Gerald, a little less steady on his feet, crawled out after him.

Maggie moved forward, but a male reporter from one of the Denver stations reached the men first. "How did you survive underground for almost a week?" he asked.

"We were able to dig our way to some emergency supplies I had stashed down there," Bob said, sounding no different to Lucille than if he'd been sitting at the bar in the Dirty Sally, discussing his plans for the weekend.

"What's the first thing you want to do now that you're free?" the reporter asked.

"Have a beer," Bob said, and grinned as the crowd responded with laughter.

"What about you, sir?" The reporter thrust his microphone at Gerald.

"I'm ready to get the hell out of this town and

out of Colorado," he said, and shoved past the startled man.

The reporter turned back to Bob. "Did you attempt to dig your way out?" he asked.

"What do you think, Junior? That we just sat on our hands and decided to enjoy a nice vacation twenty feet under?" Bob scowled at him.

The reporter flinched, but he didn't back down. "How did you occupy your time while you were awaiting rescue?" he asked.

"We managed to keep busy." He looked even cagier than usual. Lucille wondered just what he was hiding.

Gerald was working his way away from the crowd, avoiding those who called out to him, shaking off anyone who tried to stop him. Lucille moved to intercept him. "You're not going to slip away without doing some explaining," she said.

He straightened, and despite his filthy condition, she glimpsed some of the dapper manners that had so easily impressed her when they first met. "Now, you can put your mind at ease, Lucille. I don't intend to sue the city for the suffering I've endured inside that godforsaken hole in the ground, though a lesser man might take such an opportunity."

All that time underground hadn't lessened his nerve. "Call all the lawyers you want," she said. "I'll turn around and have you arrested for fraud."

"Whatever do you mean?" he asked, but his gaze slid sideways.

"What did you do with the money we paid?" she asked. "Because you obviously didn't spend it on the safety improvements you recommended."

"I think we can both agree I paid for that mistake." He raked a hand through his hair. "I've decided to get out of the mining business."

"Oh?"

"I signed over my shares in the Lucky Lady to Bob. He can explain." He moved past her. She didn't try to stop him. If the town did decide to press charges, they could probably find him, though she could see the merits of forgetting all about him and moving on.

She moved back toward Maggie and Reggie, who were standing with Bob. "Gerald said the two of you worked out some sort of deal for his shares in the Lucky Lady," she said.

He glowered at the crowd around him. "Let's go somewhere there aren't so many nosy parkers looking on."

"We can take my car," Reggie said.

Bob nodded. "No offense, Maggie, but what I need to tell the mayor isn't for public consumption."

She grinned. "I can't wait to hear the story—off the record—later. For now, I'll just say it's good to see you safe, Bob."

"I've spent so many years down in mine

tunnels, a few more days wasn't going to bother me. Old Gerald was gettin' a little stir-crazy, though. Good for him they dug us up when they did."

Maggie headed for her Jeep and Bob, Lucille, and Reg piled into his Subaru. "Where to?" Reggie asked as he started the car.

"Jake's cabin isn't too far from here. Head up there."

Lucille didn't bother pointing out the cabin belonged to Maggie now; it wouldn't hurt anything if they parked there for this meeting. In the back seat, she rolled down the window and scooted closer to it. Bob was definitely a little ripe after his stint in the mine.

No one said anything as Reggie drove up to the cabin perched on the side of Mount Garnet. Bob fell asleep, his head resting against the window, snoring softly. The poor old guy was as tough as they came, but he was obviously exhausted. Maybe she should have insisted he go home and rest; they could always talk later.

Bob jerked awake when Reg pulled the Subaru into the drive leading to the cabin and shut off the engine. "Now, what is this all about?" the lawyer asked.

Bob rooted in the pockets of his baggy pants, then turned and dumped a half dozen fist-sized rocks in Lucille's lap. "There's plenty more where those came from," he said.

"What are these?" She examined the dirty gray and yellow stone.

"Gold. Well, gold ore. But good grade. The explosion exposed a good-sized vein of it."

Reggie laughed. "You mean the Lucky Lady really does have gold in it? Pershing and his engineers were right?"

"It pains me to admit it, but they were right," Bob said.

"Does Gerald know about this?" Lucille asked.

"Oh, he knows. He and I spent the past few days digging out as much as we could."

"Then how did you persuade him to sign over his half of the mine?"

"I convinced him that if he didn't relinquish his claim on the mine, the city would sue him for fraud, and I'd sue him for endangering my life and he'd probably get to spend the rest of his life in jail."

"And he believed you?" Lucille said. "A good lawyer might have gotten him off."

"I might have implied he wouldn't necessarily live to see a trial." Bob didn't even try to look coy. "I can be pretty persuasive when I have a pick in my hand."

Lucille shuddered. "I don't want to know any more."

"Don't you dare feel sorry for the old goat," Bob said. "He got his freedom and as much gold as he could carry away. That made him happy."

"How much gold do you think is down there?" Reggie asked.

"A lot. This is a good vein—the city's money problems are over."

"And your money problems, too, I suppose, if you own a half interest in the mine now," Lucille said.

"First thing I'm going to do is find a safe vault and rebuild my emergency supplies. We ate through a good bit of them. Digging out ore with a pick and shovel works up quite an appetite."

"Not to mention you no longer have the dynamite that blew up in the explosion," Reggie said.

"Figured that out, did you? Yeah, well, that was a tactical error on my part, but it worked out. Without that explosion, we'd probably never know the gold was there."

"Gerald won't tell the press, will he?" Lucille had had enough of Eureka making the public spotlight for the wrong reasons.

"He won't tell. He knows I'll come after him if he does."

She'd gotten what she wanted—Gerald gone and Eureka's money woes solved—so why didn't she feel better about it? "I guess I'll believe it when I see it," she said. "It's going to be interesting working with you, Bob."

"Well, you wouldn't want to be bored, would

you?" He scratched his chin. "I can't think of anything worse."

"I suppose not." She sat back and sighed. Some days boredom sounded pretty attractive. She wasn't saying she wouldn't like to give it a try.

While the rest of the town celebrated the rescue of Bob and Gerald from the mine, Sharon drove home after work to a silent and empty house. Alina was with Lucas, so Sharon wandered through the rooms, fighting a dragging depression.

She had thought she'd feel so much happier here in Eureka—stronger. After all, she'd somehow mustered the courage to leave a bad marriage and travel all the way across the country and start over. And she'd counted on having her brother to help her out.

Jameso had helped her, but she still felt unanchored and lost. It wasn't just Adan missing—there was an underlying discontent. A dissatisfaction with herself she couldn't shake.

The stirring rumble of a motorcycle signaled Jameso's return to their street. She went to the window to wave and was surprised when he bypassed Maggie's driveway to turn in behind her car. She met him on the top step. "Aren't you supposed to be at your bachelor party?" she asked.

"Later. I wanted to see you first. Make sure you were okay. Can I come in?"

"Sure." She followed him into the living room, where he shed his leather jacket and sprawled onto the sofa. "You look tired," she said.

"Just a lot going on."

She settled next to him. "It's not going to get easier, you know," she said. "Babies pretty much guarantee sleep deprivation."

"So I hear." He studied her. "You look a little rough around the edges yourself. Are you sure you're okay?"

"No, but I'm hanging on, hoping things will get better."

"They will. Adan is out there somewhere."

Impulsively, she leaned over and put her hand on his. "It meant a lot to me when you offered to go look for him. Really."

"I made the offer for me as much as for you," he said. "I felt so helpless."

"Having kids makes you feel that way more than you'd like," she said. "When they're sick, or when someone bullies them at school—you want to do something for them and you can't. It's horrible. This is that same feeling, multiplied by one hundred."

"I always felt guilty, leaving you alone with our father the way I did." He plucked at the fabric of the sofa, avoiding her gaze. "Like I was a coward."

"You had to leave," she said. "I always knew that. It was worse for you than for me. He just kind of ignored me." She had memories of hiding under the bed while her father and Jameso had horrible fights—boy and man yelling, her father striking out, Jameso afterward with a black eye or bloody nose. Until he'd gotten bigger; then their father would be the one sporting bruises the next day. "And I didn't stay too long after you went away. I married Joe."

"Was that really any better?"

"It was a lot better, at least at first. Joe had strong opinions about things, and the older he got, the more closed off and paranoid he became; but when we first married, he was exactly what I needed. He was strong and protective and devoted to his family."

"When did that change?"

She shrugged. "We all got older—me and the children. We had our own opinions, and they didn't always line up with what Joe believed. And he had other people—like his friend Wilson—feeding his paranoia. I think . . . I think Joe felt the world was a very out-of-control place. The harder he tried to control things, the worse things were. He was shocked when I told him I wanted a divorce. I was a little shocked myself."

"You did the right thing."

"I know."

"Do you ever feel like growing up the way we did doomed us to make stupid choices?"

"What do you mean?"

He shifted, and slumped farther down in the cushions. "Ours was such a screwed-up family. Maybe we don't know how to have a normal life."

"Is there any such thing as a normal life?" She stuffed a pillow behind her back and settled into a more comfortable position. "Is this about you worrying about the wedding and the baby?"

"Do you blame me for worrying? I didn't exactly have the best role model for what it takes to be a good husband and father."

"You don't need to copy someone else. You just need to do what feels right to you." She smiled. "I've seen you with Maggie. You're going to do fine."

His shoulders slumped, and the hard lines of his face relaxed. "Thanks." A quick glance in her direction, then a look away. "I'm glad you decided to come here. I wasn't sure at first. It wasn't you, just . . . old wounds, you know?"

"I know." She patted his hand again. "I'm glad I came here, too. After all, family needs to stick together, even if we haven't had much practice."

"I've been thinking more about family," he said. "Now that I'm going to have one of my own, for the first time I feel like I have something anchoring me. I used to think that was a bad thing, but it feels good. Right." He looked so much more at ease now than he had when he'd first walked in. She was glad she could give him that at least.

"That's what I'm looking for, I think," she said. "An anchor. I used to think I could get that from a man, but that's not what I'm after now. I want, I don't know . . . belonging."

"Maybe it takes time, even in a place like Eureka."

She nodded. "I'm impatient, I guess. I've waited so long to feel settled."

"I haven't exactly been a big help with that."

"You've been great. It was good that you didn't help me too much. I needed to learn to stand on my own feet, but after so long depending on other people to tell me what to do, I needed to be forced into making my own decisions."

"So you're doing okay?"

"I am." She patted his arm. "It was great seeing you, but you'd better go. You don't want them to start the party without you."

"A bunch of us are just getting together at the Dirty Sally. Sort of a combination send-off for me and welcome back for Bob Prescott."

"You're not going anywhere?"

"Not physically, but emotionally, it's a big step." He stood and slipped into his jacket once more. "See you tomorrow, Sis."

"Yeah, see you."

She walked him to the door, then stood watching as he drove away. She felt a little better now, too. She and Jameso might not have it in them to be extremely close, but they could be there for each other when it counted most.

News had spread quickly about Bob and Gerald's rescue, and even Cassie had begrudgingly admitted she was glad "the old coots" had survived their ordeal. "Bob still owes fines on those detective novels he checked out last month," she huffed.

"Maybe we ought to waive those fines, considering all he's been through," Sharon said.

Cassie shook her head. "Seeing as how those books were overdue before he ever went down into the mine, I don't think so. And don't give me that look."

"What look?" Sharon pretended to be searching through the stacks of books on her desk, though she watched Cassie out of the corner of her eye.

"Like I'm some kind of ogre. People think fines are just petty cash, not worth bothering with, but charging people for overdue books isn't about the money—it's about the principle. You can't let them think they can get away with keeping stuff checked out forever. Besides, if we started waiving fines for everybody who's been through hard times, we might as well drop them altogether."

Sharon was pretty sure the library didn't collect more than ten dollars a month in fines—hardly worth the trouble of collecting the money, but she didn't bother arguing with Cassie. Better to let the Queen Bee have the final say. "I guess you'll have to talk to him about it next time he's in," she said.

"I most certainly will. Someone else I need to talk to is that Chris Amesbury. He and I were supposed to have dinner to discuss my role in his television show and he never got back to me."

"Is he still in town?" Sharon asked. She hadn't seen the director around lately, but then again, she hadn't been looking for him.

"Lucille said he left Eureka right after they pulled Bob and Gerald out of the Lucky Lady. He didn't even bother saying good-bye." She shook her head. "Some people have no manners at all."

"I wonder what Bob and Mr. Pershing will do now that they've survived their ordeal," Sharon said. "If it was me, I'd never want to go down into a mine again."

"Bob will go back. He's been mining all his life and he doesn't scare easily. As for Gerald Pershing . . . the old reprobate left town the next morning. Didn't even bother packing up his apartment, just left everything for the next tenant."

"Where was his apartment?" Sharon tried not to sound too interested.

"Oh, I think he lived in those rooms over the hardware store. Stan Adams tried to sell everybody on the idea of 'loft apartments' when he built them—like Eureka was some big city full of converted old warehouses. Honestly." She shook her head. "Of course, Gerald zeroed right in on the place. He always wanted people to think he had a lot more than he did."

"Well, I don't blame him for wanting to put such a bad experience behind him," Sharon said. "He probably associates Eureka with bad memories now."

Cassie snorted. "If people ran away every time something upsetting happened to them, no one would ever stay put. Real courage comes in staying put and facing down whatever ugliness hurt you."

Sharon studied the older woman, who had lived in Eureka all her life. What ugliness had hurt her that she'd stayed to face down? But Sharon wasn't brave enough to ask.

"Good riddance to that old reprobate," Cassie continued. "I don't know where Lucille finds these men, but we don't need any more like them here. Their kind are not going to restore Eureka to its former glory."

Sharon thought Eureka seemed fine the way it was, but Cassie compared everything to some grander past Sharon suspected was largely mythical. "I finished updating the database for the state," she said. "Next week I'll start the inventory you wanted."

"You could start tomorrow, if you weren't taking off," Cassie said. "I can't believe you're leaving when we have so much work to do."

"It's not every day my only brother gets married." On Lucille's advice, Sharon had asked for the wedding day off before she was even hired. She should have known Cassie would whine about it now that the day was here. Let her whine. Even in a small town where jobs were scarce, people weren't lining up to work for the librarian. Sharon had learned to ignore Cassie's moods most of the time. She might even say she was the perfect person for this position; she had plenty of practice ignoring eccentric curmudgeons and doing what she wanted while making sure not to attract their unwanted attention and/or disapproval. Working for Cassie had many similarities to being married to Joe, and one big advantage. When she clocked out at six each evening she was free to truly do as she pleased.

As she was on her day off. "It's going to be a beautiful wedding," she said. "I'm really looking forward to it."

"Jameso's only getting married because he got Maggie pregnant," Cassie said. "And he must not be too keen on the idea, since he's waiting until the last minute."

So much for Sharon's usual policy of not arguing with Cassie. But she drew the line at criticism of her family. "Jameso is marrying Maggie because he loves her," she said. "When they do it isn't important."

Cassie sniffed. "In my day, people had standards."

Honestly, she talked like an eighty-year-old woman sometimes. But clearly in Cassie's mind, her day was her mother's and her grandmother's time—a gentile era she'd over-romanticized, with all her talk of women's clubs and afternoon teas and fancy hats and gloves. She was a woman who really didn't fit well in modern life.

Or maybe she was just jealous because she hadn't been invited to the wedding. From what Sharon could tell, half the town was slated to be at the Idlewilde—the name Barb had given to her bed-and-breakfast inn—Saturday morning. Cassie, who liked to be the center of attention, though she would have denied it to her grave, was probably feeling left out.

"People still have standards," Sharon said, trying to keep her voice gentle. "But some of them have changed. It's not always easy to keep up."

"This world would be a better place if people followed rules and maintained a sense of decorum and tradition," Cassie said.

"Such as only naming parks after men?"

Cassie opened her mouth in what Sharon was

sure would be an angry retort, then closed it. "It's six o'clock," she said. "Go home. I will see you Monday."

Sharon left. She didn't offer to stay and help close up; something else Cassie might decide to gripe about later. But she'd had enough of trying to bite her tongue for one day.

She did not, however, head home. Instead, she drove to the hardware store, then sat in her car, looking up at the windows on the top floor of the building. She gripped the steering wheel tightly; wanting something so badly always frightened her. When you wanted something—whether it was a toy or a candy bar or a new dress or a place to live—others could use that desire to hurt you, by taking away the thing you wanted. Her father had been an expert at that kind of torture; she'd learned early on to hide her true feelings about her heart's desire.

But her father wasn't here, and neither was Joe. She was alone, and she didn't have to hide what she wanted from herself. She took a deep breath and loosened her hold on the steering wheel, then exited the car and climbed the outside staircase to the apartments.

The door opened onto a foyer with four numbered doors. She stared at the polished brass numbers and felt like a contestant in a game show. Which was the right door and what would she find behind it?

The door marked "2" opened and Josh Miller, dressed in his khaki sheriff's department uniform, stepped out into the hall. "Sharon! What are you doing here? Is everything all right?"

Her face felt hot. She'd forgotten that Josh lived here. For half a second, she debated making up some lie to explain her presence here, but rejected the idea. She didn't need to hide anything from this man. "I heard Mr. Pershing moved out of his apartment and I was hoping I could rent it."

Josh's smile made him even more handsome than ever. She looked away. "Maybe the place is too expensive, though."

"Come on. Let's go talk to the owner."

She followed him back downstairs and around to the hardware store entrance. "Stan!" Josh called as soon as they entered. "Mrs. Franklin here is interested in renting Gerald's old place."

A very thin, very tall man with stooped, knobby shoulders, dressed in a white dress shirt and bow tie, came forward to greet them. "I haven't even cleaned out the place yet," he said.

"I'll clean it, for a discount on the rent," Sharon said.

"I haven't even told you what the rent is," Stan said.

"Then tell me." Sharon held her breath, waiting.

"It's two bedrooms," the man said. "Brand new. Or it was before Pershing moved in, and he was only there a couple months."

"It has the smallest kitchen, and no fireplace," Josh said.

Stan scowled at him. "The rent's eight hundred a month. No pets."

Sharon let out her breath. If she was careful, she could just manage. "I'll take it if you'll waive the deposit—since I have to clean the place."

Stan's scowl deepened, his face practically folding in on itself.

"Sounds like a good deal to me," Josh said.

"Fine," Stan said. "But I want the first month's rent in advance."

"I'll write you a check right now."

She gave him the payment and he handed over two keys. "You can move in whenever you want."

Josh followed her back up the stairs. "I don't mean to keep you," Sharon said.

"I'm in no hurry. And I'm kind of curious to see what Pershing left behind . . . if you don't mind."

She didn't mind. Though she was proud of having found this place and rented it on her own, it had felt good having him there to back her up. She hadn't *needed* him there, of course, but having him with her hadn't hurt anything.

She turned the key in the lock and pushed

open the door, steeling herself for everything from a trashed-out room to an empty one. The reality was somewhere in between. Gerald Pershing hadn't been a slob or a hoarder. Neither had he been obsessively neat. He'd taken his clothing and most personal items and left behind the furniture, a television, and some books and everything in the kitchen, including food in the refrigerator. "This doesn't look too bad," she said. She wouldn't have to buy a sofa or beds—a big plus.

"Welcome to the neighborhood," Josh said. "It'll be nice seeing more of you."

She turned to him. "I'm glad we're going to be neighbors. You've been a good friend to me. My first real friend in Eureka."

He studied her, his face so open; here was a man who didn't hide his feelings. "Why do I sense a big 'but' coming?"

"I like you, Josh," she said. "It would be very easy for me to like you too much—to depend on you. But I've spent my whole life depending on men—my father, then my husband . . . even Jameso. I need a chance to learn to depend on myself."

He let his disappointment show, but he didn't turn it to anger. "It's not what I wanted to hear, but I appreciate you being honest with me. I hope you'll still let me be your friend."

"Of course." She offered her hand. After a

moment's hesitation, he took it, and clasped it briefly before releasing it again.

"Congratulations on your new apartment," he said.

Congratulations on your new life, she told herself.

Chapter 20

Sharon had just pulled into the driveway when Alina and Lucas turned onto the street, pedaling hard on their bicycles. She stepped out of the car to meet them and Alina waved. "Mom! We need your help."

She skidded to a halt in front of the house, struggling to right the cardboard box she'd balanced between the handlebars. The box and one like it that Lucas carried were filled with lilac blossoms.

"Where did you get the flowers?" Sharon asked. "Are these for the wedding?"

"They're for a wedding, but not Maggie and Uncle Jameso's," Alina said.

"Then whose wedding?" Sharon brushed her hands across the deep purple blossoms that filled the air with their sweet perfume.

"It's a secret," Alina said. "And the wedding is kind of a surprise."

"A surprise for the bride and groom—or for someone else?"

"For the bride." Lucas wheeled his bike alongside Alina's. "It's for my mom."

Sharon studied the two young people, their

faces flushed from the bike ride, expressions so earnest. "Lucas, it's sweet of you to want to surprise your mother," she said. "But the bride usually decides on the details for her own wedding."

"We're helping D. J.," Alina said. "Mom, please."

"Mom wants to get married," Lucas said. "She keeps saying she doesn't have time to arrange a wedding, so D. J. and I decided to arrange one for her."

Who could argue with the sweetness of that? "What do you need me to do?" she asked.

"We need to get these flowers over to their house and decorate," Alina said. "We've got some candles and stuff, too. Danielle is making a cake and someone needs to pick that up."

"Someone meaning me," Sharon said.

"Could you, Mom? Please?" Alina leaned forward, hands clasped, and Sharon remembered her as a nine-year-old, begging to be allowed to stay up past her bedtime to read one more chapter of *Harry Potter.*

"All right. Why don't you put the flowers in the car and I'll drive you over to the house; then I'll pick up the cake."

"Great. We have to hurry to get everything done before Olivia finishes up at the B and B. She's in charge of decorations for Uncle Jameso's wedding."

"I take it Janelle and Danielle are in on the secret," Sharon said.

"We had to tell them," Alina said as she shoved her box of flowers into the back of the car. "They're making all the food for Uncle Jameso's wedding, but they said it wouldn't be any trouble to put together a cake for us. They're just really nice ladies."

"Yes, they are." Sharon helped Lucas fit his box of flowers alongside Alina's. "I hope your mother likes lilacs," she said.

"They're her favorite." Lucas piled into the back seat beside Alina. "And purple is her favorite color."

"Then the flowers should be perfect. But where did you get so many?"

She glanced in the rearview mirror just in time to catch the looks the teens exchanged. "They were on public property," Alina said. "And we just took the blooms. The bushes will make more next year."

Sharon could think of only one place in town with such a profusion of purple lilacs. "Did you take those from the library?" she asked. Cassie would stroke out. Those flowers were her grandmother's legacy, and as such she considered them her personal property.

"They just dry up and fall off the bushes every year," Lucas said. "This way they'll make my mom happy."

"Cassie will stroke out when she finds out," Sharon said.

"They're just flowers," Lucas said. "She'll get over it. She's always getting worked up about something, but she calms down eventually. Besides, I read that it's good to prune shrubs periodically. It makes them healthier."

Sharon wasn't going to get into a debate about pruning versus picking flowers. "I just hope I'm not there when she sees her stripped bushes for the first time," she said.

At the house he and Olivia had remodeled, D. J. was hanging a swing on the front porch. "Hey, Sharon? What are you doing here?"

"The kids recruited me to help with the wedding. Congratulations."

His smile contained equal parts joy and anxiety. "Thanks. I just hope we can pull it off."

"Cool, a swing." Lucas plopped himself in the wooden seat and pushed off.

"I meant to put it up this last week," D. J. said. "But with the mine collapse and all, I forgot. But I know Olivia really wanted a swing for the front porch."

"Come on, you guys, you can't just stand around." Alina joined them, a box of flowers almost obscuring her figure. "We have to get these inside and start decorating."

"Now that your mom is here, I thought you and she could do that," Lucas said.

"She's going to get the cake." Alina nudged him with her foot. "Come on. We need to find vases for all of these, then arrange the candles and light them. It's going to be beautiful."

Reluctantly, Lucas followed her inside. "Maybe Alina has a future as a wedding planner," D. J. said.

"Or an army general."

Reverend Kinkaid emerged from the house next door and waved to them. "Everything all set?" he called.

"We're just putting on a few last minute touches," D. J. called.

"Wonderful. I'll see you in about an hour, then." He went back into the house.

"Convenient to have a minister as a neighbor," Sharon said.

"He didn't even blink when I told him what I'd planned."

D. J. had an air of quiet certainty that would prevent most people from questioning his actions or plans, Sharon thought. "When is Olivia due back here?" she asked.

He checked his watch. "In about an hour. I told her Lucas and I were going to be here working on stuff and she said she'd stop by with her mother; she wanted to show her the border she painted in the dining room."

"The house looks beautiful," Sharon said. "I never saw it before, but obviously you've worked hard."

"The place was a dump," D. J. said. "That's how we were able to afford it. But now"—he surveyed the red brick bungalow—"now it looks good."

The house featured a mansard roof, mullioned windows, and a deep front porch supported by squat brick pillars. Twin dormers jutted from the second story, flanked by red brick chimneys at either end of the house. A large elm shaded much of the front yard, and honeysuckle spread along the fence. "It's a beautiful home," Sharon said.

They moved inside and found Lucas filling jelly jars with bunches of lilacs. Alina alternated jars of flowers and votive candles along the mantelpiece, the sideboard, and in the window-sills. Someone had rearranged the furniture to form an aisle from the stairs to the fireplace. "The bride will come down the stairs and walk to the fireplace, where the groom will be waiting." Alina indicated the path. "The guests can sit on the sofa and in chairs and watch the ceremony."

"Are you expecting a lot of guests?" Sharon asked D. J.

He shook his head. "Just Lucille, and now you and Alina. It's plenty for us."

Alina stopped in front of D. J. and regarded him seriously. "Do you have a marriage license?" she asked.

"Yes, Reverend Kinkaid has it so he can fill out his part."

"What about a ring?"

A smile tugged at his lips. "I've had the ring for months. I brought it with me when I first came to Eureka."

"You must have been pretty certain she'd eventually say yes," Sharon said.

"I wasn't certain of anything. I just knew she was the only woman I loved, and I'd wait as long as I had to, to make her see that."

"Mom, you'd better go get the cake," Alina said.

Sharon snapped off a salute. "Yes, ma'am."

Alina flushed. "I just want this to be a really nice wedding for Lucas's mom," she said. "And you, too, Mr. Gruber."

"I appreciate that." He squeezed her shoulder. "Now tell me what I should do."

When Sharon left, Alina was directing D. J. and Lucas to move the sofa back to make room for a table with more flowers.

She had to park down the street from the Last Dollar, and was surprised that the restaurant would be so crowded. But as she walked past the Dirty Sally she realized most of the cars must belong to the bar's patrons. A glance in the window showed Jameso in the middle of a circle of well-wishers. She smiled and hurried on. She hoped her brother enjoyed himself tonight—but not too much.

"Hello, Sharon." Janelle, her blond hair wrapped in an orange and pink scarf, hurried to greet her. "Would you like a table or a booth?"

"Neither. I'm here to pick up a cake." She lowered her voice. "For D. J. and Olivia."

Janelle giggled and took her arm. "It's in the kitchen. Come on back."

They found Danielle piping the last frosting curlicue along the bottom of a round white cake decorated with sugared violets. "It's beautiful," Sharon said. "Olivia will be so pleased."

"I hope so." Danielle deposited the icing tip in a tub of soapy water. "I took an Italian wedding cake we hadn't cut into yet and covered it with fondant and added the violets. I wish I had a wedding topper, though."

"The flowers are perfect," Sharon said. "Olivia doesn't strike me as someone who's overly traditional."

Danielle brightened. "That's true."

"She's going to be so blown away by this surprise wedding she won't even notice the cake, lovely as it is." Janelle popped open a cake box and transferred the cake into it. "I think this is just about the most romantic thing ever."

"This weekend is just full of good things," Danielle said. "Bob was in here earlier and we made him all his favorites and fussed over him." She laughed. "I never thought I'd be so happy to see a grouchy old man, but we were really worried about him."

"I think I saw him just now at the Dirty Sally," Sharon said.

"He wouldn't have missed Jameso's bachelor party," Janelle said.

"Bob would have been at the Dirty Sally tonight anyway," Danielle said. "The bachelor party is just a bonus." She handed Sharon the cake. "Tell Olivia and D. J. congratulations from us. I guess we'll see you at Jameso and Maggie's wedding tomorrow morning."

"Of course. Two weddings in one weekend. Who would have thought?"

"Who knew Eureka was such a romantic place?" Danielle laughed and Sharon smiled all the way to her car. Helping with the surprise wedding was much better than sitting at home alone moping.

She returned to a living room transformed into a romantic bower. Someone—Alina—had scattered flower petals down the makeshift aisle and tied lavender ribbon to the spindles of the stair railing. Candles filled the room with a soft glow in the deepening twilight. "Did you get the cake?" Alina rushed to greet her mother.

"Danielle outdid herself." Sharon set the box on the kitchen counter and opened the top.

"Oh, it's beautiful!" Alina set a plate beside the box. "I think this is big enough."

Mother and daughter carefully transferred the cake from the box. Alina was licking a dab of icing from her finger when Lucas called from the front room. "They're here!"

Alina started for the front room, but Sharon grabbed her arm and held her back. "Let's give the family a moment," she said.

"Oh . . . yeah." She moved to the door. "But we can watch, right?"

Sharon joined her daughter at the door and they watched as D. J. ushered Olivia and Lucille into the candlelit room. "What is all this?" Olivia asked, looking around in wonder.

"You said you didn't have time to plan a wedding, so I planned one for us," D. J. said.

Olivia gaped at him. "You did what?"

"Everything is taken care of. All you have to do is walk down the aisle and say I do. That is, if you still want to."

She laughed. "Of course I want to. But I'm a mess." She looked down at her paint-splattered skinny jeans.

"There's a dress upstairs for you to wear—the lilac one you wore to Lucas's program at Christmas." He smiled. "I always thought of that as our first date in Eureka."

"I don't believe this." She looked around the room. "You did all of this yourself?"

"I had a little help." He put his arm around Lucas.

"Alina and her mom helped, too." Lucas looked anxious. "Mom, you're not mad, are you?"

"No! No, I'm not mad." She pulled him close and he allowed it. "Thank you. This is the sweetest, most romantic thing anyone has ever done for me."

"Hurry and change," Lucas said. "Reverend Kinkaid will be here soon . . . and Alina says the candles won't last forever."

"Then we'd better get to it." Olivia hugged D. J. close. "I can't believe you did this."

"Then you don't think I'm overstepping? I know most women like to plan their own wedding."

She shook her head. "The idea of pulling together a wedding just made me tired. This is perfect."

D. J. bent his head as if to kiss her, but Lucille tapped his shoulder. "Save it for the ceremony," she said. "We have to transform ourselves into a wedding party."

All four of them headed upstairs, and Alina and Sharon returned to getting the refreshments ready. Sharon found a bottle of champagne chilling in the refrigerator and set it in a bucket of ice, then arranged glasses and cake plates and forks. "Can I have some champagne?" Alina asked.

"I might give you a sip," Sharon said. "I'm betting you won't like it, though."

Alina shrugged. "I think there's Sprite I can drink instead."

"Good idea."

A knock on the door made her jump. "It's probably Reverend Kinkaid," Alina said.

They made small talk with the reverend while they waited for the wedding party to come down. D. J., Lucas and Lucille eventually trooped down the stairs. The men had changed into suits and ties. Lucille had settled for combing her hair and freshening her makeup.

"We're ready when you are," D. J. told the preacher.

"We should have had music," Alina said.

"We do!" Lucas hurried to a boom box that sat half-hidden behind a plant at the bottom of the stairs and pressed a button. The strains of the wedding march sounded. A few seconds later, Olivia moved into view.

She looked lovely in a filmy lilac-colored dress, her hair left loose to fall around her shoulders. She carried a bouquet of purple and white lilacs bound in lavender ribbon. "I did the bouquet," Alina whispered.

"It's beautiful." Sharon slipped her arm around her daughter's shoulders. "I'm proud of you," she said.

"It was fun."

They fell silent as Olivia moved down the aisle to join D. J. and Lucas at the fireplace. Sharon's eyes stung as she watched D. J. take his future wife's hands. The world could have crumbled around those two at this moment and they never would have noticed, so intent were they on each other, their love so clearly revealed on their faces.

The Reverend Kinkaid had a rich, steady voice. As he intoned the familiar vows to love and honor in sickness and health, poverty and riches, " 'til death do you part," Sharon tried to remember her own wedding so long ago. She'd been so young and so nervous, overwhelmed more by the pageantry of the moment than by any depth of feeling for her husband-to-be. She had loved Joe, but only with the love of a young girl infatuated with a handsome, strong man who had the power to take her away from a life she despised. It was all the love she'd been capable of at that time of her life; she hadn't really known more was possible, and Joe hadn't seemed to want more, in any case.

When had things changed? When had she changed, so that that shallow, young love wasn't enough anymore? As an adult struggling with the burden of raising children, providing for a family, finding out who she was, those immature feelings weren't enough to carry her through the hard times.

"I now pronounce you husband and wife," Reverend Kinkaid intoned. "You may kiss each other."

They kissed and the others applauded. Then Olivia kissed her son and her mother. D. J. opened the champagne.

"Better make it a glass of Sprite for me," Olivia said, her smile almost shy.

D. J. froze in the act of pouring. "What are you saying?"

"Alcohol wouldn't be good for the baby."

Luckily, Lucille was there to take the bottle before D. J. dropped it. He pulled Olivia into his arms and kissed her again, then peppered her with questions. "How long have you known? When were you going to tell me? When is it due?"

"I was waiting for the right moment. I'll have the baby in January, I think."

"Talk about a great wedding present." He whooped and grabbed up a glass of champagne. "A toast to my son or daughter!"

They all laughed and toasted and offered their congratulations, then enjoyed Danielle's delicious cake.

A while later, Lucas left with Lucille and Alina with Sharon. The newlyweds would spend the night alone in their newly remodeled house, which Olivia declared was all the honeymoon she needed.

Alina still bubbled with excitement as Sharon drove toward home. "Everything was so beautiful," she said. "I can't believe how pretty Olivia looked. And Lucas is going to have a little brother or sister."

"Brides are always beautiful," Sharon said.

"And grooms are always handsome. Did you see the way he looked at her? Do you think Uncle Jameso will look at Maggie that way when she walks down the aisle tomorrow?"

"I hope so." Every woman should have a man look at her that way at least once—as if she were the greatest treasure in the universe, and he couldn't believe his great luck in finding her.

"Mom, do you think you'll ever get married again?"

The question startled her. "I haven't thought about it," she said. "I think I'd like to try it on my own for a while." In the space of a few weeks she'd gone from wife to divorcée; she needed time to take it all in.

"Was it so awful for you, with Daddy?" Alina's voice was small, a little girl's voice.

"No, honey." Sharon gripped the steering wheel more tightly. "Sometimes people grow apart instead of growing together. It doesn't mean that either one of them is a bad person."

"It still doesn't seem real—that Daddy just let Adan leave." Her voice broke on the last word; Sharon reached out and squeezed her hand.

"He probably didn't believe he'd really go."

"Maybe if we'd stayed with him, this wouldn't have happened," Alina continued.

A chill swept over Sharon and she chose her words carefully, searching for a way to remove at least this burden from her daughter's grief. "I don't think our staying would have made things better," she said. "And it might have made them worse."

"You mean because of me."

"Maybe," she admitted. She pulled the car into the driveway and shut off the engine. "Your father wanted a life away from everyone. That wasn't healthy—not for him, but especially not you children."

"But you let Adan stay with him."

She closed her eyes. "Yes, and I will have to live with that guilt for the rest of my life." She turned to her daughter. "People make mistakes —parents make mistakes. I know now I should have fought harder for Adan, but I truly thought he would be all right."

Alina chewed her lower lip and stared at her own reflection in the side window. "What are you thinking?" Sharon asked. "Tell me."

"I was mad at first, about the divorce and about moving here. But then, after a few weeks, I felt"—she shrugged—"I don't know. I wasn't mad anymore. And things just felt . . . easier here. More relaxed. As if back in Vermont I'd been all stressed out and didn't even realize it. But then I felt guilty about feeling better that we weren't all a family anymore."

Sharon sighed. "Guilt is like that, but don't listen to it. It's okay for you to be happy."

"I guess so."

"Are you just saying that because you think it's what I want to hear, or because you believe it? Because if you want, we can find someone else for you to talk to—a professional counselor."

"I'm okay, Mom. But I promise to let you know if that changes."

"Good." Sharon felt wrung out, as if she'd just run a marathon. She opened the car door. "Come on. If you want, I'll paint your nails for Uncle Jameso's wedding tomorrow."

"Cool." Alina fell into step beside her mother as they headed toward the door. "I think I want to wait at least until I'm out of college before I get married," she announced. "Maybe a little longer. I think it would be good to live on my own a couple of years first."

"That sounds very wise." Maybe Alina had learned what not to do by observing Sharon's early-marriage disaster. Or maybe the girl was just smart. Sharon didn't bother mentioning that love didn't necessarily operate on a timetable. Better for the girl to believe she could control her own destiny. And why not? If Sharon had had that kind of faith in herself, her life might have worked out differently. But then, she wouldn't have Alina and Adan.

No, she decided, life worked the way it was supposed to. The trick was adapting to the changes, riding out the waves, and enjoying the smooth sections without worrying too much about the storms ahead.

Chapter 21

"Stop fidgeting. I'm almost done." Barb unwound the last hot roller from Maggie's hair and tugged the curl into place. "I swear, you'd think this was your first wedding, you're so jumpy."

"This is my first wedding to Jameso," Maggie said. "My first wedding with a baby on the way. My first wedding with a whole town full of people waiting to witness the ceremony." Honestly, at forty years old, she would never have dreamed she'd be making so many firsts. Who wouldn't be a little nervous?

"You don't have anything to worry about." Barb aimed a blast of Super Hold hairspray at the back of Maggie's head. "There. Take a look."

Maggie swiveled to face the mirror and blinked against the sudden sting of tears. She might feel old and bloated inside, but Barb had transformed her into a storybook blushing bride. "Oh, Barb!"

"You're not allowed to cry," Barb said. "You'll ruin your makeup."

Maggie pulled her friend close in a hug. "Thank you. I don't know what I would have done without you here."

"You'd have managed, I'm sure. After all, you got married the first time without me."

"I had my mother to do everything. Plus, I was just a kid. I didn't know enough to worry."

"There's something to be said for naïveté."

"Yeah, it got me through twenty years of being married to Carter."

"This time around is going to be so much better," Barb said. "And you couldn't possibly have been any more beautiful back then."

"I was younger and definitely thinner." She smoothed over the bulge of the baby, remembering that first wedding, a lifetime ago. "We were married in the Baptist church my mother attended," she said. "It wasn't nearly as lovely as this place. I can't believe you did all this work for me . . . and all while you were getting your bed-and-breakfast ready to open. I can't thank you enough."

"You know I loved every minute of it." Barb patted her shoulder. "And speaking of the B and B, there's something I wanted to talk to you about."

"Oh?" Maggie turned back to the mirror and patted her head. At least now she knew she wouldn't look awful in the wedding photos— though she'd have to beg the photographer to focus on head shots. At this stage in the pregnancy, her baby bump had grown into a baby boulder and she couldn't get away with standing behind chairs or other people. "You're already booked up for most of the summer, right?"

"Right. And I've got people calling about reservations for the fall, and even this winter."

"That's wonderful." Maggie turned back to her friend. "I knew you'd be terrific at this. You've found your calling."

"I guess so. But I still live in Houston. And I want to stay there. This past Christmas I had enough mountain snow to last me a lifetime."

Barb and her husband, Jimmy, had been stranded by the same snowstorm that had almost kept Jameso and Maggie apart at Christmas. They'd spent the holiday in a remote tourist cabin.

"I guess you could close the place for the winter," Maggie said. "Though that would be a shame. There really aren't enough places for people to stay in the off-season."

"I was thinking of finding someone to run the inn for me," Barb said. "Year-round. I'd still visit regularly to make sure things were running smoothly, but really, my fun is in decorating and planning special events—not the day-to-day hospitality stuff."

"That shouldn't be hard," Maggie said. "Do you have someone in mind?"

"Actually, I do." Barb looked steadily at her.

Maggie's heart fluttered—or maybe that was just the baby kicking a little vigorously. "Barb, no! I don't have time to run a B and B, not with my work at the newspaper and a baby on the way."

"I wasn't talking about you," Barb said. "I was thinking of Jameso."

"Jameso?"

"Can you think of a reason he couldn't do it?" Barb asked. "He's charming; the customers at the Dirty Sally and at the Jeep tour company love him. He could do all the maintenance, and I understand he cooks at least as well as you do."

"That's not saying a lot."

"He could use my recipes, and it's just breakfast. He'd have to keep track of reservations and handle the money, but he strikes me as a pretty smart guy."

Maggie nodded. "Have you mentioned this to him?"

"I wanted to run it by you first."

Maggie laughed. "I'm marrying him—I'm not taking charge of his life. If he wants to do this, I'm all for it."

"That's not the reason I wanted to ask you," Barb said. "In order to do the job, you'd have to live on-site."

"Here?" In this gorgeous house?

"I converted the whole third floor into an apartment. There's a separate kitchen and living area and three bedrooms."

"I thought that was part of the B and B," Maggie said.

"I planned it for you all along." Barb grinned. "Why do you think I made you come with me to pick out the paint?"

Maggie swallowed a lump in her throat. "I really am going to cry now," she said.

"Don't." Barb handed her a tissue. "So what do you think? Will you do it if Jameso says yes?"

"Of course I'll do it. It's the answer to our prayers. We need a bigger place for the baby— Jameso and I barely have enough room in that little miner's cottage I'm renting—and the one his sister is in now isn't any bigger. Oh, Barb, thank you!"

The two women embraced; then Barb stepped back, blotting her eyes with her fingers. "Come on. We'd better get this show on the road. I at least want your vows said before the little girl there decides to make an appearance."

"Right." Maggie hoisted herself out of the chair. "But no worries. I saw the doctor yesterday and she said I'm hardly dilated at all, so we have a few days."

"Just don't get carried away on your honeymoon," Barb said.

Maggie stuck her tongue out at her friend, then followed her to the door.

A fresh flood of tears threatened when she saw the crowd filling the chairs in the inn's front parlor. All of her friends—people she hadn't even known a year ago, but who now were as dear to her as family—were gathered: Janelle and Danielle, Rick, Katya and Reggie, Lucille, Olivia and D. J., Shelly and Charlie Frazier. Eve, the real-estate agent, and Joette, who did her hair—everyone taking time out of their own busy lives to celebrate with her and Jameso.

The organist for the Presbyterian church began playing on the electronic piano she'd hauled to the B and B for the occasion. "It's showtime." Barb took two bouquets from the table by the door and handed one to Maggie. "I love you," she said.

"I love you, too." The friends embraced; then Barb opened the door and stepped into the parlor.

Maggie had told herself she was going to do a better job of remembering this wedding than her first, which had passed in a frantic haze. But the onslaught of so much emotion overwhelmed that determination. She settled for remaining upright and fixed on Jameso. He stood beside Reverend Kinkaid in front of the marble mantelpiece, hands clasped in front of him, broad shoulders stretching the jacket of the black suit Lucille had unearthed from the stock of Lacy's and insisted on altering for him. His ivory tie matched Maggie's dress, and the columbine in his lapel echoed the cloud of blue and white flowers in her bouquet.

As soon as Barb reached the front of the room, the organist segued into the "Wedding March" and everyone shuffled to their feet. For a few seconds, Maggie's view of Jameso was blocked; then she stepped into the middle of the makeshift aisle and locked eyes with him.

All the tension she'd been holding all morning released, and she all but floated up the aisle. A man she had at times thought of as impulsive, distant, immature, and impossible now looked nothing but certain of himself and his love for her.

When she reached him, Jameso took her hand, and never let go as they said their vows. She focused on the words, determined to seal them in her mind and heart: *for richer, for poorer; in sickness and in health; for better or worse; so long as we both shall live.* She smiled when Jameso slid the wedding band on her finger, and was smiling still when he kissed her, vaguely aware of the applause and cheers from onlookers.

Then they were hurrying down the aisle. They had reached the entry hall and turned back toward the crowd when pain sliced through and she gasped. "What is it?" Jameso put his arm around her, all concerned.

She shook her head. "It was nothing, I'm sure." She smiled wanly. "Just another Braxton Hicks contraction."

"You're sure?" Jameso's brows almost met over his nose, he was frowning so hard.

"I'm fine." She turned to greet the first of their well-wishers—Bob, his beard and hair trimmed, his plaid suit looking like something out of a forties movie.

"Congratulations," he boomed. He took Maggie's hand, but instead of shaking it, pulled her toward him and gave her a resounding kiss. "Don't look at me like that, boy," he cackled at Jameso. "I'm just kissing the bride." Still grinning, he moved on.

"Bob's been celebrating pretty hard since he got out of that mine," Jameso said as Janelle and Danielle moved forward to offer their congratulations.

"You look beautiful, Maggie," Danielle said.

"We wish you so much happiness," Janelle added.

"Thank you," Maggie said. "And thank you for all the wonderful food for the reception. Everything looks too beautiful to eat."

Janelle's answer was lost to her as another pain ripped through her. "Could somebody get a chair?" Jameso called.

Barb appeared at her side. "What is it? Is it the baby?"

"I . . . I don't know." She lowered herself into the offered chair and rubbed her stomach. "Maybe."

"That's it. We're headed to the hospital." Jameso pulled her to her feet once more.

"I guess we'll be having the reception without you," Barb said.

"Jameso, we don't have to leave right away," Maggie said. "Babies take forever to be born."

"Better to not take any chances," he said. "I'm parked right outside."

"We could at least cut the cake," she protested.

"Aren't you supposed to obey me now that I'm your husband?" His tone was only half teasing.

"We didn't have those words in our vows."

"Then humor me. I've never had a baby before."

"Neither have I!"

"Then don't you think we'd better play it safe and go to the hospital?"

"I'm with Jameso on this one." Barb gently pushed Maggie toward the door. "We can cut the cake without you. And I promise to save you a piece."

"All right." Maggie looked uncertainly at her guests. Those who had figured out what was going on looked back with avid interest. She had a sudden image of herself giving birth with a crowd of onlookers. "Maybe going to the hospital is a good idea."

"You can call the doctor from the car," Jameso said, and opened the door.

"Good luck, Maggie!" "Call us from the hospital!" "Congratulations!" The cries from well-wishers still rang in her ears as Jameso started the car. She fastened her seat belt across her stomach and settled back in the seat, eyes closed.

"You okay?" Jameso asked.

"I'm better than okay." She smiled at him. "We're going to have a baby. How's that for a wedding present?"

"I'd just as soon we didn't have to unwrap it ourselves," he said, and hunched over the steering wheel and sped up.

She laughed. All the worry and fear that had plagued her earlier had vanished somewhere between "I do" and that first labor pain. Life had a way of working out exactly the way it was supposed to. She would never have planned things the way they were turning out, but she couldn't have been happier—and with a brand new husband and daughter about to make her debut, things were only going to get better.

"It's destruction of public property. You should find whoever is responsible and arrest them." Cassie glared at Sergeant Miller. What was the world coming to when she had to tell an officer of the law how to do his job?

Sergeant Miller surveyed the row of blossomless lilacs in front of the library. "They aren't destroyed. I'm not a gardener, but the plants look fine. And I don't think there's a law against picking flowers."

"Those flowers belong to the town of Eureka. Whoever took them had no right." Cassie clamped her lips shut against the dangerous wobble in her voice. To Sergeant Miller—a newcomer to town and a man—the lilacs were just flowers. But to Cassie they were part of her heritage—a living symbol of the way her family had contributed to and shaped this town. "We have laws against vandalism, don't we?" she asked.

"Yes, ma'am." The sergeant took a notebook from his pocket. "Do you have any idea who might be responsible? Did anyone see anything? Did the culprits leave anything behind that would help us identify them?"

"It's your job to determine those things, not mine."

"And you're sure the flowers were here when you left last night?"

"Yes, and when I came in this morning, they were gone."

"What about Sharon—Mrs. Franklin? Was she here last night also? And doesn't she usually open the library on Saturdays?"

"She left shortly after six o'clock. And she's off today."

"For Jameso's wedding. Of course." Smiling, he tucked the notebook back into his pocket. "I'll see if I can find any witnesses who saw anyone at the library who wasn't supposed to be," he said. "You let me know if you hear of anything, too."

"I certainly will."

He tugged at the brim of his hat and turned to stroll back to his police cruiser. That would be the last she heard from him on the matter, she was sure. People had no sense of what was important anymore.

Unable to look at the bereft lilacs any longer, she returned to the library front desk. Though the library opened at ten, she seldom saw a patron much before noon on Saturdays. This left plenty of time to devote to the exhibit about the Eureka Women's Society she planned for the front display case.

But she had scarcely opened the case when the front door opened and a tall, thin young man sidled in. He had a big backpack on his back, his nose was sun-burned, and his jeans and T-shirt were gray with dirt. Cassie wrinkled her nose. Occasionally these young vagrants passed through town, on their way to Denver or some other place where they could camp in the parks and panhandle for beer or drug money. She'd let him know quick enough that the library was not a public rest stop and he had best move along.

She moved out from behind the front desk and met him halfway across the room. "We do not have public restrooms or a phone you can use," she said.

He blinked at her, brown eyes shining from beneath the curtain of his shaggy blond bangs. "Do you have a newspaper I could read?" he asked. "And a local phone book?"

"Who do you want to look up? The town isn't that big, and I know most of the residents."

His gaze remained steady, undaunted. "Maybe just the paper, then."

"The newspapers are for our patrons. People with library cards."

He glanced over her shoulder, toward the front desk. "This is a public library, isn't it?"

"That doesn't mean any vagrant off the street is free to loiter here."

"What makes you think I'm a vagrant? Maybe I'm a tourist. Or maybe I'm a new resident." He drew himself up taller, as if his dirty jeans and worn backpack were merely a costume he'd put on as a lark.

Despite the bravado, Cassie realized he was young. His cheeks were smooth, the barest peach fuzz glinting above his lip. Dark half-moons shadowed his eyes, and he had a pinched, hungry look.

Which didn't mean she was going to let him take advantage of her. "Where did you spend the night last night?" she asked.

"That's none of your business."

"I doubt you walked all the way from Montrose this morning, so you must have camped somewhere nearby. You were probably waiting for the library to open. Did you see who took my lilacs?"

"Your lilacs?" Confusion replaced bravado.

"Someone sneaked up here last night and cut every bloom off the lilacs in front of the library. Did you see them? Do you know anything about the crime?"

"I didn't think it was a crime to cut flowers."

"So you *do* know something!" She leaned toward him. "Did you take them?"

"What would I want with a bunch of lilacs?" He started to turn away, but she grabbed his arm. He tried to shake her off, but she held on. Wynock women had always been strong, and she was no exception.

"I'll let you see the phone book," she said. "Just wait right here."

She retreated to her office and pulled the phone book from the bookshelf above her desk. Through the glass overlooking the main library, she watched the young man look through the display of newspapers in the reading area. Stealthily, she lifted the phone and punched in Sergeant Miller's number.

"Sergeant Miller, Eureka County Sheriff's Department."

"Sergeant, I have a suspect I want you to question."

"A suspect in what? Who is this?"

"This is Cassie Wynock. I have a young man here I believe knows something about the theft of the lilacs."

"Who is it?"

"I don't know his name. He's a stranger here. He looks like a hobo. But I'm sure he knows something."

The sergeant sighed heavily. She'd have to talk to the sheriff about Officer Miller's attitude. "I'll be over in a few minutes," he said, and disconnected the call.

She returned to the young man and offered him the phone book. He checked the cover. "This is from last year."

"Things don't change that quickly around here."

He set the book aside. "It won't have what I want." He shouldered his backpack once more. "Maybe you can just tell me how to find the nearest café. Someplace that might let me wash dishes in exchange for a meal."

"The Last Dollar is two blocks over. The owners, Janelle and Danielle, are softhearted enough they might let you do a few chores for them." And they would keep him occupied until Sergeant Miller bothered to show up.

"Okay. Thanks."

She let him leave, and stood in the doorway, watching for the sergeant's car. She had such a strong feeling about the young bum, as if his showing up here this morning was significant in some way. Obviously, her keen sixth sense had pegged him as the key to solving the mystery of her vanished lilacs. It paid to listen to that kind of intuition.

Ten minutes later, long after the young man had slouched off down the sidewalk, Sergeant Miller's cruiser turned the corner. "What took you so long?" Cassie asked, greeting him on the sidewalk before he had even fully exited the vehicle.

"I went on another call." He straightened to his full six foot two and regarded her over the open car door. "Where is this dangerous suspect?"

"I never said he was dangerous. Why? Do you think he's dangerous?"

"I don't even know who we're talking about. Is he inside?"

"He went over to the Last Dollar to see if the girls would let him wash dishes for his dinner. That's as good an admission as any that he was broke."

"Being broke isn't any more of a crime than cutting flowers," Sergeant Miller said.

"They took every blossom! That's vandalism."

"What makes you think this guy knows anything?" the sergeant asked.

"Because when I asked him if he'd seen anyone messing with the flowers, he stopped looking me in the eye and changed the subject." She drew herself up taller. "And because I have very good instincts about these things."

"Uh-huh." Frowning, he lowered himself back into the seat.

"Are you going to question him?" Cassie asked.

"I might."

"Then I'm going with you." Without waiting for an invitation, she opened the passenger door and settled into the seat.

"Cassie!" He lowered his voice. "Miss Wynock, I really don't need your help with this."

"If I don't go with you, you're liable to just blow me off. Besides, I can point him out to you."

"What about the library?"

"No one comes this time on a Saturday morning. If they do, most of them know how to check out their own books, and the loafers don't need me there for them to read the paper and nap." She fastened her seat belt and looked at him expectantly.

He glared at her a long moment, then clicked on his own safety belt and put the car in gear.

He parked the patrol car in a no parking zone in front of the restaurant. Cassie had to wait for him to unlock her door, but then she led the way into the Last Dollar, where a few tourists— and Bob—lingered over late breakfasts. "We're looking for the young man who just came in here," Cassie said. "The one with the backpack."

"What do you want with him?" Danielle folded

her arms across her chest, a stubborn set to her chin.

"The sergeant needs to question him about a crime," Cassie said.

"Miss Wynock thinks the young man may know something about the lilac blossoms that disappeared from the bushes in front of the library sometime last night or early this morning."

"Janelle is fixing him a plate," Danielle said. "He was waiting here when we came from the wedding. The poor boy was starved. He told us he'd walked all the way from Montrose yesterday."

"I don't have any reason to think he's done anything wrong," Sergeant Miller said. "Could I talk to him a minute?"

Danielle softened. "All right. I'll go get him."

"Would you like to sit down?" The sergeant motioned toward an empty booth.

Cassie slid into the booth and he sat across from her. A moment later, the boy she'd seen earlier, minus the backpack, emerged from the kitchen, flanked by Janelle and Danielle. "This is Josh Miller," Danielle said. "He just wants to talk to you a minute."

The sergeant's face changed when he saw the boy. He actually smiled. "Welcome to Eureka, son," he said. "I know someone who's going to be very glad to see you."

The boy halted by the table and looked confused. "I don't think we've met."

"No, but I've looked at your picture often enough. A lot of people have been looking for you. Your mother's been beside herself with worry."

"You know my mom?" The boy looked wary, ready to bolt.

"Sharon has been worried about you. I told her you sounded like a smart, resourceful kid. Did you hitchhike all the way from Vermont?"

He nodded. "I walked a lot, too. Not many people want to give a guy a ride."

Cassie fidgeted. What were they talking about? And didn't they know it was rude not to include everyone in the conversation? "Are you saying you know this boy, Sergeant?" she asked. "Who is he?"

Sergeant Miller stood and clapped the boy on the shoulder. "This is Adan Franklin. Sharon's son."

"Oh, how wonderful!" Danielle clapped her hands together. "Sharon will be so relieved."

"I thought you were living with your father," Cassie said.

"I was, until we had an argument. He told me if I didn't like the way he did things, I could leave. So I did." He turned to Josh. "The judge at the divorce hearing said I was old enough to decide who I wanted to live with, and I decided I want to stay with Mom."

"She'll be glad to hear it." He patted the boy's

shoulder. "As soon as you've eaten, I'll take you to your mom."

Adan grinned. "I already ate." He glanced at Janelle. "But I promised to wash dishes."

"Put the boy's food on my tab." Bob spoke up from his table. "Tell his mom I'm glad her prodigal found his way home."

"Thanks, mister," Adan said.

Bob waved away the thanks. "Go on. Sharon's been worried about you."

"I guess we'd better go," Josh said. "Does anybody know if Sharon's home? I could call ahead, but I'd kind of like to surprise her."

"I think she's at the hospital with Jameso and Maggie," Danielle said. She turned to Adan. "Your uncle got married this morning and his new wife went into labor right after the ceremony."

"Then I'll take him to the hospital. He can meet the whole family."

"Aren't you going to ask him about the lilacs?" Cassie asked.

Sergeant Miller gave her a stern look. "Give it a rest, Cassie. The lilacs will bloom again next year."

She started to protest, then clamped her mouth shut. All this fuss over one boy who'd obviously done a fine job of looking out for himself.

"I'm sorry about your lilacs, Cassie."

She looked up to find Danielle standing over

her. "They were beautiful flowers," the young woman said. "I smiled every time I drove past them. I know you're going to miss them."

"Yes, they were beautiful," Cassie said. "Thank you." The girl's thoughtfulness surprised her, especially since Cassie had never been particularly nice to her.

"It's too bad there's no way to get the flowers back now," Danielle said. "But at least Sharon can get her son back. That's a little miracle worth celebrating, isn't it?"

Cassie didn't believe in miracles, or in celebrations, for that matter. But she got the point. "I'm sure this will be a huge relief to Sharon," she said. "I'm glad the boy is safe. I mean, I'm not completely insensitive."

"Of course you aren't." Danielle patted her shoulder. "Would you like some coffee? And how about a cinnamon roll? There are still a couple of fresh ones left."

"I really should get back to the library," she said.

"I can wrap it to go."

"That would be lovely, then. Thank you." She doubted if she'd be able to walk up to the library for the next few weeks without a pang of sorrow for the lost lilac blossoms, but the sergeant was right. They would bloom again next year. That was the wonderful thing about a heritage. You never really lost the gift your ancestors had left you. People who didn't have that connection to history didn't understand that. They could celebrate births and weddings and reunions, but without the richer context of history to imbue those events with meaning, they must be left feeling a little shallow, shouldn't they?

Chapter 22

Sharon couldn't stop smiling at her brother. Jameso looked like an awkward giant, cradling his baby daughter in his arms, an almost comical expression of besotted love transforming his rugged face. He stroked his finger across one tiny cheek. "She's so perfect," he breathed.

"She is," Maggie agreed. She wore the smile of weary exhaustion Sharon remembered from her own deliveries. The birth had gone smoothly, the baby arriving only five hours after Maggie arrived at the hospital.

"What are you going to name her?" Alina asked. She perched on the side of Sharon's chair in the corner of the hospital room. Like everyone else in the room, her gaze was fixed on the red-faced, swaddled infant. She hadn't asked to hold the baby, but Sharon guessed by the way Alina sat on her hands and fidgeted, that she wanted to.

"We're going to call her Angela, after my mother," Maggie said.

"Angela." Alina repeated the name. "I can't wait to babysit her."

"We'll both look after her," Sharon said. She patted Alina's arm. "At least at first. After all, an infant is a big responsibility."

"Don't remind me," Maggie said. "I'm terrified of taking her home." She looked at Jameso, who was cooing to his daughter, oblivious to anyone else in the room.

"Don't worry," Sharon said. "You'll do great. I was only fifteen when I had Adan and I knew absolutely nothing about babies, but we all managed to survive."

"Everyone tells me instinct will kick in," Maggie said. "But I've never been one to trust my instincts."

Instinct was all Sharon had had to rely on with Adan—that and frantic phone calls to her mother. As a girl, she'd never even played with dolls; then suddenly, she had a real-life doll depending on her for everything. Joe was no help. At the first sign of a dirty diaper or baby whimpers, he'd disappear. But somehow they'd survived.

She hoped her boy was surviving still. He was the type who would take to the woods and avoid the police—just as his father had taught him. No telling how long before the police found him or someone responded to the missing child posters authorities had distributed.

"I guess we'll have to move all of that nursery furniture from my house to the B and B," Maggie said.

"Junior Dominick is doing it this afternoon," Barb said. "Don't worry about a thing. I even got that baby animal wallpaper border you picked out and the white eyelet curtains and every-thing."

Maggie shook her head. "I can't believe you've been planning all this for months and never even breathed a word."

Barb fluffed her hair. "There's nothing I like better than plotting."

Maggie turned to Sharon. "I'd offer you my house, but it's the same size and configuration as Jameso's, so it wouldn't give you any more room. Besides, I'm pretty sure the landlord already has it leased to summer visitors."

"You don't have to worry about me," Sharon said. She sat up a little straighter, unable to keep a smile from her face. "I've found a new place— a great apartment with two bedrooms, within walking distance of the library even."

"Where did you find that?" Jameso asked. "Maggie and I looked for months and didn't turn up anything."

"It's one of the apartments over the hardware store. Gerald Pershing was living there. As soon as I heard he was moving out, I called the land-lord and asked to rent it."

"I'm impressed," Jameso said. "How did you know who to call?"

"Josh Miller told me. He has the apartment across the hall."

"So are you and the handsome deputy an item?" Barb asked.

Sharon's cheeks burned. "We're friends. That's all." She reached over and took Alina's hand. "I want to spend time finding out who I am before I get involved with anyone else."

"I always knew you were smart," Jameso said.

A knock on the door interrupted their laughter. Josh Miller, dressed in his sheriff's department khakis, leaned into the room. "Sorry to disturb y'all," he said. "I'm looking for Sharon."

"Me?" she squeaked. Her heart pounded and she felt dizzy. She couldn't help it; the sight of a law enforcement officer these days produced an instant mixture of hope and fear. Hope that they had found her son, and fear that they hadn't. "Is something wrong?"

"No, nothing is wrong. I just brought somebody I think you'll want to see."

He stepped aside and a young man appeared in the door behind him. A tall, blond, shaggy-haired young man. "Adan!" Sharon spoke the word on a sob and tried to stand, but her legs refused to support her.

Instead, her son came to her and hugged her tightly. "Hey, Mom."

"Where have you been? What happened? How did you get here?" She cradled his face in her hands, scarcely able to believe he was really here.

"I didn't mean to upset you," he said. "I couldn't live with Dad anymore, and I took off. I couldn't remember your phone number, but I remembered the town name—Eureka. So I just decided to come to you."

"I can't believe you came all that way by yourself. You must be exhausted. And starving."

"The ladies at the Last Dollar—Janelle and Danielle? They fed me. And an old man—Bob—paid for my meal. Josh—Sergeant Miller—gave me this shirt. He said I couldn't come to you in the one I had." Adan smiled shyly. "I guess it was pretty dirty."

"But how did you find Janelle and Danielle and Bob and Josh?" She marveled at all the people who had seen him before she even knew he was back in town.

"I tried to find you in the phone book at the library, but the old lady there called the cops on me. But that worked out okay, because Officer Miller knew you and brought me here."

Sharon laughed. "Of course Cassie called the cops." But in this case, it had been the exact right thing to do. "I'm so glad to see you." She hugged him tightly again. "I'm not going to let you leave again. Not for a very long time."

"That's okay, Mom. I'm ready to stay for a while."

"Hello, Adan." Jameso came to stand beside him and offered his hand to the boy. "I'm your uncle Jay—but everyone calls me Jameso now."

"Pleased to meet you, sir."

"And this is my wife, Maggie. And our brand-new daughter, Angela."

"We're all happy to meet you," Maggie said. She tried and failed to suppress a yawn. "I'm sorry. It's been a big day."

"Aunt Maggie and Uncle Jameso got married this morning," Alina said. "She went into labor right after the ceremony."

"And now she needs to rest." Sharon stood and put one arm around each of her children. "Come on, kids. Let's go home."

"That sounds really good," Adan said.

"Yes, it does." Home. The people who said it was the place where they had to take you in were wrong. Home was the place that welcomed those who were dear to you. Where the people who mattered to you mattered to those around you as well.

She had felt she didn't fit in Eureka, that she would always be separate and outside, a woman without a family who was too damaged to know how to have a family.

But the people here had showed her differently. Family wasn't merely the people related to you by blood. Family was made up of all the people who cared about you and those you loved. For so long she'd believed her family was lost to her—but she'd found them in Eureka.

Acknowledgments

Many thanks to the people at Kensington Publishing, especially my editors, Audrey LaFehr and Martin Biro, for all their help and support. Also, I'm thankful for the friendship and support of other authors—particularly members of Rocky Mountain Fiction Writers (especially the Writers of the Hand) and the Duet Authors online group. You keep me going! Most important, thank you to my husband, Jim, who is always there for me. He is my anchor in this crazy writing life.

A Reading Group Guide

A Change in Altitude

Cindy Myers

About This Guide

The suggested questions are included to enhance your group's reading of *A Change in Altitude.*

DISCUSSION QUESTIONS

1. One of the themes of this book is loss and recovery. What things do the characters in the book lose? What do they recover or find to replace the loss?

2. If you were Sharon, would you have left your son with his father? Why or why not?

3. What do you think about people who identify themselves as preppers or survivalists? Are they harmless eccentrics or a danger to others?

4. Why is Maggie so ambivalent about her upcoming wedding? Have you ever felt ambivalent about something other people saw as a reason to celebrate, such as a wedding or the birth of a child?

5. Do you think Jameso's distancing himself from Sharon when she first arrived was a normal reaction, or was he letting his sister down? Are we obligated to help other people simply because we are related to them?

6. Do you believe in the concept of karma? Do you think Gerald got what he deserved? What about Bob?

7. Would you watch a reality television show like the one Chris Amesbury proposes to film in Eureka? Why or why not?

8. How do you feel about Sharon's decision not to date Josh? Were you disappointed, or do you think she made the right decision?